TO DEFY DEATH

"You have no idea what you're asking, what'd be involved," said Bronh, the last Tek of Kantmorie.

"It's a simple thing," Jannus asserted, for it seemed so to him: simple as sight restored, or breathing underwater, or sun at midnight, or any other necessary, impossible thing. "It's the body that's gone wrong, that's all. She just needs to be rebodied. Teks used to be rebodied five times a day . . ."

It had been then that Bronh had cut in. "You want magic," she formulated severely," not science. And there *is* no magic. What does an herbalists' and bonesetters' culture know of gene surgery or cell regeneration anymore, much less redes, bases, and rebodying? You're a thousand years too late."

"I will not accept her dying," Jannus responded. "You haven't said it's impossible."

THE HIGH PLAIN
OF KANTMORIE

Newstock★   Down★   Morgaard V.

SMITH-
LANDS

Lisle★   ★Debern K

BREMNER   VALDE'

Cliffhold
IS   ★K····   SMITH
Quickmoor★   Ardun   BAY

HAN
HALLA

NEW
SMITH-
LANDS

LONGLAND
SPUR

Dunwater I
Andras Pt   Firstlight I
Ismere I

Camarr★   Lake I
Smoke Mt
BAY
OF
ANDRAS   Keening Is

Storm Rock

Landsend
Little Storm R   Blackrock I
Turnabout I
Twin Peaks Is

Windward Is
Glatten I
Goat R
0   ·   ·   ·   ·   500   Firetop I
Lookout I
SCALE IN MILES

Summerfair

The Third Book of the
Strange and Fantastic History
of the King of Kantmorie

by
ANSEN DIBELL

DAW BOOKS, INC.
DONALD A. WOLLHEIM, PUBLISHER
1633 Broadway, New York, NY 10019

FIRST PRINTING, AUGUST 1982

1 2 3 4 5 6 7 8 9

 DAW TRADEMARK REGISTERED
U.S. PAT. OFF. MARCA
REGISTRADA. HECHO EN U.S.A.

PRINTED IN U.S.A.

Table of Contents

DEDICATED to the members of the Fiction Writers' Consortium of Cincinnati, particularly Michaele Hahn Jordan and Michael Resnick, for their interest, illuminating arguments, and shrewd advice.

I

ICE

———◆————◆————◆———

It was an odd funeral, just short of scandalous, not that Poli herself would have cared two beans, thought Dan Innsmith. Valde had no notion of how such things were properly done, not being altogether what a man could call human.

But Jannus, the widower, had no such excuse, and the funeral was his doing. And if he chose to hold the public leave-taking out in his garden, where crusted midwinter snow still showed the trodden wheel of a children's chasing game, there was nobody to prevent him.

Nobody expected a man to be altogether himself under such circumstances, but Jannus was from the nation of Bremner, and Bremneri did few things carelessly or without full awareness of appearances. If Jannus chose to display his dead Valde wife in a setting of frozen ground and bare black trees, linking her rigid immobility to that of the land, it was on purpose.

Poli's remains rested on a stone bench. The sheet that covered her left her head and her feet showing. The head was bad enough—the face wasted and the color of old wax, and glints of blown snow in the dense cottony hair—but the feet were obscene.

Faces were public, after all. But the narrow feet, undefended against the cold, made Dan shiver and look away.

He occupied himself with greeting the guests as they arrived, and saw the same reaction from each group in turn. Even with the city under the threat of siege, people expected

9

things to be done properly—a civilized reception, indoors, with a good fire. Instead, they'd been shown in one side of the entry hall and out the other, right back into the cold, confronting the draped form that seemed, with its naked feet, to radiate a glacial chill.

Each guest would halt, finding the scene an assault, an affront they were unprepared for. Then they'd notice the mug of hot spiced ale Dan was trying to hand them, and seize the distraction eagerly, as much for the civility as for the warmth. Eventually they would recover enough to crunch across the snow to pay their respects to Jannus and the five girls.

The city's Bremneri community, as might have been expected, had turned out full force. Jannus was an important enough arbiter to make that social duty a necessity, though they'd been critical enough of his outlandish marriage to a Valde while Poli was alive. There were, besides, assorted Andrans, local folk, some with red-nosed daughters in tow who were visibly put out at having to keep their fine new gowns covered and whose parents made the most fuss about the poor motherless children—all five of the poor motherless children meanwhile regarding them with black eyes as favorless as so many river stones. And there were a scattering of Smiths, mostly Dan's close kin, come either for Dan's sake or because Dan's father, Elda Innsmith, was to say the remembrance.

But there were no Valde at all. Not one.

Sparrowhawk, Jannus' young kinsman who managed the household for him, remarked on that conspicuous absence while setting down a fresh tray of steaming mugs. "They must know she's gone. Least they could do is show up for one of their own."

"They know," responded Dan. There wasn't much in the city of Ardun that could be kept hidden from any Valde who cared to take the trouble to discover it. "They just don't like the weather, I expect."

Sparrowhawk glanced up at the dull overcast before apparently realizing the weather Dan meant wasn't physical but emotional. To the empathic Valde, the moods broadcast by an outlanders' funeral would be an unpleasantness to keep well clear of, to say nothing of what Jannus—uncommonly

10

loud anyway, by all reports—would likely be contributing to that mood-weather by way of storm. Dan couldn't say it surprised him that the Valde would sooner keep well clear of that; he wasn't all that happy just having to look at it, those feet.

Nevertheless Sparrowhawk insisted, "They could have *come*, all the same."

"You be sure and say so, next time you see one." Dan turned to proffer a mug to his father, patriarch of the Free Smiths of Ardun.

But Elda Innsmith, surveying the appalling garden, remarked bluntly, "What's this, then, tell me? What in the green world's he thinking of?"

Jannus was thinking of bodies, bargains, and a bird.

"You ignorant lowlander," the bird had remarked with withering accuracy, "you have no idea what you're asking, what'd be involved."

She was the last Tek of Kantmorie, bodied like a valkyr hawk. She was called Bronh.

She'd stopped in Ardun about a month ago to visit the cache of special powdered food she left in Jannus' keeping. She couldn't hunt to eat like a normal valkyr—most of her body held brain tissue, Jannus had been told—and birdform kept her from carrying much in the way of supplies on her solitary journeys.

Though all the rest of her kind were gone and long forgotten by most of the ignorant lowlanders save Jannus, Bronh always took care to avoid becoming conspicuous. She'd come in the twilight, perching like a vague mound of gathered smoke on the garden's north wall while Jannus scuffed restlessly through the fresh drifts below her, arguing against the prospect of Poli's dying.

"It's a simple thing," he asserted, for it seemed so to him: simple as sight restored, or breathing underwater, or sun at midnight, or any other necessary, impossible thing. "It's the body that's gone wrong, that's all. She just needs to be rebodied. Teks used to be rebodied five times a day, sometimes, just to travel from—"

It had been then that Bronh had cut in with her appraisal of his ignorance. "You want magic," she formulated severely,

11

"not science. And there *is* no magic. What does an herbalists' and bonesetters' culture know of gene surgery or cell regeneration anymore, much less redes, bases, and rebodying? You're a thousand years too late."

Jannus responded, "She's *not* just tired, or bored with winter. She's dying, Bronh. She isn't but thirty, and dying of old age." Finally believing it, he still couldn't accept it; at almost twenty-eight, he was still judged a young man.

"She's a Valde. She was grown, mature, at nine or ten. What did you expect?"

Jannus only shook his head, leaning against the rough stones of the wall. "I thought you cared about Valde. I thought *you'd* understand, at least."

"Nobody cares for Valde as I do," Bronh retorted sharply in her harsh, high voice. "But I don't indulge in sentiment, to pamper one individual at the expense of the rest. There's been enough of that, whether from Teks or our lowland descendants. All Valde are valuable, independent of anyone's whims. Not pets, or Fair Witnesses, or troopmaids, or any sort of social furniture for human convenience. I care for *all* Valde, not just this one or that one who happens to attract my notice or flatter my fancy. Individuals don't matter," concluded the Tek sternly.

"I will not accept her dying." Jannus stepped away from the wall to confront the valkyr's dispassionate marigold eye. "What use is your lofty compassion, what use is all I've learned of Teks and redes and bases, if we cannot do this one thing?"

"No use, perhaps."

"No. It *has* to matter. You've said it's complicated, that I don't understand a tenth of what would be involved. All right, Bronh. But you haven't said it's impossible."

Instead of answering, the Tek demanded, "How long ago did the turning-away, the aging, start?"

"I'm not sure—she'd just say she was tired, and I didn't think much of it." Aware of Bronh's impatience at his imprecision, Jannus tried to think back. "Two months, for certain—maybe longer. Maybe since we got back from the last Summerfair. I just don't know, Bronh."

The Tek lifted her huge smoke-grey wings as if checking the strength of the icy breeze that spun snow spirals fitfully in the corners of the garden wall. Settling, she remarked with seeming inconsequence, "If ever this bird is killed or so badly injured I cannot make a meeting with the Shai, I'll be dead, no different from the least mindless sparrow."

That was what bound them, what made him an acceptable depot to this last Tek: their mutual link to the Shai, whose body was the starship *Sunfire* which hung, an anonymous and unremarkable star, a little west of the zenith, visible on clear nights.

Jannus responded, "And nobody left to care for the Valde," to show he understood her concern was not for herself but for the work left unfinished. He knew enough of Teks for that.

"Since the Shai ended the bases and the deathlessness," she went on in a musing tone, "only direct impression's been possible. From life, to life. No redes taken or stored."

"What do you want, Bronh?" Jannus was Bremneri: he knew an oblique slide toward a bargain when he heard it.

"There was a redestone," said Bronh, giving him a direct, unblinking look. "A coded molecular lattice you took out of *Sunfire*. Do you still have it?"

"Yes."

"Then I want it. My last full rede is encoded in it. My whole self—not just the fraction that this bird can hold. I want my whole self back."

Without any hesitation, Jannus promised, "When Poli is re-bodied and whole, you can have the redestone."

"Agreed."

By that time darkness had fallen and it had become even colder. But Jannus had ignored his daughter Mallie's voice calling that the daymeal was ready, to listen to Bronh explain what he must know, translating desire and will into the less comprehensible machineries of base capacities, gene replication, and rede impression.

But it was all founded on life-into-life transfer—or, as the Valde would have put it, "water into water." And before the summons he'd sent by Bronh had been answered, Poli had dreamed herself into death too far to return and had become ice.

Jannus looked now without seeing at that ice, at the cold mirror of desolation he'd chosen to surround it, so the inside and the outside would be one thing. Without attending he heard old Elda Innsmith beginning the formal remembrance.

"Her name was Poli lar-Jannus and she was a Valde, which is to say she was different."

Elda clasped hands thoughtfully behind him, feeling thick as a stump in his layers of sweaters, coat, and muffler. But standing around in the cold seemed little enough to do for Poli before she went to the fire, and for Jannus, who'd never been one to make a proper speech anyhow. They'd been, all three, strangers and exiles together in this foreign city, the last human settlement on the doorstep of the pathless forests of the Valde. As the pair of them had no proper family behind them, Elda felt he was as good a one as any to be saying the remembrance though they were no kin of his. And though it was a remembrance, and so deserved some special care, it was only another speech; and Elda had been either making or listening to speeches at Innsmith clan meetings for upwards of seventy years.

He went on, "She was born about the year 851 since the Fall of Kantmorie, some place in the east forests of Valde. An't no way to say nearer than that because Valde don't make maps nor have anything by way of landmarks we'd know, and they mostly don't count years because that's how they are—different. She was born together with five other sisters, all at the one birth like a litter of kits. Different again. And they were Haffa, which means there wasn't a brother among them. So when they got to be grown girls of about nine or ten, they all went to the Summerfair to make their Choosing. And whichever way the rest chose, Poli took the smoke into her hands, the way they do, and went off into Bremner to be a troopmaid ten years and fight for some riverstock until she won her bridestone, so she could go back again to the Summerfair and choose a husband. You Bremneri, most of you are riverstock-born: you know how it goes with the troopmaids in the she-Traders' cities along Erth-rimmon.

"Now it happened," Elda continued, surveying his audience, "that she was assigned to the Newstock troop. And in Newstock she got to know Jannus, Lady Lillia's boy. And when Poli had lived through her term, Jannus took a notion

14

to go and see her brided, not expecting anything more, him being just an ordinary youngster and her a freemaid then who'd put ten years into earning the right to marry among her own people. And except for Poli, no Valde's married outside her own kind since the first troopmaid put on some riverstock's colors going on nine hundred years ago: they'd sooner go without, the Haffa Valde, then get mixed up that way with any of us ordinary folk.

"But it happened that the one great difference that Valde have, Poli lost. She lost the inhearing, the *marenniath*—how they know whatever a person's feeling. Now that was hard— worse than being struck blind and deaf together would be for a regular person like you or me. Any other Valde hurt that bad you'd expect to just fade away and die right then, the way they do. But she lived like that, ten years and more, and was partnered to Jannus, and had children with him, and they settled here in Ardun, where Valde come and go all the time."

Looking over at the bench, Elda wondered whether Jannus was even listening to him. If not, then that was all right: Elda could repeat it all for him some other time.

"So she knew loss, and hurt, and hard times. Not so different. She had to judge by what she could see and touch and know, just like a regular person. Not so different. And she bore children and saw to their growing, and put money by, and wondered how the new year'd go, like we all done a time or two. And this, that she's come to so young, the way we measure the years, an't any different from what we'll all come to, soon or late. No different."

Elda coughed, and accepted the fresh mug of ale Dan came to hand him, warning the folk with his eyes and his stance that he wasn't done yet. Elda got some of the hot inside him, touched his sweeping white mustache dry, and nobody moved much or started talking, which was gratifying.

Elda changed his stance, then in a quiet voice he remarked, "Whatever you had of Poli, much or little, you lost yesterday. Maybe that's the way you feel. But that an't so. What we had of her, we still have. We each of us got our own piece, that's all—what we remember, and saw, and knew. But it's all still here, what we have, same as it was yesterday, and the day before. And it may be that after this one

15

time, we won't bring all the pieces we have together in the one place again. But so long as we all remember, Poli's not—"

Elda broke off short because somebody had laughed.

Then there was a stir, and Elda had just time to turn around to see the motion of two men, heavily bundled in dark, nondescript clothing, catching hold of Poli's rigid corpse and swinging it the six long paces through the open entryway door which slammed shut just as Elda's shoulder hit it. The door bounced, then closed tightly as more weight was brought to bear on the inside. Elda heard the bar fall.

Young Sparrowhawk was already dashing in long-legged strides toward the kitchen door, but Elda heard the outside street door bang before the young Bremneri had cleared the steps.

The corpse-snatchers had gotten clear away.

The figure of a young man came toward Ardun from the west, scuffing alone down the last of Lifganin's mounded white hills along one of a witch's broom of isolated converging tracks. The punch-holes of single steps became a trodden mash of snow and mud leading to the packed clear surface of Ardun's Sunset Bridge spanning Arant Dunrimmon's hurrying turbulence.

With his broad, uneven features and his waterman's braid hanging outside his rough scarf and turned-up collar, he looked like one of the rootless folk that followed the river trade, and he faded easily into the waterfront crowds.

The river was still not quite frozen, due to its swiftness, and a few score sailcraft and steam packets were loading, their masters betting they'd be able to beat the ice to the Sea with one more cargo before inland traffic was closed altogether until thaw. Though Dunwater Isle, which controlled Ardun's access to the Sea, was in enemy hands, the gate had not yet been shut: winter would do that. And few believed that Duke Pedross Rey would dare to try to blockade the mouth of Arant Dunrimmon for fear of giving the other baymasters and the lowland nations common cause to forget differences and unite against him—not for Ardun's sake but for the sake of the Valde Summerfair, whose gateway Ardun was. Everybody depended on the Summerfair: the ancient ceremony of meeting and alliance which alone was exempt from partisan feuds, the place of reliable promises. Depending on the Summerfair in a more immediate way, Ardun carried on its usual end-of-season traffic in undiminished volume, confident of eventual thaw.

The young man noted rigging, ships' names and pennants, the shapes of the goods hanging in the cargo nets. He noticed preoccupied scarlet-caped patrollers out on each dock before whom crates were grudgingly being opened. Everything interested him and he watched everything with an automatic thoroughness as he passed unremarked down the lines of long docks.

Drawcarts were busy all around him, but he didn't hail one, preferring to walk the distance to the foot of Millers' Street and renew his acquaintanceship with the City of the Rose.

He strolled slowly, taking no particular care to avoid being noticed, although he would have received a prolonged and painful welcome had the Master of Ardun known so old an enemy had been rash enough to venture into reach.

Nobody could possibly recognize him. He'd worn the pleasantly ugly, unremarkable face less than half a day.

Only Valde, by some incredibly bad luck, might have noticed him because to them he wasn't there. He had no *farioh*, selfsinging, which they could have perceived. And Valde had a way of dealing with really offensive forms of difference with violent thoroughness.

Therefore he moved with the riverside crowds, whose inner emotional clatter should effectively mask his own silence. Nobody would be looking for him: at least not for his present appearance.

He was a mobile, a bodied rede-self of the Shai whose own body was the starship *Sunfire*. He hadn't yet chosen a name for this latest incarnation. He thought he'd let Jannus name this persona; Jannus had always put such weight on names.

It was little enough to offer, arriving empty handed and too late.

The summons Bronh had delivered he'd obeyed as quickly as he thought wise and not as quickly as he could. To have ignored the order altogether was not among his options. Jannus had merely told him to come, naively supposing his own

17

urgency must necessarily inspire a like haste. However, obeying the letter of the appeal, the mobile had decided to make haste as slowly as he could.

Nevertheless he had not come without cost. He'd abandoned nearly two thousand square miles of photoelectric sailfilm, more fragile than flies' wings, bringing *Sunfire* into atmosphere again; and he'd jettisoned a perfectly viable persona, that of spymaster to the Andran Duke Pedross Rey, a position which had afforded him immense leverage over the social evolution of the lowland nations. But the mobile didn't expect Jannus to be impressed by the sacrifices he'd made in answering his friend's summons with such unpardonably calculated haste.

The mobile was glad of the opportunity to see Ardun of the Rose again first-hand. Spies' reports, however thorough, couldn't include even half of what he himself could notice on a slow walk along the west side waterfront: no spy save perhaps Bronh, his occasional ally, had anything like his data base as a vantage point for observation. Whistling tunelessly through his teeth, he surveyed with immense interest and affection the prosperous city he meant to destroy. And everything he saw was simultaneously relayed to the complex evaluative capacities of *Sunfire*, to his larger self: that ancient and immortal entity called the Shai, last remaining great artifact and treasure of the Teks of Kantmorie, servant of the Rule of One.

The mobile, like Bronh, was a fractional self: as much of the Shai's memories, nature, and capacities as a single human body could hold. But, unlike Bronh, his complete identity was a living being with whom he was in continual synaptic rapport, not an encoded pattern latent in a lump of green crystal.

Prices, he noticed, had gone up again since his last reports. That was satisfactory. Another small token, but welcome.

It would be young Duke Pedross and his fledgling Andran empire that would inherit when the Blooming Rose withered: the mobile's satisfaction was quite disinterested.

At Millers' Street he turned left and went two blocks uphill. The third house from the corner was, like its neighbors, of dressed red stone, windowless except for high ventilation slits beyond the reach of thaw floods.

On the door was a plaque dating the house from the fifteenth Master's time. Below that plaque was another listing four notable past tenants, and then a third which, in stylized lettering, identified the present holder of the lease: *Jannus lar-Poli. Bremneri. Arbiter.* That Poli was named only as an appendage, almost a suffix, merely reflected that Andrans were a patrilineal culture and that Arduners had evolved very specific notions on how things were properly to be done—even the painting of door-signs. Any new resident would be accepted only to the degree that he conformed to the strictures of custom.

The mobile's knock was answered by a young girl—one of the five daughters, he supposed—who peered up at him through the lattice of a small looksee panel above the plaques. She asked him his name and his errand with sober politeness.

Any girl-child of partial Valde blood, however dilute, would have powers of discernment beyond the ordinary: limited, but intimidating enough within those limits. *Truthtell*, they'd named it in Bremner, where it had developed.

It was exactly what the name implied, an immediate sense of the degree of conviction behind spoken words.

Brusquely, the mobile said just that he'd been sent for by Jannus, offering as few words as possible. He adopted a thick downriver accent and meanwhile stamped snow off his boots and coughed repeatedly to distract her attention from the uniquely unresonant quality she would hear in the statement, empty of intent either to truth or to deception. The fact was that the mobile never lied; but it was a fact beyond the verification of Truthtell.

The child gave no sign of having discerned anything odd as she shut the panel.

After a few minutes Jannus opened the door. He was thinner than the mobile remembered and more composed. The expression of his dark, broken-nosed, streetfighter's face had almost a Valde's neutral repose.

"Bronh reached me in transit," said the mobile at once: truth, literal and deceptive. "I gather it's too late. I'm sorry. I know something of what Poli meant to you."

Jannus made no visible reaction except to look around over his shoulder, directing, "Shut the daywing door, Mallie, and tell Sparrow to hold them maybe two minutes, if you will. Come on," he told the mobile, stepping aside.

Jannus led him across the cold, bare entry hall. On the paving was a stringsack that strongly suggested the presence of one of the Awiro Valde unless someone in the household had taken to buying salt by the block. The mobile quickened his pace, Jannus meanwhile remarking, "The city watch is in the daywing with an Awiro as Witness," confirming the mobile's guess.

They started up a switchback staircase. "Eight days ago," Jannus added, "somebody stole Poli's body. They haven't found it yet, or who took it. And with any luck at all, they won't."

The mobile followed Jannus up the steps with the troubling awareness that it wasn't too late, after all. At least Jannus didn't think so.

Jannus ushered him into an untidy but well-furnished study. Sunlight fell from a large double-paneled casement in the long wall opposite onto a scribe's desk piled with scrolls and bound ledgers. The redstone, the mobile noticed, was being used as a paperweight. *Well,* he reflected, *and why not?*

There was a small fireplace on the left wall, bracketed between sets of shelves overflowing with scrolls, their colored tapes and seals dangling, and a few printed books and leather document cases standing upright.

Stretching himself out in one of the chairs before the fire, Jannus poked at the burning shell of log in the grate, remarking presently, "What'd you do with Secolo, then?"

Secolo, publicly deceased, had been the Andran spymaster, the mobile's most recent incarnation.

"The regency was over," the mobile replied, tossing the muffler on top. "Pedross quit appreciating unasked advice long since. . . . And he always *was* such a poisonous little man, Secolo, with his charms and his augurs and his dread of 'witches'. . . ."

It'd been an impersonation forced by necessity. *Somebody'd* had to keep young Pedross in check, and keep him from being assassinated before he learned to guard himself properly. The Shai had put so much time and effort into producing just such an individual as Pedross to become the keystone of what was to come that it would have been an offense against plain thrift not to see to it that the boy was solidly mortared into place.

"How did you come," Jannus asked, "by river, or straight from *Sunfire?*"

"*Sunfire* dropped me off in Lifganin before dawn, frightening the wits out of a mara herd. But I don't think the Awiro knew anything, since they had only the beasts' terror to go by. Fairly inconspicuous, considering. There'd have been no use trying to come into Ardun wearing a face as well known as Secolo's," remarked the mobile, settling into a leather armchair to lever off one wet boot, then the other. "Domal Ai would have had word of it in under an hour; and I'd have been no help to you from his dungeon downstream on Wind Rock. . . . I let Secolo be assassinated by an agent of the most incompetent of Pedross' commanders and saw to it that splendid proof would come to light afterward. A death is too useful a weapon to waste, I've always thought."

"I'd think Pedross would more likely promote the man, having succeeded in assassinating a Chief of Assassins," observed Jannus.

"Ah, our Pedross isn't that devious yet. He'll have the man's skin first, and then it'll occur to him that the man might have been more useful alive, traitor or no." The mobile propped his heels in comfort on the curve of the warm fender, still calculating what tack to steer in these dangerous shoals, so near the blunt question *What kept you?*

He added carefully, "But I hadn't foreseen the need for a new persona quite this soon, and hadn't one in stock. This body's practically got the damp of the still-box on it. . . ."

He waited, concealing his tension; but Jannus didn't try to pin him down, having a different preoccupation: "Where's *Sunfire* now? Lifganin?"

"No, at Sea, out beyond the tidestorm limit, making back some of the power it cost to enter atmosphere." The mobile cocked an eye to see if Jannus understood or needed an explanation. Jannus only nodded noncommittally.

"Can that be cut short?"

"How short?"

"How short have you got?" rejoined Jannus, momentarily cheerful. "Actually, I suppose I'd need a day or two to get ready."

"It'd depend on what I'm to get *Sunfire* ready *for*," countered the mobile reasonably.

"It's Ardun law," remarked Jannus, after a moment, "that all dead bodies have to be burned within three days. Enforcement's very strict. It's a health thing, I'm told."

"And a prudent one," agreed the mobile, understanding at once why Jannus had staged the ghoulish abduction: to keep the corpse intact, frozen, until the mobile should arrive.

Whatever Jannus had in mind, the mobile could not have contrived to have arrived too late short of the spring thaws. That was why Jannus had so little interest in pursuing the reason for the delay. He'd already crossed that chasm, and now looked only ahead.

"Bronh said you'd need something of hers," Jannus continued with a certain ingenuous briskness, "of Poli's, to make a copy. Since I didn't know what, or how much, I figured I'd better save it all."

The mobile stirred uncomfortably. "Very resourceful."

"You're thinking, what use is the meat without the rede," Jannus guessed accurately. "I didn't know how I'd get around that either, once she was dead. But there had to be some way. I just had to keep the meat until I found a way to do it, that's all."

"Not only resourceful, but stubborn," commended the mobile, and Jannus smiled faintly. "You sound like a Tek: *meat*, indeed!"

Jannus lifted one hand and let it fall. "Bronh's the only one I could talk to about this business. Besides, I'm a kind of adopted Tek. . . . Every once in a while I recall I'm supposedly the king of Kantmorie. And sometimes it seems to me that ought to mean something."

"Kantmorie is dead," replied the mobile firmly.

"So is Poli. But I'll have her back, if there's any way to do it. It ought to mean something, regardless." Jannus was frowning past the mobile: looking, it seemed, at the redestone.

"It means something," agreed the mobile, with a certain private grimness: it meant, among other things, that when Jannus sent a summons, the mobile was obliged to come, eventually.

It had never been an easy friendship, that between the Shai

and this young lowlander who had come so oddly to hold the Rule of One whose instrument and servant the Shai was. By taking the vacant sovereignty, Jannus had been able to authorize the Shai's ending the Teks' endless nightmare cycles of reincarnation into the utter desolation which the High Plain had become. Without such outside authorization, the Shai couldn't cut power to the bases because of ancient and unbreakable convenants on how he might treat his one-time masters. The friendship had endured this long because Jannus had been wise enough not to try to make further use of the power which that dead title, *King of Kantmorie,* nominally granted him; for a king's authority was revocable only by death.

But now Jannus had decided the title should mean something because he found utter powerlessness in the face of death intolerable. He'd put aside prudence and committed himself to the disastrous folly of a conspicuous, unmistakable resurrection.

This left the Shai facing two courses, both equally unacceptable: to become first the instrument, then the victim, of that folly, a public scandal in which his true nature could not avoid exposure, to the grave harm of his effectiveness; or else to eliminate the fool to protect himself and what had been so carefully grafted onto the stock of the Rule of One in these latter decades.

There might, however, be a third way.

He could hope to turn Jannus aside, or persuade him to accept some less explosively recognizable substitute, before the issue became a choice between the Rule of One and a lowlander king, however beloved. For that would be no choice at all.

The mobile of the Shai requested sadly, "Tell me the rest of it."

"Well, I know now what to do about the rede. You know who told me? Elda Innsmith."

"Elda doesn't—"

"Of course not. Do you think I want to get tried for 'foul and self-confessed witchery'? Elda would be the last person I'd tell. As it was, I scandalized him halfway to an apoplexy, laughing out loud and spoiling his remembrance. And then, the corpse-snatchers, on top of it. . . . What do you want to be called now, by the way?"

"You pick a name."

"No, that's not right," Jannus objected, looking pleased.

"Then never mind, for now. Just tell me how you propose to reconstruct the rede." With any luck at all, the mobile thought, it would prove impractical and the whole idea could be scrapped.

"Memory." Jannus leaned farther down in his chair, lacing the fingers of both hands together in an unconsciously descriptive gesture: meshing, joining. "There are a few people who knew Poli really well. Elda knew her before I did, back when she was a troopmaid. And there's the children—the whole household, really, and Dan—anybody I can find who did more than meet her on the street. I made a list. And then there's all Bronh's knowledge of Valde itself, the ways and customs. She knows a hundred times what I do, and I've been learning about Valde all my life, or trying to. . . ."

"Bronh has a few centuries' head start," rejoined the mobile absently: his luck wasn't good today. Such a composite could be made. "And access to all the records the Shai holds, besides."

"And I'd need a redecap," Jannus continued, "that I could attach to something, a chair, maybe, to get the memories in the first place. Then it could all be put together, everything any of us knows or remembers about her. It should be possible. Isn't it?"

"It . . . wouldn't be a rede," responded the mobile slowly. "A rede is the living thing. Not just facts but patterns of facts, habits, *ways* of thinking. Not just the contents of the mind, but the motions of the mind, as well. And emotional states don't transfer. With a Valde, that would make a considerable difference. What I woke might not have the slightest interest in you at all."

That, thought the mobile, *should be a fine block to be stumbled over.* . . .

And Jannus had gone very still. He said, "Can it be done? What I've said?"

"Yes." As the stillness eased, the mobile warned, "But it wouldn't be the same."

"Is there another way?"

24

"No."

"Then that's the way it will have to be," said Jannus flatly. In a lighter voice, he inquired, "Would you take the name *Garin?*"

The mobile recognized the allusion. It was a modern, elided form of the name *Gaherin;* and Gaherin was the legendary Tek who had altered the genetic makeup of the Valde to permit human-Valde interbreeding. The modification had had the side effect of producing a ten-to-one ratio of female to male births, among Valde. Before Bronh's social counter measures—the exclusion of most Haffa from the breeding pool through troopservice or becoming Awiro—had begun to reverse it, the imbalance had come close to destroying the Valde as a viable species. It had been, and remained, a notable bit of meddling.

"Is that what you think you're doing?" inquired the mobile mildly, and Jannus shrugged.

"It's what Bronh thinks I'm doing. Particularity. Sentiment. Feeling there's a value to an individual life—"

"I know. Partiality is always a temptation and a risk," observed the mobile, as much to himself as to Jannus, who wasn't listening anyway.

Instead, Jannus was saying with a sort of sullen intensity, "And I just don't care. I will do this thing, whatever comes of it."

" 'Garin,' then. Until it's done."

Like a long obsidian reef the ranked waves had failed to mark or channel, the Shai rested in midocean, eating light. From above, his outline was most like that of a squid—elongated, with the tapering cables of his external handlers spread behind and occasionally arching, serpentlike, above the surface for a moment as they tended his nets. But most of his bulk was far below the heaving surge of the surface. The actual contours of the vessel the Shai wore were more nearly like a manta's. Below the floating layers of weed and red plankton, vast solid triangles of wings sculled lazily, producing a slight bow wave that curved away from the exposed leading portion of his black, seamless hull.

Sunfire had been the Shai's body almost as long as he could remember; and that was a very long time indeed. Yet

25

the body of his birth had also been a creature of the landless depths; and the feel of the currents and the thermal gradients against the sensors of his outer skin was pleasant and familiar.

He could have chosen any of half a dozen solid places to wait while the mobile made initial contact—all closer, many almost as isolated. But he'd come instead among the sliding hills the tidestorm winds pushed before them, as he always did, given the barest excuse.

It didn't matter that his own oceans were thousands of light-years distant, nor that he pulled his thick wings into a slow downstroke by flexing electromagnetic fields instead of muscles.

The Shai was at home in the Sea.

As, far away, the mobile stumbled while following Jannus upstairs, the Shai regretfully began retracting his nets although half a day's sunlight still remained. The fan of photoelectric crystals that floated for miles in his wake was drawn in gradually.

The receptor nets, though less efficient than the sailfilm he used in vacuum, would stand rougher handling and could be reused. But they were a terrible nuisance if allowed to tangle. The Shai took his time stowing the immense jingling bundle in a still more immense storage compartment that had once held over five hundred Teks, frozen in still-boxes, sleeping out the time of journey.

He was aware of the mobile's actions and perceptions from minute to minute, as he was aware of the blown spray against his upper hull; but the reverse was not true. The mobile was too limited to handle more than three or four completely separate layers of perception at once, or to integrate more than two simultaneously with full interconnectedness, evaluation, and prediction. Therefore the Shai didn't distract or interrupt his fractional projected self any oftener than he could help, allowing the mobile to initiate fuller rapport whenever necessity prompted.

He could have dried and cleaned the receptor nets, but he didn't. He savored their briny tang with a small portion of his attention while simultaneously evaluating all possible courses of action, monitoring outside conditions, and completing the preparations for departure.

His thought processes were associational rather than linear. Arriving, then, at a conditional solution regarding Poli's hidden body, the Shai braced his wings and retracted his outer handlers into their sockets, meanwhile enjoying the flavor of the Sea that remained on the net, fresh and pungent.

Memories, records, facts were all very well; but even in constantly shifting suspension, they could never replace the living flex of water, no two waves alike. *Particularity*. There was irony in that: except for his own unending interest in the immediate and particular condition of individuals and nations, his own immortality would have been as intolerable a desolation as the Teks' had become to them, at the last. Only a love of the flexing present made unending life meaningful and tolerable.

The Shai knew with perfect clarity what he'd be taking from Jannus in removing all hope of Poli, rebodied.

For unending life was identical to mortality in that both were lived only by an hour, a day, a week at a time, and were lived on hope. The Shai knew, with pitiless compassion, just what a desolation a day could become if hope was amputated.

But better that than being forced to kill Jannus, for whom the Shai had a most particular concern and affection.

The last reaching wave slapped the rising bulk. The manta-shape flattened, forward surfaces becoming razor-edged, following edges thickening and curving to afford maximum lift. A moment later an explosion like lightless thunder, then *Sunfire* began to climb, pressing through the turbulences of air.

One thing *Sunfire* could not do was hover. The Shai would have to grab the knowledge he needed in passing. He timed his arrival over Ardun to coincide with that of the evening tidestorm wind, which rattled shutters and howled down alleys quite loudly enough to cover his own approach.

He banked and turned into the wind to make his first pass, satisfied merely to identify that single configuration in all of Ardun's multitude that was Jannus' mind. Had the Shai not once had a rede of Jannus', he couldn't have done it. But he singled out the familiar pattern and his course looped upward again to make his second pass again from the north, over the forest, against the wind.

He could only scan surface thoughts, and only at extremely close range—a few hundred yards. So as he leveled into his second approach, his mobile asked a suitable triggering question, bringing the whole grisly abduction scheme into the Bremneri's immediate awareness. The Shai scooped it up, all unfelt, with the ease of a hawk striking a sparrow.

He pursued a lifting course south, evaluating what he'd snatched before dropping it into the general pool.

Jannus had hired one man, who in turn had hired two, all three to be gone with the tidefall that same night of the funeral, out of reach of Ardun's questioning. After the initial contact, Jannus had kept clear of the actual abduction, protecting himself with ignorance against the inevitable confrontation with either Truthtell or the more comprehensive probing of the *marenniath*. He truly had no idea where Poli's body had been hidden.

But he knew how to find out.

The arrangement had been that the man Jannus had hired would go for final payment to a certain Bremneri woman who kept a fish stall on Market Street. To her he was to deliver a sealed note he declared to be "as agreed." Unless the woman heard the assurance of good faith in the declaration, she would not turn over the payment. And in that note—still untouched and unread by anyone in eight days—was named the location of Poli's body.

The Shai could perhaps have gotten at the note itself, through the mobile or some intermediary. But the Shai particularly wanted to leave no least trace of his own intervention. So he was going, instead, to the source of the note, the man himself: the assistant cargomaster of the schooner *Westwind*, homeward bound down Arant Dunrimmon toward Firstlight Isle.

Shortly after the half-moon rose, the starship caught up with the schooner. *Westwind*, sails furled, was riding the midstream current without tacking. Arant Dunrimmon, swollen from the inrushing dam of Sea that had blocked its mouth, was again gathering momentum, and the tidefall bore the three-master smoothly along.

There were only thirty-four people aboard. At short range, the Shai could impose false information upon consciousness

28

as well as draw information from them; it was the only sort of lie of which the Shai was capable.

He identified the man he wanted and woke him by throwing a fear at him, then followed it with the thought—which the man would take for his own memory—of handing the note over. The Shai supplied the note's image blank: the man put the words in their places, and the Shai knew where Poli's body was.

Minter and Sons' warehouse on Ardun's east side waterfront.

He relayed the information to his mobile, which was best equipped to attend to the matter, himself turning meanwhile to the northwest and leaving *Westwind* to continue riding the tidefall.

The Shai cut across a corner of the tidal marshes of Han Halla, rising steadily as he approached the still-higher rim of the High Plain of Kantmorie. It had fogs about its ankles, and clouds were broken against its knees to spill their waters down deep gorges back into Han Halla.

The Shai passed over the jagged rim of the High Plain and the land fell precipitously away again. Responding to his grant of hoarded power, an abandoned Tek keep began broadcasting a landing beacon which grew stronger as the manta shape of *Sunfire* came nearer, slowing, descending. The Shai glided to a halt on a cushion of suddenly molten sand that stiffened into glass in the icy, motionless dry air.

The Shai cut off the broadcast power and the keep's voice became silent. *Sunfire* had enough stored energy to have achieved its accustomed orbit—barely. But the Shai sent out his nets of photoelectric chips, each section trundling along the gritty rock on tiny rollers until the nets were fully extended, each chip aligning itself to the moon. The Shai could subsist almost indefinitely on starlight alone.

The mobile would attend to the matter of the corpse; nevertheless, he himself wanted to stay fairly near, his entire resources available to respond to whatever consequences might develop.

When the nets were fully deployed they took with them the last lingering scent of the Sea. Regretfully the Shai irradiated the compartment and flushed the residue out with a searing breath that flamed along miles of empty passageways before the rear rotors expelled it into the outer air.

The mobile called Garin watched Jannus watching the warehouse burn down, and Poli's body with it.

It was, in its way, as handsome a fire as Ardun had probably ever had. Certainly it was the most spectacular one the mobile, in any of his incarnations, had ever set.

Poli was undoubtedly having the largest and best attended public cremation in Ardun's history.

The burning warehouse was one of perhaps a score, all more or less disused, sagging toward the likewise abandoned east side waterfront. The rotting piers pointed across the Morimmon, which barges and flatboats no longer plied, to the rank brushy hills of the Fallows: prime fertile land that had known neither plow nor harvest in several generations. Interdicted, the Fallows had become, by the will of the Valde, a wilderland like Lifganin, where stone might not be laid on stone. In the decay of Ardun's once-thriving east side, lit with the grey morning spreading above the Fallows, was prefigured what would come upon the whole city when the Summerfair up in Valde was ended and Pedross shut the gates to the Sea.

The mobile had found the warehouse nearly empty, except for the inevitable dueling among cats and rats, and except for the open-eyed corpse that lay in a hollow. Garin had left a pyre well alight before returning to his rented lodging by climbing a tree and a roof to his windowsill.

The fire had been brighter in the sky than the dawning. The street's early risers had been full of the talk of it. But Jannus might as well have been walking through a tunnel, for all the attention he gave his surroundings or other people's disasters. The warehouse meant nothing to him, burnt or whole. Not even the name and address of the place staring from the opened note had roused in him the least alarm. Not until they'd almost reached the east side docks had the knowledge visibly hit him.

Jannus hadn't said anything, just lengthened his stride, until he reached the rough paving of the river road and saw the full dimensions of the blaze. When the mobile caught up to him he was standing at the rear of the crowd that had gathered while patrollers cleared working room around the big, hissing cylinders of the steam-driven pumpers. The fire crew had given the warehouse itself up for lost and were directing their efforts to wetting down the warped roofs and sides of the adjoining buildings.

"Was that it?" Garin demanded in a medium shout, as about half the left-hand wall of the blazing warehouse fell in, dragging most of the roof down with it. "Jannus? Was that the place?"

Without answering, Jannus risked the rotten planking on the nearest dock, going out as far as the shoulder-high stump of a cargo boom. He had raised his face toward the fire when the mobile came carefully along the dock's outer edge to stay near him.

Garin tried to avoid for one more moment the unhidden desolation in Jannus' face. It was no great matter. Garin had simply underestimated the extent to which he could be affected by another's grief.

"Listen," he said, catching the side of the boom stump with one hand, "you can always use a Tek body instead. What do you need with a physical duplicate? What does it matter what she *looks* like, after all? What does the outside matter, if—"

"Shut up," Jannus responded briefly, without the anger Garin had hoped to provoke.

He'd expected Jannus to hate the idea. Such a body would have, to a lover, attractions equal to those of a figure of animated clay. *Meat*, Teks had called their bodies, and meat they were: mere dispassionate vessels. Teks had freed themselves, so far as possible, from the tyranny of glands and pain-receptors, the better to pursue the more enduring passions of the mind and will.

One result of which, Garin reflected, was that for practical purposes Teks had become extinct. Flesh had its own priorities which it was perilous to ignore.

Garin knew Tek meat well: he wore it.

Nevertheless he argued, "I've changed bodies a few times since you've known me. And yet you have no trouble accepting that it's still me, each time."

"I take your word for it. And you don't care what body you wear," Jannus responded finally, "so long as it serves your purposes. She'd care: Poli. It was mostly my fault she had nothing but the silent outsides of things, people, around

31

her: *sa'marenniath*. Should I wish on her the body's silence too? No. She couldn't live like that."

"You don't *know* that. She—"

"No. You just don't understand."

"Then as long as you're starting with a blank slate anyhow," Garin persisted, "why not produce a woman who'd really suit you? Be exactly in every detail what you'd most like? Or do you remember her as perfect now? Jannus? Have you plated her over already, in just this little while, that you've covered all the faults and shortcomings, the times she hurt you, the times you just couldn't make her see what you meant no matter how hard you tried, and how it felt then? Have you forgotten those things so soon?"

He'd caught Jannus' attention with that—either the idea or the accusation, it didn't matter which, as long as it interrupted the intolerable deadly grieving. But the mobile hadn't often found anyone who couldn't be tempted by the offer of a literal dream-lover, no matter what lopsided monstrosity such a construct would be to less partial eyes, and to itself. Dreams didn't do well in daylight.

"I remember," Jannus replied eventually. "It doesn't change anything. . . . She's not some inept speech, to be edited down to fit my liking. I'd wish the *marenniath* healed, that was hers before she came to me. Nothing else. No changes." Jannus bent his head onto his arms again, his uninflected voice becoming almost completely inaudible.

Garin thought he'd said something about its being no use, that she was truly and completely gone now.

"It was only the meat, after all," Garin argued, throwing yesterday's word back at Jannus to rouse him.

That made Jannus look again at the fire. "It was all I had, all that was left. I guess I'm not fit to be a Tek yet after all. . . ."

Recalling the absolute single-mindedness, Garin thought Jannus had probably come as close as a man could without the support of a Tek body, obedient to his will. But he didn't say so. Instead, Garin remarked inconsequentially, "I could fix that for you."

"What? Oh." Jannus murmured. "No. I earned this. It's . . . fitting. Let it be."

Garin asked, "Are you going to give her up, then?" He put

the question quietly because people were retreating in haste onto the pier, warned back by the fire crew and the visibly imminent collapse of the warehouse's front facade.

Jannus said dully, "I can't see any way to go on. There's nothing—"

Garin lost the end of that because the facade began to go: sagging forward, boards and timbers separating, all afire, striking the street stones in a mighty uprush of sparks and rebounding coals, some of which landed in the river and some among the retreating crowd. People recoiled. Some planking gave way, and people fell into and over each other. Garin got a firm grip on the heavy post and held his place; but when he was able to turn, there was a stranger in a red plaid coat beside him and he couldn't see Jannus at all.

When Jannus surfaced he was blinded by ice sludge and so confused by astonishment that, when he'd blinked his eyes momentarily clear, all he could see were senseless shapes of moving light and dark. The ability to breathe seemed to have been shocked out of him. He bumped against something, failed to catch hold, and the current drew him along, and under.

He'd never been so cold before in his life. The chill seared right through the layers of heavy clothing. He felt naked in liquid fire and moved randomly, with slow awkward gestures.

He'd never been better than a middling-poor swimmer. That wasn't going to be enough.

The current pushed him against something and he clasped it with both arms, having lost all feeling in his hands, his head above water again. He was under a dock. The planks were close above him: he could see his hand strike them but didn't feel the contact.

Nobody could see him from above.

He managed to gather enough breath to make a noise, but that wouldn't do any good either, not with the fire and the crowd. He held the piling tighter and tried to think.

There'd been at least one Valde in the crowd. He knew because she'd pushed him off the dock—deliberately, he thought. She'd struck out, being forced so near what she'd have heard in his *farioh* just then: striking out merely to shove the hurt away from her. If the water and the cold took him, that was nothing to her. He knew Valde.

He was shaking so badly he lost hold of the piling and was carried clear. For a moment he was facing the riverwall between docks. It was empty of anyone to see him or be called to. Then the ice sludge closed over him.

He was carried under the next dock between pilings, too far to touch any. By the time the slow, implacable current drifted him to the next dock beyond, he'd forgotten any thought of holding on, was adrift within himself too, trying to keep his face above the ice from bodily instinct alone rather than any coherent, purposeful effort to stay afloat.

There came to be only two conditions: being able or unable to breathe, and increasingly less difference between them. There was dark, and slow silence. He'd lost the ability to feel the cold.

Then the breathing state continued a while without choked interruptions. He came to himself enough to reach out and found he'd been carried against a slant of planking—a section of fallen dock, one side sagging below the water line, a sieve holding a mound of trapped branches and floating debris, all cased in a glaze of ice.

Belatedly the thought came that the inspeaking of the Valde had no need of breath and that he'd become, through laborious practice, an inspeaker—even an *in'farioh*, a farspeaker. Loud enough to be heard against the tumult of any mob, any fire. . . .

The knowledge didn't seem to matter. He hadn't the energy to focus the speaking attitude-sequences or even the will to form them. There was no Valde to whom he had anything to say.

Garin was frantic. Within seconds he felt certain Jannus had been pushed off into the river but what with the ice, the drifting trash, and the crooked boards of the decrepit dock itself, Garin couldn't catch sight of him.

There was no sense in his first impulse, to just jump blind. He wouldn't have hesitated to sacrifice one more mobile, but that would have left nobody to see to Jannus unless, once in the all-but-frozen water, he could locate Jannus almost at once. And that was unlikely.

There were few things more destructive than stupid heroics. He got a cry raised, which was no use either, people peering under their hands and leaning into each other to no purpose, meanwhile working his way back to the road, using shoulders and elbows indiscriminately to force a way. The collapsed bonfire that had been the front of the warehouse was a barrier across the whole width of the street. Garin ran along the unreliable stones of the riverwall until the heat was behind him, then dropped down on the paving and reached the next pier downriver. But he still couldn't see anything of Jannus.

He spotted two Awiro walking away up a cross street and discarded his second impulse, to just grab them. He was *sa'farioh,* and they'd be sure to notice that, if he were stupid enough to force his unnaturalness right in their faces. So Garin grabbed the nearest patroller instead, spun him around, and pointed. "Get those Valde. My friend's in the river, and I can't see him."

With only the briefest hesitation the patroller called to his fellow on the opposite side of the street and sent him after the two Awiro. "Can he swim?" he asked curtly of Garin, scanning the river.

"Not much. And that's no summer pool."

"Go fetch a closed drawcart. Blankets, if you can."

"You see him?"

"Not yet. Get them anyhow. No use to fish him out and then have him die of cold on the street stones . . ." responded the patroller absently, moving to check the vicinity of each pier in succession.

The other patroller was coming with one of the Valde, so Garin drifted back into the crowd, which was still absorbed in viewing the blazing destruction. At the cross street he turned and ran.

He had to go almost two blocks uphill before he encountered a shut drawcart, a wooden box balanced on two wheels, held level by the carter himself between the shafts. The carter already had a passenger, but Garin jerked open the door and hauled the man summarily out with a rapid explanation of the emergency. The passenger, a Smith, at once banked his indignation and volunteered to fetch blankets or whatever he

35

could find. The carter, turning in his harness, announced flatly, "I don't carry no deaders."

Garin said, "Double fare," which was more to the point.

"Triple. And if it's a deader, it don't go in my cart."

"Done. Get moving."

" 'F I carry deaders," the carter justified himself, pocketing the handful of coins Garin had given him, "I'll need a new cart. Word gets around. Folk don't like it, riding where a deader's been. I got to eat too."

"Just get moving!"

The former passenger, who named himself a Coopersmith, had commandeered two good-sized blankets from the shopkeeper and trudged downhill remarking to Garin how all the Ardun Smiths knew Jannus Arbiter at least to speak to, on account of old Elda Innsmith and his boys being so thick with him over the years, and what a shame it had been to lose that outlandish wife of his and then the scandal on top of it, the woman not even decently gone to the fire, just stuffed away someplace, most like, and nobody to know where till the spring thawed her out, without the cold to keep her. . . .

They'd gotten Jannus out of the water, Garin saw, by the head of a broken dock downriver. That the carter didn't object when Jannus was carried toward the box of the cart proved that the Bremneri was still alive. But Garin didn't need that minimal assurance. He'd have known, if Jannus had died.

The Awiro was still there. Garin asked the Coopersmith abruptly, "Can you see him home?"

"My place is closer. That lad needs to get into the warm right away. Not clear the other side of the city."

Though he didn't want to, Garin fell behind. He lost himself among the crowd until the drawcart had been trotted away and the Valde released to her own business by the patrollers who then returned to try to get people away from the warehouse on the downstream side of the one Garin had fired: its roof was smoldering, and the hoses were being moved to concentrate the water there.

From his agents' reports, during his tenure as Pedross' spymaster, Garin knew the Smiths occupied the whole of the Rocky Point district, the triangle at the narrow end of Ardun where the Morimmon joined Arant Dunrimmon's swifter flow. The enclave was coming to be called Smith Point. The leases of a few businesses and houses remained to be bought up, but, except for these, it was solid redheaded Smiths anywhere you looked for about twelve square blocks.

Garin hadn't caught the Coopersmith's first name, but it didn't matter. Word would run to Elda Innsmith, perhaps even sooner than to Jannus' own household. Waving over an unoccupied drawcart after walking a few blocks, Garin directed the carter simply, "Set me down by Elda Innsmith's place," and the carter started out at a jog-trot without asking any more detailed directions. Tired, Garin settled back on the seat and shut the leather window-flap.

The carter stopped in front of a substantial house, stone below, wood above, with a railing and several yards of trodden snow separating it from the sidewalk. Garin walked slowly down one side of the street and then up the other, watching for a messenger's arrival. But nobody came. So he knocked at the door and asked of the broad ruddy young woman who answered whether Elda was at home. He made no attempt at diversion because there was no Truthtell, no least touch of Valde blood, in any of the Smiths. They married only their own.

"Why, you just missed him," the woman responded, pulling a shawl more tightly around her. "What you want with him, tell me?"

"I want to find out how Jannus is getting on, is the truth of it."

That seemed to validate him in the woman's judgment. "Well, he's down to Matt Coopersmith's. Two squares down, half a square east, next past the rope-walk. That do you?"

Garin said he was obliged and started walking according to her directions.

He'd had a winter ducking himself once in another body, and remembered perfectly well how long it'd taken the meat to recover from those few seconds of bitter cold. And Jannus had been in the water far longer. And those two Valde, Garin thought, who'd been strolling away so unconcerned: Jannus, with his demonstrated strength as a farspeaker, should have been able to bring them running. Valde clear into Lifganin and up into Entellith, beyond the Thornwall, should have been able to hear the kind of inspoken shout Jannus was able to put out, by all past evidence. But the two Awiro had shown no sign of reacting to any such call. That made Garin suspect there hadn't been any.

At the Coopersmith house he again named his concern and was accepted. An older woman showed him to a side parlor, saying, "You just bide here with Elda a bit. . . ."

It had been over ten years since the mobile had seen the Innsmith; Elda seem unchanged, a solid old man like a keg of stones scowling up under thick white brows at a stranger's being shown in. Garin went straight to the fire and stooped to put both hands on the fender's warmth, without any fear of being recognized: their last meeting had been two faces ago.

"He come asking after Jannus," the woman explained to Elda, who settled deeper in his chair with a noncommittal grunt.

"I was there, when he went into the river." Garin worked at unfastening the front of his short waterman's jacket, prompting, "How is he?"

"They got him inside, there," Elda nodded toward a wall. "Blue in the face when they fetched him in, so they tell me. But breathing all right, and if nothing an't cold-burned. . . ."

"You haven't seen him?"

Elda scowled uncomfortably. " 'Tan't my house. Anyhow, bathing a man, that's women's work. It don't call for a crowd. Where you know Jannus from, tell me?"

"Quickmoor, mostly." The mobile never lied; but seldom did he tell all the truth he knew, and a careful fraction of a truth would generally do as well as any lie.

"*That* place," said Elda disdainfully, and lapsed into silence. Garin occupied himself with trying to get warm.

Presently the woman came in again carrying a crockery pitcher of hot ale and a tray of mugs. Young Sparrowhawk, entering behind her, immediately demanded of Elda, "What's happened?"

"Don't know, lad. What in the green world was he doing out on the east docks at first light to begin with, tell me?"

"*I* don't know, he was gone 'fore I was up. He don't tell me what he's about half the time, you know that," Sparrowhawk remarked to Elda without rancor. "You know what he was doing away off on the east side?"

"There was something in a warehouse there he wanted me to have a look at, see if I could use it," replied Garin calmly, turning to put his back to the fire. The mug was warm between his hands.

"What manner of a thing?" prompted Elda bluntly.

"Some diverted cargo," said the mobile, meeting Elda's staring green eyes with equanimity.

A younger woman, her copper-colored hair bound up in a cloth and her naturally ruddy complexion flushed bright pink, looked in to ask, "Elda Hildursson, you know anybody by the name of 'Garin'?"

Bracing one hand on the floor, the mobile straightened, then carefully set the mug down. "I'm Garin."

"He's bound and determined to talk to him," said the woman to Elda, half apologetically, asking permission.

"He'd best go and do it, then," Elda remarked, giving consent in a neutral voice.

Garin followed the women into a room so full of steam he could hardly see. Hot stones, he guessed approvingly, and water. Nothing better for a deep chill, if the steam itself didn't choke you.

"Shai?" came Jannus' voice, followed by a spell of unhealthy resonant coughing.

"Hush," advised the mobile softly, but found the woman had gone out again, leaving them alone. Garin felt his way forward until he made out Jannus sitting bent over a table, a blanket around his shoulders and head like a dark, cowled cape.

"Shai?" Jannus said again, with no caution whatever. "Get me out of here."

Obediently moving nearer, Garin nevertheless warned, "You'll freeze your lungs, going out from this. Think, before you make me do that to you."

The mobile had only the one drastic, final way to refuse any direct order Jannus gave him. They both had to be very careful, walking that knife.

Jannus said hoarsely, "Never mind, then," before Garin touched him. "Han Halla," he added, explaining in the same favorless tone Elda reserved for Quickmoor and such places.

He meant the fog. The mobile, too, disliked misty entanglements, with no clear sense of distance and things visible

39

only at intimate approach. "Han Halla it is. No sinkpools, though. . . . How do you think you are?"

Instead of answering, Jannus directed abruptly, "Don't go," before the coughing caught him again.

"I'm still here," responded the mobile.

"No. I mean, *stay*. Till Bronh comes back. I've been thinking about Bronh. . . ." Jannus stopped and just breathed for a while. The mobile didn't interrupt. Presently Jannus said, "I don't know how to go on, now that we've lost . . . what I was keeping. Do you? Know any way?"

"None that would serve, except for what I said before," replied Garin carefully.

"And that won't do. But maybe Bronh knows. Some other way to do it. She's got a stake . . . of her own in this. I'm not complaining. But it's not to you what it is to me. You have nothing at stake."

The mobile, with an effort, kept himself from comment.

"But till Bronh says . . . that it's impossible," Jannus went on, between short, labored breaths, "I'm still going to try. Do you know . . . where Bronh is now?"

The mobile reached along the rapport and was given the information. "She's in Valde, moving southeast from . . . all I have are surface-grid coordinates, but they wouldn't mean anything to you. And there aren't any names. . . . I know, but I can't tell you. It just won't go into words."

Garin found this frustration more than he could accept.

"I want a synaptic transmitter on you," Garin said, with great seriousness. "The locator implant isn't enough. I want a synaptic transmitter on you too, so I can *reach* you when I need to! All but near enough to touch, and no way to reach. . . . I nearly *lost* you!"

Jannus responded with ominously quiet words: "*What* locator implant?"

The mobile braced himself, realizing what he'd unguardedly gotten into.

It would have been so thoroughly commonplace a matter to any Tek that Garin had referred to it without stopping to consider that Jannus wasn't a Tek but a Bremneri, with a Bremneri's pathological sensitivity to any suggestion of having been spied on or misled—twin heritages of oppression by the *marenniath* and by Truthtell, respectively—and, more-over, that it was a matter Jannus had known nothing about.

This was going to be bad.

It had been a stupid, needless admission. Being tired and anxious was no excuse.

The mobile opened himself more fully to the unsleeping deliberation of his larger self. He said, "It's the least, and the most fundamental, of precautions, Jannus: all Tek bodies have locators as a matter of course. You didn't, so I implanted one. It merely tells me whether you're alive or dead and, within a mile or two, where you are. No more than that."

"When did you do this to me?" Jannus demanded, still quietly: waiting to decide just how angry he was entitled to be.

"Ten years ago, last summer: when you came into *Sunfire* and claimed authority over the use of the Rule of One."

"You had no *right!*"

"I had the need and the power to do it. I didn't, and don't, need your consent. I have to know whether whoever holds the Rule of One is alive or not, from minute to minute. You weren't a Tek. So I did what was necessary. Only my care-lessness made you aware of it. It's unfortunate that it offends your tribal privacy taboos. Like you, sometimes I am not as guarded in these exchanges as I ought to be."

Jannus' own carelessness was fresh enough to make him tacitly admit the justice of that. The fold of blanket slid off his head as he looked down at himself. "Where . . . ?"

"The junction between the brain and the spinal cord," the mobile informed him in a deliberately colorless voice.

"I wish you hadn't told me."

"So do I," agreed Garin fervently. "Now if we're done with *that*, I *still* want a synaptic relay implanted in you, besides the locator. You could have *died*, Jannus—for no reason at all! A fire, a crowd's flash of panic—"

"People die sometimes. For no reason at all," Jannus pointed out, with ironic reserve.

"You're not 'people.' When you took the Rule of One you gave your death over into my keeping. Irrevocably. You knew that."

"Do you resent the competition?"

"Your death is *mine* to give, when it becomes necessary. For cause. No other way. You are subject to the consequences of your choices, and to necessity. Not to chance. That's how it has to be."

"I do hear you." It was a characteristically Bremneri phrase: evasive and supposedly neutral. "And this relay-thing: what is that?"

"It's a link to your rede," responded Garin, putting it as simply as he could. "Like a permanent redecap. I have one. It's the way I can reach out to . . . to myself, the rest of me, and know where Bronh is, for instance. It would give you that same access, to all the Shai holds. And that's the way it *should* be. That's what the Rule of One is, after all: the right to choose how the Shai's power and knowledge is to be applied in the world. That requires access—"

"You say it's a link. So both ends are open. The Shai would see through my eyes, and know whatever I know, just as he does with you. Isn't that so?"

"Theoretically, but it would be up to you to initiate contact. I don't—"

"One mobile at a time is enough," said Jannus flatly.

"I *say*, the link would be under your control, once you got used to it. But in an emergency, I'd have a way to reach your rede before the body died. You'd wake in *Sunfire*, safe," explained Garin earnestly, sure if only he could make the advantages clear, Jannus would discard his stubborn mistrust and realize what a rare thing he was being offered.

"I don't know," responded Jannus slowly, and paused for another bout of coughing. "You always said . . . my holding the Rule of One was . . . nominal. That I had no business actually . . . trying to *use* it. Has that changed?"

Garin smiled, stiffly quizzical. "Who called *Sunfire* out of orbit? Who called this mobile into being? Who just said to me, *Stay here*? What do you think you've been *doing*, Jannus?"

"Trying to get Poli back. That's all."

"All you want to do is raise the dead, no matter if it means tipping the isles of Andras, and Ardun, and Valde all askew. . . . A little thing: *simple*. . . ."

Jannus admitted the justice of the sarcasm with a series of nods. "Wanting it is simple. The rest, I don't care about. I told you."

"I know that."

"Do I have to get this link-thing, to go on, about Poli?" Jannus asked, disliking it, yet prepared to be resigned if it was the necessary price.

"No. The one thing has nothing to do with the other."

Jannus was visibly relieved. "I bet you wished you could lie to me, just then," he remarked perceptively, with something near a smile.

"*I* wish you'd accept the implant. I don't want to go through this morning again. Ever."

"Nor me," Jannus agreed, both turning somber again. Pointedly shelving the matter of the implant, Jannus asked, "Can you get Bronh here?"

"She doesn't fly to *my* fist any more. Arranges meetings for food or rebodying and that's all I see of her." The Shai had refused to prevent Pedross from recruiting Valde to become a communications network among isles and ships. Bronh had broken with him over it: new ties to the lowlands were emphatically not what Bronh had in mind for Valde.

"There should be a way of catching her attention. . . . I can't *think* now," Jannus was complaining. "How long do I have to stay in this?"

"Until Elda says otherwise, in a Smith house."

"Is he here?"

"He graciously surrendered his rightful turn to me. He's waiting in the parlor. Sparrowhawk, too."

"He should be home with the girls, they'll be scared sick, *this* now, on top of Poli. . . . Tell Sparrow I said to go home, will you? No. I want to see him first. Ask him to look in here first, will you? And then Elda. Of course Elda would have come—I wasn't thinking. And you go on, too. You look awful."

Garin found himself laughing. "I'm used to being an old man and keeping regular hours."

"Oh, didn't you get any rest either?" rejoined Jannus, quite innocently, and Garin knew he had better end this conversation before he said some other irrevocably stupid, incautious thing.

"The chance to see Ardun again first-hand, so as to say, is too valuable to waste. I've always *liked* Ardun," Garin responded.

"And before that, you liked the Longlands. And before

that, the Windwards," replied Jannus, naming the most recent conquests of the late Ashai Rey, Master of Andras before his son Pedross had inherited the title. The mobile had been Ashai, two faces ago.

"I like them too, yes," agreed Garin calmly and took his leave, pausing to relay Jannus' summons to Sparrowhawk on his way out.

What most urgently needed attending to, it seemed to Garin, was to block any possible interference from Bronh by stealing the redstone. Trudging in search of a drawcart, he hoped that errand wouldn't take very long so that he could get to sleep before noon.

It was turning into one of those bright, windless days that made people imagine spring. Garin unlatched the front of his jacket, surveying Jannus' house from the street with the same deliberate care he'd have given a city he meant presently to sack.

By accident or design, the house was a small fortress, each part capable of being closed off from the others and defended separately. The only ways in were by the front door or else through the bare garden, that approach in plain sight of all the inward-looking windows. And Sparrowhawk hadn't, somehow, the look of a man who would run off, leaving five children alone, without first checking that every latch, bar, and shutter was secure, no matter how urgent the summons. The two inner doors were almost certainly both locked and barred.

There were folk in place in Ardun, a network of agents who gathered such light as came their way and passed it on; but Garin hadn't had the opportunity yet to make contact or attach them to his immediate uses. He'd have to manage this alone. He referred his evaluation to *Sunfire* for review. The Shai concurred, as Garin had expected.

So he knocked at the door. The looksee panel opened presently, showing him the gaze of bird-black eyes high enough to look directly out at him through the lattice.

"I just came from Jannus," offered the mobile. "He'll be all right. He should be home before evening. I need—"

The looksee was vacated and a piercing voice sounded in a retreating treble screech of *"Mal-liel"*

And Garin was left on the step to review his tactics. He checked that the door was indeed solidly barred as well as latched, then knocked again several times. Peering through the lattice, he saw the lanky girl returning from the passage door on the left, scowling and muttering to herself. As Garin moved back from the door, the child's face again filled the panel and she prompted, "Say something else."

"There's something of mine in his study. I can't wait till evening for it."

"Mallie *said* so, but I didn't believe it," remarked the girl to herself. "Say some more."

Garin was mildly disconcerted to conclude he was being viewed as a freak, the one with the odd voice that didn't resonate in the ways Truthtell was accustomed to hearing.

He said, "I'm in a hurry. Will you let me in?"

After several thuds and clicks, the door was opened. "I'm Sua. Sualiche. Mallie's gone back to the print shop, I guess, and the three are some place. . . . But I'm not done with my midmeal." She displayed a chunk of bread topped with a thick layer of jam. "I'm twelve," she announced slyly, to see if his deformity let him be lied to, like most people.

"You're not. You're nine," responded Garin firmly, heading across the entry hall toward the stairs. "You're all nine."

Actually it would have been easier to believe her age to be what she'd claimed. The body was long-legged and adolescent, the face with no childish roundness—thin, in fact, almost gaunt. Except for the eyes, she could have been taken for a Valde.

Garin thought, *growthyear*. At least this one of the five half-blooded children had inherited the sudden onset of physical maturity unique to the Valde.

The girl ambled across the entry hall after him; she asked, "Why do you sound that way?"

Garin started climbing. "What way?"

"*You* know. How you sound. I can't hear what you mean, or what you don't," responded Sua, in steady, unhurried pursuit.

"I sound fine to me," Garin remarked dismissively, reaching the upper landing and moving quickly to grasp the handle of the left-hand door. It jarred slightly: locked.

"Da keeps it locked," Sua observed serenely, watching him from the head of the stairs.

"Where's the key?" He only hoped she'd go away to fetch it. All he needed was one or two unwatched minutes to have the door open, snatch, and be waiting outside again when she got back.

"The Sparrow keeps the spare keys." By her tone, she was not overfond of her kinsman.

Trying another tack, Garin remarked, "You left the front door standing open. Sparrowhawk should be along any minute. Don't you think you'd better shut it?"

"I'm right here," Sua defended herself. "I can see everything." She demonstrated, leaning far over the bannister, and lost the rest of her bread. Pulling herself back, she shot Garin a sullen, embarrassed look, then started rapidly down the stairs to retrieve the dropped bread.

Instantly Garin put into the keyhole the nail he'd worked out of the frame of a drawcart, finding the wards of the lock by touch.

"What's this door doing open?" demanded a man's voice from below: Sparrowhawk.

"I was just *doing* it," came Sua's resentful reply.

"Why'd you open it in the first place?"

"That bay man. He wants something he forgot upstairs yesterday. . . ."

Garin pushed open the study door. The redstone still sat holding down a stack of papers on the desk, brilliantly green in the in-slanting sunlight.

Garin had gotten two paces into the room when the sound of the stairs being taken three at a stride told him there just wasn't going to be time. He had the door shut and was standing in the hall when the young Bremneri reached the upper landing.

"What was it that you wanted?" Sparrowhawk inquired curtly, reaching past Garin with the key.

"Some names and records that I need," responded Garin, with entire accuracy. "They're not where I'm staying, so I thought I'd better look here."

The tone seemed to diminish Sparrowhawk's automatic mistrust of finding a stranger abroad in the household. He said, "You want papers, you're welcome to *try* looking. . . ."

46

He got the door open, apparently without noticing it had been unlocked, and waved at the untidy assortment of scrolls, loose sheets, and leather document boxes covering nearly every flat surface. "But was I you, I'd wait till Jannus is home. He knows where everything is." Quite unself-consciously, Sparrowhawk crossed to the desk, picked up the redstone, and dropped it casually in his coat pocket, waiting for Garin to decide whether or not he wanted to try poking through the papers, showing no least awareness of Garin's chagrin.

"That green stone was pretty. Can I see it?" asked the mobile.

"I s'pose." Sparrowhawk displayed the redstone on the flat of his palm.

"What is it?"

"Some trinket, luck-piece, something. Now this has happened, he wants to start wearing it again. It was this morning he needed it, not now." Sparrowhawk shrugged, implying illogic wasn't any surprise to him from that quarter. "If you want to look for your list, go ahead. I can wait, and *he's* not moving any place, not till Elda says."

"That's a bad cough he's got," Garin remarked idly, staring at the faceted sides of the redstone just beyond practical reach.

"It *is*, that. He was lucky you were by," responded the Bremneri. He bounced the stone restlessly twice and then put it back in his pocket. "Well, you going to try to sort through this nest of scraps, or not?"

"Not," decided Garin, making the word a sigh. "It'll have to wait for another time. I'm too tired to begin a thing like that now."

He went to the stairs and started down. Over the bannister he could see Sua waiting for him below. As he reached the turn, she asked, "You find it? What you were looking for?"

"Couldn't seem to put my hand on it," admitted the mobile, wearily amused. "Maybe I lost it before I came here. I'm not going to worry about it."

Sua called past him, "Sparrow, I'm going to go tell Mallie that Da's mending, but old Tanner's sick and the shop's closed. You going to lock me out?"

"I'll be back in about an hour. You can tend yourself, or

47

else stay at Dan's place, that long anyhow," Sparrowhawk replied.

Garin left them to settle the question of household security any way they pleased. Once Sparrowhawk left to deliver the redestone to Jannus there wouldn't be anything in the house worth the breaking in for anyhow, nothing worth the missed sleep.

Under a pale half-moon's light Bronh circled, slowly surveying Elenin Vale, which for over eight centuries had been the training place and wintering ground of each Summerfair's muster of Valde troopmaids. Haffa who'd been moved to respond to the Troopcalling, advance to the fire and capture a bit of smoke between their hands, were led here to finish out their growthyear. Here they would await the thaws that would free them to journey to their places of service among the Bremneri riverstocks.

Instead of fifty fires, there were two. Instead of several hundred adolescent Haffa, Bronh counted twenty-seven plus a troopleader distinguishable by the fluency of her breathtalk.

Bronh decided it was time to try to rouse the Singing and empty Elenin.

She glided to a landing high on the bare north rim of the gorge—Elenin was at the edge of the timberline—and made a meal of concentrate-paste kept unfrozen against the warmth of her underside, like an egg. She'd waited a long time to loose the Valde from this, the last of their servitudes.

First they'd been the Teks' pets: pets, or slaves, or toys, meat for anybody's killing, anybody's pleasure, their numbers dwindling because of the unconscionable genetic tinkering of Gaherin of Debern Keep.

Bronh had been born into Debern Keep, on the west rim of the High Plain overlooking the lowlands of Bremner. She had chosen to be bodied female, as had become the custom in Debern after Gaherin's time—a subtle, largely unconscious preference, Bronh had come to think—an alliance with the passive and the dark, with what waited and dreamed and endured rather than with that which worked its will upon the nature of things in a more direct and immediate fashion.

It had become her custom to shelter whatever runaway Valde came her way. She built for them a sanctuary on the lowlands, which came to be called the Wood of Fathori and in whose making the whole energies of Debern came gradually to be absorbed. Most of the Debern Teks had gone, one by one, to live in Fathori, creating it as they went, so that it became a living artwork of fantastic splendor whose name still had not been forgotten.

But Bronh herself had remained in Debern, protecting with its powers what had been made from being despoiled by the impulses and whims of her peers. When a Rork Keep Tek who held the Rule of One for a few centuries set aside the vaster forests east of the High Plain to be a larger sanctuary, Bronh's smaller protection continued, unchanged. As she'd expected, when the Shai put aside that master, as the Shai eventually put aside all masters, Valde were again hunted down the mountain passes and among the trees. But no hunters could approach Fathori—not until the general rebellion of the lowlands and the sealing of the High Plain behind its force field Barrier.

Bronh had seen Fathori incinerated then, helpless to protect it or prevent the flight of its Valde into the lowlands, where they made alliance with Bremneri folk and became scattered and lost among them, leaving only a crop of half-blooded children and the legacy of the Truthtell to mark their passing.

Bronh had gone then into the eastern forests among the Valde that remained and crafted for them a culture that would keep them alive; for that was Bronh's own particular art. Whatever native culture had been theirs before the Teks landed, and before Gaherin's changes, was forgotten, lost beyond recovery. Bronh foresaw them being lost as the Fathori Valde had been lost, among the greater numbers of alien peoples; she had bonded them with shared rituals suited to their natures and the unique rhythms of their lives and perceptions. She had kept them one people, and they had survived. She had laid out a timetable and embodied it in myth to give it the proper emotional resonance of its meaning, a timetable not of years but of sequences and events which would mark the path of their return to what they had been before the first Tek stepped from *Sunfire*'s port onto the bare sand of the High Plain.

Having laid down this foundation, Bronh had been trapped

for a time within the Barrier, unable to oversee or guide what she'd set in motion. To gain escape she put on the bird and made alliance with the Shai, becoming a servant's servant, obedient to the Shai's purposes so long as he would forward hers. She had become, consciously, what she had always been: the Keeper of Valde.

She could imagine Elenin as it would have been in those first minutes of alien intrusion almost four millennia ago, before any native life knew of the invasion: empty, the snow unmarked under the vast moon, unnamed.

It was time for Elenin to be emptied again.

She spiraled down and, in a long, soundless glide, landed on a bough of a tree midway between the two fires. From both sides she heard truncated scraps of breathtalk interspersed with the humming cadences that commonly accompanied inspeaking among Valde conversing in each other's presence.

"Haffa Wir'e," Bronh called in a metallic, carrying voice, "when will the Change come?"

As one, the Haffa arose and came from their fires to surround the tree, puzzled and uncertain, a few fearful of the phantom voice coming out of the emptiness where inhearing told them nothing living was.

The Tek had had only a few generations of Valde to work upon since her escape in birdform from the High Plain: for a moment she believed not one among this group knew the response. Then she heard a blurred mutter of "Bronh Sefar'" and was reassured. *Bronh se'farioh*, her name was: *Windvoice*, for the wind that also had an audible voice with no selfsinging behind it. Teks, they'd forgotten; but the name they'd given her had been imbedded in their culture in the Lore of the Change and had endured, not signifying a Tek but instead the harbinger of what was to come.

With more assurance Bronh demanded again, "When will the Change come?"

From below and to Bronh's left, the troopleader offered the words of the ancient response: "The Change will come when it comes. In its proper season, on the wind."

"And who will say it, and confirm it?"

"The wind will say it. *Bronh Sefar'*."

The poses altered into a different tension, and there was a

soft murmur of humming, counterpoint to the inspoken exchanges Bronh could only guess at, as they felt the forces of prophecy, belief, and age-long waiting impendent on this moment of present breath.

Bronh said, "And what are the marks of the season of the Change?"

"The *in'marenniathe* will begin the Singing, and whoever hears it will answer it, and they will all be changed. Is it coming, then? Is it now?" the troopleader demanded, moving nearer the tree and staring up.

Instead of answering, Bronh asked, "Which among you are *in'marenniathe?*"

The *in'marenniathe*, the hypersensitives, were always the first to react to any change in the surrounding emotional ambiance. Bronh was mildly surprised to find almost half the group making some motion or gesture to call her eyes to them—surprised, because insingers comprised a fractional minority of the general population.

Drawing conclusions, Bronh said, "And you, troopleader, are *in'farioh.*"

"I am a farspeaker, yes. I am Callea: troopmaid to Dark in Bremner and now called to be troopleader to Slatefen."

Gently Bronh asked, "Where is your troop, Callea Wir?"

For a full troop was two hundred Haffa, not the mere handful scattered around the tree.

The troopleader bowed her head and made a cupped-hand gesture of spilling. "Few would answer my Troopcalling. I had more—a hand of tens. But I could not hold them. These remain. I do not know how I am to keep our faith with the riverstocks."

Bronh was elated to know that an *in'farioh*'s strong Troopcalling could draw scarcely a thousandth of Haffa in their growthyear, in their season of Choosing—and that a disproportionate number of those drawn had been *in'marenniathe*, the most susceptible, who rarely survived even their first year of troopservice. Resistance must have been strong.

But Bronh also sympathized with Callea's apparent sense of personal failure. Anyone expecting to attract a group of responsive, admiring followers and instead drawing only a few and then failing to hold nearly half of *them* would feel disappointment and frustration.

Callea's concern for the Bremneri riverstocks Bronh discounted. Bremner was too far away for anything that happened there to touch Callea here. It was merely the riverstocks' matriarch's own fears, repeated from habit.

It was merely Callea's pride and rank within the immediate dominance hierarchy that had been injured.

"Those who did not answer your Troopcalling, and those who left you, they were simply the smallest leaves that are first to stir when the wind rises," Bronh formulated, to salve the troopleader's hurt. "They simply felt the approach of the Change sooner, having had fewer dealings with the Unhearing to dull them. For the Change is indeed upon you. It has been gathering since the first troopmaid turned from her assigned post and walked away. You *in'marenniathe,* you know it. You're pulled this way and that, as the Change comes. Not because I say it: because it has waked, and you feel its drawing."

The humming became less dissonant, consensus, unanimity establishing itself.

Bronh said, "It's the time of turning away and turning together. Cast out whatever will not fit your harmonies, all stranger-enemies—sing what you know, what you are. Sing to the Haffa still bound to the troops, and to the Awiro: all who are outside or distant. Call them away. Call them back. The *sa'marenniathe,* the Unhearing, are last year's leaves. They have no part in this, or in you. Sing what you know!"

Though Bronh's words had reached the Haffa only through the medium of Callea's understanding, the troopleader herself reacted in opposition. She swung, challenging, to confront the surrounding ring of young Haffa. But her dominance had been overshadowed by Bronh's silence, the growing unity among the Haffa, and the intangible weight of waking myth. The Haffa were already escaping her—some eager, some slow, but united in their own harmony she could not disrupt. They were turning away, light-footed among the drifts, and Callea could not hold them.

"And what was it for," demanded the deserted troopleader sharply as the sounds of escape faded, "the ten years' service that only two hands and six of us returned from, of the two hundred?"

It had kept 184 Brotherless Valde from passing on their

marred genetic inheritance to the new generation. But Bronh didn't expect Callea to understand the pitiless culling of the Haffa which troopservice had been designed to provide.

She said merely, "Without it, the Change would not have come. It is ended now."

"But I am called to be a troopleader," protested Callea.

"Who calls you, Callea Wir?" responded Bronh, with great compassion for the Haffa's reluctance to surrender her familiar servitude: after the Rebellion, most Valde had been the same, with nothing but freedom to fill the vacuum where their Tek masters had ruled, bending confusedly to every wind of power that touched them.

"The need of the riverstocks," replied Callea, "the faith of all the Haffa troopmaids gone to the ground in keeping them safe."

"That is last year's snow, a shadow's shadow. As you stand here in this place, who calls you?"

Callea the farspeaker attended to the nightsinging of Elenin. "No one," she admitted. "They have no need of what I have become."

"Then go until you find a calling to draw you."

Callea brooded for a time, then said, "At the Summerfair of my returning I saw grown Haffa of the troops, deserters, faith-breakers who did not stay out their terms, being brided like full-term freemaids. I gave away the bridestone I had won. I would be no part of such a briding as that. I will be a troopleader, as I am called to be. If I can call no Haffa to me, I will go alone."

Bronh doubted any Valde could tolerate even a full week of complete isolation. But she didn't dispute the troopleader's brash declaration. There was no need. The long weeks until thaw would bring their own arguments of silence and unshared waiting. And, soon, the Singing would be moving throughout Valde, exerting its own power to draw and merge. Long before thaw, this Valde would have rejoined the rest.

So Bronh said only, "Burn bright, and fare well, then, Callea Wir," and left her there, standing poised between the two fires.

But Bronh had meant to leave Elenin altogether empty; and the lone figure annoyed and troubled her as she spiraled higher, trying to identify the exact nature of her disquiet.

What was one Valde, more or less, as long as the rest were drawn into mergence?

It would seem, Bronh concluded, that there were some Haffa, survivors of the troopservice and perhaps their descendants, who'd become so thoroughly contaminated by the outside contact, by alien values and behavior, that they might resist the Change though it sing to them from all sides. They'd still wish to subject themselves to the incomprehension of unhearing strangers when they could be losing themselves among their own, fully known, uncritically accepted, everything alien shut out and forgotten.

Refusing freedom for themselves, they would also attempt to deny it to others—as Callea would do, if she could. At some crucial moment at the coming Summerfair, the resistance of even one such Haffa, not even a farspeaker, might sway the multitude into discord and confusion.

The whole meaning of the Change was that all such artificial divisions as Haffa and Hafera, freemaid, troopmaid, and Awiro, be discarded, transcended. Bronh did not mean to see new divisions merely substituted for the old. The Valde must become one undifferentiated whole, all alien influence and experience shed, as they had been in the beginning or Bronh would not be satisfied.

Callea's reaction intensified Bronh's conviction that she'd need all her resources when, to confirm and validate the Change, she came before all the assembled Valde at the Summerfair as she'd promised them a long age ago, ending what she had begun—or rather, guiding and encouraging the Valde in ending it themselves: the final turning away that would leave them whole.

She would need her rede, herself as she'd been before first putting on the bird.

Bronh bent her flight southeast, toward the Thornwall and Ardun.

Garin's second tossed handful of small change—pebbles being unavailable under knee-deep snow—brought a motion to the dark study window above. Garin looked up from the garden for a moment, then returned to the central door he'd found barred beyond the limits of even his dexterity.

Presently a voice inside demanded softly, "Who's there?"

"How many folk have you *got*, Jannus, that climb in through your garden in a snowstorm in the middle of the night?" rejoined Garin with asperity, as the door was opened enough to let him edge through.

Replacing the bar, Jannus said, "Keep still. Everybody's asleep. What is it?"

"Bronh. Is she here yet?"

"No. . . ."

"Well, she *is* here, within a mile or two either way."

"The famous locator implant," deduced Jannus sourly, and stifled a burst of coughing.

"The same. It's fine, if you don't care about precision a whole lot."

Jannus was trying to control the coughing, moving toward the foot of the stairs. Garin followed. Near the turn of the stairs Jannus inquired, "How'd you know to make a noise up there? *That's* not your locator."

"Lucky guess," offered the mobile; then he added, "I don't like guessing. I still wish I had a full relay on you."

"Quit changing names. It was hard enough memorizing 'synaptic transmitter,' " replied Jannus, pronouncing the syllables with care, "whatever that means."

"Monitor. Link. Relay. Transmitter. Redescanner. You need one. Then you'd know all the names."

"Just leave off about it," Jannus directed shortly.

Going ahead into the study, Jannus lit a lamp and set it on the desk. He was fully dressed except for shoes and seemed quite recovered, except for the persistent cough, from his wetting two days before. But with a monitor implant, Garin wouldn't have had to guess about that either.

Brushing snow off his clothes on the hearth stones, Garin remarked, "I may be *sa'farioh*, but I leave tracks. Will that be a problem to explain away?"

"Shouldn't. I go out myself, some nights. . . . But nobody's likely to ask, and the snow will fill them level soon enough. . . ." replied Jannus abstractedly from beside the window.

Having bent to lay sticks on the embers, Garin judiciously began to place heavier sticks on the pile. "I wish you either knew more, or less," he complained suddenly. "You know just enough to get a hold on tools you don't know enough to be afraid of using. I wish you knew what you're doing."

Garin slid from the front of his jacket a bowl-shaped yellow object made of the high-tensile Tek glass called plarit. It was a redecap: the temporary, external equivalent of a monitor implant. Until recently, such a device had been his own only means of keeping in touch with the Shai. Garin held it up, both displaying and offering it.

"No," said Jannus, sharply annoyed.

"I didn't say anything. I just brought it, in case you'd agree you needed to understand what you've gotten us into. You can't keep blundering forward, blind, much longer."

"No. I went through that once in *Sunfire* and it was . . . it wasn't anything I want to repeat."

"It wouldn't be like that," Garin argued. "It doesn't have to be conceptual input. It could be kept to words, just like talking. You—"

"No. I won't touch it. Either Bronh will know, or she won't."

Garin laid the redecap softly on the floor. He'd made the warning as plain as he could. He hadn't really expected Jannus would open himself up to the deluge of persuasive discouragement the Shai would have supplied; and there were a number of things impinging on the present situation he'd prefer Jannus knew nothing about. But Jannus didn't know enough to ask the right questions to elicit that sort of information.

Just then, Garin could have twisted Bronh's neck with considerable satisfaction. He'd set beacons, and tried to intercept her, but the weather and the loose approximation of her position—all that the locator provided—had conspired to defeat that effort too.

Jannus, who'd had his hand poised on the latch, pulled the windows apart and open, and Bronh flew into the room.

The huge grey wings were momentarily a danger to the lamp, which Jannus grabbed and steadied while Bronh's extended talons reached to lock on the carved back of an upright chair. She slowly folded the wings against her sides, fixing Garin with a suspicious, hawk's stare.

"Yes, Bird. Another face, but still myself."

Without greeting or preamble, Bronh said, "Elenin's been emptied. The Singing's begun."

That was news of considerable import. The Shai had foreseen the approach of those events but not when they were likely to occur. Pedross would have to be told to shut the gate, set the blockade that would cut Ardun off from the Sea.

That Garin couldn't communicate directly with Pedross the mobile felt to be no more than a delay, a mild nuisance. He'd never offered Pedross access to even a redecap, and never would. Pedross had been born into a later age of the world than that which the Shai, Bronh, and—to an extent—Jannus shared: a declining age in which travel was measured in weeks or even seasons, and long-distance methods of communication were cumbersome and only intermittently reliable. But the three in this room shared the memories of the High Plain as it had been during the Teks' long afternoon of power, and had a different standard of possibility.

Jannus, thought Garin briefly, was the last of the old, as Pedross was the first of the new. Jannus still believed, as the Teks had, that anything that could be imagined could be done, if only one were willing to pay the price; once, that had been nearly true.

Bronh was saying, "What's the current status at Dunwater Isle? Is Pedross—"

"Not now, Bird," cautioned Garin, and the valkyr turned her unchanging ferocious stare thoughtfully toward Jannus who was mixing water and powder in a bowl, which he set on the floor. Bronh hopped down to feed, Jannus watching her, the redstone hanging plain against the front of his sweater.

Bronh remarked, "What's the status here, then?" before continuing to eat.

"Stable." Garin didn't intend to discuss his plans for Ardun in front of Jannus either if he could help it.

Bronh then demanded of Jannus, "What's the problem, then?"

"Poli died, and the body was burned," Jannus told her.

"That was your stupidity; not mine. I carried your message and wasted several hours lecturing you on rebodying procedures. I want my pay."

"I know what to do about her rede," responded Jannus pa-

57

tiently, and he explained the composite shaped from a synthesis of memories.

"Perfectly possible," commented Bronh, "if you're satisfied with that. What's the delay, then?"

"The body's gone."

"So what? There's Tek meat enough to be had."

"A Valde trapped in *sa'farioh* Tek meat would be an abomination," declared Jannus.

"If you won't have Tek meat, then grow your own. Get a sample from some Valde, and reconstruct from that. The cosmetic modifications would be simple enough. But I'm not going to wait around for completion, if you go that route—I want my pay now."

Jannus looked to Garin. " 'A sample'?"

"A small amount of tissue, flesh, enough for me to identify the genetic components and arrangement. Bodies are coded, like redes," Garin said.

"Then it wouldn't be Poli," mused Jannus. "Not any part of her at all, not really."

"Or if you want to go in for more elaborate verisimilitude," Bronh continued briskly, "you have perfectly good samples of her genetic code still to work from: the children. Eliminate what's yours in them, and the rest should provide what's needed for a full reconstruction, cell for cell. I'd imagine that method would have more emotional resonance and be more satisfactory, from your point of view. It would take longer, but that should be an advantage. After first thaw, people here will—"

"*Bronh*," warned the mobile, but Jannus said, "Go on, Bronh, what happens here in the spring?"

Bronh turned to Garin in annoyance. "Haven't you even told him *that*? If you're not going to keep him informed, why don't you scrap him and have it done with?"

Jannus said, "Because he doesn't want to. Garin. How did the warehouse fire start?"

One plain opposition unraveled all the rest: Garin had been afraid it would be that way. "I set it," he said, as he was obliged to.

"*Why?*"

"Because it was necessary."

Staring at Garin, Jannus said, "From the first, the beginning. The whole time. You've been against it, and I thought. . . . I should have known better," he decided with an arid bitterness. "You only care about the Rule of One. You never claimed otherwise. You'd think by this time I'd have learned what can be expected from Teks and what can't—"

"I'm no Tek."

"Same difference."

"I'm no Tek. I did what I could."

Uncompromising, Jannus responded, "You could have told me."

"You could have asked. And if I'd told you, would you have given it up?"

"No." A statement, not an admission.

"Then my only option was to persuade you to abandon it. Can't you see that?"

"You could have told me," said Jannus again.

"No. I can give you predictions about remote results of anything you care to name, but not how they'll affect your holding the Rule of One, your life. That's not permitted." Even saying as much as he had was perilously close to the limit.

Bronh said to Jannus, "Deal with me. *I* say what I please, and won't even try to protect you against the consequences of whatever irrationalities you commit. Will you promise me meat to my specifications, besides the redstone? Meat available on the ground: not prisoned in orbit, or underwater, or on some glacier the other side of nowhere—will you guarantee that? *When* I want it, and *where* I want it?"

Garin shifted and instantly Jannus directed, "Leave her alone." Jannus looked at her: a shift of attention that excluded Garin. He said, "Yes, I promise. I'll see you're bodied however you want, wherever, whenever—always assuming I'm alive then to enforce it. . . . Now tell me: why is the Shai against me in this?"

"Because it can't be done without your making yourself flamingly conspicuous; and in that light, he'd be seen—if not for what he is, at least for what he can do."

"What of it?" replied Jannus curtly. So he'd thought it through that far, at least, for himself, Garin judged. Jannus added, "Who can touch him, much less do him any hurt, now?"

"Any attempt to warp the Rule of One to favor a part at the expense of the whole will oblige him to put you aside. Permanently. He doesn't want to do that. He's already gone to outrageous lengths to keep you out of his way. What you do in your own private persona, that's your business and your risk. But whatever you try to do through the hold the Rule of One gives you over the Shai's powers you're accountable for. Isn't that clear to you yet?"

Jannus said slowly, "This is a private thing. All I want is to get Poli back. That's all."

"You still don't see it," commented Bronh, in exasperation. "Then I'll take it simply, one step at a time. I assume, by the way, that you didn't take the rudimentary precaution of concealing the death, pending a sudden recovery: correct?"

Jannus frowned, responding, "There were already too many people involved by then—five children with Truthtell and no discretion, Dan into everything. . . ."

"And," Bronh persisted, "you didn't think of it."

"I thought of it. I just couldn't. . . . All right, Bronh: just assume I'm as stupid as you please. How does rebodying Poli risk going against the Rule of One?"

"Say that you rebody her," said Bronh. "Then what? Are you imagining nobody will notice? That the neighbors won't care? That they'll all decide the news of her death was some sort of minor mistake? Somebody's sure to shout *Witchcraft*, and you're arrested and charged. Any argument?"

"It's not witchcraft," protested Jannus.

"Fine: that's what you'll say at the trial. That it was a perfectly natural procedure, a commonplace resurrection in which you were assisted by a talking bird that goes to the fire every few years to be reborn, and by the projected alter-ego of an immortal fish. And this you're going to explain to an Andran civil magistrate, some hearty lout with five luck charms hung around his neck. Fine. Then what?"

"It's the truth," Jannus burst out. "We're not all fools here, Bronh—"

"How many executions for the proven practice of witchcraft have there been in Ardun in the last year?" rejoined Bronh with scathing patience. "An approximate figure."

"Eleven," replied Jannus tightly.

"Out of how many accusations?"

"Sixteen."

Sufficient comment, Bronh apparently judged, on the enlightenment of Ardun's civil courts. She remarked, "So you're obliged, by a combination of direct questions and Valde Witnesses, to put forward this wonderfully truthful defense, and the Witness confirms you're deranged enough to believe it. Then what?"

Jannus lifted both hands. "I'm released. Whatever I may be, I'm not a witch. In Ardun the truth matters, even if they don't understand it. They know it when they hear it."

"Commendable. Then how do you propose to explain away a fetch?" That was what folklore named the walking dead: what'd been "fetched" back from the far side of the fire. Bronh meant Poli. "If it's not witchcraft, what is it?" Answering her own question, Bronh said sternly, "It's power. Public as a bonfire, visible from here to the coast and beyond. Do you think you can make that kind of fire of yourself and not be seen? Do you think that, whatever the legal technicalities, anybody's going to care whether it was done with magic or with spit and string? Whether you're released on the charge of witchcraft, that's arguable; what would happen as soon as your defense got around, that's *not* arguable. Don't you realize you'd be pounced on by the agents of some baymaster, some riverstock Lady whose troopmaids are deserting, somebody with an immediate need for power as vital to them as yours seems to you? Take the most likely case, that it's Domal Ai who does the collecting. What do you think Domal Ai wants most in the world?"

"Pedross dead," replied Jannus, with concise accuracy. He was, Garin thought, beginning to see.

"Exactly," said Bronh. "The Shai then has two choices: to free himself of you, or let himself and the Rule of One be put under the orders of some upstart lowlander who won't know or care whether he's commanding a Tek cyborg or a fire elemental with lightnings for hair, serving his own tiny purposes at the expense of everything the Shai has been doing for longer than you've been alive. As soon as you've made such a public spectacle of yourself, the rest follows. There's no stopping, short of somebody's dungeon."

Garin put in without inflection, "My best estimate is eight days. Before I'd be obliged to have you killed. The variables are the skill of the torturers involved and the endurance of all concerned."

Jannus said slowly, "I can't imagine a dungeon on the continent the Shai couldn't get me out of if he chose. . . ."

Garin shook his head. "Not with *Sunfire.* Not at all. It would become as conspicuous as Poli herself, and, eventually, as fully a warping of the Rule of One to private purposes at the expense of the welfare of the whole. No. If the Shai had to get access, it wouldn't be to *rescue* you. . . ."

After a minute Jannus remarked, "But even at the worst, it's only me. Whatever came, at least she'd be alive. . . ."

Bronh put in, "She'd just die all over again, becoming unpartnered."

"You may know Valde," rejoined Jannus sharply, "but I know Poli. She survived being *sa'marenniath* all those years. She'd survive that too, if she had to. If the *marenniath* were healed, so she'd have the living world to hold to, she'd manage." To Garin, Jannus said, "You can't prevent me from starting, at least, bringing her back—"

"No. I can't. Jannus, it wouldn't be Poli. It'd be a construct, body and *farioh.* Other people suffer losses as bad, and worse, and manage to tolerate them—"

"They don't have a choice," Jannus replied flatly. "I do. Suppose," he formulated slowly, "that I agreed to accept your wretched implant, monitor, whatever it is. Then the Shai could pull me out of any situation before anything irrevocable had happened. Like the river. And if something was added to it—"

"An incendiary," suggested Garin unhappily.

"Oh, is that how you're doing it now? All right, then: that. Then you wouldn't have to even put yourself to the trouble of hiring assassins or getting access, if things went that way. I know you'll find some way to make it impossible, about Poli, unless we came to some sort of terms. I don't understand enough of the procedures even yet to prevent the Shai from ruining things if he wanted to. You've been going on and on about that implant—what's it worth to you for me to agree to it? Enough?"

"And afterward?"

"Afterward, I'll take care of myself," Jannus replied curtly.
Garin consulted with the Shai.

With such a link implanted, the Shai could indeed retrieve
Jannus' rede as easily from a prison as from a river, at any
distance, and wake it safe in *Sunfire*. It needn't even be Tek
meat that the rede would wake in: from the single sample
Jannus would be providing for another purpose, endless cop-
ies could be produced.

For his own reasons, the Shai viewed the prospect of such
a rebodying almost as unenthusiastically as Jannus did the implant itself. The Shai simply had never found Teks particularly likable. He'd only realized that recently, never having
had, before, any basis of comparison. He didn't look forward
to Jannus' making that particular transition. But it was inevitable, if the relationship were to continue more than a paltry
half century or so. All bargains had their price.

Garin reported, "All right. It's still unsafe and unwise, but
we can try it."

"And Bronh's entitled to her meat, as she said."

"Agreed."

"Then how much is 'a sample'?"

There was a startled moment before Garin realized Jannus
was still thinking exclusively about Poli and hadn't even begun to consider the further ramifications of the link. Measuring the end joint of his least finger, Garin replied, "Less than
that much. I could take it without your even noticing."

"Do you have what you need to take it?"

"The Shai does. I can get it by tomorrow night."

"And how long would it be, after that?"

"Till the construct could be wakened? I've never tried anything at all comparable," Garin mused. "Say, two months.
Till thaw."

"Appropriate," commented Bronh.

"The rede will take a few days," Jannus calculated. "I'll
have to find pretexts to get all the people I want into contact
with the redecap: fix it some way, in a chair back or something. . . . But the Shai can have everything I remember of
Poli right now." He came across the room and stooped to
pick up the yellow plarit redecap.

II

MEMORY

When Poli woke, it was in the usual way—body finding its balance and coming to a sitting position in a single lithe motion before her eyes were ready to open or her mind to attend. That she woke from death rather than sleep made less impression on her, in those first seconds, than the continuity of habit.

She remembered being dead, as something she'd been told. She had no memory of the thing itself, not as an event which she'd experienced. Though she didn't doubt it at all, it didn't matter except that it was the cause of this strange place's reverberating with unmodulated welcome. The jubilation seemed to her a condition of the place, like the pale directionless light, until she noticed Jannus sitting on a sort of stool at the foot of the glass container that was her bed: close enough to have touched her, not touching, except with the stronger grasp of his *farioh*.

Too loud, as usual.

Good morning, came his inspoken remark, both greeting and affirmation.

The power of the gladness moved her like being infected by giggles. His feeling became indistinguishable from her own. She reached out to him then, answering welcome for welcome, contact for contact, in ways that could reach him, Unhearing as he was. The language of gesture came easily to her, the ways to steady and reassure, not even needing the responses of his *farioh* to know the effect. She'd been

67

sa'marenniath, used to using guess, familiarity, and imagination to reach what she could not know directly.

And now, the knowing was there too. Again.

That was the first element of her condition to surprise her in the least.

"How was it healed?" she asked, aloud.

"The inhearing? It was because we weren't working with a rede, with true memory. Think back to the High Plain."

Poli reached back for that time, the summer of her becoming *sa'marenniath.* She found a very clear sequence of events—how they'd gone onto the High Plain to reclaim Jannus' rede from the Shai, and how the massed Teks' passionate yearning to escape what their lives had become had driven her into an Unhearing state impervious to these Screamers' torrential deathwish. The facts were there. She just didn't remember ever having lived through them. They were merely something she knew, as she knew she'd been dead, and that this place was Downbase, in *Sunfire.*

"No resonance," remarked Jannus contentedly into her hair. "No hurt, no scar. No need, now, for the defenses. But look here." He took her right hand and traced a white line scoring the back of it, another near the curve of the elbow: dueling scars, from her time as First Dancer to the Newstock troop. It took Poli a moment to understand she was being told that the marking of these outward scars had been a matter of choice, that it could have been otherwise.

It was an odd feeling.

His voice said, "They're yours. You earned them," while the inspeaking invited/directed *Behold yourself.* There was suddenly in the center of the featureless room an image of herself, leaning as she was leaning, reposing on the air. As she straightened, the image did likewise: not flat like a mirror's reflection but exact as a second self.

She stepped down and circled the mirrorless reflection once around. When she cautiously reached out, she touched nothing. *Marenniath,* too, affirmed that the air was empty.

She turned her back on the image, less interested in it than in the fact that Jannus had called it into being. He'd done it: she could tell. The Shai, she knew, could command illusion; but what had that to do with Jannus?

She asked, "What have you sold this time, to buy me free?"

He braced himself for disapproval. "Same old thing—my rede. Just on a continuing basis, that's all. A link. The Shai wants to keep better track of me. But he's left me alone so far, at least as far as I can tell. . . . A little power goes with it, at least here in *Sunfire*. . . ."

In counterpoint, his *farioh* was hoping she'd accept what he'd done, accept the image just as a means to view herself, regardless of how either the image or the body it showed had come into being.

Gifts, whose costs should not be inquired into.

Dubiously she again regarded the illusion, to please him.

She saw a Valde, full-grown and long of limb, winter-pale all over, the mass of unbound curly hair making a triangle connecting head and shoulder-points. The face, too, was triangular, the cheekbones sharply defined, the expression a bit blank except for the suspicious gaze of grey-green eyes.

It could have been anybody.

Yet Poli didn't need the confirmation of the scars, to recognize herself. Jannus' acceptance of her had already supplied all the confirmation she could need. People were the only mirrors she'd ever needed or cared about.

With *marenniath,* she tried to reach out to the five, her children, but could hear only Jannus and, diffuse as smoke, some larger presence: the Shai himself.

Reacting to her tense abstraction, Jannus queried, "What?"

"I can't reach outside. Is that how it's—"

"No, it's not you: it's *here*." Smiling, he rapped the shiny sand-colored wall behind him. "*Sunfire* shields us, the way the Tek foundations of Newstock did. Let's go." He collected a basket from the floor, commenting, "I brought some clothes. If you want something in particular, I'll bring it out later."

"We're not going home?" she inquired, deducing from his clothing that the cold weather must be past. She laid out a loose undyed shirt of summer-shear mara wool, green trousers, and a warm cape of the same shade, the common dress of an Awiro.

"Not just yet," Jannus replied. "I thought I'd best wait and find out what you thought about it. Pedross has shut the door to the Sea. It can't last past Blooming, the beginning of Summerfair, at the longest, before the baymasters and maybe the Smiths make it too expensive for him and break the blockade, the way they've always done when anybody tried to block off travel to the Summerfair. . . . But, all the same, it's not a good time to get accused of calling back a fetch." A wry smile softened the blunt phrase. "Anyhow, until the balance of things falls more in our favor, I made a place for you to camp out here in the Fallows. I built you the most frighteningly crooked lean-to shed you've ever seen, all by myself—Dan would have a fit for sheer contempt if he ever saw it—and with a fire it ought to do until—"

In the middle of his rapid chatter and quite without self-consciousness he was crying, struck all over again by the wonder of their both being here, so unremarkably. Then he said, "I've been here, some part of the day, for ninety days. Otherwise, I don't know how I could have managed."

"Hush, now. It's done. Tell me what the five have been up to." Poli leaned against his side, her arm tightening to bring them closer, as they passed through the place where the image had been.

A round door irised opened in what had been a blank wall as they approached and they walked down a long curving passageway, a tube unbroken by visible doors. The floor was very slightly resilient: their feet made little sound. But the strip of flameless lights along the ceiling kept unobtrusive pace with them, fading and going dark as soon as they were past. The way ahead was always plain, the way they'd come a dim stretch and then utter dark.

When Poli paused, the lights directly above stayed bright. The vague sense of the Shai's presence was stronger but remained directionless, neither nearer nor farther any way she turned.

Interrupting his account of Sua's growth and recent doings, Jannus inspoke an unshaped inquiry.

"Nothing," Poli responded, proceeding again the way the lights led them.

She'd never been in *Sunfire* before. But she knew what it was: the Shai's body. It was, she thought, like a cave. She didn't remember caves, not really; but she knew about them, in the flat, factual way she knew about having been dead. Even recalling the children was that way—in fact, everything before this morning, before she'd wakened.

Odd, she thought, passing through the hollow hill that watched her pass.

A larger portal opened before them and they stepped out into cool morning daylight. From the top of the ramp Poli could see Ardun, or at least the upper third of the Master's tower rising above intervening wooded hills. More immediate, though, was what engulfed her inhearing the instant she stepped beyond *Sunfire*'s shielding: an intoxicating many-layered flood of living voices, more sudden and pervasive than the burst of sunlight. The voices feared, or hungered, or were at brief peace, or craved mergence, or merely *were* and *grew,* all together and without pause, extending as deep as the least final thread of root-end and high as a lifting lark, everywhere. The concept *daysinging* came to her, vividly fulfilled. That was what it meant, then, this wondrous jumble: the daysinging of the Fallows.

It was too rich, too dense, too multitudinous, and as basic as air damp with the scent of new growth. It was almost too wonderful to be borne.

Jannus, aware of her reaction, followed her down the ramp with a self-effacing calm, not intruding. Yet, in spite of the tumult of the daysinging, Poli was aware of his deliberate quiet, the reliable support of his mindfulness of her. With it, she could reach out toward the overwhelming abundance of the world's life which, however marvelous, had no knowledge of her in turn, nor care.

"How did I live," she wondered softly, aloud, "in lack of this?"

A stirring, a wincing away, immediately suppressed beyond her hearing. He said simply, "I don't know." But what he was feeling was closer to *You didn't.* And Poli had no answer for that.

As she became more accustomed to the engulfing daysinging she reached cautiously farther, ready to retreat at the first stirring of acknowledgment, contact, reply. She realized, "There aren't any Valde in Ardun."

"I told you things were unsettled," Jannus responded. "Valde don't like unsettled things very well. They've been keeping clear, more and more. And the fewer Valde there were, just casually abroad in the streets, the wilder Ardun started getting, so the more Valde left, and so on." He pulled off a dry stalk of last year's feathergrass as they continued down the gradual slope. "I don't claim Arduners are any better than other folk—"

"Yes you do: frequently."

"Well, they're more careful, anyhow—living by the Summerfair traffic and trade, on Valde's doorstep. They're polite, anyhow, for fear of bothering the customers. But they've started to realize they can get away with things—losing the awareness that any Valde who cares to, or that the patrollers collect, can point the finger and fix the blame. Truthsayers are fine for trials, once somebody's been caught, but they're not a whole lot of use in finding out who did the thing in the first place. . . . And Arduners don't feel the same way toward Truthsayers as they do about Valde anyhow: *you* know. . . . Anyhow, Arduners aren't so careful any more. So, as I said, the wilder it gets, the more Valde are inclined to stay clear of us, round and round." His hands mimed the cycle. "Once the blockade is broken, things will settle down again."

"But what started it, to begin with?"

"How would I know? I don't know half of what's been going on just in Ardun, and understand less. I've been busy," he remarked pointedly. "Here it is halfway to Blooming, and nobody's come down from Morgaard to set the stakes of the Summerfair Path, and I don't recollect it ever going until this late before. . . . I don't have to understand it. I just manage however I can."

"Like the link," she suggested, and got a quick sidewise glance in reply.

"I'm getting used to it," he asserted, calmly enough. "I end up with a headache, sometimes, but it's been easier to learn than the inspeaking—nothing like the nuisance I was afraid it'd be." He went on, "And it has its uses. He showed me how to build the shed, for one thing. He's promised to keep the link a shut door except when I open it myself, so as to say, and call him. And I have no reason to suppose otherwise. It's not that bad, Poli."

He hated the link. She didn't need to pry under the surface control to know that. It was the continual dread of being spied on, the heritage of all riverstock men, intensified, confirmed to a certainty. She couldn't imagine his willingly surrendering privacy so utterly, ever, for any reason. And yet he had.

"I don't know," she said.

"It doesn't matter."

"I don't know," she said again; and he made no reply.

They'd come down from the open hillside into dense brush fully leafed out beneath trees showing the first haze of green and knobby with buds, no screen against the warming sun. Poli noticed that they were following a path that circled around the rougher north face of the hill. She thought, *ninety days, every day*, and walked silent behind him on his path.

Before, the branches hadn't mattered to him, walking alone. Now he caught each one and held it until she was ready to catch it in turn, so that she seemed to herself to be continually arriving, continually greeted.

She began to wonder how long it was going to take before she would finally have arrived.

They came to a wedge of open ground above the soggy, lush margin of a stream, where some Arduner had once cleared land for a furtive garden. Tucked into a sizable overhanging bank and surrounded by the massive, dappled boles of a stand of yellowwood was the little shack he'd built her: a lean-to faced east, its wood not yet weathered to neutral grey. Swinging the basket, Jannus went on ahead so she could inspect his handiwork at her own pace, in her own fashion.

It was too solid and elaborate a structure to have been intended for just an overnight shelter. It might, she concluded, be some time before she could go home.

Inside the lean-to she found a tripod, a few cooking pots, a bucket, and a latched box that proved to hold provisions. *Quite some time*, she corrected herself. Hungry, she took a handful of dried fruit and munched pieces distractedly.

Toward the back of the lean-to was a string bed with a wooden frame, and a rolled pallet and blankets on it. From a nub of branch overhead hung her own bowcase and quiver. *Maybe years*, she thought, increasingly oppressed by the prospect and by the evidence that she'd been waited for with such detailed premeditation.

Stooped near the firepit with his back to her, Jannus remarked, "Deer come down to drink here, and rabbits, and

73

some grasshens. Seems like the hunting should be fairly good. . . ."

More premeditation. Even the stream calculated in terms of her sole convenience. Tight-throated, she said, "I keep seeing you setting these posts in the cold. No sound, nor anything moving but just you. . . ."

"Kept me busy, gave me something to do besides just wait," he commented mildly. "And I could always talk to the Shai anytime I wanted to." A flash of self-mockery invited her to join him in ridicule even of that pain too, his chafing awareness of the link.

"No. It's cost too much," she declared violently. "Nothing's worth that, what it's cost you."

His mild voice commented, "Seems that's up to me to say. And I'm satisfied. There's nothing I'm waiting for, or expect, that I don't have right now. So don't be sudden with yourself, Poli, any more than you can help. You haven't had the time I've had to sort things out and get used to it all."

Poli gradually was able to share his calm and her agitation departed. She began sorting among the confused raucous manysingings of Ardun, blocking and dismissing all strangers, seeking her children. She couldn't distinguish them; and, with a sense of startled stillness, she realized why. She'd been sa'marenniath since before they were born. She'd never known them except from the outside. She could no more identify their selfsingings than those of any other strangers. It felt odd, thinking of it.

What she was beginning to think of as her dead memory contained facts galore—Sua's sulks, and Mallie's stubbornness, and that Liret wouldn't eat cabbage. But it wasn't the same as *knowing*. All that she truly knew were Jannus, and the daysinging of the Fallows, and the distant turbulence of Ardun. Everything else, everything before, was no more than mirror-shadows.

She began to feel how truly strange a thing had happened in the unfelt interval between her sleep and her waking.

On the morning the construct was to be wakened, Garin had risen at first light to watch the revolution taking shape in front of the Market Street granaries—by no coincidence, not half a block from his window. He expected to enjoy the insurrection and his breakfast sweet rolls from the same chair.

The carters' guild had begun it. Coming out of the lean months, from the threat into the actuality of blockade as the thaw floods receded, the carters had exhausted their reserves and begun to starve, with no prospect of ships to be unloaded, goods moved, or floods of visitors to be hauled about on their pre-Summerfair business. Having taken counsel among themselves, the guild sent a deputation to Domal Ai demanding aid in the form of a regular ration of grain from the public stores. Wisely or unwisely, Domal had granted their demand. Something in excess of eight hundred carters had shown up to collect their rations. Within minutes there were, as well, several thousand beggars, which hadn't surprised Garin at all, since he'd been spreading a rumor of free food all the previous day. Not unexpectedly, therefore, it had turned into a riot, with great ill feeling on all sides.

Quite satisfactory.

In the six days since this first preliminary riot, a political aspect had been developing. There had been for years a faction in Ardun which had never accepted the loss of the Fallows. They called themselves the Greenleaf Federation and were notable for their banner, the Blooming Rose of Ardun flanked by two green leaves representing Lifganin and the Fallows, which the Federation advocated unilaterally annexing; and for parading every spring to perform the same futile rite of symbolic planting, to the east and to the west, in colorful costumes they then packed away until the next twenty-first of Greening.

With the fact of blockade and virtual siege, cutting off all outside aid, the Greenleafers' nostalgic yearnings suddenly were accepted as a practical necessity by such pragmatic folk as Elda Innsmith, for example, who publicly declared that, to stand, Ardun had to be prepared to stand alone. He, for one, had no intention of marching across Sunrise Bridge, planting a morsel of wheat, spitting on it, and persuading himself he'd done anything worth the time or the spit. The Fool-Killer visited the lovers of empty ceremony, he said, or words to that effect.

Overnight the Greenleaf Federation gained twenty thousand members, a considerable treasury, and an entirely new organizational structure.

When the carters returned to their vigil before the granaries, it was with Greenleaf banners and a demand: not, this time, for a ration to make bread but for the whole store of grain, as seed. To plant the Fallows with. They sustained their vigil with sack lunches provided by the Federation, which had pledged to support the guild until the first crop was in. They would wait, they said, until the twentieth of Greening for the granaries to be opened to them; after which they'd open them themselves.

Garin was intrigued with the predicament in which this left Domal Ai, commonly known as "Old Four-eyes." Either Domal could abrogate Ardun's ancient, treatyless relationship with Valde and thus jeopardize Valde's Summerfair, which was Ardun's whole excuse for existing, or else he faced civil insurrection of hitherto undreamed-of magnitude, which would mean that many of the most powerful men and women in Ardun would be actively seeking his downfall. Garin was interested to see which set of enemies Domal would choose.

Blowing on his tea, Garin settled on the sill of his open window. Past the arcaded sides of Market Street was the broad interval of Market Square. Beyond, instead of arcades, there were the openwork concrete walls of Factors' Row and the upper stories of the factorages visible behind—the high central spine of the city. The granaries flanked the square on the east and west—vast old piles, windowless, patched with every color of brickwork the centuries had provided.

Garin had chosen his lodging chiefly for the view. In any siege, granaries and public markets always became centers of unusual activity, sooner or later.

He was looking down on heads. Solid people, not only filling the square but backed up Market Street and down Factors' Row. It was a Tenday morning, after all: nobody had to go to work except those to whom today's work meant today's food and other people than Garin were interested in the choices of Domal Ai.

Like flocked with like, whether nationality, race, or guild. It wasn't hard, for instance, to spot the familial clusters of Smiths, or the bare shoulders of carters in their open vests, or the starched white headdresses of Bremneri women, Traders out of the more conservative of the riverstocks. There were no flaxen heads, no Valde, anywhere to be seen: whether drawn by the phenomenon Bronh termed "the Singing" or driven by Ardun's turbulence and snatching reliance on the last-goers, all had now apparently departed. Nor did Garin find any of the scarlet capes that would mark the city watch either: they were otherwise occupied, or else under orders to stay scarce until the present crisis had been resolved. It promised to be a really edifying riot, no matter what happened. Garin had been looking forward to it most of the week.

But Tenday was also market day—except for the half-holiday in midweek, the only chance many working people had to shop. So, behind the unmoving crowd, trade was going on more or less as usual in the diffuse early light: fish stalls opening and pushcarts of produce, from the precarious rooftop greenhouses that made Ardun glitter even from orbit, being eased into position beneath the arcade arches.

Jannus sidestepped around the back of a flatcart, threading his way as expertly as any pickpocket. Avoiding a woman stacking cheeses, he was gone under the shadow of the opposite arcade.

Circling wide of the square, Garin surmised, on his way across town to Sunrise Bridge and the scheduled reunion: afoot, because all the carters were otherwise occupied.

Garin continued looking the way Jannus had gone, but didn't catch sight of him again. It was perhaps the third time he'd seen Jannus since the implant and Bronh's departure for Bremner—all just chance sightings like this one. Well, there was no need for them to meet anymore, since the link functioned properly. And not meeting roused no awkward questions anywhere. But the link was to the Shai: Garin had no part in whatever exchanges Jannus grudgingly initiated.

Garin was about to turn back to the square when a second figure ducking around the chicken cart caught his eye—notable both for the stares she attracted, and the wild mass of fair hair that provoked that attention. *Not* a Valde: Sua.

Leaving his tea mug steaming on the sill, Garin banged down two flights of stairs and hit the street in something less than a minute.

Garin had no trouble catching up with her because she was being held. A large man with a towering rack of pies strapped to his back had both hands clamped around her arm and was shaking her, crying, "—and he's been gone *two days,* Mistress. You have to *find* him, I—"

Without discussion Garin hit the man under the short ribs, ducked the tilting rack of pastry, and got Súa away. Shoving her through a gap between stalls into the dimness under the arcade, he demanded sternly, "What are you doing out all by yourself?"

"Oh," she responded flatly, "it's you." The roustabout's face might not be familiar, but the odd uninflected voice, she'd recognized at once. She disengaged herself, frowning past him at the street. "People are stupid," she declared rancorously. "They just look at the outside, and that's all they see. He thought I was some mossheel. Do I *look* like a woodsrunner or a woolchaser, tell me?"

What she looked like was a spring cattail gone to seed— tall, fragile, and fluffy on top. But it would have been hard, objectively, to have mistaken that animated dark-eyed face for the neutral repose of a Valde's countenance. And her dress was almost aggressively Bremneri: bright green, with a thickly embroidered panel in front—a stylized Ardun rose, Garin realized.

He said, "People see what they want to see. You could always wear a scarf. . . ."

"Like some proper Quickmoor matron scared to death of being mistaken for a whore? Not likely."

Whereas she, a ten-year-old who looked at least sixteen, had an adolescent's horror of looking *too* proper. Understandable.

Finding the coast momentarily clear, she darted through the aisle back onto the street, leaving a wake of turning heads. He couldn't catch up with her until she'd reached the less congested cross street and turned east with long strides.

Walking fast to keep pace, Garin pointed out, "He's long gone," because it had been immediately obvious Súa was following her father.

"I'll make up the time on the far side of the bridge. I can climb hills faster than he can," she responded absently.

"Oh—you know where he's going, do you? Then why bother to follow?"

"Because I *lose* him!" Sua burst out. "All of a sudden he's just *gone*—and there's no place to be *gone* to! Just a plain hill, I've been over it and over it, but he's just *gone* and I don't know *how* . . . !"

Reaching through the link, Garin was informed that Sua's pursuit had indeed brought her at least twice within the circle of illusion the Shai maintained for a few hundred paces in every direction around the hill that was *Sunfire*'s landing site. The Shai had wound her in intricate rambling circles up and down the hillside below the unseen black mass of *Sunfire*'s hull until he judged her sufficiently discouraged to give up.

"How can a person get lost in broad daylight on a bare hill in plain sight of the Master's tower, tell me?" Sua complained. "But I *was*, one whole afternoon—come back to the same stinking place no matter which direction I tried to go. I nearly *starved*, and my feet freezing off, and *he* didn't care, didn't even know I'd been out. Because I had Mallie check for me afterward: *he* didn't know." Sua sounded as though she couldn't decide which was the greater offense—having been inexplicably trapped, or ignored. "There's some place that's just not *there*, that he has a way into and I don't. . . . *You're* not there," she reminded herself suddenly, her expression one of speculation, "not like everybody else. Mallie says you're *sa'farioh*, that a mossheel couldn't hear you at all. Do *you* know how to get inside that wretched bewitched hill?"

Avoiding a direct answer, Garin replied, "That's none of your business."

"All right, *don't* tell me," she said haughtily, striding along with no sign of noticing the stir her unheeding passage continued to provoke. Shopkeepers sweeping doorsteps did double-takes. A young man carrying laundry tied up in a bedsheet started diagonally across the street in pursuit. Either Sua's oblivious intentness or a level unfriendly look from Garin was enough to thwart the plain impulse to accost this supposed Valde.

And Sua was saying, "Nobody else tells me anything either, treating me like a *baby*. . . . But I'm not: *I* know why he sneaks off to the Fallows," she declared darkly, challenging.

"All right: why?"

79

"He's got a *woman* over there," Sua announced with such triumphant distaste that Garin burst out laughing. "He does! It's not funny. It's *dis-gusting!*"

"He wouldn't have to hike five miles and back for just that," pointed out Garin, still vastly amused. "He could contract with a companion and not even need to leave home. Much more convenient."

"He *wouldn't!*"

"He hasn't," shrugged Garin amiably. "But not for lack of your permission, I think. And whatever his interest in the Fallows may be, I don't think he'd be at all pleased to learn he was being spied on. Bremneri don't like that."

"Don't you tell me about Bremneri. *I'm* Bremneri, and *I* don't like secrets. People sneaking around and never *saying* anything. . . . What's the use of Truthtell, tell me, if nobody will *say* anything?" But she was, after all, uneasy about Jannus' reaction, because she flicked around a quick black glance, demanding, "You going to tell on me?"

That glance, at least, was ten years old, defying the body's precocious maturity.

"Not unless he asks me. And if you quit and let me see you home now, it isn't likely he'll ever ask. Hasn't anybody told you the streets aren't safe anymore?" Garin asked, meanwhile fending off two more approaches without having to do more than look.

The knobby, river-drifter's features could settle quite intimidatingly: it'd been a useful face, and he'd put off changing it—so far, without repercussions. Establishing a new persona was generally a real nuisance—contacts and ongoing plans all had to be renewed or started from the beginning.

But the persona was young. That Sua so easily shrugged off his admonitions brought home what a disadvantage that could be. He began to think he'd prefer something more dignified, less approachable, older, for the authority and distance it would grant.

"There's some trick to it," Sua was muttering. "A password or something, and then the hill opens . . ."

Garin remarked, "And Dan Innsmith: does he have 'an arrangement' too?"

Sua replied carelessly, "Of course not, he's waiting for

Mallie. I mean— None of your business. And anyhow, it's a secret."

Garin glanced back again, found Dan only a block behind, and was satisfied. He could hand Sua over into Dan's accepted authority. At the same time, Garin was examining the intriguing revelation of Dan Innsmith, at twenty-six or so, secretly planning to handfast himself to a Bremneri child of ten. *That* would rouse a storm, down on Smith Point, fit to start fights for ten generations.

To keep the conversation going until Dan could catch up, Garin remarked, "No wonder nobody tells you anything, if you're in the habit of blurting secrets to strangers in the middle of the street."

"Well, you're different," Sua justified herself uncomfortably.

"Yes, I know: *sa'farioh*. By the way, that's supposed to be a secret too."

"Not just the voice, not just that," she mused, unheeding, and gave him a longer, direct look. "I don't know. You're just different, that's all. What's your name, anyhow?"

"Lately I've been going by 'Garin.' "

"Not 'Garin Somethingson' or 'Garin Tradename'? Or 'Garin Mind-Your-Business'?"

The flash of teasing caught him unprepared; and the appraising look that went with it was older than ten, or Time itself.

The preposterousness of it made him laugh out loud a second time, and that was once too often: Sua lengthened stride, turning angrily, threatening to escape. Then she spotted Dan, and really decided to run. Garin grabbed and anchored her there, though she immediately chopped at his neck with a hand bladed stiff, evidence of some close-combat training—a First Dancer's child, after all—and would have wrenched free in another instant if Dan hadn't hurried and hauled them apart.

Swinging Sua protectingly behind him, Dan gave Garin a hearty shove that sent him staggering halfway across the street. Sua pried futilely at Dan's hand, not daring to try on him the tricks she'd unleashed at Garin, which was probably sensible: Dan wouldn't have hesitated to slap her silly, in spite of the fact that she was the taller by a full head. Sua

81

protested, "You turn *loose* of me, Danna Eldasson Innsmith, this minute, or I swear I'll make you sorry!"

"I'm sorry already," responded Dan, watching Garin rub at the sore places and return his impassive stare.

Garin inquired in bored tones, "Do you think you can get her home without going through Market Square?"

"I believe so," Dan replied reservedly.

"And keep her there?" persisted Garin, over Sua's renewed objections.

"I expect I can."

Garin nodded and started back up the hill, hoping the digression hadn't made him miss the revolution. And he was thinking that he was inclined to change faces at the earliest opportunity. Sua's unguarded impulses could become a serious danger. *Something austere,* he thought, *and venerable. Preferably with a long, white beard.*

He strolled unhurriedly back toward Market Street, conferring with the Shai on the cosmetic modifications to be made on one of the spare Secolo bodies left over from the previous persona. Secolo's enemies and rivals had most often employed poison, and the mobile had used up more meat keeping that persona viable than in any previous incarnation, incidentally earning Secolo a reputation for possessing an infallible charm against poison. He'd been killed, that final time, for an amulet, a trinket of carved mara horn rumored to be the charm in question; and the man who'd ordered the murder had indeed escaped poisoning while in possession of the amulet: specifically, for three entire days before Pedross had him first strangled, then skinned.

The mobile still enjoyed the tidiness of that.

Anyhow, there were a few spare Secolo bodies left over, all nicely lined and wrinkled, needing only minimal facial modifications to be ready for use. Nobody recognized bodies anyhow except lovers, and Secolo-meat was in no danger whatever of that sort of recognition.

Garin looked back casually to learn what sort of progress the other two were making. Dan appeared to have extracted from Sua some sort of promise of parole because she was lagging along unheld, slowing at every sort of food-selling establishment and apparently demanding to be fed. But Dan paused only to haul Sua away from some importunate petitioner every ten paces or so, plainly as anxious to get her home and off his hands as Garin had been.

One petitioner was a large man who objected to Dan's intervention and wouldn't be explained to. And while Dan was shoving the man off and trying to keep clear of a fight, two women pounced on Sua and tried to drag her off in another direction. Garin stopped, ready to become involved if it seemed necessary; but Sua was by this time angry and perhaps frightened enough to deal with the women abruptly. A few chops and kicks freed her. And once she'd moved on, Dan's antagonist lost interest and Dan was able to turn and follow.

Garin strolled across the street as Sua approached, and fell into step beside her.

"I don't like this," Sua announced, scanning the people ahead warily, looking ready to bolt if any of them looked back at her or started to approach.

Garin took a wadded bandana out of his jacket pocket and held it out. After a minute Sua took it, to bind around her hair.

"What we need," declared Dan, catching up, "is a closed drawcart." It was an offer of temporary alliance.

"Whistle for it," responded Garin tersely, because only privately owned and official carts were still moving.

"I got kin in the square," Dan calculated, and looked past Sua at Garin, suggesting, "You go wide: down Tailor to where the Row meets Miller, and then down Miller. I'll cut through and collect some help and meet you either at the Row or the top of Miller, soon as I can get there."

"If you have trouble getting clear of the square, we won't wait," Garin warned.

"No, don't. All right, then?"

"All right," Garin confirmed, and at the next corner they separated, Garin and Sua turning left on Tailors' Street while Dan continued on toward Market.

Garin remarked to Sua, "You stay close, no matter what, unless I tell you otherwise. But if I say *run,* you head for whatever Bremneri factorage is nearest, yes, and *stay* there till somebody you know comes to fetch you. Understood?"

Factors occupied almost the position of ambassadors, and

their factorages enjoyed special exemptions from local authority: it was the safest place Garin could think of.

Sua nodded, still jerking her eyes around like a skittish deer.

"Then say it back to me," Garin directed, and was satisfied when she did so correctly. Garin made sure the Shai was aware of the situation and would inform Jannus of the arrangement if anything untoward happened.

In the Shai's view, there could hardly have been a less opportune time to interrupt Jannus with news of an emergency as yet only possible and, moreover, one which he was too far away to do anything about. And there was the Shai's promise that, except for the continuous low-resolution monitoring, he wouldn't contact Jannus on the conscious levels without invitation.

Garin felt that was all very fine, but it was only a promise, after all, not MacElroy's Constant. Jannus wouldn't want such a promise kept, not at Sua's expense.

In the short run, no, the Shai admitted; but in the long run, over a few centuries perhaps, a broken promise might work more harm than a broken child, regrettable though the latter option might be.

There was no use arguing. But sometimes Garin felt his alter-ego's remote objectivity made him slight the importance of immediate things. Conversely, the Shai always considered his mobiles too prone to becoming enmeshed in trivia, transitory complications, because of their more limited viewpoint.

It was an old, old dispute, one that was unlikely ever to be resolved.

Sua said abruptly, "Why is it like this? It was never like this before."

"You don't remember Quickmoor."

"I was just a baby, of course I don't."

"Most places are like this, most of the time," Garin formulated slowly. "And many are worse. All you've known is Ardun's summer and the good weather. But summer's done."

"I don't like it," she said again, unreconciled. "*Places* shouldn't change, shouldn't have to change or die. That's people, that get old and die and trick you—not *places*. Places, you can depend on. They're solid, they're *there* . . .

84

except for that blasted hill," she added, with meditative venom.

"The hill's there too. You just can't see it the way it really is. It won't let you."

Sua looked around. "It's on purpose? The hill's alive?"

"After a manner of speaking," Garin admitted, and sighed.

"Is it a troll hill?" Sua whispered. "Is it *really truly* magic? I knew it! I knew *somebody* was doing it on purpose. But it wasn't Da, he didn't even know I was there. So I couldn't see who it could be, if it wasn't him. But it was *her:* the troll lady!"

"No," contradicted the mobile irritably, despairing of being able to tell the truth, not sure he even ought to try. Maybe it *was* a troll hill. There was no law a starship couldn't be a troll hill too. It was just a matter of perspective, and perhaps of nomenclature, after all. And anyway. . . . "And anyway," he said aloud, "what *is* a troll?"

"*You* know. It's a *troll*, that's all."

"But what *is* it? What does it *mean?*"

"Well, a troll is an earth-power," Sua began, still watching to see whether he was teasing or really didn't know. "It trades with men sometimes, jewels and metals and such, but it can be mean, too—make you lose yourself on open ground till you die, or invite you in and you get *old*, old all in a night because time's different inside a troll hill, and a night can be a hundred years outside . . . or else you wake up in the morning and it's everything *else* that's old: all the places just ruins and the people you knew just *bones* and *dust*. . . ." Sua recited the folklore with relish, especially the grim parts, as was proper. "Or the troll can give you treasure, just for no reason at all, and it's *real* treasure, but it's always poison some way and terrible things happen to whoever tries to keep it or use it, because of the curse."

All in all, that seemed a reasonably accurate description of the Shai. Garin decided heavily, "It's a troll hill, then. Really, truly."

"I knew it!"

"But it wasn't the woman who tricked you," Garin continued. "She was asleep, waiting till it was the time for her to wake up. She didn't mean you any harm. Neither did the troll, not really. He just wanted you to go home and be safe."

Sua's look turned scornful. "You're lying, just because I can't tell. How would *you* know what the troll wanted?"

"Because I'm the troll's brother."

She moved aside, but only to consider him critically. "You don't *look* like a troll. . . ."

"*I'm* not the troll. Only his brother. That's why you can't tell if I'm lying or not. Besides, what does a troll look like? How do you know all trolls don't look like me?"

"Trolls look like . . . like Dan Innsmith," reported Sua, and giggled, "only littler, and hairier."

"How do you know Dan's not a troll himself, then?"

"Don't be silly. Besides, he doesn't even admit to trolls, no more than Da. The Sparrow does, though. . . . And besides, I know when Dan tries to lie."

"I guess he's not a troll, then," admitted Garin, while suddenly thinking, *What if "souls" are just a matter of terminology too? Teks are different from other people:* narrower, somehow. Colder. . . . *And what if magic isn't the process, the machinery, but the whole configuration of intent, act, and result, the* meaning *of it, whatever the means?*

What if the Teks were wrong and the Smiths right, after all this time?

Two patrollers came out of a doorway, seized Sua, and took her inside before Garin had a chance to do more than swing around.

Following, he saw Sua being herded up a flight of sagging wooden steps by the two patrollers, Sua protesting, "But I'm *not* a Valde, I don't even *like* Valde—"

Another red-caped figure appeared at the landing above: a district inspector, who told Sua, "I know you're not a Valde, Mistress Sualiche, but you're a Truthsayer, and that will do almost as well. Come this way, now."

The inspector led Sua off, and Garin, halfway up the stairs, could offer to her look of appeal only the assurance that he was there, and was concerned. It wasn't the time to do anything drastic, not yet. Ardun's civil watch were not sinister folk who pounced on young girls whenever authority began to break down. Not yet.

Garin climbed the rest of the way, told the patroller outside the sole open door, "I'm with her," and was allowed to pass.

There was a man dead on the floor, halfway under a cheap table. Messily dead, slashed, with blood drying on the boards and red handprints on the tabletop and low on one wall, under a glassless, uncurtained window. The sharp unmistakable smell of blood overcoming the fetor of cooking, bodies, dirt.

A woman with braids hanging like plumb lines and blood on the hem of her wrap, twining bare feet around the legs of the chair she sat in, saying, "—and then he ran off down the stairs, I was trying to make Tom lie still but he wouldn't, he kept trying to go after him because it was our last, it ain't *my* fault, I been sick and they don't like the coughing, too *fine,* too *picky*—"

Waving aside the recording scribe to make room, the inspector finished guiding Sua around an unmarked stretch of floor, saying to the woman, "Stop, now, Mistress Elma, we have a witness here to get the basics settled—"

From the doorway Garin shouted, "You moron, she's *ten years old!*"

The inspector signaled the nearest patroller, who bent Garin's arm back in a way that should have been painful but which Tek meat made it possible to ignore. Garin held his ground, demanding, "Aren't there Bremneri factors, scribes, Aihall functionaries, you could drag into this instead of a ten-year-old child?"

"Her age has no bearing," began the inspector as the woman came out of the chair, scooped up the knife that lay on the table, lunged at Sua.

Sua, with remarkable presence of mind, shoved the inspector against the woman and ran, rebounded from the table, and kept running, coming toward the door, the woman an arm's length behind, and Garin disabled the unready patroller in time to step forward to meet the knife, with no more pain than from a light punch. But when the woman, glaring into his eyes, dragged the knife down, *that* hurt. But Tek meat had its advantages. Pain could be controlled.

While the inspector finally pinioned the woman's arms and hauled her back, Garin held himself still, lost for a moment in a flashing relay exchange with the Shai, monitoring, calculating, predicting, at the same time thinking, *What if each persona is a self, an unrepeatable excerpt of the whole, modi-*

fied by immediate experiences, choices: a twin, not an identity, unique as a single wave?

What if I'm all the I I've got?

He stabilized his breathing and remarked to the inspector, "You don't need Sua now."

It wasn't a question.

Deciding he couldn't have seen what he thought he'd seen, the inspector said, "I suppose—"

"Fine," Garin cut in curtly, took Sua away from the patroller who'd caught her, and started back down the hallway. He didn't like the look of those stairs. He said, "You remember where I told you to go when I said *run?*"

"Yes, but—"

"Then *run.*" He gave her a push, not quite hard enough to shove her off the landing. Those stairs were just not going to be possible.

"But you're *hurt,*" she protested, balanced between steps, staring at the arm he held tight over the wound.

"No I'm not." *I'm killed, Sire, and smiling. . . .* the quotation ran through his mind in sardonic counterpoint. "Can't you do what you're told, just this once? Get out!"

"No, you come with me," Sua's voice demanded, from a considerable distance, and the meat finally had its own way after all. Dimly there was a sense of falling, a remote impact, and Garin thought, *Good-bye, Troll.*

The Shai received the Garin persona back into himself, disposed its elements, experiences, attitudes back into the Sea of his own personality. And the Sea changed.

The process was catalytic. In the enormously complex colloidal suspension that was the medium of his conscious thought, linkages of fact-molecules dissolved and made other attachments, creating new compounds with fundamentally different properties and values. The medium shivered, once, as the change swept through it.

But the Sea of himself was after all very large, very ancient, and very stable. The persona had been only a small fraction and had not had time to diverge very far from the elements of its beginning. The term of Garin's life had been a little less than that of Poli's death, an interval so brief as to be practically meaningless. The medium stirred, yes: but the stir passed, and the Shai could feel, taste, perceive almost no difference when the process had worked its way through the whole.

He focused attention on one of the bodies in the base area beyond the seal he now retracted, since Jannus and Poli had departed and were making their way to an outside port. The body in its still-box began to undergo a metamorphosis. Shinbones began to thicken and lengthen, and the clavicle broadened by minute increments, building bone tissue from elements supplied by the fluid that surrounded and supported it. Meanwhile the head was changing. Eye sockets thickened, and the skull itself lengthened and adjusted. The flexible flesh reflected the structural changes beneath and gradually ceased to be a recognizable portrait of the spymaster Secolo. Muscles and tendons modified their attachments, at jaw and cheek particularly, altering the tension of the overall network of wrinkles.

The flesh itself was in fact young: unborn. Bones had not yet fully hardened. They would accept molding, remodeling. Only when the still-box drained and opened would the meat begin to age.

There were other stations in the base: ten, altogether. It was, by Tek standards, a modest facility, fitted only to serve the needs of Shai and king. One station had been devoted to the production of the construct. Of the other nine, five were occupied. One held an unmodified Secolo replica beside that which contained its no-longer twin. A third, divided in half, held what looked like two large plucked chickens with overlarge scimitar-beaks: reserve valkyrs for Bronh. Feathers tended to deteriorate with long holding; in flight, that would matter. Therefore the Shai inhibited the feathers' growth until the meat was to be used.

In the fourth station, the shape of a dark boy seemed asleep, unbreathing. It looked about two years old: there was as yet no urgency to prompt the application of the forced-growth procedures used on the construct and now being applied to the new mobile. Jannus hadn't authorized any replicas being produced from his sample; but, as in the matter of the locator, the Shai didn't need his consent to proceed with this most basic of precautions. The implant was in place, so the rest followed.

In the fifth box was the body Bronh had commissioned. It was ready any time she should arrive to collect it, when she'd finished the last of the errands she wanted to accomplish in birdform. It was a woman's body—that, almost, of a young troll, the Shai reflected now, recalling Sua's description—it was smaller than Dan Innsmith, and hairier. The hair was an apricot auburn shade and floated around the head like a sunset auriole. The body was heavy-boned and deep-breasted. Even floating, it had an appearance of weight and strength. The overall impression was not one of beauty but of vitality: crude female strength. It was what Bronh had ordered; the Shai thought it remarkably ugly.

The Shai's own notion of beauty was far otherwise than this vulgar damsel. His love and admiration was always for the productions of time: what was alive and unpredictable, essentially transitory and profoundly mortal, never the work of only his own electromagnetic hands. . . .

The new mobile, he judged, was ready for impression, with the requisite long, white beard. The container began draining.

The Shai blocked off most of his store of memories, leaving immediate conditions and concerns in full detail, and the inclination to remember. He suppressed awareness of his own bodily form, retaining his satisfaction and confidence in the physical aspect. Then what remained, the essential patterns of personality, focused for one instant on the empty, receptive convolutions of the passive brain: burning paths linking a myriad of synaptic channels, blocking and searing others, etching pathways of habits and inclinations, spreading awareness and self-consciousness like a running spark until it became a microsecond conflagration of union: a Sea of raw psychic energy pouring itself into a vial.

The mobile breathed, bodily systems coming to full function. The Shai withdrew, becoming a mere attending presence, to give the mobile psychological space to integrate his elements and know himself to be alone, separate.

The mobile took a deliberate breath, puffed it out—a comment—and levered himself briskly out of the box, giving directions about clothing and equipment. "White, I think, and fairly austere. No staff: they're always getting snatched or mislaid. But a first-rate bag of tricks: anything portable, so long as it makes a noise or a flash to awe the yokels. No more of this bare-handed business. And you're still wrong about the link. But I'll tell Jannus myself, about Sua. That's what a mobile's for, to run errands, walk errands, ruin trysts. . . ." The mobile patted the damp mound of beard hanging against his chest. "Yes, that should make a difference, that's better. Very suitable for a reputable wizard."

While being hustled down the length of the Aihall portrait gallery, Sua wished her body were a paper so she could shred it; or a stone, so she could throw it away. Its past offenses were nothing to what it had inflicted on her today.

It had gotten her attacked for a Valde, gotten somebody killed dead in its defense (a thought very quickly shoved aside), gotten her dragged off to the Aihall for no reason— after all, *she* hadn't done anything—and all the stupid body cared about was that it was *hungry:* painfully, obsessively, demandingly *hungry*.

With equal intensity Sua wanted never to eat anything ever again, to punish the body for its thousand humiliations of appearance, growth, and appetite; and she wanted several large pork chops with raisin dressing, rice, and two vegetables.

Sua returned the glare of successive austere painted faces peering down as her escort of patrollers dragged her past: all the Masters of Ardun back to the Laying of the Stone. All of them committed to being Valde's doormat where folk could scrape their feet clean before venturing onto the venerated dirt beyond the Thornwall. *She* was a Greenleafer, *she* knew Valde were nothing all that special, and corn cake would have been nice, too. Or even plain bread, with jam.

"It's not fair!" Sua shouted as loud as she could, and the fools of patrollers of course didn't understand at all. They just babbled about how she mustn't be upset, it would only be for a little while and a unique chance to be of service to her city, and such things. Sua had no idea what they were talking about, but she was quite sure she didn't want to be "of service," not to the Aihall, anyway, because she was a Greenleafer and they were against the Aihall and the fawning dependence on Valde. She was almost as sure she wasn't going to be given any choice in the matter, the way the patrollers were hanging on. And she was absolutely positive that,

91

whatever Old Four-eyes wanted with her, it would prove to be the fault of the wretched body again.

She wouldn't admit to being hungry, she promised herself, not if she starved right away to nothing.

But, then again, maybe she should ask for just a little something, just enough to make the body shut up. . . . A dry crust. A *large* dry crust and just enough tea to dip it in. No honey in the tea. Almost a punishment, just in itself. . . .

It wasn't *fair!*

The patrollers dragged her up the turns of what must surely have been fifty flights of stairs and thrust her, breathless and drooping, into a large room that showed her reflections of herself from every wall and even the ceiling. A little old man as bald as a turtle looked up from some papers to ask the leader of her escort, "Are you certain?"

The patroller said, "She's Bremneri. One of Mistress Poli's—"

"Yes. Well, she'll have to do if none better can be found in time. We can still hope. Meantime, have this one prepared."

The little old man was Domal Ai, Master of Ardun. She had recognized him at once by the glass circles he wore in a frame over his nose to aid his dim sight. Those glasses were almost as universally known as the Master's tower itself.

While Old Four-eyes continued giving directions as to how she was to be "prepared"—it sounded like a roast—Sua blinked at all the sullen reflections and tried to get her breath back. It wasn't two minutes before her escort turned her around again and took her back down all those stairs.

In the special watch cart they'd brought her in, Sua again confirmed that it had no handles on the inside and lattices over all the windows. She slumped back on the hard wood seat, discouraged. Then she realized she was being taken back to Market Street again. But she couldn't see very well and it wasn't but a few more minutes that the cart stopped. She was pulled out and then through a door held open against the cart, so she had no chance to see anything. She didn't know where she was, except that it had to be somewhere near to Market Square: but certainly not Factors' Row. It wasn't like any of the various factorages, which were elegant and full of doors, that she'd ever been in.

This place was vast and dim, with sunlight falling in solid dusty bars from ventilation slits away up by the high roof beams. Steps seemed very loud in the enclosed silence. But there were voices ahead, conversing quietly but so many of them that they made a steady sound like water flowing. There were people, hundreds of people strolling or standing or sitting in a sort of enormous alcove with board sides rising out of sight—one empty bin of the granary, Sua realized, and realized too that the shut bins, the other ones, must therefore be full.

She laughed to think that she was surrounded by such an enormous weight of food she couldn't touch. It was an angry laugh, and made some of the people look toward her. Immediately there was a stir, people rising and moving toward her as she came into one of the bars of light that leaned like braces between floor and upper wall.

"No," called the patrol leader generally, "none have come back yet. This is Sualiche, daughter of the lar Haffa Poli and the Bremneri—"

"Of course she is," interrupted a slender woman clearly. Taking Sua around the shoulders, the woman walked with her away from the patrollers, saying, "Do you remember me, Sua? You're grown so, I should say, 'Mistress Sua'; and you must call me just Marlena."

Being welcomed with such gentle condescension by Marlena Singer, the most famous member of the entertainers' guild, quite disarmed Sua's brooding indignation. Mistress Marlena had only been at the household once that Sua knew of, for a memorable dinner party about two years ago; had there been other times, Sua would surely have remembered.

Sua asked, rather shyly, what all these people were *doing* hiding in a granary at midday.

"Oh, some of us have been here for almost a week," replied Marlena, in her lovely, unmistakable voice.

"But why?" Sua insisted.

"The Valde have left us because we didn't want them to stay badly enough," replied Marlena, in a pensive, sad voice. "We've been taking them for granted and going our own ways, forgetting that Ardun must be a joyous and serene place for them to care for it as we do—a place all made by hands, all dead stone with so little that sings in the voices they can

93

hear, so much that's divided, dissonant. . . . So those of us who care are trying to balance that discord outside, in the square, do you see? And we're trying to call them back. Perhaps there aren't enough of us yet, or we're too unused to attending steadily to any one thing . . . or perhaps they're already returning, our Valde, though we don't know it yet. But I wish we could learn how to better tune ourselves to a harmony. It's hard to *sing,* so as to say, if you can't *hear.* . . . Do you have the inspeaking? Could you teach us?"

"No." Sua scowled, abruptly less charmed. "I'm no mossheel."

"Of course you're not," agreed Marlena at once, approvingly. "You have the best of both—the beauty, and the wit as well. Because I've sometimes thought—and don't tell anyone—Valde can be the least bit *vague:* do you know what I mean? Just not interested, not curious enough to wonder about things, the way we do. But of course in a way that's good, or otherwise, none of us would have any secrets left at all."

That was said with such a smile and so much soft laughter in the voice that Sua, half unwillingly, had to smile back.

It would have been unpardonably rude to have said she didn't want to be here, didn't care whether the Valde came back or not. If the mossheels wanted to just go off and desert Ardun, then *let* them: that was what Greenleafers said. Ardun didn't *need* Valde or the Summerfair. They could manage, all by themselves.

Sua said, "I don't want to be here. I want to go home."

"Of course you do, and you *will,* just as soon as this trouble is settled. Help us call a Valde, just one, and you can go home right away. But we—"

"*No!*" Sua jerked away from the woman's light embrace and went into the darkest corner she could find.

She felt that if she joined that attempt at summoning she'd have made some irrevocable surrender that would leave her no defenses at all. And she felt that to just out-and-out *beg* like that, to humble herself before what after all were only *people*—different, but not all *that* different, just as old Elda Innsmith had said that time—was just a thing she *would not* do, not even if it was the price of getting out of this place. Without turning she stated harshly, "I'm hungry."

"We all are," came Marlena's reply from close behind her. "It helps us keep mindful of what the poor carters have been going through, what's made them desperate enough to bring things to such a pass."

"But you're against them," objected Sua, in surprise.

"We're only against letting bad times make us forget the long love between Ardun of the Rose and the People of the Trees. We're against becoming so angry and desperate we not only stop loving but stop being lovable. Nothing's worth that," replied Marlena, grave and gentle.

Sua began to cry then, and found she could afford to allow herself to be comforted.

The day grew stranger as it went on. Sua became lightheaded and dizzy and, apparently alarmed, Marlena argued one of the patrollers into going to fetch some stall food. It was only a cold rice ball with some blackberry conserve dabbed into the hole on top, but Sua ate every bit and was given cold tea out of a jug somebody had; but instead of feeling better, she felt increasingly vague. She ceased to care very much where she was or what these people expected of her.

When Marlena suggested it was too chilly in the granary for what Sua was wearing and produced shirt, pants, and cape such as an Awiro might have worn, Sua listlessly changed in a corner without any sense that she was doing anything strange in surrendering so docilely the Greenleafers' emblem she'd stitched so laboriously last night while Mallie was finishing the banner Dan had wanted. But she wouldn't let go of the bandana she'd been given for a scarf. And she still wouldn't help with the summoning.

Whenever the anxious edges of things started to come back Marlena would give her some more tea. All around her, people were muttering to help them concentrate on how much they wanted the Valde to come back and not desert them.

But Sua wouldn't do that. Valde had nothing to do with her anymore. Valde died young. Sua herself was just a plain Bremneri, like her sisters: she'd decided that, months ago.

Domal Ai came in and looked at her again, though she hadn't noticed him arriving, and then everybody left the alcove and went to the great doors at the far end of the granary. One of the big doors had a little door in it, and ev-

erybody went outside through the little door except for Sua
and Marlena and two patrollers. They had to wait, Sua didn't
know why.

Presently the noise outside dimmed enough so that Sua
could hear Domal Ai talking in a very loud voice. He was
saying that the Greenleafers ought to wait, that word would be
coming soon from the forests and the Sea. A deputation was
expected any day now from Duke Pedross Rey, to say what
price he'd take to end the blockade. Buying him off would be
cheaper than fighting him; and Ardun could buy and sell any
islemaster ten times over, for all that they called themselves
arrogant names while Ardun's master was content, proud, to
be merely Ai, Administrator. Baylords were just a bunch of
lazy ambitious greedy thieves, declared Domal Ai, cat and kit
alike, and always had been. They'd outlasted the cat, Ashai,
and the kit, Pedross, had stretched himself too thin, over-
reached this time for sure. Already there were rumors that
the Windward Isles, off away west, had thrown out Pedross'
governor and chosen themselves a duke. He would come to
terms, would Duke Pedross: it was just a matter of waiting,
Domal insisted.

And another delegation, one from Ardun, had been gone
six days now into Entellith, the forest on the far side of the
Thornwall, to discover what complaint the Entellith Valde had
against Ardun, their neighbors: offering to submit any dispute
which couldn't be resolved on the spot to any arbiter they'd
accept, with no bond posted. Another party had gone out, on
the same errand, into Lifganin, seeking the Awiro. Domal
had hoped at least one of these groups would have returned—indeed, had delayed as long as he possibly could,
hoping to be able to bring them all definite word of what was
wrong, why the Valde had felt compelled to leave them this
way.

"But I look at you," said the sharp, accusing voice into the
increasing quiet in the square, "ready to break a marriage all
but a thousand years old between Ardun of the Rose and the
People of the Trees, and I don't wonder any more why
they've left us. What are we becoming? What have we done,
to turn Ardun into one vast street market—snatching, raucous, and greedy? They flee us, as they fled the loathsome Old

96

Ones of Kantmorie. We're no better—not if the gentle Valde can't even tolerate our presence."

Sua had the sudden feeling that her mother was beside her and had just responded with half-heard sarcasm to the reference to "gentle Valde." Any troopmaid who couldn't hand any opponent his head in under three minutes stood a poor chance of surviving the riverstocks: Sua wondered what Valde Domal Ai knew that she didn't. But it had only been Marlena saying something to one of the patrollers.

Domal Ai was going on now about how they'd been taking the Valde and the Summerfair for granted, as a right. "We have always been guests in Morgaard Vale, and we're guests *here:* the first stone of the Aihall was laid by consent and not by right or by conquest. The Summerfair has never been ours, though Ardun has grown rich as its doorway, and though all peoples depend on it—the reliable promises, the verified contracts, the festering feuds that are healed and settled in the truth: the heart's truth, not merely the mouth's, you Bremneri. The Valde are the clear windows whereby we can see each other and, at need, the walls that keep us from each other's throats; and what do we offer in return? What need has any Valde of us, or of anything we make or do?

"But we can't live without Valde. Just in a few weeks, it's begun to go bad," continued Domal in a dark, brooding voice. "Haven't you seen it, felt it? A curse of dark-heartedness, infecting everything it touches? Do you like it, what we're becoming? Do you think Valde will tolerate forever such a howling shadow as Ardun's becoming, crouched on their very doorstep? Stop it now. If we want our Valde to return, if we want it with all our hearts and strength, if we're truly sorry for what we've allowed ourselves and our city to become, they'll be moved to take pity, and forgive, and come back to us. They will! If we all call together, they'll hear us wherever they are and return. Those of you who believe me and those with the gift of telling that I've been speaking the truth I know as clearly as I can, all of you, be quiet a little while and want them back. *Believe* they're coming, and they'll come. I swear it, by my life. *Try!*"

And he had believed it, every word: Sua would have known, otherwise. There'd been just the one different one,

97

with the voice she'd have known in a thousand, and he was gone. . . .

Sua twisted the bandana slowly into knots.

Outside, in the complete silence, somebody had begun humming. Presently the humming became singing without words—one of the songs of the Blooming Festival, when the dense rose hedge beyond the Aihall Square, the Thornwall, came into flower and marked the beginning of Summerfair, a renewal and a welcome and a shared gladness deeper than its cause. Beside Sua, Marlena joined in the singing in her wonderfully true voice with nobody to hear but just Sua (the patrollers had gone off), and tears ran down Marlena's face. The singing gathered voices to it, not all of them tuneful or even on key; but the individual flaws became lost in the multitudinous sound: a windsound of poignant unseasonal longing that grew louder or softer but continued, until it seemed less a song than a natural part of the evening, like the vermilion light shining through the ventilation slits.

When Marlena said, "It's time to go now," Sua didn't question it but followed the slender woman back through the granary, away from the voices. And, as she'd expected, they turned west: toward her own house. It was time for the daymeal, time to be going home. So she was surprised when Marlena wanted to turn back toward the singing again.

"It's all right," Marlena assured her. "They won't hurt you now."

Except for a little while this morning, it had never occurred to Sua that people *might*. But she'd known only the summer, and the warm weather. She thought of Garin saying that to her. All day, she'd shied away from thinking about him—about the knife, and the way he'd fallen. . . . She wouldn't sing, but the singing made it somehow possible to risk grieving for the two terrible losses she'd suffered in her life. It no longer seemed necessary to hold them tightly against herself and not feel them, lest they begin bleeding and refuse to stop. Sua went the way she was led, with the singing all around her.

People touched her but no one tried to grab or hold her. Vaguely she was aware of their moving aside, making a way for her to walk. Marlena wasn't with her anymore. Sua glanced around confusedly, but the opening corridor showed her the way she was supposed to be going and she followed it.

There were steps, and the way closing behind her, so she climbed the steps and found herself on the loading platform of the granary. Farther on were Domal Ai and the crowd of summoners who'd been in the alcove inside with her. And before her was the crowd. She couldn't see them very well with the level red light shining full in her face. But they saw her. And slowly she began to understand what they were seeing, were meant to see, what fraud her wretched, deceiving body had gotten her into this time.

"Wait!" she shouted, as loud as she could, but nobody heard her and Domal Ai started toward her. She turned, daring him to lay hands on her in front of all these people he was trying to fool. But he kept coming, the two glass circles flashing red, his eyes invisible behind them.

Making motions of greeting, he said in her ear, "Keep still, or I swear by my life you won't be breathing at moonrise."

He didn't scare her, or not much—not when she had a father who knew a troll, and the troll's brother had done what he'd done on her account. Sua freed her arm from his fingers and hit him as hard as she could across the face.

Into the shocked silence she yelled, "I'm *not* a Valde, or only half. I'm Sualiche. My father is Jannus Arbiter and I'm Bremneri. You know me! They don't care, the Valde. They're gone, and *let* them go! We can manage, all by ourselves!"

Then the riot started.

The summoners were after her, those that weren't trying all to jam in at once through the little door in the big door. Sua jumped off the dock into the crowd while Domal Ai was still trying to get his glasses straight, and tried to keep from being shoved or stepped on in the rush toward the granary. From the other granary on the west side of the square, patrollers were jumping down onto the street stones, fighting, and more were behind her, coming out the little door so that the summoners were swept away. Sua just ducked and dodged, trying to circle back toward Factors' Row. She should run for the nearest Bremneri factorage, just the way she should have when Garin told her to. But she hadn't realized then what was truly going on.

Somebody was moving with her. She almost struck out before she realized he was fending people away from her, using elbows and stiff-bladed hands with a really remarkable efficiency that seemed almost casual. The people seemed to drift away of their own accord. Sua stayed with him, using what skills she had, and presently found herself jammed against the openwork concrete wall at the head of the Row, the young man blocking the people pushing heedlessly past them by wedging one of his arms into the wall.

He was nobody she'd ever seen before—a middle-sized young man, about the Sparrow's age, she thought, about twenty. He had dull black hair worked into a waterman's braid that swung as straight as string when he looked around warily. His short beard was dark too. That was odd, because he was fair complected, even a little sunburned across his forehead and nose. And he had eyes as green as a cat's.

Still scanning the mob, he asked, "Where were you supposed to go?"

"A Bremneri factorage. . . ." replied Sua uncertainly, because he was frowning at her and seemed to expect some different answer.

"No, you have to get clear of the city altogether. Old Four-eyes'll have you broken into little bitty pieces for that bit of prize mischief . . . if he catches you. Wake up: where are you supposed to be?"

He had, Sua noticed, a strong downriver accent—like Garin's when he'd first come; afterward, though, Garin had mostly lost it. And this man had a perfectly ordinary voice, with the underhum of conviction in what he said.

"I can go past the Thornwall, into Entellith—" she offered, but he cut her off with a sharp negative gesture.

"No. It's not safe. Some place else. I'm sure. Can't you *hear* that, Sua?" he asked, with a tense grin.

"Do you know me?"

"After a fashion. You were a Truthsayer against me once, you and the rest. I know your father and I want to get both of us clear of this in one piece. Now can you hear *that*, Truthsayer?"

"Yes. . . ."

"Come on, we've got to move," he directed, pulling her into a trot, heading down along the Row. Glancing behind, he dropped to a fast walk, then paused to sneeze about five times into a hastily snatched cloth. "Damn inland weather," he remarked, staring around him, clearly not knowing one street from another.

When Sua turned decisively east and downhill, toward the Fallows, he went along, seeming to know just by the way she moved that she'd thought of some place safe, someplace where neither Domal Ai nor anybody else could get at her.

She'd decided to go to the troll hill.

"Who are you?" she asked presently. "Why'd you help me get clear?"

"Because," he replied, and grinned mockingly. Then he changed his mind. "I got you out because I had the chance to, and after I heard you yelling out who you were, fit to scare crows. I figure maybe it's worth enough to your da for him to trade for something I want that he's got. Or I think he's got, that's mine. Favor for favor."

Sua nodded: that was true. Besides, it made sense. "But I asked, 'Who are you?'" she reminded him.

"Personally, my own self, I'm Duke Pedross Rey, Master of Andras. I'm in disguise," he explained, looking around at her.

And that was true too: or at least he believed it, every word.

Sua said, "Oh," and wondered just what sort of insanity he suffered from. Because even if it *was* true, what he believed, nobody but a crazy man would leave his nice safe blockade to stroll through Ardun, not even knowing the streets. Either way, he had to be crazy.

But the troll could keep her safe a thousand years, so she didn't try to duck into an alley and lose the madman, which she thought wouldn't have been too hard. Because if he really *was* Pedross, and was caught abroad in the city, Domal Ai would do something even worse to him than to her, if there *was* anything worse.

She wondered if there'd be anything to *eat*, in a troll hill.

The current headache was going to be a blinder. Well, Jannus thought resignedly, there was no help for it.

He continued walking toward the Morimmon and Sunset Bridge, trying to piece together the best way of handling the situation Sua had become involved in, which Jannus had learned from the new mobile. The old man had decided to call himself "Simon," having been argued out of his alternative choices, *Merddyn* and *Nostradamus,* which Jannus considered outlandish noises. "Simon" sounded like a Smith name, but at least it was something Jannus wouldn't feel foolish saying.

Though Poli had wanted to come with him, they'd finally agreed it was imprudent. So Jannus was returning alone, the mobile having gone on ahead to assess the situation further and take word to Jannus' household to stay indoors.

He'd gone perhaps halfway to the river when he felt a sort of pressure imposing itself through the rhythmic pulse of his headache.

The pressure resolved itself into words:

—Jannus?

He found a flat place on the hillside and let himself down. —All right.

He'd agreed to that, that the Shai initiate contact, persuaded by Simon's arguments that the former arrangement had been overscrupulous and potentially dangerous. Jannus wanted no wider rapport; nevertheless, at need, he'd do what he had to.

The Shai continued—Sua's clear, and coming this way. With Pedross.

Jannus opened his eyes and looked blankly about him, half blind anyway with the red sundown staring him in the face through the naked treetop silhouettes. —You sure?

—Well, he's in disguise: that is, he's dyed his hair black, replied the Shai, with restrained derision.

—No, he hasn't the gift of being inconspicuous, has our Pedross. What do you make of it?

—Serially, or conceptually?

—No more conceptual input! directed Jannus at once: it had been taking in all of Garin's day, and all the Shai's interpretations of events in Ardun, that that had earned Jannus his present headache. —Never mind. I'll ask him myself what in the world he thinks he's about. Put it this way: were you expecting him?

—Not as a high probability. Scarcely as a remote one.

—All right.

—You shouldn't still be having that sort of reaction to the

implant. If you could just stop trying to reject it by sheer force of will.

—It's my head, I'll do with it what I please. Now leave me alone or I won't be able to walk straight for an hour.

Jannus sat with his eyes shut, waiting to be sure the Shai had closed the rapport and trying to recover enough sense of what he was doing to interpret this news. It was true he'd found the link easier to learn than the inspeaking. But it was also harder. The necessary concentration was nearly as difficult to hold as breath, and tended to leave him exhausted and disoriented afterward in all but the briefest exchanges.

And conceptual input, that the Shai was always after him to consent to, just meant *headache*, as far as Jannus was concerned. It meant getting direct knowledge of complicated things, and all their interrelationships and implications, all at once, in one massive indigestible lump. The Shai insisted that Jannus was capable of handling information that way: Teks had.

Teks didn't get headaches, Jannus had retorted. Or, if they did, they didn't care.

He wanted to let Poli know what was going on, but found that the headache interfered too much for him to find images that would say what he wanted. His head felt like something empty and dry and hollow, with a tight strap holding it together.

Just the same, his mood had lightened considerably, and not just because of Sua's escape. The fact that Pedross had come told him a lot of things, all satisfactory. Not least of these was that the Shai really wasn't using the link to spy beneath the agreed levels. Finally, Jannus could allow himself to believe it. One of the multiple uses of this matter of Pedross, was to be a test of that.

Pedross was the foundation of the afterward, which Jannus had promised to see to himself, independent of the Shai and the Rule of One.

But he couldn't manage to focus the inspeaking at all, he found. The two modes of concentration were too different. So he initiated contact and, when the Shai answered him, directed— Relay for me, to Poli. She's in your range. Give her an image of somebody to talk to: Ashai, maybe. She knew him. And tell her about this, about Sua.

Without needing to think about it, Jannus knew she'd hate a projected image of himself, *sa'farioh* and intangible, appearing like some visitation by an importunate ghost anxious to deliver some dire message. Even mobiles unnerved and annoyed her.

He added, —And relay back to me anything she wants to tell me. He rested his forehead against his knees for a while. But it seemed Poli had nothing she wanted to say to him, not through the link anyway, by means of Ashai's fetch. It didn't especially surprise him. Poli liked things she could touch; and, if necessary, hit.

—Jannus

—What?

—Domal's dead. He was pushed off the loading platform of the granary and broke his neck. An interesting development.

—Isn't it. Tell Poli.

—All right. Take care, Jannus, what you get yourself into, with Pedross. He's got no business even being here. No master of Andras can afford to turn his back on the isles for even a day without some insurrection or other hatching behind him.

—I do hear you, Jannus responded noncommittally.

So the Shai had put all the coincidences in the pot and found the arrangement significant. It hadn't taken him long. But that was the Shai's special skill, after all. As long as he didn't decide Jannus' private tinkerings around the edges of the Rule of One merited blowing his head off with the incendiary, Jannus figured there was no cause for complaint.

The headache was definitely easing. They took their own time—none of the usual remedies seemed able to touch them at all. But eventually, they all passed. The trick was not to care, and still hold on to the sense of what he was doing, in spite of the pressure.

It was the first of the twilight before he heard the two of them, Pedross and Sua, coming up the far side of the next hill and roused himself. He'd almost fallen asleep, he realized. Well, that was no wonder, considering he hadn't slept all last night. He'd wanted to, but it just hadn't been possible.

The headache had ebbed to no more than a bruised tenderness at the base of his skull. Rubbing it seemed to help now.

The approaching pair came over the top of the hill and started down, circling among the trees. Pedross saw him first, and slowed: so Sua, running, reached him well ahead of her more cautious companion.

Jannus interrupted her agitated and largely incoherent account of her adventures to say, "You had no business being out on the streets alone to begin with."

"I *wasn't* alone, Garin . . ." she began, and then stopped, chastened.

"Precisely. Take more care what you do, Sua. What you do is beginning to have consequences, and they involve more people than just you. Don't start what you can't see, or what you're not prepared to take the consequences of. Because the consequences come, whether you want them or expect them or not." Having been, he hoped, sufficiently stern, he got hold of her hand and pulled her down to be hugged.

"But I can't go home, not now," she went on as Pedross was arriving to stand against a tree a few paces off. In his own fashion, Pedross knew how to be inconspicuous enough, Jannus thought. Sua was saying, "So I thought I'd go to the troll hill."

Troll . . . ?

When Jannus reached for it, the knowledge was there—almost like something he'd heard himself and was remembering, an item from the concentrated mass of conceptual input he'd taken in earlier.

"That's probably best, until this business settles down. . . . I'm surprised to see you," Jannus greeted the young man politely waiting to be noticed. Jannus avoided using any name, in case that was part of Pedross' disguise, like the bronze-gold hair dyed that unconvincing black and the beard he'd managed to grow since Jannus had last seen him. Jannus wondered what Pedross supposed himself to be disguised *as.*

Pedross nodded to himself, as if that unhesitating recognition told him something he'd wanted to know, confirming some guess. He said, "The old man."

Realizing all at once that he had to be *much* more cautious around Pedross than around most people, Jannus replied unhelpfully, "The old man *what?*"

"You know." Pedross glanced very slightly aside at Sua, who looked from him back to Jannus perplexedly.

105

Of course Jannus knew: recognition meant prior warning, meant mobile, which meant the only person they'd seen this side of Sunset Bridge. But Pedross wasn't going to say so in plain words in front of Sua.

To simplify matters, Jannus asked Sua, "Who's this?"

"He says he's Duke Pedross Rey. . . . He helped me get clear of the square."

Helpful, even if demented, that seemed to mean. "And what was he doing in Ardun to begin with?"

"He wants to trade helping me for something he thinks you have, that he wants."

Pedross remarked lightly, "I thought I'd bring a Truthsayer, in case we needed one."

"And I'm obliged for it. I haven't any I can spare." Jannus put his arm around Sua's back.

"Five ought to be enough for anybody," rejoined Pedross. "Well, they turned against Domal, the way you said they would."

"It wasn't that hard to predict," rejoined Jannus mildly. "The Greenleafers aren't exactly neutral, and it's mostly Innsmith money behind the Greenleafers. . . ."

"And you've worked out an arrangement with Elda Innsmith," concluded Pedross, and looked surprised when Sua stifled a laugh.

Jannus reached, and got that reference too; it was merely that Pedross' choice of words had, for Sua, an unintended and ludicrous double meaning.

"Elda and I understand each other fairly well, yes," agreed Jannus noncommittally.

"But your fallback was terrible," commented Pedross, a professional judgment of applied tactics. Reading from Jannus' expression that Jannus didn't know what he meant, Pedross explained, "The fallback—getting her out of it once she'd gotten the riot going properly. She wasn't even sure where her primary fallback position was supposed to be."

Jannus regarded the young man very coldly for a moment, then reminded himself that Pedross had only appearances to go on. With restraint, Jannus told him, "I didn't send her into the middle of that. I didn't even know she was there until a little while ago."

"For a fact," said Pedross, with a covert glance over at

Sua, to see if she'd reacted to a deliberate lie in any way he could discern. "Then your planning and intelligence are terrible—almost as bad as mine have been since I lost Secolo."

"For a fact," Jannus responded, cautious in his turn.

"I'm not stupid, Jannus," declared Pedross provocatively, walking a few paces and then swinging around. "I notice, when my weather predictions suddenly turn so unreliable that I lose two ships in a storm nobody knew was coming. I notice, when I've been getting the best intelligence of any baymaster, and then I start going through the actual paper those reports were purportedly based on and find not a tenth of what there should be to have generated what I'd been taking for granted. It was Secolo, wasn't it?"

He'd discovered the substitution. No, he wasn't stupid: it had only taken him six years. Of course, he'd had powerful reasons *not* to notice that his spymaster was just another incarnation of Ashai Rey, his father: he'd hated Ashai, and with some justice—mobiles were never the easiest of companions. But once Secolo had "died," Pedross had been obliged to take notice and free to think.

Jannus considered carefully a moment and could see no sense in denying it. "He's decided to call himself Simon this time," he replied mildly.

"And all the while, it was him, when I thought. . . ." Pedross bent, yanked up a fistful of dry grass, and flung it aside. "As a father, he was unbearable. But as a spymaster, a chief of intelligence, he's irreplaceable. I want him back," he announced, with a sharp, direct look. "And don't think I don't know how funny this is, either," he went on, with a face that forbade laughter, "because I know it. What do you imagine I've been thinking about, sitting on that damn wet footstool they call Dunwater for weeks, waiting for a delegation to arrive inviting me to become Master of Ardun, which they didn't do yet, by the way."

"It just took awhile to make everybody see Domal was in a box with just two doors, and then make him open one of them—the wrong one, as it happens. . . . You didn't have to come, though. You'd have gotten your delegation presently."

"And now my Valde signalers are deserting, and the troopmaids up in Bremner," Pedross responded heedlessly. "That your doing too?"

"Are they? I didn't know about that. . . ." Jannus

107

frowned: he'd assumed that once the blockade and its consequent unrest were settled, Ardun would once again become tolerable to its neighbors, the Valde. But what Pedross said suggested a more general withdrawal, its causes unknown but surely not attributable to Ardun alone. But Ardun and his immediate problems were all Jannus felt prepared to consider just now. Absently, he said, "It's not my doing, no," and saw Pedross look down at Sua again. "Sua, am I lying to him?"

Sua scowled up at Pedross indignantly. "Of course not, and if you did I wouldn't tell."

"Tell," said Jannus.

"Then, no."

"It's so nice to be sure," commented Pedross dryly, and sat down cross-legged, facing Jannus. "The bargain stands?"

"The bargain stands," Jannus confirmed. "You'll get your deputation. Elda agrees with me: better you as Master of Ardun than Ardun just cracked between the two shut doors and thrown away like . . . like some folk we know have planned. To any sensible man, Ardun as a live money mill should be preferable to Ardun as a dead enemy—"

"A waste," Pedross agreed, "just for the sake of old spite. I've put aside more than one old grudge for the sake of what was at hand." Jannus nodded, knowing that was so; it was one reason he'd thought Pedross might agree to any reasonable plan that would put the key of the money mill in his hands. Pedross asked, "But how long? I can't hang around waiting forever, I've got the Windwards to see to."

"A week, maybe. No more than two. Then you'll get your deputation, as agreed."

Pedross had, besides his cool pragmatism, one other great attraction for Jannus as a prospective Master of Ardun: he didn't believe in witches and had no patience whatever with those who did. The only way, Jannus had judged, to be a demonstrable witch, married to an indisputable fetch, in Ardun, was to make witchcraft and fetch-hood legal and respectable. That was the other part of the bargain, the personal part. Pedross had promised that, in return for Jannus' help, he'd remove witchcraft from the list of possible civil offenses.

"But I want the mobile besides," Pedross declared abruptly, the good humor suddenly fallen away.

"That wasn't what we agreed."

"It wasn't part of the agreement that you steal my eyes, my right hand, either."

"What makes you think I stole him?"

"Don't be absurd. Who else *could?*" rejoined Pedross baldly.

"The Shai. . . . But yes, I called him away from the isles. . . . Poli died, you see. I needed special help in getting her back."

"Did you get it?" Pedross asked, after a moment.

"Yes. . . . Today. This morning. It took awhile," Jannus explained. Pedross had seen Ashai dead at least three times, and Secolo once. He knew such things were possible.

But, plainly, he didn't like to think about them any more than he had to.

"All right," Pedross said. "I guess that was important to you, enough to be worth the trouble it's been to me. But I want him back now. That, or no bargain."

Jannus couldn't easily decide what to say. There were advantages and rights to be considered on both sides of the question—too many to resolve all in a moment. But, beyond that, it seemed to him that it wasn't properly his to decide. The Shai chose his own masters. Even trying to interfere might be dangerous. Eventually he said, "You'll have to ask him yourself. We'll go in a minute, but just be quiet a bit, will you?"

Settling his head in his hands, Jannus made the necessary effort of concentration and directed the Shai to consider Pedross' demand and relay it to Simon, as well; and, through Simon, to let Sparrowhawk know Sua was safe, and with him, and that he might not be home until late—maybe not until morning. And he told the Shai to have the Ashai-fetch tell Poli they were going to have company that would need to be fed.

Slowly recovering, he asked Sua, "You hungry?"

"Yes!" The word was fervently emphatic.

"Then let's go. It's not too far."

As he pushed himself to his feet, Sua said, "I know," meaningfully, and he regarded her a moment, smiling.

"You don't know everything you think you do. But then, neither do I. Neither does the Shai—your friend, the troll."

Pedross made a face at the word. Then he said, "Is *it* there? The ship? *Sunfire?*"

"Yes. . . ."

"Good. I've always hoped that I'd get a chance to see it."

"You may even do that," commented Jannus obliquely; for the Shai didn't show himself unless he wanted to, as Sua had discovered. Jannus would leave that choice, as well, up to the Shai's own discretion, feeling such family tensions were best settled without the interference of outsiders.

But he thought it likely that the Shai and Pedross would work out some kind of accommodation in regard to the mobile. After all, it was to *be* so served that Pedross had been begotten, born, and trained to his present formidable pragmatism. And who else would it be worth a mobile's time and unique talents to serve? Certainly not Jannus, who could employ Simon only as an assistant housekeeper and messengerunner. . . .

What Sua and Poli would make of each other, he had no idea. That, too, seemed to be a matter he would be wisest to keep out of, and let it settle itself any way it needed to. A considerable part of learning to use power, he was discovering, was learning its limits and what ought to be left alone.

Poli was learning to spot the holes.

Pedross, the boy she'd just been told was coming, was an empty place in her memory. She'd met him, she knew, in that distant way of knowing. She'd presumably been at least sufficiently acquainted to have recognized him, the way Jannus had. She'd once gotten angry at Jannus when he'd wanted to help Pedross some way she'd thought too dangerous. And Jannus had once fought a troopmaid in Quickmoor on Pedross' account and gotten his nose broken, among other things. Nothing, really. A hole.

Sua's hole was more deceptive: full of facts, empty of meaning.

Poli attended closely to the distant selfsingings, determined that before the two strangers arrived, she would know them down to their very bones. Because Jannus was with them, and she *knew* Jannus—really knew him—she could tell them apart, the strangers, by his reactions, and theirs to him.

But for Poli relationship remained the only true mirror.

110

And she was deeply afraid of meeting Sua and finding, in Sua's eyes and selfsinging, no relationship or reflection of herself at all: as if Poli weren't truly there, were just another deceiving appearance modeled by Tek tricks onto the air.

Poli wasn't sure she could face that.

She checked that the water in the kettle was boiling and tipped in the chunked meat of two rabbits today's snares had caught in a thicket on the far side of the stream. As Jannus had predicted, hunting should be good here.

But it wouldn't be enough, not with two more mouths to be fed, and one of them Sua's.

Poli took a burning splint and, by its light, checked through the provisions in the box. As she thought she recalled having seen, there was a bundle of dried fish: hand-sized slabs like brittle leather. She sat down by the fire and set about reducing a few of the slabs to powder, pounding them between two stones.

Presently she said aloud, "Shai, why is everything that happened before today like so much sand?"

The false Ashai began to form, shimmering in the dark across the fire, but she said, "Take that thing away. I know you don't need it to answer." She'd never liked Ashai much even when he was alive.

"Jannus said—" the false Ashai began to protest.

"Jannus isn't here." Poli reached to slide the powder into the pot. "I'm not going to be frightened into fits by a voice in the air. Not by comparison to that thing."

The false Ashai twirled somehow, like a flame, and went out. There was only the dark, and the firelight, and the pot boiling above it. From the place where the image had been, a voice remarked, "There are precedents with a certain relevance to this situation. The consensus of their advice seems to be that it's wiser not to look back."

"You ought to be scooped out of your shell," responded Poli firmly, slivering carrots. "You've been in that cave too long, Shai."

"I'm used to it. You might as well tell Jannus he ought to get out of his skin."

"He changes skins often enough by himself. He doesn't need telling. You do. You sent out mobiles, yes—but you

111

stay home in your safe cave. You'll go blind in there pretty soon."

"I can look into the sun," retorted the voice.

"Now?"

"No, it's on the other side of the world now."

"Well, then," said Poli, measuring pebbles of dried corn from a sack. She identified the right twist of herbs by smell and dropped two pinches into the water.

"A day old, and already you can refute me," observed the voice, with mild mockery. "I scarcely know you any more, you've grown so shrewd, just in the one day." The Shai sounded more serious toward the end of that, as if he was thinking about something else too.

"What's the matter with my memory, Shai?" she asked again.

"You wouldn't understand."

"Could that bird understand?" She meant Bronh. A name covering another hole.

"Probably."

"Could Jannus?"

"Again, probably."

"Then what am I, some incompetent . . ." She searched for a word. ". . . *fetch?* The fact is, you don't *want* to tell me because it was a mistake. It wasn't supposed to be this way. Was it," she challenged.

"You'd have liked the alternative even less. Or, rather, the fact that you can notice the difference at all means that you were made *right*. Well. Whole. From the moment of your waking."

"But not before."

"There *is* no before. There's now."

"The before is the shadow it casts. Who took the measure of my shadow, Shai?"

That was a witch trick, so-called, to gain control of somebody.

"I did," stated the Shai, no apology or uncertainty in the voice.

"Then why are there holes in it?"

"Some things," answered the voice slowly, "nobody knew but you, yourself, alone. And I couldn't ask you."

"Because I was dead."

"Yes. If you're whole enough to try to call me to account, then you're whole enough to live with the gaps. After a year, or twenty, like today, it won't matter so much to you. And some gaps will be filled. Sua, for instance. Pedross. Jannus himself. That was just memory too, until you woke."

"That's *now*. That doesn't mend the shadow."

"My advice is still, 'Don't look back.' "

"And mine is still that you should be shelled like a clam. With your wonderful eyes, can you see how far away they are?" She needed to know when to throw in the rice; and, beyond broad perceptions like *near* or *far*, the *marenniath* made no distinctions.

"I can't see through hills, woman."

"Then what use are you?"

The Shai laughed, sounding genuinely delighted and amused. "But my ears are good, too. Say, five minutes."

Poli threw in four good handfuls of rice, considered briefly, and added a fifth. Chipping a small chunk of salt from the block in the lean-to, she dropped it in the pot and clapped on the lid. That was done, then.

She admitted offhandedly to the air, "Considering everything, I'd rather be alive."

"That's small enough thanks," complained the air.

"Did you expect thanks?"

"If I always got what I expected, the world would be dull beyond enduring."

"Did you want to do it?"

"Yes," replied the Shai, quite definitely. "In a way, I'm even sorry it's done."

"What makes you think it's done?"

When the air said nothing, graciously allowing her the last word, Poli realized the nature of the game she'd been drawn into, that the Shai had been playing so that she could win. She felt, thought about, the subtle kindness of that.

"Thank you, Shai."

The air remained contentedly silent about her.

Poli walked to the edge of the firelight to meet them all when they came. One daysinging, fully known, had healed all daysingings, remembered; maybe one meeting would heal all the holes in Sua too. Poli no longer felt she must either lunge at the child and encompass her, defend herself from hurt by a species of attack, or else flee at once into the dark. If there was no reflection, she'd make one. It was just a matter of getting acquainted again. After all, she'd been away.

III

ROSE AND THORN

When Simon learned, one morning, that another floater had been found, he left his offices at once to inform Pedross. The mobile took the most direct route through the Aihall's turnings, accompanied only by his reflection appearing in sudden flashes as he passed mirrored panels.

Some people used power to gather an entourage to attend their slightest thought or motion; Simon used that granted him as chief of intelligence to the new Master, Duke Pedross Rey, to buy the rarer treasure of solitude.

But its price was the complete forfeiture of anonymity: he was able to pass unchallenged and unhindered along the Aihall's ornate corridors only because every servant, scribe, and page had learned in fourteen days to instantly recognize the gaunt striding figure and avert their eyes, pretending they saw no one at all.

Across the length of the principal audience hall Simon saw Pedross seated in the official Master's seat enduring the obligation of having his portrait painted. Around the chair moved the usual frantic swirl of scribes, clerks, mid- and upper-level functionaries, aides, their assorted servants and bodyguards, and pages circulating with trays of food. In an alcove five inconspicuous musicians played twittering inconspicuous music suitable to an informal morning audience session.

And Pedross himself was held still in the center of it by the eyes of the painter. Gesturing, talking, intermittently eating, interrupting himself to dictate another snatch of letter

117

to his governor of Camarr, Pedross would suddenly remember his captivity to the discerning civilian eye of the painter. Then he'd locate the empty volume of air he was supposed to be occupying and balance himself back into it until he forgot again. Simon noticed as he passed that the painter had beside her a sketch pad filled with detailed studies of hands spread in gestures of reaching.

Waiting for Pedross to finish a conversation with a man on Simon's list of possible ministerial appointees, Simon reflected that this foolish detour into Ardun would eventually have its uses. Pedross knew how to sack a city and order it afterward but hadn't yet had the leisure or the opportunity to learn the weapons of civility. Conquered cities permitted a certain brusqueness of action possible only amid violent chaos. Ardun was another breed of cat altogether: cosmopolitan, cultured, occupied but unconquered, long accustomed to invasion by seasonal migrations of strangers to be humored, entertained, and controlled; and it was watching most intently this stranger it had invited, under duress, to ownership. Pedross could suffer no harm from learning the uses of ceremony and the tactics a civilized populace could use to transmute virtual occupation to a favor they'd been minded to do the occupier, however unworthy he might be, though of course they'd be too civil to say so aloud or to his face.

Approaching the chair at the next opportunity, Simon reported tersely, "Another floater. You asked to be told."

The expressive hands of which the painter had taken such special notice tightened fractionally. "Have you seen it yet?"

"I'm going now. It's relatively fresh, I'm told. There may be something to be learned this time beyond the fact it's dead."

Pedross swung around in his chair. "Which river? Morimmon, or Arant Dunrimmon?"

"Arant Dunrimmon. By the pumping station above Sunset Bridge. A woman fishing snagged it about first light."

Pedross deliberated a moment. "Invite the Lady Poli to view it with us," he directed.

Nobody in Ardun had the power to command Valde, as both Pedross and Simon knew perfectly well. Nevertheless Pedross expected Simon to manage it.

It was one of a series of challenges or tests Pedross had

devised since regaining the service of the mobile he now knew to be such. Often the occasions were trivial but the reasons were not: Pedross meant to learn how far he could rely on this unique and powerful ally who served by his own whim, not through any strength Pedross possessed to compel him. Simon found Pedross' many-faceted wariness quite reasonable, under the circumstances.

The two who had once been father and son looked at each other a moment, confirming their understanding. Then Pedross turned to amending his morning schedule to make room for this excursion, and the mobile moved away.

Consulted, the Shai declined to transmit such a trifling request through the link. Unsurprised, Simon called a message runner and formulated a summons Simon thought would suffice. The runner was just departing when Pedross separated himself from sleeve-catching interruptions, bringing in his wake a small entourage—his personal bodyguard, a duty squad of five marines and their officer—and Pedross' official Truthsayer who was at hand during all daylight business.

Pedross' Truthsayer was Sua.

It was an appointment popular with the Greenleafers, whose mascot and living banner Sua had become since the granary insurrection nineteen days ago. She also served as an excellent de facto hostage: Pedross didn't altogether trust Jannus either. And, in lieu of the lately deserted Valde of his signal corps, Sua would detect any substitution—Pedross was mindful that Secolo had once been an ordinary living man before the Shai had decided to steal his face and manufacture a mobile in the spymaster's image. If it could happen once, it could happen twice: Sua was Pedross' protection against such impersonation. She'd be listened to if ever she claimed Pedross was not himself but a *sa'farioh* imposter. From Pedross' point of view, Simon judged, Sua's attractions were manifold.

And of course Sua was eating it all up with the most obvious relish. She was very likely the most famous and generally popular individual in Ardun at the moment, and wore her white Truthsayer's tabard with delighted aplomb.

As they began descending a broad spiral stair, Simon suggested quietly to Pedross, "Leave her here."

"Why?"

"You don't need a Truthsayer to interrogate a corpse," commented the mobile with unemphatic calm. "And you want her to *like* your service—an overt hostage would be awkward just now. The Greenleafers, among others, wouldn't like it. Drowned bodies aren't sightly objects even at the best, and she's unacquainted with them and half your age, in spite of appearances. Why invite needless complications?"

Simon continued to take the stairs at an even pace, letting his comments hang lest by multiplying reasons he rouse resistance. Argument was a tactic he preferred to avoid whenever possible. Irrationalities tended to intrude in indignant disguises.

After about ten steps Pedross said indifferently, "That makes sense," and paused and turned to dismiss her.

Simon would have fabricated some errand to let her feel she'd been sent *toward* rather than *away* . . . but no matter.

As she turned dejectedly he noticed a tape of blue cloth tied arond her right wrist. It was from the bandana casually lent her by the Garin persona. She always had some bit of that cloth about her somewhere, and Simon suspected that nobody but himself noticed it or knew what it was. At least she'd never mentioned it either to him or within his hearing.

When she'd asked, at their first meeting, he'd said he was Garin's older brother: for of course she'd known him as *sa'farioh* the first instant he'd uttered a word in spite of the changes in voice and appearance. She'd looked at him searchingly a moment, there at the edge of the inauguration activities, then demanded, "Is that true?"

"Nearly," he'd replied, and presently she'd drifted off into the crowd—to be made much of, he expected, by some jubiliant Greenleafers. . . .

It was a windy morning—warm within the sunny confines of the Aihall Square but blustery as they walked west toward the riverside between the Thornwall and the hedges of the Seven Houses, the mansions, each a block wide and two blocks long, that had been built in the days when lots could be bought outright and were now the only privately owned estates in the city. Three of the Seven Families were Greenleafers; the other four were Loyalist and had guards and ambling nackers—knee-high cousins to wolverines—patrolling their perimeters. The duty officer ranged his squad on that side to discourage any needless incident, leaving Pedross and Simon strolling alone in the middle of the road.

But Pedross was thinking about other things than Ardun's factions. Regarding the impenetrably tangled expanse of the Thornwall, he voiced his continuing anger at the desertion of those members of his Valde signal corps whom he'd brought inland with him. "I'm not some Bremneri riverstock nor yet Ardun, to collapse for the lack of them," he went on, frowning, "but it galls me, all the same. They were so *handy* . . . ! It galls me, to build up that network the best part of six years and enforce general tolerance and then be back to runners, hand signals, and heliographs again. . . . What's the *matter* with them?" he demanded, looking up at Simon sharply. "I treated my people well. They were Awiro anyhow, they contracted with me freely, they had no lack of regard or food or bed partners on shipboard or ashore. . . ."

"Perhaps they got homesick," offered Simon.

"I don't want *perhaps*. I want *why*," Pedross shot back. "The isle network's still in place, or most of it, and I want to know if it's worth the work of rebuilding, recruiting all over again, or if they'll just take a fit of absence too and be gone without so much as a 'by your courtesy.' "

"Don't put too much hope in the isle network," advised the mobile mildly. "I expect it's only the lack of transport keeping them in place. And *that* won't last. . . ."

Pedross nodded grudged agreement. He knew Valde could no more be held captive than mara. They just pine and die on you, no earthly use to anybody. "This has been such a crazy business," Pedross remarked after a moment. "Catching hold of one thing means losing hold of another. I get Ardun, but the Windwards revolt. I get you, and lose my signal corps. Is it coincidence, or have I got all the balls in the air I can juggle these days?"

"A little of both. You should have maintained the blockade. Turning your back so long on the Windwards—"

"—was a gamble," Pedross cut in. "I want information, not second-guessing criticism. I'll see to the Windwards as soon as this can be trusted to boil without tending." His glance included the Thornwall and the Seven Houses.

"Ardun won't concern you long," agreed Simon, consciously ambiguous.

121

"And how long will it be before I can get decent weather predictions again? There was a force-ten storm dropped on Firetop with no warning and dismasted three schooners, and one of them was mine, though it took me four days to hear about it. . . ."

"Not till *Sunfire* goes aloft again. That needs high-altitude scanning."

"And what's that waiting for? Jannus?"

"Bronh."

Pedross nodded without further comment. He'd known Bronh, with steadily decreasing affection, since childhood and had been acquainted with most of the details of her current activities as they related to the termination of the Secolo persona whose loss had caused him so much personal annoyance.

Simon reached along the link to the Shai to learn what effect his summons was having and was informed that both Jannus and Poli were coming in the closed cart the Aihall had put at their disposal. That was satisfactory: Poli was beyond direct coercion, but Jannus was not. And a threat to lift the protection of the four squads of marines that, in alternate shifts, prevented the virtual siege of the house on Millers Street from blossoming into overt attack was enough to enforce Jannus' compliance with the summons, just as Simon had expected.

To the Loyalists, Poli resurrected was anathema. In their view an abomination had been done in Ardun and all subsequent ills, however coincidental, were thus seen to be its fruit. They dated the beginning of their troubles, the first desertions by Valde, from Poli's death and the scandal of the disappearance of her remains; and with her public return, they'd gotten Pedross, three divisions of marines, and no visiting Valde whatever. The proposition demonstrated itself. No Valde could be expected to share a city with the walking dead, those who raised them, or those who tolerated their presence.

Legal means to lift this curse being denied them, social means were at work, both overt and subtle. Some, like hurled bricks, were merely more overt than others.

Fortunately this was neither Simon's problem nor his concern, except as it affected Pedross. In the long term the Loyalists could of course be relied upon to work toward a coup; but there was no need to be concerned with Ardun's long term.

It didn't have any.

If Pedross was determined to take a stint playing helmsman and sailmaster to a foundering craft, Simon saw no reason to antagonize him by making an issue of the unwisdom of it. Pedross could be trusted to abandon anything that proved past mending and to get well clear before the first wave broke over the settling deck.

The corpse had been laid out on the grass near the intermittently creaking wheel of the water-powered pumping station, attended by an impassive trio of patrollers the duty officer dismissed from their vigil. As the initial report had stated, the woman was quite freshly dead. The water had not disfigured her much and the series of ascending cascades that began a little distance upstream had not found the unresisting limbs worth the breaking. She was in better condition than any of the other six known floaters that had drifted down the lazy Morimmon, whose snags detained any corpse to ripen into foul bloat on which fish and small scavengers dined at leisure and selectively.

There was little remarkable, at first glance, about the corpse save that she was a mature Valde and still wore the insignia of Pedross' signal corps.

Looking up in startlement, Pedross exclaimed, "You didn't say she was one of mine!"

"She may be," responded Simon conservatively: clothes, after all, could be lent or taken. "Do you recognize her?"

Pedross studied the slack features earnestly but their inertness defeated him. "No," he replied tightly, quite aware that he was admitting he couldn't tell if this face had belonged to an Awiro who'd been in and out of his presence for years, perhaps an evening's bedmate on occasion. But he declined to duck into guesses or a fraudulent claim to certainty.

Simon settled down to examine the corpse. Contrary to his initial impression, there were broken bones—in an elbow and the arm above it—but the condition of surface abrasions and the absence of any contingent swelling classified these as having occurred after death. He needed to look deeper. Extracting a long, needlelike probe from a pocket case, Simon inserted it slowly between the ribs. The Shai reported to him what the probe found.

The sum of the findings suggested drowning as the probable cause of death, but prior injury, poison, or drugs were not absolutely ruled out. So nothing was proven, especially since this corpse was one of a series of at least seven and it was likely the actual number was far greater. There was no telling how many had floated by under the surface or by night, unnoticed, or had failed to drift as far as Ardun but were just as dead for all that.

What was needed, as Simon had expected, was a thorough autopsy down to the molecular level.

His pocket case contained an implant—not exactly the sort which Jannus had received, but a related instrument. In appearance it was a hair-fine rigid rod perhaps half the length of a finger. Exposing the nape of the corpse's neck, Simon located with his probe the proper insertion site at the junction of brain stem and spinal cord and delicately eased the implant through the probe-tube and into place.

Unbreathing and livid, the corpse opened its eyes and sat up.

Approaching noise informed Simon he'd judged the timing about right. While a following crowd was restrained by a shifting line of patrollers and marines—cooperating for once—Poli stepped down from the drawcart just as the corpse tottered to its feet.

Simon judged it would be an excellent chance to demonstrate beyond any possibility of mistake what a fetch was, and wasn't.

In the abrupt silence, the corpse stilted its way up the slight incline and advanced on drawcart and crowd, slackjawed and staring. Though its balance was uncertain, maintained only by muscular feedback and the twitching energies the Shai was channeling through the deteriorating synaptic network, the corpse did not extend its arms for equilibrium or make anything approaching a human gesture except for the controlled fall of the act of walking itself.

Leisurely, Simon followed. He pointed at the cart, and the corpse made a hitching adjustment in its course. The crowd would see and remember at whose bidding this fetch moved. Or they would, as soon as they quit running and screaming themselves hoarse, as if a creature that was with difficulty making a speed of perhaps a block an hour were likely to spring into lithe pursuit and lay its mildly bloated hands on their fleeing backs.

Standing her ground, Poli viewed the approaching corpse with slightly less distaste than she showed the mobile.

"This," announced Simon didactically, "is a dead body. I am merely *sa'farioh*. Does the distinction become clearer to you?"

With some difficulty Jannus was stepping down to the street stones, holding onto the cart's open door as if he needed to: he'd been into the link, Simon surmised, to understand what was going on.

A gust of wind made the corpse teeter and lean. Simon put out a hand to steady it from behind, remarking to Jannus, "I don't think either the Loyalists, or anyone else who might take an interest in such things, will as readily presume it's you who goes around raising fetches. I'm already a bonfire, and have certain protections of position you don't."

Having halted in front of the open cart door, the corpse abruptly folded forward and made ineffective scrabblings on the cart's floor. Jannus, rousing from abstraction, lent a reluctant hand to pushing the lower half of the body inside, then slammed and latched the door, muttering, "That's awful. That's really awful," and wiping the hand on a sleeve until Poli caught the hand and stopped him.

"Nobody obliged you to touch it," remarked Pedross, who hadn't, and was quite as pale as Jannus and angry about it.

Jannus sent him an opaque glance, then told Simon, "I prefer favors I ask for first."

"It needs a thorough autopsy," Simon responded firmly. "The favor, even if effective, is incidental."

"You could have used a litter. It didn't have to walk."

"*Do* teach me about the proprieties of transporting the dead," invited Simon, and Jannus declined to pursue the issue further, wandering down to the riverside.

Simon called over one of the duty squad, a stolid man he remembered from the Longlands campaign, and arranged for the inconspicuous transportation of drawcart and corpse across the city and into the Fallows, from which point it could make its way unassisted to *Sunfire*. The marine, not recognizing in Simon his former commander, accepted the order because he was patently more afraid of the mobile than of the cart's contents, which was as it should be.

Pedross meanwhile had waved the remainder of the squad out of earshot and had begun skimming stones on the blue-gray sliding water, having tossed his cloak aside on the bank to free his arms. "They should have come back by now," he remarked suddenly. "It's quieted down—no more riots, no more worry about the blockade. They should have at least started to come back. Without Valde, without the Summerfair, Ardun's a city at the edge of a cliff with only the drop beyond. What's the *matter* with them?" he demanded, with a certain frustrated plaintiveness. "It's not *us*—we're what we've always been, and I, at least, am not about to crawl and wail and accuse myself of loving them too little. I always treated my people well. They were content in my service—I *know* that. And now one's come back, dead. Maybe they're all dead, my Awiro signalers. And I don't know why. You, my head of intelligence: can *you* tell me what's happening beyond the Thornwall?"

"Not in detail," replied Simon.

"In general, then?"

"An ingathering of Valde. A periodic multi-resonating mood echo that Bronh refers to as 'the Singing.' A—"

"And do you have the least idea what you're talking about? Or is it just what it sounds like: words?" Pedross hurled his last stone and, continuing the motion, swung around to face Poli. "Can you tell me?" he demanded of her.

"In this life, I haven't contacted another Valde," she replied slowly. "And to me, *mood echo* is just words. I knew once. I don't, anymore."

"Do you want to?" Pedross asked provocatively.

Jannus cut in, "Pedross, what are you after?"

Poli reported, "He wants me to go into Valde for him." Her tone was listless and she was looking off toward the edge of the Thornwall. "I know," she said, apparently in response to something wordless, "but that's what he wants, all the same. And he thinks he can pressure you with . . . with the threat of arrest, and that if you two both agree, I'll be influenced enough by what you want to do it."

There was nothing like a Valde, Simon reflected, to banish all delicate opening maneuvers and go straight to the fight.

126

"I have your word," Jannus said to Pedross, controlling obvious anger, "to eliminate witchcraft as a prosecutable—"

"I said it," Pedross interrupted, "and I'll stand by it. The charge would be corpse theft."

Jannus was a moment assimilating the weight of that threat. "You can't prove it," he said finally. "You don't know enough to ask the right questions and force answers."

"Maybe. *He* does, though." Pedross nodded toward Simon. "It would be interesting to find out just whose spymaster and right hand you are, Simon-Secolo-Ashai."

Pedross, it seemed, had also learned to construct multi-purpose configurations, where all moves became either useful or revealing.

Thus forced to choose sides, Simon chose as he was obliged to. Folding his arms, Simon showed Jannus an impassive, unhelpful countenance. If Pedross lodged that charge, Simon would supply the information needed to prosecute it.

Through the implant link, which gave a final, irrevocable escape from any coercion, Jannus had been given all the protection the Shai meant to offer him. Regarding any lesser unpleasantnesses, Jannus would have to fend for himself however he saw fit, unless he was so unwise as to demand the Shai's intervention; and Simon's face showed him how such a demand would be answered and what it would lead to.

Simon's options were likewise circumscribed. Whatever his own feelings, he was, first, last, and always, the mobile of the Shai who alone lived forever and whose choices were predicted on the Rule of One, which permitted no favoritism.

Though untrained in the discipline, Jannus could read stance and gesture well enough to recognize non-support when he saw it. Taking in Simon's position, Jannus looked past him to Pedross. "If you want to know what's going on beyond the Thornwall that badly, *you* go," he challenged bluntly.

"I would, if I thought there'd be the least use in it." Pedross caught up his cloak and swung it back across his shoulders against the chilly wind. The sun had disappeared under the leading edge of a shelf of unbroken cloud. "If I had the eyes to see, if I had the *marenniath*, I'd go," Pedross continued, so untroubled by the implication of cowardice he didn't even attempt to defend himself. He was merely explaining why such a course would be impractical. "Domal Ai sent six people past the Thornwall six weeks ago. None has come back. There's no welcome in Valde, just now, for the Unhearing. I need a Valde."

"Bronh would know. . . . Where's Bronh?" Jannus asked the mobile, who reached down the link for the information, sparing Jannus the effort.

"Currently she's in Bremner. Recruiting troopmaids to abandon their posts, by all present evidence."

"Is there any way to get her here?"

Jannus, of all people, should have known better. "She flies to nobody's fist."

Pedross said, "Bronh wouldn't do, anyhow. She may think she knows what's going on—but she doesn't *know*. She's as deaf as the rest of us. *And* she lies, any time it suits her," he added, with meditative venom, freeing his waterman's braid from the cape's collar. The dye of his disguise removed, his hair shone almost as fair as Poli's in the overcast light. "A plain traders' bargain, Jannus, to buy news. If Poli can go in just far enough to get it and come back—after all, she doesn't have to get within touching distance of anything: who ever succeeded in sneaking up on a Valde?—I'll make you governor of Ardun in five months' time."

Jannus found that funny. "That's a worse threat than trial—don't you know that yet? I like my quarrels one at a time, with labels, not in lots of twenty and all together." The amusement evaporated. "No," he said, had finally been forced into saying.

Into the silence of threat and stalemate Poli remarked, "There were two groups Domal sent out, if I recall . . . ? One went into Lifganin. I'd like to learn the grass hills again, and the mara. . . . And maybe the Awiro know what's happening to us." She was talking, it seemed, as much to Jannus as to Pedross. In the same tone of idle unconcern, she continued, "It's a week, afoot, to the edge of Han Halla. A week or two away from the reception Ardun's given me would be *nice*." That last word was spoken with surprising and unmistakable bitterness.

Jannus met this proposal with no arguments or defenses of the Arduners' unwelcome into which he'd brought her—at least none Simon could overhear. And, perhaps, none at all.

She added tartly, "Or would you sooner stand public trial for stealing my corpse, with that poor twitching thing I just saw, shown by way of example of what a dead Valde ought to look like? While I sit in the gallery and—"

"All right," Jannus said to her: not agreement, but capitulation. "I've walked Lifganin a time or two—"

She cut off that proposal with a "No," as absolute as his had been. "I can call mara to me and be safe from anything that goes on legs. Ten days, altogether, if I ride."

Again, Jannus had no arguments. Ten days was less, and less dangerous, than twenty; and nobody but a Valde could persuade a mara stag to serve purposes not its own. Jannus studied her as though trying to judge how much real desire, silent so long as it had no acceptable outlet, underlaid her suggestion.

Of Pedross, Poli inquired, "Will that serve?"

Since it was obviously the best, indeed the only, bargain likely to be offered, Pedross accepted with expressions of gratitude. He was, after all, genuinely troubled about Valde; and seven floaters in under two weeks were just too many to ignore or pass off as accidents.

Simon undertook to walk them home rather than call a drawcart: "I think you'll be safe in the streets after this," he observed to Poli, who made no reply and seemed unimpressed with his achievement of acceptance for her based on a comparison with an awkwardly animated corpse. Passing the grounds of the westernmost of the Seven Houses, the mobile next remarked to Jannus, "You'll never make a strategist. All you know to do is set your feet and stand fast."

"What should I have done, then?" Jannus responded.

Gratified that Jannus didn't consider this betrayal irrevocable either, Simon advised briskly, "You should have made a counter-threat."

That roused a wry, incredulous smile. "What, for instance? All I had to bargain with was Ardun, and he's *got* that. I don't want to threaten him. He's just where I want him, right now."

"You could have threatened to take me back. That's what he was waiting for you to do. He isn't sure of me."

"Who is? But that's no threat: I couldn't deliver. You're

129

the Shai's to dispose of . . . and your own, if there's a difference. Not mine, anyhow."

"There's a difference. And if it was a good threat, you wouldn't have to deliver. Truthtell has ruined all you Bremneri for bluffing."

"Elda always claimed we couldn't lie worth warm spit. . . ."

"Or threaten to withdraw Sua," Simon continued, thinking aloud. "He wouldn't like that. She's very useful to him now. And that, you *could* deliver on, and there'd be no legal way he could prevent you."

"Sua'd have a fit, missing all that free food, not to speak of the attention. And how do you figure I'd keep her home, Simon: lock her up for a week at a time?" By his more somber expression it wasn't chiefly Sua he was thinking of but Poli's term immured in the household besieged by its neighbors.

"No trouble," Simon pointed out, waving toward the pedestrians who dropped their eyes and ducked away like Aihall pages. There were uses to the right kind of conspicuousness. "No mob reforming, scrambling over each other to shout names."

Breaking her long silence, Poli observed, "There's more ways than one to call names. If you could hear what I hear, you wouldn't be so blithe."

"If a little hate could kill you, you wouldn't have lived out your term of service," countered Simon hardily.

"That's not the trouble," she replied. "The trouble is to keep from hating back."

There were a few paces of awkward silence. Then Jannus declared abruptly, and with restraint, "Simon, I'm not mad at you. Now will you just go away?"

Stopping at once, Simon let them get about a block ahead—walking in matched slow paces, not talking as far as he could tell—before drifting along behind to make sure his prediction of safety was holding. He felt he owed them that much.

He was obliged to Poli for suggesting an acceptable compromise. Otherwise, he was virtually certain Pedross would have proposed that Simon be the one to go into Valde.

A mobile could be slaughtered and yet return with news: Pedross would reason that Simon might acquire some valuable observations before he was observed in turn and cut down for a *sa'farioh* abomination. Rather than prosecute Jannus, about whose powers and options of retaliation he was still unsure, Pedross would (apparently) send away the sinister subordinate who had so publicly established himself in the popular imagination as a raiser of fetches that Jannus was unlikely, hereafter, to be considered in that context at all. . . . Yes, Pedross would have liked that alternative fallback plan.

Probably everyone would have, except Simon himself.

Simon considered the back of one hand, noticing the ridge of each tendon, the pattern of wrinkles across each knuckle, the muted indigo veins. He might not justify a portrait—too old, too lean, too austere—but he was all he had. What he had, he meant to keep as long as he possibly could, like any other prudent breathing soul.

In the middle of the night Jannus ended a prolonged contact with the Shai, falling into the reality of an agony of confused reorientation and the realization that Poli wasn't asleep after all.

He confined his deep contacts to the late, dark hours when his absence wouldn't bother her, though the aftereffects which persisted well into the following day made plain enough what he'd been about. He wasn't trying to hide anything: merely to make his withdrawals as little troubling to her as he could.

It was awhile before he could see well enough to discern the contour of her profile against the dim lines of the shutter slats. Slowly it came to him that the sound he heard was the hiss and beat of rain.

He hitched his elbows behind him against the pillow and asked aloud, "What roused you?"

After he broke rapport, it took hours before he could manage the inspeaking at all. But the headaches weren't as frequent now, or as bad.

The spoken words sounded odd and echoing to him, the necessary motions of tongue and lips seemed wooden, like things he needed to practice.

"They're across the street at the bakery tonight," Poli reported dispassionately. "Wishing me gone, all together. Really, they're getting quite good at it, for *sa'marenniathe.*"

"I can relay to Simon and get him to scatter them. ..."

"On what pretext? It's not illegal to hate fetches, not that I ever heard about. Let them alone," she concluded wearily, and lay flat again.

He had to reach out to find out if she'd put her back to him. She hadn't.

"I've been learning Lifganin," he mentioned presently. And none of it had settled yet either. He knew all the shifts of all the streambeds for several thousand years, and ten thousand plants and their needs, seasons, and uses, and insects innumerable, all of it a blur jumbled like discarded glass. ... "Did you know mara were a created species, not native at all? Debern Teks made them for Fathori, just two pair. Never meant for use at all, only to be large and beautiful. ..."

"It's past time for the first-warm shearing," she mused. "I wonder how much wasted wool is rotting away on the hillsides, tufts caught on twigs. ... You know there aren't any Awiro in Lifganin, nothing to learn."

He knew. It was why he'd consented to the compromise.

"Nothing in range, nobody, as far away as I can reach," she went on in the same slow nighttime voice. "That's how it's been ever since I woke into this life. ... Reaching out, and no reply."

"Why don't you want me to come with you?" He found it difficult to ask.

"Why do you go off into the link, hours at a time?" she rejoined, a pointed enough comparison.

"I have to," he responded at length, an apology. "I didn't know you were awake or I wouldn't have."

"*They* woke me. The Choral Hating Society." It was what she called the collection of Loyalists who brought their antipathy into the closest possible range, hoping to drive her out by the sheer force of their wishing her gone. "And you weren't there, empty as that glib self-satisfied thing that calls itself. ... The Shai, he's tolerable. Under all that shell, there's something at least alive. Inside *Sunfire* I can even hear him in spite of all that shielding. But there's nothing to Simon *but* shell—"

"There is. Just because you can't hear it doesn't mean it's not there. Partly it's a matter of glandular balance—"

"I'll give you *glandular balance*," she exclaimed, and slung her pillow in his face.

It was, among other things, an appeal and an invitation; but rapport starved that set of responses too, like all his other senses. The body seemed increasingly like something he'd leased, with no necessary connection with the self it housed.

Meat.

But he could respond to her in less direct ways, and the inner closeness could be the rest. *Touch-loving*, Valde called it, whatever form it took. And when it was done, he was the one who was crying: the morning of her return suddenly with him again as sharp and urgent as dreaming.

That happened less often now, and always unexpectedly, catching him by surprise and as deep as he thought he probably went.

He gentled her comfortably against his chest. The image of the hideous pitiable dead thing Simon had roused came to him, but it had no power and contained no comparisons, because he'd made himself touch it. He could touch anything and not be defiled or overwhelmed. He felt that he could love a tree, each least leaf, or be set in the middle of the Sea and be balanced so perfectly that each wave would carry him patiently nearer wherever he wanted to go, however far.

"I have to," he murmured, with her living breath warm on his skin. "Otherwise, I'll drown."

She made a soft inquiring noise.

"I mean, it seems I've got so far out now I have to become it all, or it'll kill me."

Simon was wrong. Jannus didn't fight flat-footed, merely enduring. He could do that, *had* done it in the bad time at midwinter, and in bad times before. But that wasn't fighting. That was just refusing to be beaten.

He fought by joining, as he always had.

He was trying to encompass the Shai. He couldn't be a minor fragment in that enormous wilderness of personality and still survive. The Shai would engulf him and never notice the change, or that anything was lacking.

That the Shai didn't see it didn't mean it wasn't there. It just meant that the Shai had a different sort of eyes. The Shai didn't even understand his own mobiles. It *made* a difference. . . .

Poli was asleep now: he was certain.

Letting his head and shoulders lean into full relaxation, he prepared to renew the rapport. He couldn't have slept anyhow, or else he would have been visited with dreams of horrible transformations that would have disturbed Poli almost as much as they did him, maybe as much as the Choral Hating Society, gathered for its nightly vigil. She needed her rest. In the morning, she was leaving.

Seven days after setting out, Poli returned out of Lifganin in haste astride a mara stag. One hand fisted into his coarse back-blowing mane, she guided him with the tilt of her body and the drive of her impatience to be delivered of her news. She'd have ridden the stag all the way to the Aihall Square if she could, to save walking; but the stag was a volunteer, the fourth of a small herd of bachelor bucks she'd conscripted to carry her. And his slowing gait and yellow slit-eye looking around at her echoed the reluctance in his selfsinging to go any nearer the city and its strange, busy canyons visible beyond the river at the bottom of the slope. Poli accepted it, and the stag halted to let her slide down, stiff and lame, and collect her bowcase, quiver, and blanket roll from around his shoulders. Then the stag—a tall, cream-colored, lance-horned beast of the deer-kin—turned and set out at a rocking, easy gait to rejoin his fellows, halted at the crest of the ridge. Poli put various straps over her shoulders and started walking. She didn't remember ever having ridden so long at a time—from the margins of Han Halla in a night and a morning. She felt it now, in every muscle.

The patrollers stationed, with a marine officer, at the bridge knew her and let her pass without overt comment; but Poli had yet to become resigned to the slap of that sort of recognition. It came in two flavors: *the arbiter's fetch,* and *that Valde who hasn't run out on us yet.* Either image was enough to make her wince and stiffen.

As she turned north toward the Aihall, repetitions of those same two reactions struck her like a continuous bombardment of windblown hair. She didn't distinguish individual voices. It was just a moving storm-line of unwelcome that accompanied her progress through the busy streets. But Ardun had regained its manners to the extent that nothing more tangible than antipathy struck her. It was quite enough. She felt raw, inside and out. A breeze, it seemed, would have raised a bruise.

But what she heard around her had at least the virtue of being familiar; she was fresh from a general welcome imbued with more menace than anything the Choral Hating Society had ever tuned themselves to.

She deflected some of the ambient roar by concentrating on Jannus' selfsinging, using it as both barrier and guide. That rapport alone was exempt from distance or, indeed, any separation save that which occurred when he went by means of the implanted link into the exclusive and jealous company of the Shai. And that, he'd not done while she'd been gone. She herself had felt no separation; it had been as if she were merely out of sight and touch, as if in another room.

Entering the Aihall, she found her way by means of the rapport to a sixth-floor chamber in the administration wing and found him hearing a case involving smashed pottery of some sort. So strong and unquestioned had been her sense of unbroken contact with him that she was shaken as well as startled to discover how ill he looked: drawn and tense, tiredness having intensified during her absence to outright and obvious exhaustion. Reaching for a pen, he needed two attempts to set his hand accurately on it. But he found the inkwell and went ahead to make the needed notation with no frustration or impatience registering inwardly at all: nothing but the deliberate calm which had been her companion throughout all the past days and nights.

She couldn't have told what upset her more—the terrible fatigue itself or the fact that he'd somehow shut her out, kept it from her.

The transcript scribe called Jannus' attention from the potter droning on about damaged greenware, whatever that was, and pointed to the door arch where Poli stood.

There was a slow moment before what Jannus saw roused any reaction at all. Then there was a rush of recognition, surprise, and a clear uncomplicated gladness. He came down the row of benches, touching perhaps every third benchback to steady himself, and said to her, "I didn't expect you for another three days yet. What's happened?" While Poli hesitated he asked again, more soberly, "What's happened?" meaning *what's wrong?*

She, at least, would share whatever came to her.

She asked, "Can you get clear of this?"

Jannus slowly considered the question, looking around at the people on the front benches. Then he went up to speak to the scribe and told the waiting complainants that he'd been called away. While the people argued about the broken proceedings—none had yet noticed her, mostly concealed by the angle of the arch—Jannus returned, remarking, "There's a retiring room down this way I've been using. . . ."

There were three other arbiters in the retiring room and twice that many scribes, the latter playing cards and discussing the defects of drains. Poli recognized them all, and, from their reactions, they'd all been to her funeral. They wished her decently dead: she wished them the same. She had to clasp her hands together to control the desire to turn impulse into act.

Slowly absorbing the realization that this room wasn't going to do, Jannus went to collect something from one of a line of cabinets and stood blankly perplexed at finding the cabinet empty. One of the scribes, a man named Hallan, rose from the card game, yanked open a cabinet farther down, and resumed his seat without saying a word.

From the scribe's reaction Poli could tell Jannus hadn't merely misremembered where he'd stored something: it had been moved.

Finding in the second cabinet what he'd been looking for, Jannus took out a small case, tucked it under his arm, and made sure both cabinets were properly shut. Remarking, "Obliged to you, Hal," he rejoined Poli and calmly headed for the stairs.

The incident seemed to have made no impression on him at all. If she hadn't been present, Poli would have known nothing of it, shut out completely.

Nevertheless that same calm, combined with the immediate aches and twinges produced by descending five flights of tiled stairs, effectively cooled her temper. Calm nearby had more influence than distant malice and antipathy.

Into folds of the bordering Thornwall were tucked carved

benches among a succession of tiered fountains. Setting the case on a vacant bench in an alcove free of passersby, Jannus made a methodical business of taking out a small stoppered jar, shaking a measured amount of granular greyish powder into a cup, and dipping from the nearest fountain enough water to make the powder drinkable.

Replying to her unasked question, he said, "Something Simon put together for me. It isn't Fathori wine, but it serves. So it wasn't me that brought you running back three days early. What was it, then?" Adding some water, he swirled the cup briefly and then emptied it.

Carefully she said, "Are you going to keep doing this?"

"If I have to," he replied mildly, replacing cup and jar in the case with the same intent deliberation with which he'd handled the pen. "It keeps me from pushing you off balance too."

"If there's trouble, I'd rather have the trouble than be shut out."

"You have enough trouble of your own without mine on top of it. And I've been catching most of what needed to be seen to, in the meantime."

"Yes: I can see how you're catching it," she rejoined tartly.

Smiling a little, he sat down beside her. "Never mind that now. Tell me something interesting."

He wouldn't admit that she was entitled to the trouble, wouldn't do anything but continue with that implacable dull calm. She was beginning to be very angry at him. In a sharp, displeased voice, she said, "Well, the delegation Domal Ai sent into Lifganin have been butchered by Awiro. The ground-rats and such have cleaned them down to the bones." She slapped into his hand the token she'd brought away: the scrap of knotted scarlet cord that denoted ministerial rank. "That *interesting* enough for you?"

As he pulled the cord through his fingers she could feel him reluctantly moving against the weight of emotional inertia, trying to understand, trying to care. "Awiro. You sure? Not just an unpartnered herd?"

"I can still read a piece of ground. And I know an arrowpoint when I see one. They were circled, shot, and then mashed flat: in that order. Hardly a whole bone left among them. Mara are still shying away from coming anywhere near

137

the place. I even found some that were part of it—mara, not Awiro, because the Awiro are gone. They went north, into Entellith, beginning sometime in the deep cold. They were welcomed, and glad. That's all that the mara know about it."

"Yes," said Jannus, finding a pocket to stow the cord, "that's interesting. . . . What could they have done to make Awiro turn on them like that? Mara, I could see. There have been people run down before this. But those folk were sent out to *beg*, Poli—I'd as soon believe Marlena Singer had gotten into a murderous rage and been knifed by a midwife. What could they have done, that Awiro could have taken it for consent to a general massacre?"

"Valde have done murder. That's all I know about it. Not a duel, or a fight and a killing. Murder: without consent. I didn't think any Valde could have become so dark-hearted and not gone into the turning-away, much less been welcomed among Valde afterward. I don't understand it at all. . . . And there's more. I came in range of some Haffa deserters. They'd been camping just inside the edge of Han Halla, resting after the crossing. . . . Jannus, I just don't know how to tell you what it was like. . . . It was like a Troopcalling and a spinwind and a swarm of hornets, all together." And that this had been the food to break her long fast made it that much more bitter; Jannus' selfsinging let her know at least that much of the encounter was quite plain to him. She continued, "I tried to inspeak to them and there was no single one I could reach. And then they reached back at me. . . ." Poli blinked in the sunlight, seeing nothing of the square. "Now I know what a mood echo is," she said finally. "It's like being turned inside out. Pulled out of yourself into the spinwind, lost. . . . But there weren't enough of them to hold me, and I'm . . . different enough now that the resonances and attitudes weren't quite the same, I still knew myself—"

She spread her hands, despairing of making it any clearer, and he responded quietly, "I follow well enough. Go ahead," fully attentive now, reachable in spite of the powder, comprehending at least her misery.

"There were three insingers among them—*in'marenniathe*? weavers?—and when they couldn't make me fit the harmony, they struck out at me. So I'd just not *be*, still unfitting. . . . I think . . . I think if they'd been nearer, close enough to get at me, or if they'd had even one farspeaker among them, or if I'd been afoot instead of mounted, to get clear of them *fast* . . . they would have *killed* me! Wiped me right—"

He interrupted by taking her hand with a deliberate firmness: both support and warning, for he then bent his head and went *away*. Into the implant link. Breathing the slow breaths of sleep: absent, *sa'farioh*, silent, leaving her alone.

If he'd been so when she'd reached out to him yesterday, making of that rapport a means of breaking free of the demanding, welcoming, devouring spinwind, she would have been lost. The thought made her feel cold. The idea, the fact, of separation deeply troubled her. She pulled him to lean against her side, holding him until he was suddenly *back*: stirring vaguely, confused, in pain the powder did nothing to mute because it was only secondarily the body's pain; and, hurting with his hurt, Poli thought with absolute certainty, *He cannot keep on like this. This is intolerable.*

Presently he collected himself sufficiently to wander across to the raised lip of the fountain and duck his head in the water, his selfsinging moving in uncontrolled swoops and checks. Still leaning against the rim with his back to her, he said, "It's Bronh. Something she's set going. They've gone away now because the first spin's inward. Pulling. But afterward, a few seasons or a few years, the spin will turn out: against us. And they'll come back. Across Lifganin, the Fallows, Han Halla. . . . Into Bremner, maybe: silencing things, whatever won't fit. The only places sure to be safe are the isles. Therefore, Pedross. Therefore, the new empire of Andras. Therefore the urgency about starving Ardun out and then stripping it of everything worth the saving—like setting a backfire to scorch away everything in the path of the wildfire to come. Pedross doesn't know. I didn't, because I didn't know enough to ask until now and force a full answer. But the Shai's always known this was coming, soon or late. He and Bronh have a sort of bet on it," he reported, with arid precision. "She thinks the Valde will exterminate us all, every one, clear to the Sea. The Shai thinks there are too many of us now and we'll turn and exterminate them instead. . . ."

He swayed, leaning harder against the fountain's edge; and

139

as Poli went to steady him until the spasm of dizziness passed, she caught the least thin susurration of something unfamiliar, something strange.

Beyond the body's fusion of shock and calm, beyond the jagged agitation of his selfsinging, there was something else which was neither of these: a sense of presence, formless, diffuse, with no language in it, nothing she could hold to or interpret. Beyond her grasp but not quite beyond her reach, whether new or only newly perceived, it was not unlike what she'd caught at times within *Sunfire*. Then, it had been the Shai. Now she was somehow quite certain it was not.

She asked, "What's Sparrow been about? I can tell he's pleased with himself, but not why."

Reacting to the blank banality of the question, the other thing, the strangeness, dissipated or was hidden behind nearer motions. "Sparrowhawk?" he responded, in bewilderment. "He's been doing summaries and first hearings."

"Oh, did they conscript him too?"

"Everybody who knows anything about arbitrage, to try to settle the mess that was left after the riots. . . . What's the Sparrow got to do with anything?"

"Nothing," replied Poli composedly, satisfied: he was entirely with her again, nothing hidden or strange or out of reach. "I just wondered what he was being so proud of. So he's an arbiter in his own right?"

"Beginning, anyway. . . . Poli, I can't think about that now," Jannus complained, pulling free of her. "I've seen it. Now what's to be done about it? That's what I've got to get clear somehow without crossing the Shai's damn Rule of One and getting my head blown off. . . . I knew they hated Screamers, but I never thought. . . . Bronh, she's been tied up in the business from the beginning. She'll come for the redstone. We—what?"

"Bronh Sefar'," murmured Poli again. "The wind's voice. 'The *in'marenniathe* will begin it, and we will all be changed. . . .' Except some of us," she ended tightly.

"I've heard that. What is it?"

"It comes before the Troopcalling, every Summerfair. The Lore of the Change. *Bronh Sefar'*. I never thought. I was touched by the Singing and didn't even know it."

"*Singing*. That's part of it. . . . But what is it?"

140

"Spinwind," replied Poli slowly. "Troopcalling. Madness. A rage of madness." She looked from the cherry-brick face of the Aihall to the Thornwall's green buds and told Jannus, "We're going home. Now."

"I have to talk to Pedross about—"

"Let Simon tell him—he's his spymaster and, anyway, that's what mobiles are for. We're going home. And you're going to eat an entire meal, fruit to sweet, and sleep a whole night. And a whole day besides, if you need to." With a dire stare at the case, she added, "No more eating ashes. If we're going to last this out, you're going to start looking after yourself. You look more like walking death than I do."

"I suppose I can," he responded uncertainly. "When Bronh comes, I'll know it. I'll surely know it. All right. Let's go home."

When Bronh soared in from the northwest on the rising midday thermals, the Shai, plainly expecting her, extended the tapering cable of an external handler as a perch. Alighting on it, Bronh was carried smoothly toward the retracting iris of a port. An internal handler ending in four bundles of hair-fine digits offered itself from beyond the three layers of port seals. Bronh stepped across, and the seals spun shut behind her.

"Where's Jannus?" she demanded at once, as the handler carried her rapidly along the inward spiral of the corridor it served toward the next transfer node. "I want the redestone."

"Of course you do," replied the Shai's projected locationless voice.

"Well, is he here, or not?"

"The locator gave us notice of your arrival," said the Shai.

"And what's Pedross' banner doing on top of the Aihall?" Bronh demanded, moving to the next handler, and felt its digital filaments slide around her legs, pinioning them firmly to the perch.

"Ask him," suggested the Shai.

She was swept past the base area inward to the main bridge, where she found herself awaited by a reception committee of three: Jannus, Pedross, and a Valde she assumed to be the reconstruction of the lar Haffa Poli. With the ubiquitous and impalpable presence of the Shai, a tribunal of four.

141

The handler set her down on the sensor display console that circled the round room like a low wall; but as soon as her legs were freed, she flew to alight on the short crosspiece surmounting the director's station in the middle of the inlaid flaming sun that was the power grid. She wanted height, to secure whatever psychological advantage there might be in making the three look up at her.

She said flatly, "I was promised my meat when and where I said. I want it now. This minute."

Taking a chain from around his neck, Jannus laid the redestone in a small opening that everted itself from the inner rim of the sensor console, replying formally, "As you say."

The power surge from the sun disc below to the matching plate above, vaporizing everything organic between, was too sudden for Bronh's nervous system to even begin to react before the valkyr had ceased to exist.

From her point of view she merely found herself suddenly elsewhere, opening eyes whose unaccustomedly dim sight showed the lid of the still-box retracting above her. Finding her body resting horizontal was both strange and not-strange. Her sitting up was an abrupt motion too spasmodic for the length of torso, and it took a moment's thought to remember hands were for reaching, not feet.

And yet the familiarity was present and increasing: the part of her she'd lost in putting on the bird reasserting influence and, gradually, dominance. Thus her third action was to shut her eyes and meditate on her condition, recalling and employing techniques of relaxation and, in apparent stillness, relearning the balances and strengths of a human body. Only secondarily did she consider her immediate situation and the deferred meeting still awaiting her.

"I gather Pedross has decided Ardun, intact, pleases him better than Ardun destroyed," she remarked, finding the sleeve-holes in the plain grey garment a handler had taken from a storage niche. "Does that please you any better than it does me?"

"He'll abandon it when it becomes necessary," replied the Shai's voice.

"Is that a reliable projection, or a hope?" said Bronh, trying to remember how a knot should feel to the fingers as she went toward the place where a shimmer at the violet edge of sight marked the sterile field of a port. Passing through as the plates retracted, she found that her sleeves were sufficiently voluminous to permit tucking her hands entirely out of sight. That was good: hands connoted act, power. Hers, she'd keep hidden and humble; or, if she were permitted a seat, she'd lay them passively in her lap.

"It won't help," remarked the Shai, but Bronh ignored his comment as he'd ignored hers. She was quite aware that, within *Sunfire* and for a short radius beyond, the Shai had direct access to her rede—could, in effect, read her mind from moment to moment. It didn't matter. Her tactics did not operate on rational levels. The Shai might explain them as fully as he pleased and influence their effect not at all.

And the Shai had done her no disfavor by supplying her simple clothing fit for a penitent or a pilgrim—not that present cultures knew anything of such roles: but the immortal images were always there to be invoked, beneath superficial layers of current usage, containing their own inherent power. The role of a pilgrim was not unsuitable for one who'd traveled so far, in distance and in time, as herself; and the subordinate image of penitence could also have its uses since she felt accusation was in the air.

From body-poses, she could tell that the three visible people awaiting her had had time to grow impatient—the two humans, especially. Jannus' regard was thoughtful as she advanced to a position nicely calculated between visual isolation and familiar encroachment. He inquired, still formally, "Are you satisfied, Bronh?"

How like a Bremneri, she thought: wanting a plain receipt for goods delivered, contracts performed. She replied, "Quite satisfied, thank you, Jannus. The bargain is fully kept. And you: are you satisfied?"

He looked a bit startled—taken aback, probably, by the change from the ferocious bluntness which was all her former fractional self had been capable of—and leaned unconsciously nearer the Valde reconstruction. "Well satisfied, Bronh. Without you, it would not have been done. I am obliged to you."

Bronh only nodded, not stating the obvious fact that, had it not served her purposes as well, he'd have gotten no help from her. Since it was probable that the Bremneri would be the only one present who might harbor sentimental scruples

143

against destroying her, she would not refuse gratitude or any other leverage he might offer her.

Bronh didn't need to ask the reconstruction herself if she was satisfied: reservations all but shouted from her rigidity, the frowning tightness of the planes of her face: thoroughly contaminated, that one, by alien influences in her lifetime and now scarcely to be considered a Valde at all. Nevertheless Bronh greeted her in the ancient Valde manner, "Burn bright, Poli lar-Jannus."

"I hear you, Bronh Sefar'," was the grudging response, interesting chiefly for its combination of recognition and hostility.

Thoroughly contaminated—like the troopmaids, fully a fifth of the total, whom Bronh had failed to budge from their self-imposed servitude to the Bremneri riverstocks before she'd exhausted her last cache of food and been obliged to return. *In'marenniathe* were few, among the troops: not many survived past their first seasons of service. Rousing the Singing had been more difficult, though not impossible, without them.

Well, if a fraction had to be lost, then they'd be lost. Bronh had done what she could to free them.

She looked then to Pedross, whom she'd known from infancy. His pose revealed nothing at all: he'd retained that much, at least, of what she'd taught him. Then he went into an absolute paroxysm of blinking, shifting, ear-rubbing and the like, an intentional semaphore mocking the language of gesture and pose she'd taught him to read while at the same time an acknowledgment of it. The wry salute finished as a repose with one arm draped over the top of the sensor console, asserting, unconvincingly, his confident familiarity with this place and its powers. Bronh let him see she doubted his assertion; he shrugged and remained as he was. Bronh lowered her gaze and tucked both hands farther into her sleeves.

It was Jannus who responded to the signal, saying abruptly, "What have you been doing to the Valde? Why are they leaving everything, even the mara, to gather—"

Pedross broke in, "I've lost all the signalers I brought upriver with me, which should make you happy."

There was a momentary pause while Jannus controlled his annoyance and deliberately waited so Pedross could go on if he chose. When Pedross gave no sign of understanding the courtesy, his bland gaze still on Bronh, Jannus continued, "There's been murder done. Valde have been hunters always but never killers, to murder any living thing without its consent."

"Except Teks," the Shai's voice pointed out. "If one cares to count the *sa'fariohe* or the Screamers as living. . . ."

Really, Bronh thought, they might as well all shout that they were at cross-purposes and be done with it. She said, "The greatest weakness of Valde has always been their difficulty in separating themselves from the emotional surround." She kept her tone quiet, didactic. "It kept them the Teks' passive pets until Teks themselves broke that bondage by becoming *sa'farioh* and thus no longer part of that surround. Valde found then that they could strike out, strike back, without suffering the hurt themselves. And when madness intervened, and the *sa'fariohe* become Screamers, there was still no mutuality, no sharing—and so, no need of consent to free the killer from the repercussions of participating in violent death.

"As for my part in it, that was no more than to gather and preserve the Valde as one people so that, by contrast, they might learn what they were, to know and value their own uniqueness." Shifting her gaze deliberately from Jannus to Pedross, bypassing Poli, Bronh went on, "And, knowing themselves, they have slowly come to know you, the Unhearing, for the intruders and aliens you are. Your mere proximity is offense enough to warrant your being silenced. You don't belong here. You are both Screamers, and abominations, to the sensitivity of the *marenniath*. You, Jannus, have the added distinction of having made of yourself an *in'farioh*: you can pollute the daysinging for miles around with your wretched, trivial wants and greeds." Though Bronh saw Poli's protective fury translating itself unhesitatingly into act, she continued, "And you, Poli, chose to become and remain *sa'marenniath* rather than tolerate his—"

Poli backhanded her solidly across the side of the face and would have pursued the attack had Jannus and, more cautiously, Pedross not dissuaded her.

The incident was its own object lesson in how little it required to goad a Valde into attack. Bronh, having intended it as such, was satisfied.

145

Pedross, moving warily clear, plainly understood it. Jannus, distracted by subjective concerns, was arguing in incomplete phrases with Poli about the accusation. His own lack of indignation suggested it hadn't, to him, been an entirely new idea, whereas Poli had the Valde tendency to respond with either full-scale attack or retreat to what could be neither ignored nor tolerated.

A very thorough reconstruction, Bronh judged. That would be the way the Valde would strike out beyond the Thornwall when the time came.

Her right eye was watering from the blow. Absently she wiped it with her sleeve. She ignored the stinging as she ignored the admonitory tingling of the power grid under her bare feet: the Shai warning her against precipitating any more object lessons. Bronh had no intention of repeating herself. The point had been made, for anyone with the eyes to see it.

Pedross, who had such eyes, remarked, "If we're such revolting, outlandish monsters, just what does that make you?"

Bronh thought briefly of replying, *The appointed and acceptable sacrifice*, but didn't. That had nothing to do with anyone here. They had no sense of mythic imperatives.

When Bronh continued silent, Pedross declared, "Valde managed to put up with me well enough until you set the Singing going. It was a good, practical arrangement, with both sides well served. Wherever I came from, or my parents—on either side," he added, with a brief up-tilted glance, "I'm here now. I'm not going to be forced off the mainland for the sake of what was done a few thousand years ago: not without fighting for every inch that's mine. I have a right to be here, and alive. If you want your Valde to survive another few thousand years, you'd best tell us now how to stop this division before it goes any farther."

"I didn't start it," replied Bronh mildly. "The division is self-evident. You are interlopers and aliens. The Singing would have begun of itself whenever the proportion of insingers became sufficient, when its season had come. It cannot be stopped."

"That's what's to be done, then," Pedross remarked to Jannus. "Get rid of all the insingers."

Both Jannus and Poli reacted with open aversion, Jannus

146

saying, "Is that the only way you know to deal with a thing: kill somebody? skin somebody?" while the Shai's voice observed, "Impractical. You'd have to locate and identify them."

"We have at least one Valde," Pedross replied to the Shai, ignoring the other comment. "There'll be others, maybe among the riverstocks, who haven't been caught up in this spinwind, this Singing. They could mark out the insingers for us."

Bronh listened to the debate, untroubled, with her hands quietly folded. Any Valde venturing beyond the extreme outer limit of the full Singing would be absorbed and held. Pedross would catch and silence no insingers.

The Shai, either arriving at the same conclusion independently or picking it up from the surface of Bronh's thoughts, said as much. Jannus abandoned his objections and Pedross turned a perfectly blank look on Bronh, remarking generally, "If that's all she has to offer, all the reasons this thing can't be stopped and why it's futile to even try, I don't see any further use to her."

"What she knows isn't necessarily all there is to know," argued Jannus. "Her believing it doesn't make it so."

"That isn't quite what I meant," said Pedross, and proceeded to demonstrate by flinging a weighted throwing-dagger at Bronh's throat.

With the least instant's warning from Poli, Bronh moved just enough so that the blade struck her collar-bone rather than the hollow of her throat and didn't bury itself deeply enough to support its own weight. It clattered to the gold of the power grid.

Directing, "Guard her," Jannus scooped up the blade and slapped it onto the sensor console. "What's on it?"

"Cyanide-derivative," reported the Shai after an instant, "but Pedross is right. She can't help, and surely will hurt if she can. Your obligation ended—"

Paying no attention, Jannus half guided, half shoved Bronh into the sensor-nexus, the director's station, and made her sit there. "Fix it," he ordered the Shai. "No delays, no discussion. Just fix it. Now."

Aware of the onset of the paralysis that was the poison's initial symptom, Bronh composed herself. She'd intended that the gift of her death be the fitting completion to the gift of

her life, and that as many Valde as possible receive the bene-
fit of participating in it. But if that was not to be, still her
purpose would accomplish itself without her.

The numbness of her extremities advanced to middle
joints, then progressed no farther as whatever antidote the
Shai had administered, unfelt, through the sampling and
monitoring capacities of the station, the chair, began to contest the poison's effects. Bronh aided the process by keeping
respiration slow and disciplining muscles to relaxation.

Pedross asked the Shai coolly, "Anything useful?"

"No," said the Shai. "Only more of the same."

Jannus wheeled to face Pedross, saying in a deadly quiet
voice, "Don't you ever play games like that anywhere around
me: do you hear me?"

"In *Sunfire*," Pedross replied, "you can enforce that, I
guess. But outside, that's another matter. That's *my* ground.
And I'm not about to lose the whole of the mainland for the
sake of your squeamishness. Bronh: wouldn't you like to
come for a stroll with me?"

Bronh tested the flexion of one hand. Sensation was sufficiently restored, she judged, to permit her to stand. Rising,
she said, "I presume I may leave. . . ."

"You leave," confirmed Jannus flatly. "We're done with
killing games. Pedross, you stay put until she's well away."
As a sudden afterthought, he added, "Shai, has he got an ambush set, outside?"

"Of course," replied the Shai's reluctant voice.

"Are they in range of the illusion field?"

"No," said Pedross, for himself. "Safely outside, if my information's worth anything."

"Shai?" demanded Jannus, refusing to take merely Pedross'
word for it.

"They're beyond the reach of the projector," confirmed the
Shai.

"Then I want to know what ways they can be kept clear of
Bronh without killing them. Use the link." Jannus leaned
away as if from a slow shove, supporting himself against the
seat Bronh had left. He settled into it while Pedross prowled
irritably around the curve of the console and Poli stood still,
uncomfortable at siding with Pedross' view in this and so doing nothing. Jannus said, "Use the flash, then. Enough to

blind them for an hour or two, not longer. Don't burn their eyes out: understood?"

"It's done," responded the Shai laconically, and Jannus rolled his head around to see Bronh.

"You have a clear way, for the time being. Shai? Let her out, and no tricks, no flashes, nothing. Just let her go her ways: understood?"

"I do hear you," said the Shai glumly.

"Bronh, there's got to be some way, some decent way, to stop this. Past the Thornwall, they're *dying*—"

"What can't adapt is being eliminated," Bronh told him calmly, and he abandoned the appeal.

"If you go away," he said, "and leave the thing to settle however it must, I'll try to keep Pedross from hunting you down out of simple spite. Except for you, there'd *be* no Valde: I haven't forgotten that. But if you interfere any more, I can't be answerable."

"You're not," Bronh assured him. "You have no power in the matter whatever. Without power there is no responsibility."

"Get out, then," Jannus said wearily, and looked away.

Finding the glow of a port, Bronh walked toward it steadily until it opened. A little distance from the hill, she passed unremarked among the dazed soldiery wandering around in blinded alarm and, once past them, followed the fold of the land north toward a place where a convergence of game trails marked a good place to cross the Morimmon into Entellith beyond the Thornwall.

Because it was obvious the alliance would fare better if Jannus and Pedross kept out of each other's sight for a while, they left Pedross coping with the wreck of his ambush and followed the new dirt road that led from the margin of the forest, through the planted ground, to Sunrise Bridge.

In the middle of the bridge Poli stopped, looking up along the division made in the high walls of foliage by the broad, slow-siding river. She was looking toward Entellith, southernmost of the forests of Valde.

Jannus, turning to lean against the parapet beside her, asked, "Something?"

She shook her head. Nothing. Only the noise of Ardun.

She remarked pensively, "There must be a lot of Haffa there who remember the troopservice. . . . Not deserters: full-term troopmaids. Lar Haffa. *And* their mates, *and* their children. . . ."

Jannus waited to hear what she was getting at.

"There must be some who were caught up in the Singing against their own wish, the way it almost happened to me," she continued obliquely. "I'd bet they'd be glad and able to get free of it if they just had something steady to hold to. . . ."

Setting his back against the parapet, Jannus regarded her. "Like what?" he inquired ominously.

"There are more kinds of link than one. A farspeaker to hold to, that'd be a lot."

Believing he'd misjudged her intention, he responded, "If they're that far off, whatever I could inspeak would just blend into the daysinging. I'm loud, but I can't hold onto what I reach because I can't *hear* it. Like a blind man fishing with a string and no hook."

"Well, there might be a way around that," she mentioned.

"That's what I *thought* you were getting at!" Jannus walked off with a sharp crosswise gesture, cutting off the proposal. "No. You're not going to play bait. No. Absolutely."

"Not bait: hook," she corrected, ambling after him, brushing aside inspoken refusals. A period of abstinence from both the grey powder and any but the briefest superficial contact with the Shai had done wonders for Jannus' temper. "That's fine," she told his back. "That should carry for a day's run, just like that."

He wheeled and said with great distinctness, "No." Then he proceeded on, refusing to turn again.

Unhurriedly pursuing, she caught up with him at the intersection with Market Street. The way was blocked there by a construction of tiered seating being set up across the whole width of the cross street by a group of Smiths. They turned south to detour around the foot of Market Square where the parade route began and the streets would be open. "I didn't know they were going to go through with it anyway," he said, referring to the Blooming Festival. "Without the Summerfair, seems like it'd be having the party though the marriage has been called off. I suppose it'd be more trouble than it's worth for Pedross, to stop it; Domal always let the Greenleafers march. . . ."

"Do you figure you're still in *Sunfire*," she put in, "to say *No* and that's the end of it? And if you just keep a nice steady flicker of 'emotional surround' I'll just forget about it, like a proper featherheaded Valde?"

"When Pedross brought it up, it was a stupid idea. Your deciding all of a sudden to bring it home and adopt it doesn't make it a bit the—"

"This is something else, and you know it. What if we could bring Haffa clear of the Singing? They're not as lucky as I am, to have somebody outside and deaf to it, to hold to. I got clear of it once that way. And you're a farspeaker. If I could get somebody into range, they'd have almost the same hold I do, don't you see? I bet I wouldn't hear any more *arbiter's fetch* thrown at me if we'd brought a troop of Valde back to this side of the Thornwall."

"That sounds like the sort of thing Sua would think up."

"If you'd ever come near being lost in a thing like that, you'd want to do anything you could to pry free anybody else who wanted to get free," she responded earnestly. "If it could shut up the Choral Hating Society too, so much the better."

" 'Back past the Thornwall' you say, blithe as somebody setting out to stop wind with a line drawn in the dirt. The Thornwall's no protection. Pedross' signalers were this side of it, and a fat lot of good it did them."

"They've drawn in since then, the Entellith folk—out of range of Ardun. I get a drift of the Singing here now and again, but not enough to pull," she asserted, not altogether truthfully: her life as a Valde among Valde remained the most profound gap in her dead memory. The yearning to fill some part of it had been continually with her since her waking; and the distant communion of the Singing from which she withheld herself intensified the feeling, keeping it a fresh homesickness that had its own power to draw. She continued, "If a Haffa could get to the edge of it, and wanted to get clear, it couldn't pull her back against her own wish—otherwise, I'd have been gone a halfmonth since."

"A Haffa wouldn't be nailed down to me, on a short tether," replied Jannus, with curt dispassion. "But all right. Suppose you did get somebody clear, draw them to your own

Troopcalling. They'd bolt south as quick and as far as they could. They wouldn't risk getting caught a second time, *they've* got enough sense for that, anyway. And that might make Pedross happy, to have his own flock nesting out among the isles again, but it wouldn't do Ardun a whole lot of good. And by the time the firestorm's burned its way clear to the coast, what'll it matter if there are a few Valde roosting out among the isles or not? Is that worth the risk, to keep Pedross in signalers?"

"They came to Quickmoor once, to keep faith. And Quickmoor hasn't the claim on Valde that Ardun does," she argued.

"Ardun's just the open door that the street noise comes through. The handiest place to trade for salt. They don't care anything about Ardun. They'd bolt for the coast."

"Maybe they wouldn't. Maybe they'd stand. It's full-term troopmaids I'm talking about, not lawless Awiro. Anybody who's lived through harvest season in a riverstock's not about to be bothered by a little noise." remarked Poli, from the midst of that noise. Trying a different approach, she said, "Jannus, you were willing enough to agree to my coming into Ardun when anything that even looked like a Valde was in danger of being mobbed. So why have a fit about this."

"I know Ardun. Entellith's different."

"I know Entellith—or I used to. We walked the stakes of the Summerfair Path enough years—"

"Entellith's different," he insisted stubbornly. "In Ardun, I at least understand the chances and the risks. But I really don't understand Valde at all, and I know it. There's a limit to what I can understand, just being told about it, never knowing it myself. There's a limit to what I can imagine. And past that limit I'm damn well terrified. There's no way I'll accept your walking off into close range of that spinwind I can't even feel and hardly imagine. . . . Suppose you didn't come out again. There wouldn't be a single thing I could do about it, even to know what had happened or where you'd—"

"You could just make yourself another copy," she suggested coolly, and was astonished at the anger that comment roused.

He stopped, turning on her a long level glance, everything

in him readjusting to the weight and scope of that fundamental outrage.

After what seemed like a long time he started walking again; and, shaken and abashed, she followed, silent.

After they'd gone almost a block he said, "I couldn't. Not twice. This time, it's you. I believe that. But a second time it'd *be* a copy, a puppet, a fetch, to me too. And what would follow then, I don't even want to try to think. This time, it's you. Things have changed, we've changed, but not past the point . . . past—"

He couldn't find words for his awareness of the fragility of his belief that she was, indeed, herself: identity continuous, back past her first waking memories, to that other Poli he'd seen dying and dead and consumed by fire so that no least fragment continued in direct, unbroken transferral.

The possibility of Jannus' ever turning away from her— with regret, perhaps, and even compassion, but irrevocably and forever—was one which had never even occurred to her. His was the one absolute reflection, the unquestioning acceptance that held her steady against all changes and denials, even her own. Who would she be if even Jannus didn't know her?

She found the notion terrifying to contemplate. That it could happen made her feel obscurely that it already had.

Finding her so dismayed, Jannus quoted her to herself, remarking with awkward lightness, "You just have to have faith in what you can't believe," and put his arm around her; but that didn't change anything.

There was some reassurance in knowing she was not merely an item in a potentially endless series, a sort of Polimobile created or destroyed at the whim of its maker; but not enough.

They walked some while, each preoccupied with an intolerable threat of loss. Then Jannus said suddenly, "Before you woke I made up my mind not to expect anything, make no demands. Whatever you were or did would be all right with me, so long as you were alive in the world. I had it all clear. You were to be free," he announced wistfully; but the half-formed images that came were of isolation, of her alone in the middle of a glowing fog undefined by any relationships at all.

153

It was striking enough, and beautiful in its way with the glamour of his wishing upon it: but nothing a person could really live in, nothing she'd ever wanted herself.

"Freedom like that," she commented slowly, "I can do very well without."

Jannus only shook his head, refusing to argue. "Whatever you wanted, then. Whatever it turned out to be." The imagined figure blurred, faded into nothing. "But that was what I meant it to be like—no conditions, nothing you had to do or be. Not like *this*. . . . And I haven't budged you a bit anyhow. You still want to go. The only thing to be settled is whether, and how, I'm going to support you in it: right?"

It was her turn to shake her head. "I can't do it without you," she said soberly. "I want to do it. I think it needs doing, and there's nobody else who could—it needs a Valde and a *sa'marenniath* farspeaker, and that's us. But if you won't or can't accept that. . . ." She let the remark trail off.

"I'll try. I can't change the way I feel about it, but I'll try. I'll support you any way I have to, any way I can. You just have to teach me what's to be done and how I'm to keep from going through the roof without even the powder to help, because that would wipe me out completely as a farspeaker. . . ."

He broke off because she was hugging him hard around the neck, her jubilation overcoming his grudged and still reluctant agreement. "It'll be all right," she explained, "you'll see!"

Walking more briskly, they set about the dull but vital business of casting ends into means, specific strategies of act, sequence, equipment, and time. Poli was prepared to be encumbered with however many protections he could think of for the chance to pass the Thornwall and come again within the embrace of Valde.

In the first half-light before dawning Poli came free of the last of Ardun's fading, distant mutter and shortly thereafter encountered her first Valde. They were one arc of a hunting relay: a *hafkenna*, a childpack, in pursuit of a deer.

First came the deer, springing through the fern in the four-footed bounces of deer's running. With little underbrush in the tended forest to hinder him, he kept a straight course among the massive, spaced boles of silverbark that made him appear tiny as a fleeing mouse. He knew himself as quarry, not yet as prey. Receding, he disappeared among the trunks which, at the limits of sight, seemed gathered into a solid palisade chalked on a fog.

The eagerness of the hunters pursued him, and then the hunters themselves. Out of the misleading perspectives of distance they ran in long, floating strides: a pack of young parentless Haffa racing as much with each other as with the doomed deer, each wanting to be the first to overtake, to touch a straining flank and catch hold. There was no speech or sound among them, only the intense communion of the hunt.

Among them ran their leader, their *hafra*—literally, *older brother*, but they were tied to him not by blood but by attraction, the fierce exclusive love of children. Neither quite brother nor lover, as much captive as leader of his pack, he turned them to intercept the deer's course rather than run blindly at its heels. He wanted to bring the deer down before it entered the territory of his nearest rival, whose *hafkenna* waited to take up the pursuit. The *hafra* would stop well short of that intangible border lest any of his pack find the power and arrogant skill of his rival more attractive than his own.

Intent, therefore, on other things than the deer's terror racing before him, he responded to Poli's inspoken hail with a particular curiosity whether or not she was Awiro. When she identified herself as a Lar Haffa—too old, partnered, and not interested—he called his pack into a flying line so she could appreciate what she'd be missing: a young man in the first rush of his grown strength who could call to him such a *hafkenna* as this, wild and fierce as banded hawks, none lamed nor ill nor starving. . . .

Poli declined this adolescent display too and tried to ask which way was *inward*, where the family clusters would be on whose outer fringes *hafkennae* ranged. But the *hafkenna* had taken notice of her and drowned out her question in a contradictory swirl of indignation at her slight to their marvelous daystar, the finest anywhere, and jealous warning against finding him *too* marvelous because he was *theirs* and they'd have the eyes of any grown Haffa who tried to use her unfair advantage to steal his attentions to herself alone, they'd as soon run her down as any deer, and old Haffa were *slow* and *dull* whereas they themselves were a whirl of splendid wildfire. . . .

That last derogatory comparison was a diminishing silent shout. The pack had already passed out of sight.

As Poli continued through what seemed an ever-opening glade with ever-denser forest just beyond, she mused that adolescence was a spinwind of a sort, but no present threat. Of the true Singing, she'd had no sign all night. Perhaps there'd been a faint drift of it just as she was setting out, at moonrise; but that might have been no more than a projection of her own eagerness.

He'd certainly been an optimist, that *hafra*, though—he should have known perfectly well she was partnered and had outgrown such attractions as he had to offer. Her eagerness was of a somewhat different order.

But *hafrae* were always fishing deep water with the wrong bait—it was the age. They seldom caught anything but a passing Awiro with a casual itch—the *hafkenna* saw to that. Awiro were no threat, but the *hafra* would find no deeper, permanent bonding, that which opened the way for children, until he and his *hafkenna* had outgrown the need to own by being owned and dominate by following.

Poli didn't remember her own *hafkenna* at all, but it likely would have been just such a one as this, and its focus a young man just as harried and self-important. The memory wasn't truly hers, but it made a beginning, a first spider strand across the empty place.

She jogged on as the dawn stirring of all life that lived by the sun increased in every direction—the high life first: trees angling their leaves to catch the first light, and birds rousing. Then, more gradually, insects began the day's frenzy of devouring and mating, and the birds ate them. And, from burrows and dens emerged meateaters and browsers, and the daysinging assumed its full volume of hungers and seekings. The air was filled with the immediacies of appetite.

Far away, the deer was brought down and broken; the united exultation of a *hafkenna* in full cry could carry a considerable distance. It was, Poli realized, like a thin single strand of the Singing. For a moment she thought she felt something stirring, waking, as the day had wakened—all colors seeming momentarily brighter, all shards of peeling bark implicit with meanings another moment would reveal. Then the peremptory tingling of the bracelet around her right wrist distracted her for the instant it took the feeling to scatter into the randomness of the daysinging. Poli was left unsure there'd been anything more than the imagined glow caused merely by her own consciousness of the brightening day.

She'd promised to contact Jannus at sunrise. If he was anxious and impatient, it was her own fault for letting herself become so absorbed in the daysinging that she'd not exactly forgotten but put off the agreed schedule. There wasn't any urgency about it—the button-thing on the bracelet relayed to him all nearby sounds down to the beat of her blood, as she understood it. So he would know nothing in particular was happening to her—*did* know it, but wanted to hear her saying so, all the same. And the pressure of his reasonless anxiety was more of a distraction to her than the signal-button's nagging tingle.

She had arrived near the west shore of a long narrow lake. She set her bundle down on a rock near the sedgy margin of the water, and held her hand awkwardly upright near her face. "I'm inside the outer circle," she reported: feeling like a fool talking to a Tek trinket cobbled onto a quartz bangle. But the tingling stopped, and his selfsinging reacted to her message, relayed to him by the Shai and through the mobile, who put it back into words. A cumbersome, corner-bounce business, but it worked. "It's farther in from the limit of Ardun's *als'far* than I expected, and the center must be almost as far again, halfway to the meadows, because I'm still out of range and I haven't reached any Haffa yet either, except a *hafkenna*."

The signaler couldn't speak back to her, but it didn't need to. She could hear Jannus well enough—if anything, too well: his anxiety was powerful and infectious.

He couldn't help it. His agreement notwithstanding, he still hated the whole idea and that reluctance and dread were a dark undertow affecting the whole of his selfsinging. And he couldn't use any of the usual aids or distractions. Anything that disrupted or muted emotional intensity would likewise ruin him as a farspeaker. And, unlike her, he couldn't interpose casual intervals of attending only to immediate, unimportant things. He had to be ready, at her signal, to support the calling she'd come to send out, give it a tether-post and a direction; and, if need be, to be ready in an instant to help her hold herself against the riptide pull of the Singing.

But it wasn't just the waiting or the unremitting tension. He'd always been like that. He loved her desperately. She loved him with many things—joy, passion, amusement, affection, loyalty, acceptance—but never desperation. He'd always reacted to any but the most trivial and temporary of partings between them, any indefinite absence, as though it were utter loss and abandonment. From the beginning, he'd had a conviction of precariousness.

Had he been different, he would never have pursued her either into marriage or beyond death. But that inability to accept reasonable limits had its dark side when, as now, it became anxiety that was beginning to rub them both raw.

Jannus had to keep himself steady, so that she could be so. He understood that. But doing it, for hours at a time, was proving to entail discipline and difficulty beyond what either of them had expected. Midwinter had scarred his confidence, Poli thought: he now *knew* she could be lost, and his overriding desire was to drag her back from the edge she was determined to at least look over.

"I'm eating soggy bread and honey," she told the wretched bangle patiently, "and a blue wader just speared a fish. Nothing's happening. Nothing's wrong. It's only Entellith."

When, in about two blinks, that reached him through the relay, he managed to enforce a bit more calm. He was managing the best he could.

"I know," she assured the bangle, wishing he could be here with her, that they could have done without this cumbersome, awkward arrangement of bangle and relay and simply have come into Entellith together as they had, year after year, on their way to the Summerfair. She wanted him close, in touching distance, not away the other side of the Thornwall. But without him to be outside as anchor and beacon, she wouldn't have risked getting into range of the Singing again—not for all the disaffected Haffa in Entellith, not for all the holes in her dead memory, and surely not to keep Pedross supplied with signalers. . . .

Sighing, she went down to the water's edge and swished her hands to get the stickiness off. It had to be done together, this calling, or not at all. And they'd do it—she'd come this far, and the sky hadn't fallen. . . . But she wished she could have found some way to reconcile him to it, so he could have been easier about it now, accepting the risks as necessary though they be *her* risks, which he could neither evaluate nor protect her from. . . . She was trying to decide whether to go on, until she made actual contact with the inner family clusters, or to begin her calling here and maintain it until somebody by chance wandered into her range.

The latter course was safer, but more difficult. The concentration would be harder to maintain—particularly for Jannus. And it would probably take longer. The Entellith folk weren't ranging abroad, hunting and gathering, in their usual scattered way, or she'd have contacted somebody besides a wandering *hafkenna* before this.

And she couldn't ignore or properly weight her own inclination, which was to go on, to stretch this foray as far as it would reach and recover for her memory as much of southern Valde as she possibly could. She still savored her meeting with the *hafkenna*—too much, maybe. It was hard to balance desire against prudence.

Lifting the bangle nearer her face, she described these choices to Jannus, ending, "You call it. I'm already farther than I expected to have to come. I'll go on, or start the calling now—whichever you want."

By the reaction, he was consulting Simon about risks and tactics—probably sensible. She wouldn't have thought of it. Then he inspoke clearly that she should stay and begin calling where she was. The other choice would still remain if, after a reasonable time, her hook remained empty. Or, he suggested, she could come home and try some other time: for instance, next spring. Then, flatly, he requested confirmation.

"Clear," she replied. "I'll give it a try here. Then we can see. After all, I only brought food enough for two days. . . ."

His response was the inspoken equivalent of a wince combined with a rude noise.

She went back to the rock, smiling to herself: equilibrium, if not harmony, reestablished.

It was a broad general seeking she was after, not the specific, exclusive rapport of what was generally called duel-trance. Although she had no particular person in mind, she had quite a clear notion of the sort of person she wanted to contact—a Haffa, who had known troopservice and the Bremneri river link, but most particularly one who was herself seeking a handhold, a way out.

Absently Poli directed, "Begin."

She began locking away whole categories of things, chunks of the daysinging, starting with the more complex awarenesses and ending with the reaching of seeds. Soon, in the silence, there was only the summons Jannus was sending out in his deaf, unmodulated farspeaker's shout: *Listen. Come out. Come to me. Listen.* Poli fined and focused that summoning, shaping it to its target. Her counterpoint sang, *I am lar Haffa, come to fetch out whoever will come. Come to me here, where I am. I am lar Haffa, out of Ardun, come for anyone who will come.*

After a time and by almost imperceptible degrees the flow of Jannus' calling began to alter. It wasn't some Haffa stranger that he wanted but herself, Poli. She tried to keep the calling to its course, shunting it away from her, adding more specific images of the troopservice and the river link that connected all Haffa of the troops wherever they served. But eventually all calling and counterpoint had diverged too far to be a unified summoning.

Poli broke trance and braced herself against the renewed roar of the banished daysinging, buffeting and chaotic. Presently she remembered to lift the bangle and say, "Stop, now. That's enough, for one try. That was good," and felt Jannus lapse into a like exhaustion.

Breaking trance was always hard without the support of a troop to fall back into, to drift with the eddies of their moods until the energy came to break free and be separate again. And harder, she knew, for him than for her: without even such support as the heedless daysinging offered, without anything but silence and his own sole self. All the rest, he had to take only on trust; and maintaining such trust, she thought now, must be the hardest thing of all.

160

Presently, as she continued to rest, someone inspoke to her, *Wait. We're coming.*

"Caught something," she said, and Jannus was instantly alert, wanting to know more. "Wait," she directed, trying to sort through the layers of contact.

There were undertones of desperation, of being, if not pursued, at least in a long, staggering flight, confusion. . . . Two people, a man and a woman lar to each other, the woman with their firstborn growing within her. Coming more slowly, in the greater haste, the woman demanded over and over whether Slatefen had fallen, as though that had been her sole concern for so long that she could not leave off asking to attend to the answer.

Poli finally made her understand none of the Bremneri riverstocks had even been attacked this year, much less wrested from their Truthtelling Ladies. Planting season gave the farmstead men no leisure to organize such an assault. It would be harvest season, and the grain barges coming east to Erth-rimmon from the inlands, before the dangerous time would begin. And it wasn't as though the riverstocks hadn't had several years' forewarning, after all, since the first of the desertions. Most were walled now, and had offered their young men inducements to stay and learn fighting skills from what troopmaids remained: not all had thrown aside their trust so casually. . . .

"Troopmaid or freemaid," she reported to Jannus' impatience, "I can't tell, worried sick about Slatefen, of all things, and her lar, they're coming. . . ."

Poli caught sight of them presently on the far side of the lake. The man's left arm was bound in a sling made from one strap of the woman's troopmaid's harness. Her tabard, or what remained of it, was the blue and white of Slatefen, and those tatters so muddied and streaked that Poli could only guess at the colors. The man was in no better case: they both looked as if they'd been sheltering on the wrong side of a tree since thaw, all moss-smears and snow-wrack and no new growth to hide it.

The woman discovered the lake's barrier with as heavy a dismay as though it were a bottomless pit or a mountain cliff she despaired of descending. She wasn't *that* pregnant, nor the man *that* crippled, to justify such consternation.

Meanwhile the man was wondering at Poli's lack of recognition. Because he knew her. He was of the Morgaard community and had come south, at first thaw, as someone from his family group had always done, to set the stakes of the Summerfair Path. For several seasons he'd been among Jannus' Fair Witnesses at the Summerfair sessions.

Frowning across the water, trying to make out his features, Poli realized she could put a name to him: Oflernan. She *did* know him! Four summers ago her children had run with his *hafkenna*. Three seasons ago he'd lost all but two of his *hafkenna* to growthyear, and had made a great fuss of running errands, fetching food and such, because the Morgaard Valde took their Summerfair hospitality very seriously and he'd come to consider himself the special host of the odd Bremneri farspeaker and his odder lar Haffa mate, being intrigued with strangers of all sorts. She remembered how vain he'd been of his fluency in the breathtalk, continually underfoot at all hours. . . .

She called across the water, *"Of-ler-nan!"* and scared up a flapping explosion of feeding ducks which carried their protests farther up the lake on whistling wings.

There was a little island, just big enough to support a single tree, about two-thirds of the way across the lake. Disregarding chaotic warnings, Poli skidded down to the shore and waded out. She went cautiously, puzzled by their dismay, but found the bottom sound and the lake shallow quite a distance from shore. She had to swim scarcely twenty strokes before her feet brushed weed, and soon she was touching bottom again. She climbed out on the island, holding to a low branch of its tree, and found the pair watching her across the remaining distance with an agitated resignation. The woman wanted her to come fast now, as long as Poli had been rash enough to come this far. Poli asked why, but all they wanted was for her to come *now, hurry*.

She stepped down and crossed to the far shore without the least trouble.

Oflernan offered his good hand to help her across the muddy edge, saying, "You shouldn't have done."

"But why not, in the name of the green world?" she rejoined in exasperation. "It was plain enough you-both weren't going to come across to me."

"If it catches you in the water," said the woman curtly, "you drown. If you're climbing, you fall. If you're cooking. . . ." She pulled back a sleeve and displayed a raw red burn across her forearm. When Poli looked back at her pack, sitting in plain sight on the rock where she'd left it without a moment's thought, the woman directed sharply, "No. It's not worth the risk. This rest won't last forever. Make what distance we can while it lasts."

Poli found herself pulled into motion by the woman's grim authority, still looking behind her at the pack—bowcase, fire kit, blankets, food, everything, across what the Haffa was absolutely convinced was an impassable barrier.

When Poli started to name herself, the Haffa responded, "I know of you. I was new-come to Dark-stock when you were First Dancer to the Newstock troop. I am Callea who was to be troopleader to Slatefen for the new term. Bronh Sefar' brought the Singing down upon us in Elenin and I lost my troop. I came this far before we-both were caught up together, trying and trying. . . . I was a farspeaker once," she added, another burst, each brief and coherent in itself but communicating a sense of a willed lunge out of some intense confusion, cast in breathtalk rather than the inspeaking for the sake of the clarity, each word separate and in its proper order.

Oflernan, whom Poli recollected as a brisk, mercurial, rather otterlike youngster, at least externally, seemed to have developed a detachment, a distance; he was alert only to collect anything that could serve as food. Whatever he scavenged—mosses, green shoots, two unbroken eggs from the wreck of a fallen nest—he stuffed indiscriminately into a sack hanging at his side. Occasionally he was roused by Callea's hard-edged angers or purposes, but otherwise he was drifting, neither bored nor interested, amiable, empty-eyed.

He was aware of Poli's assessment, as he was of the wind. Both passed by and nothing was changed.

Poli asked him, "Do I seem much different to you?"

He didn't understand what she meant.

"Different," she repeated. "Changed, compared to when you knew me before."

"I know you," he offered uncertainly, willing to give her

whatever reaction she wanted if she'd just make plainer what that was.

"But I was *sa'marenniath* before," she reminded him, seizing on the most obvious change she could think of.

"Not now," he commented, feeling Poli's inhearing to be no more remarkable than his own or anybody's.

If she wanted to pursue it, that was all right. If she wanted to sit down or cover herself over with leaves, that would be all right too, and wouldn't surprise him at all.

She wondered how he'd injured his arm. He didn't know: he'd just found it that way. Since Callea had insisted on splinting and binding it, it didn't hurt unless he ran. When it didn't hurt, he didn't mind it.

They neither one of them looked likely to do much running, Poli observed—Oflernan ambling along in his placid, vacuous way, Callea moving at a choppy, forced pace and managing to stumble on every available dip and rise because there was no flexibility in her to adjust to anything but perfectly level ground. They were companions: Poli found she could not see them as lovers. They didn't even particularly like each other. Yet they were bound, lar, caught in a relationship as choiceless and irrevocable as that between parents and children. Thrown together by accident and the defeat of their separate purposes by the Singing, they had each become no longer themselves but a portion of a third thing, a lar, alive, with its own hungers and imperatives and whose term now defined their own.

It happened that way sometimes. No, Poli thought, it happened that way all the time. One was drawn, drawn into mergence, regardless of plans or suitability or what you'd always expected to find yourself wanting. Everybody, she thought, married strangers: except some of them knew it.

They passed a sturdy peeled wand standing upright in a mound of ferns—just the one. Oflernan turned aside a few steps to touch it lightly, with a diffuse sadness, and then went on. He'd tried three separate times, he recalled, to set the stakes of the Summerfair Path this spring. The last time, two Awiro had been walking just behind him, snatching up and tossing away each stake as soon as he'd set it in the ground and moved off. Sometimes they'd contested a single stake for a whole afternoon, warring without ever touching. "They must have missed that one," he said aloud, looking briefly over his shoulder. "Or the Singing came, and they forgot. . . ."

Poli offered to carry the sack. They might go faster that way; and, besides, it was the only service she could think of to offer him.

But his refusal was immediate and, for him, sharp. "You don't understand yet. This is today's gather. It stays with us. I won't break a cairn unless I have to."

He was right: she didn't understand.

Presently Callea stumbled to fall, and a resting time began. Oflernan at once set about finding a good springy sapling to hold a snare of knotted grass twine. It puzzled Poli: she didn't expect they'd be returning to check it. "Somebody will," replied Oflernan. "Or else a rain will spring it." Either way, he didn't mind. Poli let the question go.

The bangle tingled, just briefly. Jannus had been very patient, following as much of the spoken conversation as he could, waiting through the long silences with only the reassurance of the steady sounds of motion and, she supposed, her steady heartbeat.

Poli felt a bit shy at the notion of talking at the thing in the presence of other Valde. Just the shyness alone made Callea lift her head and look over at Poli curiously. So Poli said generally, "If we're going to stop awhile, I could try another calling." It seemed to her that her current catch—a pregnant freemaid and a dazedly drifting man with a broken arm— wouldn't impress anybody much when she brought them back along the Rose Way down the middle of the Aihall Square. She'd envisioned something at least a bit more *numerous.* She'd be glad to bring anybody clear, of course, but. . . .

But the two instantly objected with the sudden energetic unanimity they'd shown about the lake. Their warnings came together, a tangle of breathtalk and inspeaking it took Poli a moment to separate into sense.

They were afraid of rousing the Singing.

"Anything can," Callea said, pushing to her feet with renewed haste, "anything—a child, fresh lovers, a *hafra* calling, nothing at all. It catches you, and who knows what began it? It just *comes.*"

"We came to you," mentioned Oflernan, letting the sapling

spring up, the dangling snare unset, "partly to shut you up, and him. And that I knew you-both. . . . It's been a long rest, this one," he observed mildly, following Callea. "Longer than most, I think. . . ."

Feeling well and probably deservedly squelched, Poli asked the bangle, "That need explaining?"

No more calling. She could almost hear that, the very tone of voice, the snap of satisfaction. He wanted her to come, now. She could link as well with the slower-going pair from ahead of them as beside them, he could come out himself a way and meet her, unlikely to meet anybody else, it seemed. The Shai hypothesized the eruptions of the Singing were getting fewer because there were fewer fresh arrivals setting it off irregularly; but it was probably also assuming a regularity, a pattern: fewer, but longer in duration, the term determined by the collective ability of the Valde to sustain it, endure it. And it had now been at least a night and half a day since the last seizure subsided. A rest, Oflernan had called it, and longer than most. . . .

Jannus wanted her back; now; running.

"I'm coming," she assured him, and caught up in a few strides with the pair ahead, then slowed to match their rambling stubborn haste. Poli thought such encouragement as she could offer from a distance to others at risk would have lost a certain helpful urgency.

And in spite of the pauses to rest or collect sour wingwort they'd gone quite far, within sound of the cascades of Arant Dunrimmon, before the Singing roused in full jubilation and engulfed them.

Lighting a lamp would mean admitting it was getting dark in the tower room and might therefore be tactless. But Simon couldn't see to read. He let the scroll curl back on itself and sat fiddling with a ring, knowing Jannus couldn't maintain his concentration indefinitely but not wanting to be the means of breaking it.

When the mobile could no longer see the pattern of the parquetry or Jannus' motionless seated figure on the far side of the large triangular room, he rose silently and lifted the chimney of a big hanging oil lamp. He set the wick alight with a spark spat by the enameled ring whose crystal could capitalize, for a microsecond, the body's electrical potential.

The lamp's springing flame woke echoes from polished wood and made the windows seem abruptly dark. Jannus didn't stir. Simon sat quietly down again.

Of all the Tek devices at his disposal, save *Sunfire* itself, the ring remained his favorite: dramatic, simple, and utilitarian. Without question his least favorite at the moment was the sound transmitter he'd fused onto a quartz bangle whose piezoelectric capacities he'd adjusted in a manner similar to those of the ring. Jannus of course had refused to hear of using anything as intrusively *gadgety* as a plain implant; when he had leisure, he'd be sure to think of that. Simon wouldn't remind him.

It had been well over two hours since the hybrid device had gone silent: the opening parade of the Blooming Festival had still been going on twelve stories below, in the Aihall Square. Now, it appeared, they were singing. . . .

The bangle was silent because it was no longer in contact with a living body.

It could have fallen off, or been discarded. It could have been whacked incautiously against a rock—one of quartz's frustrating properties was its tendency to fracture along the lines of crystallization. It broke. Or, of course, it might yet be in place but had no electrical potential to amplify and draw upon because Poli's nervous system had stopped functioning.

No explanation was intrinsically any likelier than the others. *Probability*, thought Simon, *stopped at the Thornwall*. But with no messages—no sounds, even, now—to be relayed, Simon had nothing to do. There was a certain value in being absolutely sure of that, that he had no necessary or even useful contribution to make. Jannus didn't even have that assurance. For all Jannus knew, his continuing inspoken call was the single thing which gave any hope of separating Poli from the compelling multiple rapport of the Singing. Or it might be no help at all, or altogether futile because Poli was in no condition to receive it.

There was no way of knowing. Jannus could only continue. As long as he could. Simon pushed back the upper part of the scroll and continued reading. The Shai could have absorbed and evaluated the information for him in less time than it took Simon to find his place again; but Simon followed the cursive script along with a finger, preferring to make his own evaluation of the report, with no trivial item or turn of phrase discounted.

The door banged open and without looking around, Simon knew it had to be Pedross: Simon had impressed the tower steward with dire results should anyone ever enter his personal chamber on any pretext whatsoever, including a warning of fire.

He let the scroll furl itself and looked around. Jannus had changed position; but his concentration had apparently withstood the intrusion, and he meant to continue ignoring it. And Pedross had checked, clearly surprised to find Jannus here: Simon had simply said he meant to try an experiment to bring Valde back past the Thornwall, making no mention of Jannus at all. It would seem less apt to provoke a contest over Simon's undivided services that way.

Pedross balanced a moment, reading what the poses and the quiet told him, then crossed briskly to a window embrasure on the north. As he looked down, his stance indicated that there was something notable to be seen. Simon rose and joined him.

There were torches all around the square, and colored lanterns on high poles. Resumption of the more active phases of celebration was apparently waiting for moonrise and the conclusion of the evening meal. The celebrants had been engaged in singing the sun down, as this morning they'd sung its rising: even from the tower the lifted voices had been audible, the cadences and the pauses, the old, old songs of renewal and welcome before the blooming rose hedge that, this year, returned them no answer.

They were singing still, but there was some commotion up at the head of the Rose Way. It was too far to make out individuals in the torchlight, but Simon could see people alternately crowding and making way, and then, briefly, he could see why.

Some people, he thought wearily, used sophisticated equipment, and others used forethought, effort, and stubbornness; and then some sailed right through on blind luck alone.

"Jannus," Simon called, "you'll want to see this."

For the Thornwall had answered after all. A ragged **man**

and woman, both Valde, were being ushered along the Rose Way against the tide of people who wanted to touch them, greet them. As the central cluster came nearer, Simon could see a third fair head moving behind the others, but it turned quickly and red ribbons flung out from its motion. Sua. Simon had spotted her earlier, during the parade. He'd watched partly to find out what sort of numbers the Loyalists would be able to turn out with the strength of a sentimental ritual behind them.

Feeling Jannus behind him, Simon stepped aside to make room. Pedross moved with him, retreating to the center of the room and working the situation out for himself. "A good trade, two for one," he muttered almost inaudibly. "And maybe four for two, later. But two, or twenty-one, isn't a Summerfair. . . ." Glancing up at the mobile, Pedross added, "I came for you myself because you've terrorized the servants to the point that they won't set foot on the tower stairs. Do something about that. And I need you downstairs in the hall when I talk to them. If neither one has the breath-talk, I might as well try to push string. . . ."

"You're in luck," replied Simon quietly. "One's a freemaid and the other's been a Fair Witness."

Pedross' look said that he required Simon's presence anyhow: and he was right. A chief of intelligence, even a *sa'farioh* one, belonged at such an interview. If Simon kept within earshot but out of sight, they'd be unlikely to notice his silence.

Past Jannus' shoulder Simon could see the head of the Rose Way quite plainly now. It was empty, and nothing was moving but the flames of dropped torches and the branches of the Thornwall bobbing and stirring in the last of the evening tidestorm wind.

Addressing Jannus' back, Simon assured, "If anything's heard, or if anything comes or is likely to, you'll know it."

"All right," Jannus replied without inflection and without turning.

On the stairs, Pedross asked, "Who should be sent for?"

"A bone-setter, probably, and a cook—"

"Not for them," rejoined Pedross irritably. "For *him*. Who should be sent for, that he could stand to have around him now?"

Simon thought at once of Sua and at once discarded the idea. Whatever that child-woman might be, she was not a comforting presence. After a few steps he said, "I don't know."

"I can't keep track of the names," muttered Pedross to himself vexedly. "The other four."

"Fealis. Ami. Liret. Amalia. . . ."

"*That* one: Mallie, the one that's mixed up with the Smiths. Get her. And the Lisler, whatever his name is—"

"Sparrowhawk," Simon supplied humbly. The idea should have occurred to him, and hadn't. But the Garin persona would have thought of it. That confirmed for him something about himself he'd suspected and would rather not have known.

"*Him*," agreed Pedross, satisfied. Then he demanded and got a fully detailed account of the fishing expedition. That occupied them the rest of the way to the audience hall.

The two Valde had little to say; or, rather, the woman little, and the man nothing at all. They'd lost contact with Poli in midmorning, when the Singing first roused, and knew nothing of what had become of her afterward. Both were far too spent and despondent to attempt contacting her, through trance, any time soon. Gradually the audience became a reception as upper-level officials and factors and such were admitted. The two Valde seemed to shelter in the increasingly noisy company, sitting small and silent, eating what was brought for them but mainly drinking glass after glass of water.

Again Simon found there was nothing to be done, nothing to relay. When he was notified the child had arrived—the runner had as yet failed to locate the Lisler—Simon left the reception intending to take Mallie upstairs himself. He wouldn't trust a servant to do it; and he preferred them terrified. It saved accidents. He would, he thought, put in a speaking tube, the sort used aboard ship. . . .

Finding Mallie escorted by a highly suspicious and initially antagonistic Dan Innsmith, Simon shrugged, deciding it wouldn't be worth the effort of prying her away from her companion, and led them both up the tower stairs. As they went, Simon supplied the barest outlines of the present impasse so they wouldn't be altogether unprepared. But there

170

was no need. Jannus had gone, having tidily set the latch to fall and lock the door behind him.

Pedross made the proper noises and even remembered most of what was said to him—those things were automatic. But he was so full of delighted admiration he found it quite impossible to stay still. He roved from cluster to cluster in the packed audience hall listening to the consensus shaping in voices and new configurations: inveterate Loyalists exclaiming to enthusiastic Greenleafers, locals, imports, indiscriminately, sharing astonished wonderment with whoever chanced to be at hand.

Valde had returned to Ardun and Sua was getting the credit for it.

It was better than watching a rope-dancer. She should fall, there was no reason whatever why she shouldn't, and yet she never did. And the glorious part of it was that she wasn't in the least aware of the precariousness underfoot.

Her triumph was obvious, from a particular skewed angle. The summoning in Market Square had failed, and Sua had been against it. The festival chorus had succeeded, and she'd been among the participants. Change each *and* to *because* and the conclusion became inescapable.

Pedross could feel the general wonderment quivering like the glowing freefire that scarved rigging and mast-tops sometimes during summer storms out near the tidestorm limit. It had to have a ground, and it was shimmering, thrown by hundreds of eyes, to the beribboned girl in conversation with her tiny, dark sister, herself so far oblivious to the rising adulation which she'd done absolutely nothing to merit save to be alive in the proper spot at the proper time.

Pedross found it wonderful, absolutely delicious. Her awareness of issues and factions might be rudimentary, but her instinctive balance among forces was absolutely infallible when anything involving Ardun was concerned. As some ladder rose, she would happen by just in time to stroll up the lifting rungs and pick the fruit. Then the ladder would begin to dip, depositing her on the grass, and she'd never miss a step, notice the ladder, or consider the fruit more than her due: after all, she'd wanted it.

She considered herself a Greenleafer and yet could not be

171

persuaded to see any contradiction between that and taking part in the Blooming Festival. It was everybody's, she'd contended, and always had been, and anybody who thought otherwise would probably try to fence spring.

Pedross had refused to get involved, preferring to remain an interested spectator. And if Pedross wouldn't stop her, nobody else could.

Some intuition had kept him from mashing Ardun's infatuation with Sua at the outset, when he'd first realized she was being given more credit for unseating Domal Ai than himself, his blockade, or the coincidental withdrawal of the Valde. Those things were too abstract, mundane, or disturbing to attract the ambient freefire. But Sua had defied Old Four-eyes, and hit him, and he'd fallen utterly: that was simple, direct, and satisfying. The entire population of the city had either seen it or else gotten a vivid first-hand report.

Pedross had stifled his initial annoyance at the illogic and unfairness of it and instead put her at his side, where if she shone, she'd shine on him, and where he could watch her.

He'd thought of bedding her, both for the fun of it and to put a handle on that marvelous irrational force she attracted to her. But it had seemed better to keep his distance for a while and discover what her unaided luck would bring her. Besides, bed partners were an unreliable lot in his experience, prone to sudden resentments, quarrels justified and unjustified, whereas his relationship with his Truthsayer was serene.

He didn't want her for an enemy: she was so much better as a banner. And sometimes he wondered, if she were ever to point at him and declare, "That little man's been bothering me," how many stern faces he'd see turning his way—even among his own people. She had won the city watch already: there had been, incredibly, fights over who admired her with the unmixed idolatry, the patrollers or his own marines.

Even the mobile showed her special consideration, and she in turn treated Simon with a casual lack of awe unique among the Aihall personnel. And just from a glance at Simon's back, Pedross could always tell whether or not Sua was in the same room.

Simon theorized that all Ardun's frustrated and bruised devotion to Valde had chosen to light on Sua—half Valde in truth, wholly Valde in appearance except for the dark eyes, and wholly theirs, an Arduner born—as all their execration had been dumped on Poli. But that didn't account for the marines, or the fascination she roused in Pedross, and least of all for Simon himself.

Circumstances conspired to reward her far beyond her deserving. Pedross was now quite beyond resentment or envy. He'd never seen anything like it, knowing well from his own experience what labor, patience, and ready, measured ferocity were needed to take power and what vigilance, to hold it afterward; but with Sua, it was otherwise.

Pedross knew that continuing to indulge her was dangerous play. Nothing bound her to him, and she could turn on him at any time, either urged by some enemy or simply on a whim. But while she could shine, she'd shine. Pedross hadn't the heart to stifle such a genius for self-display and enjoyment. Likewise, if the Loyalists wanted to march, celebrating a Summerfair season to which they'd not been invited and which would be recoiling on them so cruelly, he'd not prevent them: they could march and sing the day's unfolding and closing, and greet two Valde refugees as though they'd been a thousand all decked with garlands.

For Pedross was very much aware that there'd come an end to it: the slow, jagged, bitter retreat to the coast, every stage of which he now spent most of his waking hours blocking out—plan, and counter-plan, and fallback, and the counter-attack afterward from the secure footing of the isles. There would be dark enough then for everybody; and Sua would learn what Poli knew, what it was to discover she wore the face of an enemy to everyone around her and to receive hatred as undeserved as this present adulation.

While she could shine, she would shine, and Pedross would interpose no shadow.

The mirrored walls of the audience hall extended the crowd to the limits of sight, as though this one room were the whole world. Pedross worked his way among the groups, exchanging what words he had to, until he could get to a window. They were dancing now, down below in the square—circle dances, two rings moving in opposite directions, suddenly dissolving and reforming like patterns that came and went in water. He watched for a few minutes, thinking about Sua, and Ardun, and how alike he felt them to be. Then he decided and called for attention. When only a few people turned he took the signal-pipe of the nearest of his bodyguards and blew piercing blasts until everyone was looking at him.

"Some of us are new here," he said, "and are slow to take up new ways. By your courtesy, those of you to whom these are old ways will teach us. I say all of Ardun will keep Blooming Festival—"

He had to pause because of the noise. It had been the right thing to say.

"—All Ardun will keep the Blooming Festival, and all strangers be free within the city, and all guests find the welcome Ardun always has given" (*all paying guests,* he thought, but did *not* say), "to celebrate this sign we've been given that the estrangement between Valde and Ardun of the Rose won't endure forever." He was watching his words: there were other Truthsayers than Sua present. "Perhaps, as the Greenleaf Federation contends, Ardun could survive alone as merely another city of men. But the Loyalists have insisted that it wouldn't be Ardun without the strangeness and the wonder that visits freely from no farther than beyond a river, the far side of a hedge. Without Valde, the welcome and the dreaming would have gone out of things, the city founded on trust and consent, on the Summerfair. . . ."

He was thinking about what this place would look like, whatever might be left of it, at the end of the retaliatory wars.

He went on, "The last Master, Domal Ai, always called it a marriage, the bond between Ardun and the Valde. I see now that is so." (He'd seen some odd marriages in his time, too, his parents' among them.) "For helping me to see this and for drawing the first of the Valde to return to us, I declare a prize of honor and of ten thousand marks. It is awarded to Mistress Sualiche."

Approval was immediate and uproarious. It didn't matter that the Valde were refugees from whatever turmoil Poli had apparently disappeared into nor that the end of Blooming Festival would bring no Summerfair, no welcome, no trade. It didn't matter that whoever might have deserved such a prize—whether Poli, Jannus, Simon, or some combination of

174

the three—it certainly wasn't Sua. It didn't matter in the least. Nobody wanted fairness. They wanted Sua.

Pedross went to where she was, nodded his guards to elbow him a bit of open space, and displayed her, meanwhile noticing that the two Valde were looking a bit brighter—the food, likely, but maybe the mood-weather was helping too. They might yet be of some use, if only for their information. Making his way toward the doors, he remanded the pair to the care of his chief steward—they of course could have practically anything in the city for the asking, but it might not occur to them to ask.

As he brought Sua past Simon, Pedross received from the mobile a look he couldn't interpret. He returned the look, wondering if there had been some news; but Simon disengaged and moved aside, and the squad of following bodyguards gave him the widest berth possible.

Turning within Pedross' guiding arm, Sua asked, "Why'd you do that?"

She didn't seem as pleased about the prize as he'd expected—mostly puzzled. He couldn't imagine any qualm about being undeserving: whatever she was given, she'd take. Lightly, he answered, "Why not?"

"That's not a reason. You do things for reasons."

So it was his liberality in question, not her worthiness. He said, "I wanted to."

"It's something you're after from Da or the troll, isn't it? Something—"

Genuinely astonished, Pedross stared at her. "No," he declared, mindful of Truthtell weighing the words, "nothing to do with them at all. I never even thought of it."

"Then what?"

"You've given me the Loyalists."

That got a meditative frown and a moment's silence. "All right," she said, accepting it. "And what else?"

"Isn't that enough?"

"I want to know what you expect to get back for it," said Sua, more Bremneri at the moment than Valde. "Two years' lease isn't cat-scraps. I want to know what you think you're buying."

"I'll think of something," replied Pedross, with a private smile, adding at once, "Child, money's the cheapest thing to

give. And it isn't even my money. Might as well do somebody some good before it all blows away. . . ."

She hadn't liked that *Child*. Well, he wasn't delighted to
look level at her chin. It kept the balance the way it ought to
be. He said, "Do you know the dance they're doing?" as they
descended to the portrait corridor, the dignitaries behind kept
from crowding by his buffering layer of bodyguards, the
bright square before them.

"Which one?" she responded, and it was a reasonable question.

He saw there was more than a single dance in progress
now. One was a precessing type, with lines advancing and retreating from each other and couples briefly pairing off into
turns. Another was the round dance he'd seen from above,
and still a third, beyond, that he couldn't discern the shape
of. Each moved to separate musics that nevertheless over-
lapped to a single complex rhythm that defied his fingers' attempt to keep time.

Pointing to the precessing dance, which seemed least intricate, he said, "That one."

The dancers stopped, finding themselves unexpectedly
joined by their enemy and overlord, who had held himself
aloof thus far from all their activities. But solemnly Sua held
out her hand, and solemnly Pedross took it, moving as the
pressure and balance directed; the music wove itself among
the other musics again, and, around them, the others found
places, and the air seemed luminous in the Aihall Square under the huge, round moon.

For Jannus everything had become very simple and altogether dreadful. The one intolerable thing had come to pass:
what had lurked behind years of nightmares or kept him
wakeful with its nearer approach.

He moved among the thick trees of Entellith in indirect
moonglow that made everything seem no more than shadows
made visible: unreliable, insubstantial.

He was not moving altogether at random: at last contact,
Poli had been within hearing of the cascades of Arant Dunrimmon. Therefore he kept to the steeper ground that bor-
dered the Red Mountains that Teks had once called Eastwall
and which. . . .

No!

The random eruptions of remembered facts, the accretion that encumbered his least thought, that meant nothing. He thrust it away each time it began, triggered by the shape of a leaf, a scurrying among the stones. He cared nothing whatever about mean rainfall or erosion rates of the spectrographic components of moonlight. But the figures kept popping up.

He never should have stopped the rapport sessions, no matter what she'd said. He couldn't get it sorted or keep it within bounds, and his head hurt unmercifully though he'd taken no conceptual input all day, or the day before. He couldn't, not and handle the inspeaking too. And yet the pressure had been growing all day, until he'd come to feel that whatever would have shut up the body's clamoring, he would have done instantly and without a moment's hesitation.

She couldn't do this to him, not again: he couldn't endure it, wouldn't tolerate it. And he had nothing left to sell or barter. He felt there was nothing left of him at all except the pain and the deluge of meaningless information falling and falling in sudden intervals of confusion.

He followed the sound of the river. Creatures he couldn't see fled from him. Increasingly, he kept his eyes shut: picking a path and then following it by touch; but there *were* no paths in Valde, everybody lost but the animals, which sensibly followed the same routines of feeding, drinking, and return (the habits of marmots, weasels, owls intruding before he could make it *shut up*). Animals needed to know where they stood and have a choice of predictable dangers (rabbits, three varieties of tree rats). Everybody made paths except Valde alone, out of sheer perversity.

He didn't need eyes, or paths either, beyond those he made by choosing them. All he needed were the sound of the river and solid things to touch, stand upon, hold to. Things with no names, no shapes beyond where he touched, no identities to topple another stack of associated facts. Insofar as he could, he stopped thinking.

He heard the sound of his own name spoken from just beside him. Startled profoundly, he straightened and stared in every empty avenue among the ranked trunks until the word was repeated and he realized it wasn't outside but within him: the Shai knocking at the door of his mind and asking admittance.

No!

It wasn't even a word, just a focused slap of refusal, and probably the implant didn't even notice it, because the knocking went on:—Jannus. Jannus. Jannus. Jannus—until he couldn't tolerate the sound, the repetition, and wrenched his mind around to the opposite polarity. He'd gotten no farther than—Don't—when the burst arrived, so compressed it barely escaped being a conceptual configuration.

—Thisisuseless, thisisdangerous, theriskisn'tworthit, goback.

—*Shut up.* I can't do both. *Get out.*

An emptiness, a silence. Jannus rested against a tree (yellow beech, deciduous; tree-ring dating) and tried to encompass the aftereffects of contact, find the center again.

If she couldn't hear him, she couldn't find him. If he couldn't keep calling, he couldn't make her come.

Maintaining the calling through the day had been no effort at all. He couldn't have stopped if he'd tried. But there was just no keeping the Shai out of it, the implant burrowed in beyond removal, part of the meat now, inescapable.

But it didn't matter, nor did anything else except keeping within sound of the river and continuing. The Shai didn't matter either, it was nothing to *do* with him except for his wretched toys that didn't even *work* and the other toys that worked too well and were worse.

—*Troll!*

It wasn't a summons but an accusation; nevertheless the Shai seized the chance to renew the contact with another burst.

—Inabouttwodays/wecantry/tolocateher/withtrance/wait

—Don't initiate contact. Don't reply. Leave me alone!

For all the savage anger impelling it, the formulation was clear, precise beyond mistaking. If the Shai couldn't hear the rage, nevertheless he had the absolute order. Again, silence.

Feeling as though he'd been picked up, shaken, and dropped sideways, Jannus tried to realign himself to the inspeaking but pieces of things kept intruding: not information but fragments of touch-memory, sound-memory, sensations of pressure and of release that struck his attempts into confusion. He tried deliberately to call up the day of her waking

178

but could get no nearer than the waiting, the ice of midwinter, the cold garden. These alone would resonate for him.

And yet he was quite certain she was alive; that, Singing or no Singing, she was hearing his attempts to regain control and waiting to be compelled to attend and come. Nothing had held her this long but his absolute refusal to let go. She wasn't going to do it to him again, leave him with most of his life bleeding away from the places where the separations were. Which were everywhere. Linkages beyond counting, each rooted tight to hold her there, bind her to him. . . .

He was Valde enough for that at least, he thought with great bitterness: to feel the parting as countless wounds, all memory altered retroactively: all joy transmuted and all sorrow become molten and searing. But a Valde wouldn't have had the sheer stubbornness to force her back or wait out the interval—even supposing, impossibly, such a Valde could have had the means, or the wherewithal to buy them. If she'd accepted one of her own she wouldn't be alive now. But then, maybe she wouldn't have needed recalling to begin with. Valde sometimes lived to be as old as forty, with luck and serene lives. And whatever he'd had to share with her, offer her, very little of it had been serene. . . .

The Choral Hating Society whose practice on Poli had given them the unanimity to catch themselves a freemaid and a Fair Witness. . . .

The lethargy of hanging in dark water. . . .

He couldn't concentrate. His hand was a fresh ache: he must have hurt it against the tree somehow. He stopped and just listened to the rush of the water like a distant sound of wind. And eventually it became simple again, the complexities and confusions fallen away. He went on, calling her to come—first words, but soon the inspeaking too, and then no need of words.

His feet slid on steep, pebbly ground, and he was so intent on keeping himself from a fall that he didn't at first realize he'd been pushed. But when he looked around, there was a slim shirtless man above him on the open slope. The face was utterly expressionless but the pose was one of challenge. And beyond, above, was a stir that resolved itself into smaller moving figures coming over or around rock outcroppings: a *hafkenna* then, and the man an adolescent of twelve or thirteen, their *hafra*.

(Peer competition; territoriality; systems of conserving the orphaned, comparative; dominance hierarchies.)

Shaking away the fresh cascade of information, Jannus turned aside. But the *hafra* glided each time Jannus moved, remaining before him, blocking the way.

"It's nothing to do with you," Jannus called hotly, then saw the unchanged, uncomprehending mask of the boy's face. No breathtalk.

The *hafkenna* were descending on Jannus' left in an irregular scampering line, silent except for humming murmurs accompanying inspoken exchanges. Their backs were the fragile narrow backs of children or young cats, showing every rib, every knuckle-lump of spine. The moonlight gave their skins a greyish cast against the mottled indigo ground. Small gaunt faces occasionally lifted a glitter of pale eyes toward him as they slid among rocks and tree trunks farther along the slope and below him.

He was being stalked.

After the one scanning look, Jannus ignored the pack because they only turned to their leader's spinning. He slapped the boy with an unformed contemptuous dismissal drawn from his smoldering fury at Valde itself, the baited trap that had lured Poli beyond safe limits, beyond contact, and then snapped shut.

The boy stiffened and leaned away, then rebounded in a downhill rush. But this time Jannus stepped aside, leaving his leg for the boy to trip over, which the *hafra* did, sliding down in an ungainly sprawl. And Jannus swung to meet the pack's expected snatching attack, cuffing them aside with no particular gentleness. Before he'd made them keep their distance he'd been bitten and slashed by short bone or flint knives he hadn't suspected until the first one was dragged along his arm, elbow to wrist.

He'd been too busy keeping some stooping child from hamstringing him to be concerned about what might coat the blades. And by the time the pack pulled back to regroup, the time for concern had already passed. If there'd been poison he'd have known it already.

Licking the back of a hand both bitten and scored, he

180

assessed the boy, who was now leaning against a rock taller than himself and rubbing a banged elbow. That the boy didn't return his stare, seeming to ignore him, didn't mean anything: cats looked away too before suddenly swinging to strike out. Valde were not so fixed on sight as the primary sense as people, *other* people.

As that further junkpile of facts dumped itself into his thinking Jannus was almost blinded by frustration and fury at himself, the useless mindless *stupidity* of it; and the pack sprang in again.

This time they clung and the blades jumped from one narrow hand to another faster than he could follow or reach in trying to disarm them. They had hurt each other badly, he and the pack, before he got free of them a second time.

Instantly he started for the *hafra* himself.

The pack was quicker, scrambling across a gully and forming up as a solid barrier between Jannus and the rock atop which the boy was perched at his ease. Jannus couldn't get at him. But a better way to hurt him suggested itself.

He hadn't been able to disarm the pack. But he could disarm the *hafra*. The boy's weapons were the *hafkenna* and Jannus could take them away from him. There was real satisfaction in contemplating that.

Jannus found a large rock of his own to lean against and put himself away from the bounding pain in his skull, the countless shallow wounds soaking through his clothes, and inspoke, *I'm louder than he is, and older, and stronger. What I take, I keep. I have a use for you, Ardun wants you more than he does. I want you. Come here.*

That had jarred the boy out of his insulting nonchalance: he abruptly sat straighter, and the pack was shifting like leaves caught in a windy corner.

Watching the boy with relentless malice, Jannus told them, *I can bring you out of the* [Singing]. (He hadn't an image for it: he called it "the-snatching-away.") *I can hold you against it. He can't. I can keep you fed all through growth-year, never hungry, never cold, never wet when it storms. And after you grow, he'd be gone. What I take, I hold. No Choosing would come, no change. Leave him. Come here.*

The pack divided. About a third of them started slowly uphill toward him. Some had blood black around their

181

mouths and most were visibly sore. Two stopped and wavered and were drawn back. The other three came to him, staring up into his face with their smeared masks lifted to the moonlight, patting at him as if perplexed that he didn't answer them, hear them.

He told the rest, *Why chase after one skinny kit that can't even keep you fed when you could each have a pack of grown men to chase at your heels because you're different, special, you know things the breathtalkers don't. Your own parents went to the ground, left you, you were scattered from your own, you hang onto each other but it's not the same, nobody knows how special you are, one by one. All he wants is the number of you, to swell him up. One more, one less, he doesn't care. When one of you was lost from the you-together-pursuing, did he go into the turning-away? You're hurt now because of him, because he doesn't care. I don't want you hurt. I do my own fighting. Come here. Come to me.*

All but three started up the hill then, and the tuneless humming intensified all around.

Jannus called to the boy, voice and inspeaking together, "*Get out.*"

The boy slid down from the rock into a stiff stance, and whatever replies he might be making had neither eloquence nor effect. With some interest Jannus waited to discover if the boy would come up and offer his skinny frame for the breaking, Jannus being too lame to chase him.

The boy whirled and took his three away among the trees, down among the vague spaces.

And Jannus considered his winnings, with their smeared idiot faces and wicked fingers, none standing taller than his shoulder. Now that he had them, he had to think what to do with them. There had been intense satisfaction in the getting. But the having was cold and pierced with sharp, stinging recollections of contact.

He couldn't take them. . . .

And he couldn't go. . . .

But he had to hold and order them into a movement, and settle himself to it immediately, because they were beginning to stir and hum short phrases among themselves like a community of shrill fowl not quite uneasy enough to rise in a burst.

Then it came to him, quite simply: he'd send them after Poli.

He began to make them understand what was wanted, describing Poli not as he was to the eye but the inwardness of her, so they'd know her when they came into contact: the new deliberation grafted onto the old aggressive suddenness, the quick turn of her moods, the reaching, always the reaching—

The knives all went home, deep, the pointed shoulders crowding him against the rock, pinning him to his astonishment, so the wet blades could be jerked free to strike again.

When they stepped back from him he fell, and the surprise went with the blood. Then the practiced knives returned, and before the cutting was finished the *hafra* had come back with his three to carry away what they could use, leaving the rest strewn at random around the blackening hillside where nothing moved except the shadows shifting by slow degrees opposite the moon's descent.

A little before dawn the incendiary implant was triggered from far away. A burst of stellar incandescence blazed below the boulder until its overhanging projections ran and dripped, and both low furze and the high boughs of the nearest trees were crisped in an instant and then consumed. When the fury of the blaze ended, rock congealed and cracked in cooling. There was nothing below the boulder but a few shapeless blobs of dull metal and a faceted green stone that teetered and then rolled a crooked course into the nearest gully, where it lodged and remained among the springing weeds.

Somebody was hurt.

Somebody was hurt and afraid and anxious. Perhaps it was herself. Poli couldn't be sure; because someone was also hungry and delighted and comfortable and dying and sliding bloody into the world of breath: all together and at once.

The daysinging had been somehow magnified into a complex unity of everything and everyone it contained and the whole of it was beautiful beyond any expectation: accepting and affirming in passion all the life it encompassed into an overriding we-together-at-this-moment, a fusion beyond time or sequence, a present unending as long as it lasted, containing no awareness of anything beyond itself, either before or to come.

It was the ecstatic fusion of inner and other: the full impact of entire loving, infinitely prolonged.

It was, at last, the Singing.

Poli remained fully able to perceive her immediate surroundings. But whatever she felt or knew about those surroundings had no priority even for herself. Someone's satisfaction or someone's sliding by degrees into the final turning-away had exactly as much importance as her own attitudes and perceptions. All were woven into the whole, and only the whole had meaning. She had become the space framed within an open doorway.

When the first rapture faded, she found herself in a glade in late afternoon, the trees' awareness her clock. She was in the near company of strangers: four adults, and five young children with muddy knees. None of the adults was a parent to the children. When the children raised an immediate and unanimous howl of hunger, one of the adults, an Awiro, bolted for a cairn of three stacked stones and came up with a handful of limp onion stalks and some lumps of odorous meat which she jammed in the children's hands. Poli was meanwhile inspecting first her wrist, then the nearest ground, searching for the quartz bangle so she could both reassure Jannus and make him *shut up*. There was an expectation around her that made her know this was the least breathing-pause and would last only until some stronger gust of feeling swept it away.

The bangle was gone. She understood then that the urgent calling wasn't going to end, and she understood why. She had to make contact somehow and let him know he must *stop*—

And a new spasm of the Singing caught her up and even his calling became part of it, but balanced and woven among all the other voices, with no personal connection to her above any other.

Her second emergence into isolation was even briefer. From an exhausted tranquility she was snatched in the dark by an ambush of violent connectedness: a seizure so thorough and demanding she felt it as attack but so close she couldn't fend it off. She was jolted into a private rapport against which she had no defenses, a turning jagged loop of echo and re-echo like a bruising fall down a rocky slope, momentum beyond her controlling. She didn't know whether the Singing was renewed then or later.

Nor did she know when it passed. She had collapsed into sleep that was an annihilation, without dreams.

It was thirst that woke her, and intense loneliness. Chilled and shivering, with the morning dew dried on her face, she found her way unsteadily to the nearest water, a small cold brook. She could reach across and thump the heel of her hand down on the far side: anybody who could drown in *that*, she thought, deserved to.

Thirst at last satisfied, the other need took priority: more urgent than her need for food or physical warmth, akin to both. To wonder was to know: she was surrounded by an interconnected lattice of rapport—light, tentative feather touches of contact: stiff, careful of bruises. The center was *that* way, the way the warm was, bounced back to her from others who were nearer.

Any lump in the ground was apt to make her stagger like a newborn fawn. That reminded her, and she tried to reach out toward Oflernan and Callea, to learn how they'd fared. But she couldn't summon the energy even to stretch the distance she could see across. It felt like the trembling collapse of overstrained muscles. Trance was utterly unthinkable. She scuffed through the leaves, crossing the distance between one tree and the next and then pausing to lean before going on. Into the loose lattice of touches she sent a wondering whether anybody was in contact with the pair, but nobody was in much better case than herself except the insingers at the center who of course had floated on the Singing like so many ducks, or like fishes, rather, that could breathe what surrounded, supported, and fed them. Insingers were never *out* of the Singing. They couldn't understand what all the fuss was about.

Poli inspoke to them, *You should have enjoyed harvest season in a riverstock*, and got in return friendly incomprehension at Haffa's insistence on treasuring scars and believing that those who lacked them had missed a treat and were to be resentfully pitied. Haffa were always preoccupied with things far beyond knowing, either in time or in distance. *Now* was quite enough to handle for anybody not too numb-dumb to know it fully, thank you kindly. . . .

The insingers were always the center, enclosed, insulated, and protected with all manner of concern because through their fragile, resilient sensibilities every daysinging was fully, continuously noticed and affirmed and given meaning, all of it interrelated, balanced, and cherished.

They were the weavers of tangible things, too: Poli began to pass the raised, protected sheds where the twice-annual shearings were deposited, brought either from Lifganin or the meadowlands between the forests. The sheds should have been full, in spite of people dropping by to collect their share to card and clean and twist into yarn to be returned to the center for dyeing and weaving. Everything came and went from the center, which alone never moved.

But the sheds stood empty, or nearly so. The first-warm shearing had apparently been about the fiasco she'd assumed.

Assorted confirmations reached her. Awiro were always as wild as a starving *hafkenna*, and when the Singing had loosed them from their lifelong exile they'd arrived wilder still, eating everything, disrupting the cycles maintained regarding game, especially the first hatchings of ground-nesting birds; leering at the *hafrae* until every *hafkenna* in Entellith was in a constant jealous flap, and not two handfuls of wool among the bunch of them. . . .

And even the exasperation was accepting, amused, annoyed, like Sparrowhawk explaining how one entire pie had disappeared while Sua had coincidentally been passing through the kitchen.

This was what Poli had hoped for, needed, and failed to find in Lifganin—indeed, anywhere. The feeling of being connected to everyone around her, known as she knew them, all knowing the daysinging together in casual awareness, without effort or strain, as it happened about them.

If the awesome rapture of the Singing was what it cost to find this ease, it was very nearly worth it, though she suspected she'd never come to plunge into it with the unhesitating enjoyment of an insinger, or even some of the children she knew were about her, converging. It never hurt while it lasted, she'd found: only its ending hurt, the rediscovery of separateness.

We are turning, she reflected, *into a nation of drunks*, and got various responses: most cheerful as assenting shrugs, but some less so. These were more distant, indistinctly relayed or faintly inspoken. These battered voices came from the outermost fringes and they reminded Poli again of Callea, of Oflernan's calm hopeless drifting, numb almost to the point of descent into the turning-away, the withdrawal that ended in death. But they too were coming, those outskirters: at the center was fire, food, company within sight, within touch, the fundamental warmths. Away were only the dark and the cold. When Poli asked about the pair again, the other outskirters either didn't hear her or were too indifferent and self-absorbed to reply.

She could see people now, stumbling along as she was doing. They gravitated toward each other and there was much holding and patting, leaning into mutual support, sharing the strengths of their weakness. Little breathtalk, and not much inspeaking either, just presence and company, occasional outbursts of silliness or anxiety about some absent child being sought for, but neither very intense nor very lasting. Everybody was simply too tired. . . .

With an inward sigh Poli did what she'd been avoiding, putting off: attending to learn what Jannus was about. Generally she took about as much conscious notice of the flow of his selfsinging as she did of her own heartbeat: it was there, and could be attended to at will, and it was her life; but she seldom thought about it as long as the rhythms continued undisturbed and unremarkable.

For a mercy, the calling had stopped. At first she supposed that he was still in such a sleep as hers had been, like being hit with a brick, oblivion.

Unconcerned, she'd come among the conical hives and bake ovens at the perimeter of the large clearing before she tried for a clearer contact. Even then, her first thought was that he'd had recourse to some new concoction the mobile had cooked up on demand. But nothing could produce such absolute absence except absorption into the implant link. But she'd wakened with the dawning and already the air was warming; she'd never known him to maintain link for so long. But then again, she'd never known he possessed the irresistible volume and intensity of a farspeaker until circumstances had roused him to try.

Still only puzzled, she accepted the hot food the insingers were handing out, feeling mildly guilty she'd brought nothing herself to add to the general supplies. Most people, she noticed, had gathering sacks they emptied on arrival. The three-stone cairns, she understood now, were for emergencies, not to be touched otherwise, free to all comers.

When she finished eating she volunteered to collect fallen branchwood and note any damaged or greedily encroaching trees for future cutting. She didn't find much. The others had been right: the Awiro, the frequent concentration of people in this immediate area, were stripping the local forest bare, disrupting the usual cycles of supervision and selective harvest. She found clumps of raw dirt where bulbs or plants had been roughly grubbed up, disintegrating nests, and a few tumbled piles of bones where Valde were going back to the ground.

And all the while she was waiting for the familiar shock of Jannus' returning presence. In spite of her lassitude, the conviction was growing that something was dreadfully wrong.

When she returned to the clearing, people were going, scattering back toward their own accustomed places carrying a coal or a burning twig to nurse on the way home and rekindle their own fires. And the mood was harsher, darker: the outskirters were arriving, drawn irresistibly to the lessened isolation by the same hunger Poli had known. And there were seekings for people still uncontacted, ungathered—children, mostly, but some late finding themselves alone, calling for replies that hadn't come. A farspeaker, slowest to recover, was seconding, with her strong shout, those voices whose hopefulness was greatest, repeating one, then another, of the intimate callings at a volume that felt like the push of hard wind.

Poli began inspeaking the demand, *Who knows anything of my lar, the* sa'marenniath *farspeaker? Who knows anything of my lar since the Singing ended?*

The outskirters had heard him, together with a cacophonous *als'far* arising from the Noisy-deaf between the rivers, each drowning out the other by turns, a terrible turbulence. But the Noisy-deaf had quieted to its usual grumbling at last, and the unhearing farspeaker too, and that was all they knew of it.

The nearby folk knew nothing, hadn't heard him at all, though some Awiro knew who he was, that she was lar to. . . .

Her need and insistence were finally able to win the attention of the fresh farspeaker who'd taken over when the first one had tired. This farspeaker conveyed the sense of an older man, more deliberate and cadenced in his inspeaking. And about noon he got a reply from the edge, relayed from the farthest of the *hafkennae*. And Poli learned then how Jannus had contested with a hafra for his pack and won, and then had expected them to seek out and recover his own lar, and lost.

They'd flown at him in a rage of jealous indignation and betrayal and cut him down. Of course, naturally, they had.

Poli sat on the ground repeating helplessly, "Oh, my dear, how *could* you—" knowing at once how he could, *would* have committed such a monstrous foolishness. And yet she said, "Oh, my dear—" and all the color went out of the day, and none of the continuing drifts of tired laughter could touch her. She was alone, turned in another direction.

IV

———◆———

THE FAR SIDE
OF THE FIRE

Pedross sorted through the stack of charts until he found the one he wanted, a city map of Ardun he'd had made up. Landsmen all, no Arduner had done more than keep district lists to make sure all the leases were paid to date. Pedross never felt comfortable until he had an overview to put his elbows on, to see it whole and all its parts in proper connection and subordination.

Running a finger down the line of Arant Dunrimmon and up the angle of the Morimmon, he sketched a channel connecting the two, parallel to the Thornwall but beyond it: on the Valde side. It had been flooded there anyway, while the rivers had been high during the spring runoff. A locked channel, *there*, which could be opened to let the rivers meet and become a moat, and Ardun would become an island: and Pedross knew a great deal about the methods of defending islands. Walls *there* and *there*, on the opposite banks, and a new bridge upriver from Sunrise Bridge. . . .

He took a pen, dipped it, and began sketching in lines.

"You'll lose the isles," commented Simon flatly, having finally responded to Pedross' summons. "You've lost the Windwards, and now there's this trouble on Blackrock. And there are two letters from Camarr you ought to see." He set down a pile of papers on the chart. Pedross pushed them aside and *x*'ed in another wall. Simon continued, "If you lose the isles, you lose it all. They'll be in the middle of the usual cycles of civil war Ashai brought them out of, either among themselves or resisting reabsorption into the empire, when this thing breaks. There'll be no way to reunify them in time, not even enough to handle the waves of refugees—"

"This month?" Pedross shot back without looking up. "This year? I'll *see* to the isles, as soon as I can: throw that self-styled duke Stefan out of the Windwards—"

"And Blackrock? And Camarr? How many wars do you propose to undertake at the same time? They're held together by dread, greed, and promises as it is. The longer you amuse yourself up here—"

"I said, I'll *see* to the isles," interrupted Pedross as a steward and two pages arrived with trays of food they set down on the clearest end of the long table. Collecting a hot sausage roll, Pedross sat on the table's edge and continued, "As soon as Ardun's been put in a defensible condition, the immediate things at least begun—"

"Outwalls, three to four years, if they're stone," said the mobile dispassionately, touching the lines Pedross had inked around Ardun's perimeters. "Fifteen months, at least, to construct a serviceable wooden palisade; and Valde *do* comprehend the uses of fire, you know. . . . And what's this—a moat? You think you're going to get engineering crews working past the Thornwall without two years' preliminary debate?" Simon shook his head slowly. "And then there's the morale problem, and the fact that Arduners are entertainers, artists, merchants, negotiators—anything, everything but fighters, which they have *never* been: they've always hired it done."

Pedross heard it out, all the reasons why he could not do what he meant to do. When at last Simon paused, Pedross set down his wine cup and met the mobile's eyes. "Ardun's mine. I didn't inherit it. I won it myself. It's not going to fall if I can prevent it."

"Have you been listening at all?" rejoined Simon sharply, frowning. "Ardun is not defensible. It was never built to be defensible. It will take three or four years to make it defensible, and you simply don't have three or four years before the Valde turn outward against you. If people are here when that happens, they'll be lost as well—a needless and perhaps crucial waste. Save what can be saved and let the rest go." When Pedross merely continued to look at him, refusing to argue,

Simon remarked slowly, "It has a bearing on the Rule of One, what you're proposing to do. You're aware of that?"

"I don't care two beans about the Rule of One."

"That's increasingly obvious," replied the mobile tightly.

Finishing his wine, Pedross continued, "And I'm not Jannus, balanced on the Shai's pleasure with a long way to fall. And you can't just put me aside and put some copy in my place, the way you did to Secolo. . . . I want you to prepare another list of questions for Raimond to interview those Valde again. If I'm going to send a strike force into Valde, I want to know what I can expect."

"If you're going to *what?*" rejoined the mobile, visibly startled.

"You heard me. If I need to buy fifteen months, then that's the way to do it. Disrupt them *now*: before they're ready, or armed, or organized. I'm going to send a strike force up the Morimmon to Morgaard Vale and hit them as hard as I possibly can. And you're going to lead it. You," Pedross added calmly, "I can replace."

"No," declared the mobile, the witch, the terrifier of pages: "I'd be killed. I am not expendable."

"It needs a *sa'farioh* in charge, to give the orders. Otherwise, there's no chance of surprise, of catching them all massed in the one place. None of the strike force will know what's intended, and I'll make some other pretext for sending them. But I have to have a *sa'farioh* in charge. You're the only one I have at hand."

"No. I won't do it."

"Then what use are you?" inquired Pedross, casually, coldly, again meeting the old man's eyes.

The worst threat, Pedross had realized, wasn't of punishment or any physical harm: those things must be meaningless, to a mobile of the Shai. The worst threat was to ignore him, refuse his service. For there was no rival even approaching Pedross' stature to whom the mobile could go in the limited time remaining. The worst threat to the Shai must be that of finding his aid irrelevant, rejected, and himself impotent to alter the course of human events, with nothing left to deflect the boredom of eternity.

Wiping his hands clean, preparing to go back to working on his planned defenses, Pedross said, "The expedition will leave in three days. With you, or without you. If it's without, don't come anywhere near me again—not in this face or any other. There'll never be a time I won't know you for what you are. . . . Raimond's scheduled that interview for the thirteenth hour. He'll need the questions as soon as you can get them ready. Listen in on what's said and report back to me afterward." Pedross put dishes on the map to control its tendency to re-roll itself and heard the mobile leaving.

If Ardun was to send some sort of harmless-seeming embassy upriver to the Summerfair, Pedross was thinking, Sua would be a good one to ask what form it might take. Pedross had found her instincts in such matters infallible so far and intended to make use of them. Moreover, he felt that the risks he was committing himself to for Ardun's sake, his commitment of his own fortunes to those of the City of the Rose, were deserving of a reward. And at the moment, he couldn't think of anything he'd enjoy more than the deferred pleasure of Sua's intimate company. He felt he'd earned it. Besides, Sua was lucky. If he got close enough, there might prove to be enough luck for two; and he was quite certain he was going to need whatever luck he could get.

He went to the door, called a runner, and dispatched her to locate Sua and deliver his summons.

Simon returned to Pedross in under an hour and told him there was imminent, immediate danger of an assassination attempt which none of Pedross' marines would be any help at all in preventing. He refused to give any precise details, except that it involved fire, that it hadn't been determined from which of Pedross' enemies the threat arose, and that the only sure way of preventing the threat from being carried out was for the mobile never to be farther than arm's reach from Pedross—not even for a pair of seconds.

There were some ways Pedross didn't trust Simon, but matters of intelligence and fundamental security were not among them. Pedross accepted the warning even though it required him to also accept being tied, wrist to wrist, with the mobile by a bit of red cord to prevent inadvertent separations, Pedross having an unfortunate habit of lunging into unpremeditated motion. Simon told him that the matter would be settled before Pedross' deadline for departure, one way or the other. Pedross accepted that too; as Simon reminded him repeatedly, no mobile had ever told anyone a direct lie.

It at once demonstrated itself to be an awkward, frustrating, and frequently embarrassing arrangement, but Simon assured Pedross that absolutely nothing else would serve. That he was believed relieved him greatly: it gave him at least a breathing space to deal with the imminent peril.

"Is it Granddda Troll?" Pedross muttered the following morning, ill-tempered after a night sharing his bed with his chief of security—plainly not at all the company he'd had in mind.

"It's possible," conceded Simon, and reluctantly agreed that the cord could be undone at least long enough for Pedross to be dressed. Simon kept a hand on either Pedross' neck or hand the whole time. It would take no more than an instant's inattention. He felt much better when the cord was again securely tied and took care to make his presence as unobtrusive as being tied to a desperate old man could possibly be for a young, active, and impatient one.

Fortunately Pedross was ambidextrous. Breakfast wasn't as much of a farce as it might have been.

When Sua arrived for the start of the morning's business, Pedross explained to her that he was going to send some sort of aid to the Summerfair to help settle the troubles the Valde were currently going through, and that he'd wanted to consult her about what form that aid might best take.

Instantly, Sua declared "*Food!*"

Having commended the suggestion at considerable length, Pedross turned away to other matters, letting Simon set up the details: which really meant letting Simon articulate the necessary lies of omission, avoiding any mention of why a mission of mercy would require such a considerable escort of reliable, disciplined marines. Simon did it. He had no choice.

During this process Sua laid her hand tentatively on Simon's, remarking lightly, "Is it a handfasting?"

"It's necessary," said Simon, and tucked the bound hand and wrist under the table, the abrupt motion winning him an annoyed glance from Pedross.

And later, during midmeal, Sua commented softly, "You look sad. Can I help?"

"Yes," replied the mobile, after a moment's thought. "Stay away from me! Get out, Sua: run."

"All right," she said, pushing back her chair. "Until when?"

"You'll know when," he responded, then added, less obscurely, "I'll send word. Myself. And not a factorage: someplace else."

"I'll do it right, this time," she assured him, and circled quickly and unobtrusively around the side tables.

Simon was relieved when she was gone. He protested inwardly to the Shai—The fault's in the source: is the fascination for that child *my* doing? The fault's in the source!—but the Shai ignored him.

After midmeal he and Pedross retired to a conference room to discuss privately such matters as which division of marines should be sent, and how many barges, and how many big steam-powered paddlewheelers to draw them. They settled on three steam packets, each drawing five barges loaded with bread and carrying marines ignorant of their eventual role in the journey upriver. This consultation went well, partly because Simon interposed no further arguments against the planned foray he was supposed to head.

For the Shai had endorsed Pedross' preemptive attack. He also endorsed the mobile's leading it, provided that Simon saw to it the force inflicted the greatest possible damage before they were themselves overwhelmed: but they had to be overwhelmed, with no more than a couple perhaps escaping to bear news of the disaster back downriver. But, preferably, none at all. Only a silence, and then the sudden retaliation against the unprotected and unready city from beyond the Thornwall. Anything else, Pedross might yet contrive to interpret as a success. If Pedross refused to see that Ardun couldn't be defended, the Shai would demonstrate it for him, unmistakably. If he wouldn't leave, he'd be driven out: back to his proper sequence of concerns.

Simon had very few choices left, and they were becoming fewer by the hour. The Shai would tolerate little argument, and no overt opposition, from any of his mobiles. Simon did whatever was necessary, and whatever Pedross told him to, without any demur so long as those things could be done tied wrist-to-wrist with the Master of Andras and of Ardun, whom the Shai did *not* consider dispensable. He sent out streams of runners. And Pedross, to his credit, lost his temper that afternoon only at those who deserved it and made no direct complaint about the cord.

The guildmistress of the bakers' guild responded to the summons sent her and explained at length how bread could be baked to stay good through more than a week's journey upriver, and what it would cost, and how soon it could be done in the quantities required. She expressed herself as delighted at the thought of so generous a gesture toward Valde on Ardun's part—obviously, a Loyalist—and if she noticed the cord or considered it all odd, she at least had the sense not to say so.

The next conference was with the commander of the chosen division, who assured Pedross the men under his command could be ready to move at sundown, let alone sunrise two days hence. After he was dismissed with his orders, they met with the three rivermasters whose paddlewheelers Pedross was proposing to lease. Of all the folk so far, only these three rivermasters showed the least consciousness that even a mission of mercy could be dangerous on a river untraveled by anything larger than a raft in almost seventy years, using charts all but hopelessly outdated: all rivermen knew that rivers were living things, changing their courses and the location of their bars and shallows almost daily, to say nothing of the changes worked during a full lifetime. And the Morimmon was, moreover, a river interdicted to foreign travel by the Valde themselves. The rivermasters delicately made clear that they wanted no part of what some people might ignorantly interpret as an invasion, without firm assurance that the Valde would not strenuously object to their packets' passage. Firm assurance, of course, required a Truthsayer; but Sua, it developed, was not to be found.

Pedross had to settle for a Bremneri scribe called away from magistrates' sessions, and chose the words of his assurance with extreme care: obliged, this time, to do his own lying, though what he said was accurate enough—it was all in knowing how and what to evade.

"Where's Sua?" Pedross asked Simon, while they were all waiting for the most recent charts of the Morimmon to be located and delivered from Archives.

"I don't know," replied Simon, reading through the terms

of the proposed lease agreement. The rivermasters were insisting on a damage clause which, if invoked, would have rebuilt their packets twice over, as well as hazard pay for master, steersman, and crew. Simon wondered if it was worth trying to argue them down to a more reasonable figure: agreeing would only tend to confirm their suspicions, which were entirely justified. He decided Pedross could worry about that.

"Find her," directed Pedross as the chief archivist tottered in with the charts.

Obediently Simon dispatched runners to every likely place except Dan's small household at Smith Point; and all the runners reported back, before daymeal, that Sua had still not been located.

During daymeal a man named Territ requested immediate audience for himself and a friend. As his friend was Marlena Singer and Territ himself head of one of the Seven Families and a Loyalist besides, Pedross granted the audience, though the fish course was just being brought in.

Word of the expedition had gotten around even faster than Simon had expected—Simon suspected the head of the bakers' guild had been busy, since morning, with other things than bread. In any case, Territ proposed that the expedition take along a few members of the Loyalist persuasion, who, after all, had the greatest concern for reestablishing good relations with Valde, to say nothing of humanitarian interests. "Meaning no criticism, Master Pedross," he explained, "none of your people know Valde as we in Ardun have come to know them over the centuries. It would be in both our interests if we could be included in your planning and perhaps help prevent the expedition's intent being misinterpreted."

Pedross accepted the suggestion with unfeigned enthusiasm: a body of Loyalists would render the foray that much more innocuous, and, when the time came to act, they'd be no great trouble to merely push aside. As Simon had remarked once, Arduners had never been fighters themselves, and that inexperience showed in Territ's overestimation of how much deterrent he and his companions would constitute to any overt hostilities. Too, his context included only an ambitious new Master of Ardun who'd presided over the bloodless annexation of Lifganin and the Fallows and had still to learn the economic facts of life in Ardun. He certainly wasn't envisioning a preemptive attack on an enemy massing at Morgaard Vale for what would eventually become a war of wholesale annihilation waged by Valde against all non-Valde: probably even the Valde themselves weren't aware of what the present ingathering portended.

Pedross offered Territ wine poured from his own carafe, and they discussed details and numbers while Marlena Singer performed three songs gratis and a capella, graciously pointing out that it was still Blooming Festival, when she was accustomed to sing just for the joy of it.

Simon concentrated on cutting his fish one-handed: he had a poor ear for music, and concerns far more pressing.

While Marlena sang, the mobile continued the ongoing argument with the Shai he'd been carrying on, intermittently, all day:

—The Rule of One is fallible, and its implementation based on predictions that are only approximations, not certainties. And you yourself can be wrong. What a mass of error that can add up to! You expected a tidestorm of war to be set off by the looting of the Tek keeps, by the Tek tools and weapons falling into lowlander control. It never came. It didn't happen, Shai, and everything done in that false expectation, all the deaths and conniving and backstabbing alliances, remains utterly unjustified by anything more than "that it seemed a good idea at the time." The Rule of One is fine, if you're a Tek dealing with Teks, considering nothing but a Tek's rigid sense of order and as rigidly self-limited possibilities. But lowlanders are different. They're not so easily predictable as Teks, not in the mass and certainly not as individuals. The Rule of One, supported by the best approximations you can formulate, can nevertheless be just plain wrong, and *has* been. Such a flawed conception doesn't deserve anybody's service and isn't capable of justifying the murder of a mouse. Jannus knows it. I know it. Why don't you know it?

And he argued—I'm a living being, complete in myself. I have as much right to live as anybody, and to try to preserve my life any way I can. You have no right to kill anybody for no other reason than that they're inconvenient, or get in your way. Valde do that. Teks did that. Are you willing to justify yourself by standards that haphazard and egocentric?

And he argued—The fault's in the source. Another mobile would feel the same as I do. If you dispose of me, you'll have no mobile at all, and what becomes of your precious Rule of One then? Are you going to start trying to intervene among the lowland nations in person? What will you do if you can't send out mobiles? Better to come to terms with the one you've got.

Simon argued because he was *not* going to lead the expedition up the Morimmon, *not* going to suicide for the convenience of the Rule of One as interpreted and enforced by the Shai.

As long as he kept Pedross close, the Shai couldn't signal the incendiary without destroying them both. And the Shai could not afford to lose Pedross just now, the way things were. As long as the cord held, Simon was safe.

He had, he judged, one more day to persuade the Shai to abandon either his conviction of the expendability of mobiles, his endorsement of Pedross' plan, or the Rule of One.

After the daymeal, Pedross jerked at the cord to call Simon's attention and said, "Let's go up to the tower. I want to talk to you."

"We can talk here," replied the mobile, still idly spooning at his custard.

"Now," said Pedross, rising; and, perforce, the mobile had to rise as well unless he wanted to try a wrestling match in front of all the guests and the servants.

Pedross managed to keep silent all the way to Simon's tower chamber. But once the door was shut, and he was perfectly certain they couldn't be overheard, Pedross rounded on the man he was tied to and let his anger show.

"No excuses, no failures," he said levelly. "When we go back downstairs, you're going to send word, to the *right* place, this time, and get Sua here within one hour. Is that understood?"

"I don't know where she is," replied the mobile. "I don't know what makes you imagine otherwise."

Recent dealings with Truthsayers had been teaching Pedross just and how evasion need be no broader than the least fraction of a hair and yet go undetected. He said, "You mean, you don't know exactly what corner of what room she may be in at the moment. Give me the most likely place for Sua to have gone, that you *didn't* send runners to."

The mobile looked down his long nose at him awhile, then remarked, "Could we sit down? Old bones—"

"Don't give me *old bones*: not you. Answer me."

The mobile raised his free hand to rub his eyes. "I'm tired, Pedross. I'm not exempt from that."

Glaring, Pedross dragged out a bench with his foot and the mobile settled onto it with every motion of hesitant, feeble age, which deceived Pedross not at all.

Pedross demanded, "You know what I think? I think this damn cord is just a ruse to keep me away from Sua. I didn't think it was possible, but I have eyes, and when I think to look, I see what's to be seen. You're after her yourself. Tell me: have you bedded her yet?"

"It's not like that at all," denied the mobile wearily; and Pedross waited because, as far as he knew, no mobile had ever told him a direct lie. Pedross wasn't going to act on his suspicions and cut the cord until he was absolutely sure what it was tying him to, and from.

"I have an . . . interest in Sua," continued Simon, "which I inherited. I don't want her hurt, or made unhappy. Rather like a daughter. I wouldn't want her to take a weasel for a pet either, but if she was determined to do it, I—"

"So I'm a weasel," interrupted Pedross. His hand was on his belt-dagger and the impulse to use it, not on the cord but on Simon himself, became all but irresistible.

"I withdraw the implied metaphor. I merely mean that you've acquired skills with women over the years. Caring for them, unfortunately, is not one of your skills. The Lady Ketrinne of Quickmoor bore you no sons, and you turned her away with a pension."

"That was the agreement," replied Pedross curtly. "And what business is it of yours who my bed-partners may be, or how I contract with them? Was your relationship with my mother full of such remarkable 'caring' that you have the unbounded gall to criticize *me*?" It was the first sime since he'd realized the Ashai/Secolo/Simon continuity that Pedross had mentioned the profound grievance he'd carried against his father almost as long as he could remember; he could feel himself flushing.

He would have whirled away, but the cord caught him and reminded him, and he wasn't yet prepared to risk cutting it. His whole arm ached from being held still all day.

"There was no caring," admitted the mobile, rubbing at his eyes again, "and not even an agreement that she understood or had any say about. She knew nothing of what she was getting, save a rising baymaster who could help her hold Camarr. I'll offer no excuses for my treatment of her. It seemed the proper thing to do at the time," commented the mobile with a peculiar smile, "serving the best interests of all concerned. But I know more than I knew then. And to the degree my . . . inclination toward expediency has contributed toward yours, I regret it. I'm sorry to have hurt you so, out of sheer imperceptive ignorance. I won't ask your pardon—"

"That's good," Pedross broke in, "because you're not likely to get it, not matter how many faces you go through."

"—but remember that I said it—that in this one regard, at least, I'm sad to learn what I've made of you. Remember it, Pedross. It may help, eventually—"

"I say, this cord is a ruse," interrupted Pedross, avoiding any more pointless probing of such old wounds to return to the matter at hand. "Unless you convince me otherwise in one quick hurry, I'm going to cut it and find—"

"Don't do that!" broke in Simon urgently, closing his hand over the cord where it bound their wrists together, his fingers against the blade of Pedross' knife. "Sua's down at the Point, I think, with her sisters and Dan Innsmith. Unless I personally send her a summons, she won't come. And if you try to take her, you'll have a fight on your hands that. . . . But you know Smiths. You know she's out of practical reach."

"Send for her, then," Pedross ordered tightly.

"Perhaps. But first answer me one question, Pedross, as truly and completely as you can."

"Why?"

"Because I ask it," responded the mobile quietly.

"What, then?"

"Tell me," requested the mobile, "what there is that you'd die for—not just risk it: actually *die*, knowing that was what it'd mean—just on the chance of protecting it, keeping it safe."

It wasn't the sort of question Pedross had expected, or recalled ever being asked, or even ever having asked of himself. Slowly he lifted his knife and settled down on the bench, trying absently to find some way to position his arm that didn't make his elbow ache and then abandoning the effort. "Any ship I commanded, while I was aboard," he replied, frowning, trying to be absolutely precise. "Any isle I'd promised protection to and which had kept faith with me. And Ardun, I suppose. Yes—Ardun, too."

He looked up to learn Simon's reaction and found the mobile regarding him with unmistakable sadness and what might have been pity.

"What's the matter with that?" Pedross flared, furious to have been honest and yet receive such a response.

"Nothing at all, as far as it goes," Simon told him. "If there'd been even one person among that list, I would have sent the summons. But you might as well cut the cord, because I'm not going to send it."

In an instant, Pedross had freed himself. He had the door open when the blast of heat hit him. He launched himself in a sprawling dive down the spiral stairs but managed to catch himself against the first curve of wall. Flames were pouring out of the open door above, which had itself begun to smoke.

The whole tower was going to go: seven stories of wood floors, ancient beams thicker than a mast-base, set into the layers of brick: oh yes, Pedross thought, the tower would go. In fact, it would be a miracle if it were only the tower.

Pedross dashed down the stairs and grabbed the tower guards, giving one orders to spread the alarm and evacuate the place, sending the other to alert the duty squad and have the duty officer fetch from the barracks every available pair of hands to strip the Aihall, get as much as possible of the movable contents out into the square. Smoke billowed tentatively around the edges of the tower door as he slammed it. Then he ran off in search of the chief steward, who would know what the really precious things were.

There was no miracle. It was a clear, bright night, and the evening tidestorm wind was still blowing. Before long, the flames had burst from the top of the tower and licked out of windows on the top three stories. The fire had all the encouragement ample air, moving fast, could provide.

Pedross stood in the middle of the Rose Way, keeping things coordinated. He sent away the five pumpers that were dragged up, when he saw the pressure couldn't lift the stream of water higher than the seventh story of the Aihall proper, to say nothing of the tower. When the tower floors began collapsing, pulling in the brickwork, Pedross gave a deadline to the eighth-floor relay crew passing out chairs and tables and manhandling wardrobes and large chests down makeshift skids laid on the stairs, and began instead concentrating on the lower floors.

The chief steward had to be dragged out bodily when smoke began appearing at seventh-story windows, and the same treatment was applied to the chief archivist, frantic at the utter disruption of centuries worth of filing. The silly old hen should be glad they were getting the paper out at all, and they would all be lucky if half of it didn't blow away. . . . Pedross shoved somebody to redirect two men carrying a rolled carpet and lay it on top of the mound of scrolls and loose sheets. Filing could wait.

When the fire reached the ground floor the chief steward cried out, "The portraits!" and made a dash at the central arch, which was filled with brilliant shifting smoke; but, obedient to Pedross' orders, the cordon of marines Pedross had thrown around the piled treasure caught him and carried him back, shouting and weeping. Collecting himself, the steward came to Pedross, who said curtly "Not now."

"But it's the portraits of all the Masters—"

"—back to the Laying of the Stone. I know it. Now shut up and let me work."

"But there are some quite near the door, almost in reach. I could—"

Pedross jerked a thumb at the nearest of the duty squad, who clasped arms around the old man and carried him, sensibly, over to where innumerable bottles of wine had been laid out in ranks on the stones of the square.

That struck Pedross as a good idea. He sent another of the squad to fetch him a bottle and cracked its neck on the back of a carved chair. The wine was full of sediment and would take days to settle, he thought. He drank it anyway.

And he thought that, whatever he might eventually end up dying for, it wouldn't be a bunch of furniture or some old pictures, or even the Aihall itself.

Representatives of the Seven Families arrived with offers of transport and of storage under guard in assorted warehouses. They were prepared, as well, to keep the really priceless things in their own homes, so conveniently nearby.

"I'll just bet they are," Pedross muttered, but took advantage of the offers all the same. He sent the representatives to the chief steward, whom he directed to see to inventory and appropriate division of the goods. But the man was incapable. His assistant took over, surrounded by scribes wearing strap-desks. Marines held torches for them to see by.

His own people had done well, Pedross judged. Most were veterans of the Longlands campaign and had had plenty of practice in quickly and efficiently stripping burning buildings of their contents. All skills had more uses than one, Pedross thought.

At least it didn't look or feel like rain. Though with the smoke, he couldn't smell anything else, certainly not any tinge of damp in the air. But it would be the crowning unfairness if, arriving too late to do anything constructive to the fire, rain should ruin what had been salvaged.

Abruptly and violently, Pedross missed his Valde, his signal corps: they'd have been able to tell him if it was raining anywhere between here and the coast, and how fast the front was moving, if the network had still been in place.

No Valde, no mobile, and the Aihall in flames. The Council Wing, he saw, was beginning to fume. The wind jerked the smoke about, and Pedross' eyes stung even more.

No Grandda Troll, either: Pedross had to judge that the Shai couldn't have withdrawn his support much more definitely than by choosing this method of withdrawing the mobile.

Pedross tried to think what it might mean, the mobile's being removed this way, and what to make, now, of the threat of assassination. But since Jannus had apparently disappeared, no one remained who could interpret to Pedross the Shai's present intentions.

It was safe enough, however, to guess that the matter of Ardun was being left in his hands.

Presently Pedross discovered the red cord still around his wrist. He picked at it, but the knot was too tight. He set the bottle down carefully and slid his knife blade between cord and wrist until the strands parted.

A runner arrived bringing word that one of the rivermasters he'd met with earlier wanted to know what effect this unforeseen disaster would have on the proposed journey up the Morimmon. Pedross replied shortly, "Tell him, none at all. It goes on, as planned," and the runner departed with the message.

Pedross had already decided that the only way the expedition could continue was if he commanded it himself, with or without the Shai's endorsement or aid.

The Shai crouched in the middle of his fields of light-receptor nets in the arid starlight of the High Plain about halfway between the place that had been called Down and the mountains.

He was seriously perturbed: so much so that he refused to receive the Simon persona back into himself, closing off the link during the instants of the mobile's termination.

He didn't want to give that fraction of his personality any further encouragement or reinforcement. He even considered, now, that it had been a mistake to receive the Garin persona, whose aberrations had become more ominous in retrospect, Garin's budding mysticism and independence harbingers of Simon's outright rebellion.

But he'd *always* reabsorbed the whole personality gestalts of his mobiles. It was his main, practically his sole, means of acquiring experience, as apart from information. But if he was now to assume he could no longer take his mobiles back into himself without reinforcing those facets of his basic personality he had the least confidence in, progressively distorting his perspectives, then what was he to do for experience?

The alternatives of either stagnation or uncontrolled change had abruptly superseded the gestation of the war between lowlander colonists and native Valde as his main preoccupation: petrifaction, or else cancer of the self.

Garin had been the first mobile he'd ever sent out without a specific mandate, or on a purely personal errand. That had been his first mistake—leaving the mobile too much to its own devices. And Garin's idleness, intensified into Simon's ineffectual marking time in Ardun, reflected accurately the Shai's own preexisting predicament. He'd been operating at so specific, minuscule, a level that he couldn't bring his full powers to bear. That had been true since the beginning of the collapse of the Teke empire. Like Garin trying to steal the redestone, he was continually thwarted by the merest trivialities, too small to be accurately predicted or controlled. He'd become cramped. Myopic. Bored.

The only really absorbing thing, the only project he'd really taken enjoyment from working on in a very, very long time, was the Poli construct. Bored, preoccupied with minutiae, to so enjoy the reconstruction of the personality traits and quirks of a single unique individual of no particular importance except to her intimates. . . .

Simon might be shut off, shut up, but his accusations continued to rankle because some of them, at least, were demonstrably true: the fault *was* in the source, in himself. In the mobiles, the essential problems were merely more visible, concentrated, freed of their concealing encumbrances of context. The progress from Ashai to Secolo to Garin to Simon only reflected his own progressive dissatisfactions.

Therefore he'd send out no more mobiles until he'd resolved that central problem of power—resolved it properly, at the source, so that no mobile need suffer for enacting or articulating it.

And perhaps their deaths *were* proxy suicides, each death a real death, and final; surely Simon's had been. The Shai had cut him off utterly. The notion of having sent out a series of replicas to be modified by experience and choice, and then having discarded them without qualm either to expedience or to feed off their very differences now struck the Shai as something akin to psychic cannibalism, and of one's own children, at that.

He'd assumed that things equal to the same thing were equal to each other; and, until Garin, so had the mobiles. But it seemed that people did not conform to mathematical theory. And it had, moreover, become blatantly plain to him that Ashai was *not* Secolo, was *not* Garin, was *not* Simon, and none of them identical to himself after their first moment of separate breath. Mobiles were excerpted from different

209

moments in his life. Different in inception, one from another, each was different, as well, in environment and experience, different in the choices formed by circumstance and the consequences of those choices. Mobiles *changed* in the world— learned, developed. After all, that was their whole purpose: to interact with the living world of men, as he could not—not as a part of it, only as an alien intruder.

He'd even begun to doubt the Rule of One, which stated that power was single and indivisible, and that responsibility was proportional to power. The Rule of One had sustained and guided all his actions for tens of thousands of years. But if the Rule of One was imperfect, and was further warped by the service of an admittedly imperfect being, himself, what became of his justification? And if the Rule of One was unworthy of service, then what better thing was there, if any existed at all? Myth? Magic? Random patterns of cause and effect?

He materialized a phantom projection of Ashai Rey before Jannus, who was seated in the director's station in the main bridge, alternately dozing and idly watching recorded orbital views of the continent—seasons changing perhaps once an hour, days flickering like light through leaves. Through the projection, the Shai said, "Pedross is going to send marines to the Summerfair and kill whatever's within his reach."

Jannus' eyes focused slowly. Finally he said, "Why tell me?"

"I should think getting hacked to pieces by preadolescent girls would produce a certain interest in what occurs in Valde, the one way or the other," rejoined the Shai tartly.

"It doesn't seem to work that way."

Trying another tack, the Shai mentioned, "Poli will probably be there, by the time the marines arrive. . . ."

"Probably," agreed Jannus, without emphasis.

"Some of us," commented the Shai disagreeably, "can't afford the luxury of anesthetized detachment," and Jannus' expressionless dark eyes stayed on him for a couple of unhurried blinks.

"This wasn't my idea, you know."

The new body was younger, the face beardless and the hair shorter than its accustomed length: in the haste of impression, there had been no time to advance the body's ap-

pearance to match Jannus' actual chronological age. There
was an appropriateness to the two facing each other as they
were doing now, illusion of flesh and illusion of light: Jannus
was, at least to the eye, just as the Ashai-mobile had first encountered him over ten years before. Only the expression had
altered. The remembered face had been tense, anxious and
more than a little suspicious; the present face was as calm
and blank as a portrait modeled in wax.

For Jannus, there'd been no equivalent of an involved and
overwrought farspeaker to attend at the waking, to rouse the
startled mind to emotion. Only the Shai. And emotional states
didn't transfer. Theoretically, without the impediment of Tek
meat, they should revive spontaneously as soon as the immediate trauma of transfer had passed; theoretically, Jannus
should have adapted painlessly to the link, too. That the
stunned inaction and lack of initiative had continued this
long was to the Shai a source of concern.

Only recently had the Shai become at all interested in others' subjective states as anything other than intelligence data
enabling him to predict and thus subtly manipulate the actions of certain key people. Only since his adding to his
equipment the illusion-feedback device had the ongoing
processes of others been available to him at all, as distinct
from a rede's static and selective record.

With new eyes, as it were, he'd come to see new things,
and so, apparently, had his mobiles.

"No," he admitted, "it wasn't your idea. It was mine. Preferable, I should think, to the alternative. . . ."

But Jannus didn't rise to that bait either, merely waited for
the Shai to get around to whatever it was he wanted to say
by this unnecessarily cumbersome means; for the prohibition
on conceptual input had been lifted. Jannus was now fully
adapted to the link.

So the Shai dispensed with the civilities of even the illusion
of presence and transmitted his current predicament in its to-
tality. Then, on Jannus' request, he recast it into its com-
ponent parts and communicated them singly. When Jannus
had absorbed and sorted it all, he observed, "Simon was
right. That's what I make of it. But what do I know?"

"It's not a matter of knowing so much as of assigning
values to what's known. I need a more bounded perspective."

211

"Then I'd say you have a genuine impasse. Can't do with mobiles, and can't do without them."

The Shai responded with a complex request, with relationship bonds and responsibilities all clearly defined and weighted, and got an immediate reaction: incredulous laughter.

"Me? As your mobile? I have enough trouble trying to avoid tripping over the Rule of One as it is: it has this distressing habit of *shifting*, Shai, right underfoot, from one day to the next. If even your own mobiles can't walk that rope now without falling off, how long would I last? Even Bronh broke with you, and she never walked the knife I walk. And I'd make a terrible mobile, Shai—I don't even believe in the Rule of One, and never have. I'm not that badly in need of a project to keep my mind occupied." In a familiar wry gesture, Jannus lifted a hand to rub at the bridge of his nose. Then he recollected and let the hand fall.

The Shai had offered to break the nose nicely for him again, at just the proper angle and with just enough force, assuring him it wouldn't hurt at all and would heal quite quickly. But Jannus had declined, saying it didn't matter, just to be the better copy. He didn't expect to confront anyone who would notice this most visible discrepancy, not anytime soon.

"Then just go and look," responded the Shai. "So I can have some idea of what's going on out there. It's only about a week's walk—two days across the High Plain east to the mountains, and then along the Morgaard Pass. What more can you lose?" he asked baldly.

"Nothing," Jannus conceded; but it wasn't agreement.

"Otherwise," added the Shai, "I'll have no alternative but to go myself. . . ."

That threat worked because Jannus knew for a certainty that the Shai could and would deliver on it. And the interventions of which *Sunfire* was capable were all, and only, drastic ones.

"All right. I'll be eyes for you," Jannus replied finally. "I wouldn't think too well of your deciding to flame the whole valley, or poison the air. I wish you'd just leave things alone."

"The minimal interference is always the best," said the Shai contentedly. "Otherwise, the more that's controlled, the

212

more that has to be controlled, in geometric progression. You've come around to my way of thinking."

"Maybe." Jannus pushed himself out of the massive throne-like seat.

In the high meadows beyond Entellith that were blue with drifts of skyflowers and blooming lavender heathers, Poli and her companions deflected a charging rock goat off a precipice. The youngest of the Awiro was deflected as well and joined the goat at the bottom. She didn't die at once, and her agonies set off a fresh interval of the Singing. When it dropped them, about noon the next day, they found themselves somewhere else and the lare pair was missing, as well. So the remaining six hunted no more that day but spent the pause getting down off the steeps into less precipitous country, the low meadows whose flowers were white and yellow.

Two of the group were Awiro and two were defaulting Haffa troopmaids. There was also a *hafra* who'd fallen in with them after his *hafkenna* had scattered beyond his reach in the forgetfulness of the Singing. The Awiro and the Haffa were always trying to get him off by himself, trying for a permanent bonding. He'd begun to look rather hunted, and stayed close to Poli, who occasionally noticed him.

Whenever one of the Haffa or Awiro waylaid the boy and teased and nudged him into full arousal, Poli was quite aware of the progress of their touch-loving but aware, as well, that it did not include or involve her. When a nearby group killed, Poli's hunger was not thereby satisfied. Only in the Singing did such separations disappear.

In the Singing, Poli didn't miss Jannus at all; or, if she did, it was only the undifferentiated general grieving, one part of the Singing, that she suffered: not the particular knobby hole the presence of only the one person would have filled. It had eventually occurred to her that some *sa'farioh* copy of Jannus would be running around by now. But she wasn't lar to it. She couldn't hear it, so it wasn't there, not in any way that mattered. The living rapport had died in Entellith.

When the Singing encompassed them, there were no individual concerns. When the Singing fell, they were hungry; and after that, filled or, more often, hungry still, there was a return to the dreamless abyss of sleep. Poli conformed to the pattern with no wish to reach beyond, or even very far into, the daysinging of nearby life. What was done by goats she couldn't catch, or what rock chucks felt as they were whacked against the handiest boulder, were not things about which she cared to know any more than she had to. Of the three states, she preferred sleep.

They killed whatever they could find. All waking hours were consumed in hunting. Once, they surrounded a band of wild hogs in a thorny covert and killed a sow and two piglets with clubs, though a boar opened up the leg of the younger of the Awiro; she later fell behind and was forgotten. But from the two other groups of Valde that gathered to the plenty of the kill, three youngsters remained—a brother and two sisters, ravenous with growthyear, who were persuaded by a few hours' satiety that the group Poli was part of would be better providers than the group they'd been part with before. They ate almost as much as all the rest combined, and were driven away with unwelcome several times, but always drifted back whenever the group had killed.

It wasn't much like war; but it wasn't much like peace either. Had Poli been suddenly confronted by the Choral Hating Society, she could not have answered for what responses she might have made them.

She'd never imagined herself slaughtering a mara either.

It had been at the edge of a sloping green meadow that they'd found a mara doe helpless in unseasonal birth. She-animals with suckling or unfledged young had always been exempt from becoming prey, the bond of need between such creatures being too strong, precluding consent. But consent didn't seem to matter when a certain plateau of hunger had been reached. It had never been a law or a rule, only an inability, an impossibility. And with the advent of the Singing, anything had become possible—even murder, whether of a mara or a man.

Mara meat was stringy, and tasted of salt.

After the mara-kill, the three children never went far, convinced such bounty would continue forever because it had come twice, now. Poli understood: there was today, and maybe yesterday, and maybe tomorrow. Everything else was a mist of distance. She, who'd come past the Thornwall at least partly in hopes of recovering her own past, now appreciated the futility and pointlessness of her attempt. There *was* no past here: only passing. It was a mark of how alien she'd become that she'd even tried. She'd stopped trying, now. She drifted with the general flow, enduring the pauses of waking isolation that obliged her to feel for herself, if only dimly and through distractions.

The need to be together was drawing them together in progressively expanding groups: need not only for companionship but need to form, from this ingathering, a new consensus to order the present unendurable savage chaos. They followed the insingers, who reacted to the need most strongly and who went the fastest, their journeying uninterrupted by the spells of the Singing.

Poli's group moved more slowly and intermittently, but to the same end: toward Morgaard Vale, the familiar seasonal gathering place: toward the Summerfair.

The *hafra*'s name was Aran and he was good at slinging. When no larger prey was available he could often bring down a bird or sometimes a rabbit or a tree rat. Poli collected stones for him. When she found him gone one afternoon, she threw the stones away and then regretted it when he turned up the next day with purple bruises and it was instead the boy in growthyear who was missing. The two sisters attached themselves to Aran and screamed off the advances of the grown Haffa and Awiro. Aran looked much more cheerful and generally left Poli alone except when he needed some stones.

It was all one to Poli. It didn't concern her, either way.

They came into a fir forest, got sore feet from the carpet of dry needles, and were veering back toward the meadowlands for that reason when a slow-moving node of calm and attention, ahead, drifted to them like the pungent smell of the evergreens themselves. The very strangeness of calm was enough to draw the group nearer. And there was a strangeness beyond the calm, a rapt attention, a deferring, like that which would have surrounded a troopleader among her troop. Eventually they saw a group of Valde larger than their own. These were walking and conversing silently around a voice that spoke aloud.

The voice was saying, "It's all yours to begin with. Valde hunted west of Erth-rimmon, where the Bremneri farmsteads

215

are now, before there were any farmsteads or any Bremneri to score the furrows. This once, you must remember where you have come from, what's been done to you—back to the beginnings. If the land belongs to no one, then whoever has the greatest need, quickness, and skill will have the hunting of it. If it was stolen, take it back. If you only lost it, find it again. If you forgot it, remember. It's all yours, to use or to leave fallow. You're nobody's pets, but free predators. With almost two hundred generations of troopservice in your culture, you are the finest predators alive. Whatever moves is yours for the hunting. You *know* that, already."

And the surrounding Valde were reacting, not with belief, exactly, but with acceptance: after all, this was Bronh Sefar', the Bringer of the Change.

As Poli's group drew nearer she could see the Tek, trudging along in the midst of the taller Valde who were attending to her by means of those among them who had the breath-talk.

It wasn't just that Poli hated mobiles, and all such empty *sa'farioh* creatures, although she did. And it wasn't just that Bronh praised Valde, with evident pride, as cleverer, more dangerous animals, although she'd just done so. And it wasn't, either, merely that Bronh was engaged in a blatant attempt to precipitate the terrible hatred of all strangers which she and the Shai had both foreseen and which moved in the Singing already; but if that outsweep of annihilation was to come, it wouldn't be because of such a thing as Bronh.

Poli advanced in quick, long strides to put an end to that voice.

But she was held, prevented. Nobody touched her; but they were full of awe to be in the foretold presence of Windvoice, and unwilling that any hurt should come to her, or any interruption; and their unwillingness was so strong a unanimity that Poli's lone hatred could not breach it.

Unheeding, ignorant, Bronh was continuing—talking now about mood-echoes, and the way every child learned to avoid that sort of reflexive, self-perpetuating link by diverting attention into a solitary trance-bond: focusing exclusively on something, generally a tree or a single plant, but something *sa'marenniath* which would remain utterly unmoved until the impulse to shared hysteria had passed.

216

(That was, everybody knew, no use at all against the Singing. It came so suddenly, and, once caught up in the recurring cycles, everybody was too exhausted during the pauses to even attempt trance, or endure being alone and trying to commune, as one Hafera put it, with a banner bush.)

"What you need to learn now," Bronh went on, over the Hafera's inspoken comment, "is just the opposite. Be together in the Singing. Embrace it, the way insingers do. Ride on it like the wind, the way birds do. Watch the moving things, and whatever moves on that which moves—on wind, or on water. Because whatever tries to sink roots will be broken, dragged out, swept away. The Singing's too strong for any rooted thing to endure."

Somebody inspoke something about storms so fierce that even the birds took to hiking, and roused a brief twitch of general amusement that became warning as Poli seized the opportunity to advance a long step closer.

"Whatever comes," Bronh said, "use its strength to lift yourselves. Watch how a hawk balances: against the wind, letting the wind do the work of lifting. On the flow of the Singing, you can coast all day and never tire, and strike down anything with the momentum of the unity and not just your sole strength. A hawk can kill a rabbit three times its weight. Learn what hawks know and nothing will be able to stand against your strike."

Poli pushed another step nearer, and the combined groups turned on her: rejecting, dismissing, with an animosity as ready as her own—a casting-out, an attack that needed no touching but would *become* touching unless it was instantly heeded.

They were the stronger. Poli stopped, and the merged groups continued on without her. But before they'd passed completely out of sight, Aran and his tiny *hafkenna* turned aside as well, and there was the tingling all around, and feeling of wonders stirring, that was the leading edge of the Singing.

When, in almost moonless darkness, the Singing faded again, Aran and his two Haferae greeted Poli with a fat brown hen, struck down in lumbering flight and already nearly plucked. There was even a fire borrowed from a pot of coals Bronh had been carrying. They'd learned how to ride on the Singing.

It had been like a perfect dream of hunting, they reported: everything shining and sure, the stone flying unseen toward where, in an instant, the hen was bound to be, tracked and located with nothing save *marenniath* and in the midst of the Singing.

They could have killed twenty hens just as easily, they exulted, except that they couldn't find twenty hens. But it had been easy, wonderfully easy to become a single entity, share the single will of a hunting pack, once they'd known it could be done, once they'd learned how to catch the lift. The next time the Singing came, they said, they'd show her how it felt, how it was done.

The three packets had moored along the east shore. Sounders went ahead in two rowboats to cast their lines and find clear water between ripple-covered sandbars to the one side and the upended roots of the kind of snags called witchheads to the other. Sua went up the stairs from the water deck to the second deck and slipped through the rail to climb out onto the wheel housing where she could stretch out in the sun without anybody stepping on her or making tiresome remarks.

The sun was very pleasant, and she was delighted not to have to hide anymore in Marlena's cabin. Pedross had practically had a fit when he found out Sua had come aboard with the Loyalist deputation, but they'd already been two days on their way by then, too late for him to do anything about it but fume, which was about how Sua had figured it would go.

But anybody who knew her at all would have known that if anybody was going to the Summerfair this year, even Loyalists, she'd want to come too. Anybody would have *asked* her, and given her a cabin all of her own, instead of making her hide away like a thief. But she already knew Pedross wasn't too bright about things like that.

He was aboard *White Gull*—a silly name for a ship with no sails—the sternwheeler that went in the lead and bore his sunburst banner. Most of the Loyalists were on the two sidewheelers: *Kam's Luck*, with the red stacks, and the *Lady Marya*, with the blue stacks and the carved figurehead on the

front of the wheelhouse, up on the master's deck. Sua liked
the figurehead, a woman with outstretched arms emerging
from back-curving waves, and was glad to be aboard the
Lady Marya, even though the packet always went last, having, she'd been told, the deepest draft. Tidelift was no help,
this far north: what *got* stuck *stayed* stuck until there was a
heavy enough rain to float it free, or unless there were two
other packets to drag it back into open water.

The sounders had marked the best channel with white
sticks in round wood floats, with lines and sinkers holding
them in place. *White Gull* was casting off bow and stern
lines. The steam whistle blew one resounding blast and the
paddlewheels began swishing around. Angling away from the
bank, *White Gull* began to draw its barges in a curve toward
the first set of floating, upright poles.

The poles reminded Sua of the Summerfair Path, the
stakes never following the same course two years running.
Sua thought about the days and days of walking, the night-
shelters spaced so that you had to set out at a good pace at
firstlight to get to the next one by nightfall, and *then* no
proper beds, nothing more than a roof against rain, and food
waiting. . . . She thought about the factors they often traveled with, and the tale-telling, and the being-a-family-to-
gether, and the strange silent woods that knew who was
passing, and how many, and where, always just enough food
waiting at the next night-shelter. . . .

This was the proper way to go to the Summerfair, Sua had
decided: taking your bed with you, and your kitchen, letting
the paddlewheels, with their hundred flat feet, walk on the
bright surface of the water. . . .

Kam's Luck had cast off and begun to thread the passage
when arrows began descending on the *Lady Marya*. Sua, on
the side farthest from shore, found out about it only when
the wheel beneath the housing rumbled into motion and
about ten Loyalists came dashing around from the shoreward
side of the deck. A woman had an arrow through her shoulder, and everybody was hollering, except Sua couldn't hear
what because the rivermaster was blowing short hoots of
alarm, drowning out all lesser noises.

Before the packet had reached the first of the floating
stakes, Pedross had come aboard, having commandeered one

of the rowboats to bring him from *White Gull*. Pedross immediately had the wounded tended to, then began attending to the worse injury, that to the Loyalists' confidence. *Scared*, that wasn't the half of it, Sua judged, having climbed back onto the deck to keep track of what was going on. The Loyalists were scared green, Marlena weeping and Territ insisting that all three ships turn back immediately, since they plainly weren't welcome.

Pedross refused, gave reasons, refused, gave some more reasons, then had Territ, Marlena, and two other prominent Loyalists escorted into the nearest cabin and applied some additional persuasions Sua couldn't hear through the window glass. But Pedross was standing still—always a bad sign—with his arms folded, and the four Loyalists took turns jumping up from chairs for a while, then sat still. They emerged from the cabin babbling to everybody that it had all been a mistake, that a message had miscarried, that they all had to begin concentrating full time on the kindly nature of their mission and their undimmed admiration for Valde.

The first two declarations were outright lies and the third one had a suspicious flavor, like somebody trying to convince himself.

Sua, having retreated to the rail before the door had opened, decided she approved of the lies. She turned to watch the sounders taking up their markers as the *Lady Marya* slowly churned by each set.

"Well?" demanded Pedross, leaning on the rail next to her.

"They expected a friendly snackout on the grass," replied Sua. "I didn't. Did you know Marlena hasn't been to the Summerfair, ever, not even once? If they all get scared and mad, the woodsrunners will just get scared and mad right back. Somebody's got to have sense enough to know that."

After a minute, Pedross said, "If you knew there was going to be trouble, why did you come?"

"For the ride," replied Sua, smiling at him, lying. "Better four scared than fifty," she formulated, "and better scared of you, more than of *them*." She tipped her head toward the shore.

Pedross decided to smile back. "I *do* like you," he remarked, as if reminding himself. Watching her in the sharp-eyed way he watched people he didn't trust, he asked, "Do you like me?"

Sua shrugged. "Sometimes."

"But you liked Simon better," he said in a voice that wanted to be contradicted.

"Sometimes. The other one was nicer, the one before Simon. *Old man*," Sua muttered rancorously, wondering what he would come back as next time, the troll, and tugged at the blue cord around her wrist. She'd started wearing it to remind Simon that he could have come back as Garin, and hadn't, and that she wasn't about to forgive him for it, either, because it wasn't fair. It was a cowardly thing, to pretend to be an old man: it hadn't fooled *her*, not one second. It had been just cowardly hiding.

It hadn't bothered her a bit, hearing how Simon had gotten burned up in the great Aihall fire. She understood, now, about such things: people came, and went, and came, but the people you really cared about never really left—it only seemed that way if you were too young to understand. Sua felt much older now, and wasn't the least bit anxious about any of the absent people that belonged to her.

"I never saw him," observed Pedross, still watching her, "the one before Simon. What was he like?"

"Like you," Sua decided. "Only nicer." And then she smiled, to let him know he was being teased on purpose.

And Pedross smiled back, only a little sourly. "Come up to *Kam's Luck* with me," he suggested, and, before she could answer, he added, "Help me lie. There's about thirty more people to be persuaded nothing's wrong and we're welcome as springtime."

Sua could see the sense of it, put that way. Turning from the rail, she said, "Don't lie any more than you can help. It sets my teeth right on edge."

Ahead, *Kam's Luck* hooted, passing the last of the stakes with its barges trailing behind.

It was as though it had rained people, or snowed people, or the tide had brought them in shoals to cover the floor of Morgaard Vale on either side of the Morimmon and make the distant heights restless with their movements.

Pedross had seen crags where shorebirds congregated to nest that were less densely occupied.

Taking the long-glass from his eye, Pedross frowned in uneasy meditation: he hadn't reckoned on such a number. Even half so many would have given him pause; but this was unimaginable.

In the back of his mind, he imagined the mobile's voice pointing out, "I told you." Pedross muttered aloud, "I don't need your damn doom-crying." The rivermaster, hearing him, turned inquiringly. Pedross shook his head, again raising the glass to scan the banks and the river ahead.

Following his prior orders, the steersman was taking *White Gull* along dead slow, so that the packet scarcely advanced against the current. There was plenty of time for Pedross to locate the stone foundations of the old landing stages marked on the charts. Like burned-out houses, they lined a considerable stretch of bank on both sides of the river. But it hadn't been fire, only weather, determined neglect, and season after season of thaw floods that shoved them gradually into disordered rubble, more of a danger now than a help in landing. Without the chart notation, Pedross doubted he would have been able to guess what they'd been: relics of the fat, busy days of continual river traffic on the Morimmon and its tributaries before the Valde had found the intrusions of outlanders increasingly annoying and had closed it down altogether.

"See how close you can get to that slab," Pedross directed absently. "We ought to be able to moor to that."

Scraped into rounded, grooved contours, the granite slab was grey and dry and at least twice a packet's length: clear of the shore, with fast water on both sides. An island. Pedross found he'd developed a most particular liking for islands; and mooring to this one would commit him to nothing. All his options remained open save the option not to be here at all. And he was thinking, too, of what Callea had told him about the new hesitation of Valde to approach water that was deep, or swift, or both. And Morimmon was both.

The innumerable throng of Valde was, in practice, halved by the river. The farther side, to the north, seemed to Pedross both broader and more densely crowded than the steeper, nearer shore. They were his potential adversaries, those tall fair folk gathered beyond the rock, among the trees: a mass less daunting if only because it was less than the whole. The width of the river would guard his back.

White Gull, having turned a bit toward midriver, made the swing so that the bow approached the rock. "Long cables," directed Pedross, and the rivermaster reversed the wheels' motion. The packet drifted to a halt just short of the slab, and deckhands ran out the descending gangway to fix mooring lines to rock-nails they drove into cracks in the diagonally striated stone. Pedross, modifying his plans rapidly, had signals waved for *Kam's Luck* to tie up on *White Gull's* downriver side but for the *Lady Marya* to pass by and moor farther up the rock; if any packet had to be left behind, it would be the broad-beamed sidewheeler, not either of the two more agile craft.

As it occurred to him that he was already weighing matters in terms of retreat and of what was expendable, Pedross grimaced, but didn't pause in blocking out various fallback strategies adapted to the terrain and the convergences of circumstance he considered the most likely.

No Valde, he noticed, were streaming down to inspect the intruders. They didn't need to, he thought. They'd know the packets were there, well enough. Likely they just hadn't decided what they wanted to do about them yet.

Or perhaps they were cut off, by the incomprehensible bond of the Singing, and hadn't attention to spare for so minor a thing as an invasion by slightly over twelve hundred strangers. The more he thought about that, the likelier he thought it—there was something *absent* about them, even through the glass. They moved with slow underwater gestures. He couldn't discern a single one doing anything so ordinary as twining a bowstring or even scratching a fire alight—as though they'd *all* been drowned and pushed into motion by some tinkering mobile, with nothing alive behind their eyes.

Pedross folded the glass together and put it in his pocket. He'd seen all that was necessary, all he could use.

When the noise of the paddlewheels had all been stilled and the excess steam vented, Pedross noticed how remarkably silent it became. All those Valde, and no sound of voices. You'd think just all that *breathing* would make a noise a man could hear. But there was nothing—only the voices of his own people and the Arduners gathering on the packets' bows in uneasy, gesturing clusters. The Loyalists weren't so blind they couldn't see the lack of greetings from either shore, or so inexperienced that they didn't know a mischancy situation when one was spread out as far as they could see.

They hadn't expected to find themselves confronting a nation of fetches. Well, neither had he, not precisely. But if not now, then later; and so, better now.

He made sure the deck watch had been posted and gave orders that steam in the boilers be kept up, then went down the bow gangway to the rounded middle of the rock where, presently, the Loyalists came to surround him.

It was Marlena Singer who worriedly voiced the obvious: "We haven't brought enough."

All those pale incurious faces on the shore were hollow-cheeked and gaunt, the elongated forms more like storks than people, with their inhuman silence and calm. . . . There wasn't enough bread in Ardun, Pedross thought, to feed the hunger he saw before him. Meanwhile he assured them briskly, "It's the attitude that counts. We brought what we could. Now, there's no need for anybody to leave this rock. They can hear you fine from here."

"How are we to give them the bread, then: throw it at them?" sharply responded a man in a carter's vest.

"I'll see to that," said Pedross. "And it's not exactly the best place to lose tempers in."

As one, the Loyalists glanced toward the nearer shore. Then Territ observed, "Nevertheless, it's not what we'd planned."

"Suit yourselves, then. You have till the first barge is hitched up to decide."

Pedross moved a few paces off and, through the long-glass, followed the progress of five marines sent in a rowboat to moor one end of a heavy cable to the trunk of a large thorn-oak about twenty paces in from the shore. The cable's other end was being fastened to the cargo boom amidships in *Kam's Luck*. The shore crew hitched a pulley-block threaded with lighter line to the tree as well, below the guide cable. They went about these duties in workmanlike fashion and the nearby Valde didn't give them so much as a glance, as far as Pedross could tell.

It was all in the attitude. He hadn't alerted the archers yet, or taken any but the most routine precautions to secure either the mooring site or the ships themselves. All calm. He wanted at least one barge delivered without any hitches. The bread had changed, in his calculations, from a pretext to an essential: it had become bait.

Even on the near side of the river, there were far too many Valde for him to attack. But if, pulled by the lure of food, they attacked him, he had a fine moat and an island, deep water all around him, and, at the last, a clear line of retreat with the current behind him.

The south shore was well within bowshot. Pedross looked along the cable several times, visualizing how an arrow would fly: no more than a cool evaluation of distance and trajectory because attitude was everything. He hadn't a mobile's detachment, but he didn't fly into raptures of terror or enthusiasm at the prospect of a fight, either—nor did any of his people.

And then the thought came that the Arduners were his people, and that bothered him a bit. But it took no more than a long look at the shore to persuade him it was true. Compared to *that*, a naked Fisher was his close kin.

Returning to the rowboat, the shore crew were pulling back toward the rock with quicker strokes than were strictly needed; and a barge had been freed from its chain and attached to both guide cable and pulley. Pedross turned to learn what the Loyalists had decided.

A glance told him: four stood clear of the rest; or, rather, the rest had moved away from them, the four who meant to go. There were Territ, and a broad woman in bakers' guild colors, and a man who was both Territ's chief bodyguard and some sort of minor kin. The fourth was not, as he'd expected, Marlena Singer but, as he *should* have expected, Sua, braced for argument.

Pedross looked at her for a couple of blinks, feeling tired. He would have expected it, if he had thought about it, if he'd put aside juggling marines and islands and Loyalists and bread and a couple of hundred thousand ravenous silent Valde to think just about her and her whims and her continual precarious game of rope-walking.

It was too much to expect, he thought, with a growing anger and resentment: too much for anybody who wasn't a mobile, to interweave twenty lines of thought all together and with full attention, every detail in its place, and yet continue to walk and talk and eat and make all the motions of a man.

Territ meanwhile was commenting that the far end of a long rope didn't seem, to him, an appropriate place from which to deliver a gift of friendship and concern. The sentiment was generally applauded.

Pedross was thinking what would happen if he flatly declared that nobody was going, that he'd changed his mind. That line of action ended with an irrevocable falling out between not only himself and Territ, but between the Loyalists and the marines. Territ had locked his pride too firmly into facing the risk now for him to accept being overruled. Pedross could tell by the way the man stood, the sound of his voice.

Pedross wasn't prepared to cope with a pocket rebellion just now and certainly not for the sake of just Sua's waywardness.

And to single her out and try to prevent her alone from going would be worse. Argument would have no effect at all; and Pedross had seen at Market Square that she could by no means be dismissed as a barehanded fighter. It would take at least four marines to hold her without doing her serious hurt; and Pedross wasn't sure even his own personal guard would answer to such an order, at least quickly enough to be effective: the river was only a run and a jump away, and the shore no great distance. . . .

If anybody laid hands on her, it would have to be himself, alone. And Sua was balanced as if she knew it, beyond range of a sudden grab. Idly, not looking at her, Pedross moved a sidewise step, to test this, and as idly she put two oblivious Loyalists between them. So.

If he'd had a mobile's resources, or been willing to spend nine-tenths of his time just thinking about her, he would have seen this coming and forestalled it in time. He would have prevented her from sneaking aboard the *Lady Marya* in the first place. But if she needed a mobile for a keeper, that was too much—more than Pedross was willing to demand of himself or feel was demanded of him. There were limits.

Turning his anger toward an easier target, he pointed at Territ's bodyguard and said, "He stays. Nobody goes on orders."

But the man himself rejoined calmly. "It's not on orders. I'll go, so please you."

In an exchange as automatic as it was impersonal, Pedross' glance went to his Truthsayer for confirmation, which she gave. Pedross nodded. That was that, then.

As the four started across the curves of the rock toward the barge, Pedross trailed along behind. Across the Baker woman and the bodyguard, he said to Sua, "Don't. There's no need." The effort of constraint roughened his voice.

"What else are we here for?" she rejoined. "Why else did I come?"

"To show off," replied Pedross bluntly.

She gave him a cool look, then glanced toward the shore. "They're my people too. I'm not going to start being afraid of them now."

"Start. They're nobody's people but their own."

She said merely, "No," and continued on to where the barge waited.

Pedross gave the signal, and crewman aboard *Kam's Luck* began hauling on the pulley line. Held against the current by the heavier guide cable, the barge was drawn away from the rock and toward the shore.

The two women and Territ climbed rather hesitantly onto the bank. Then Territ's man began passing up the large, flat, oval loaves, and the others began handing them out to whichever Valde were nearest—or trying to, since some loaves had to be offered several times before being somnambulistically received, if not accepted. Presently there came a sudden rise of alertness, however—a general motion of faces turning. Pedross saw it clearly even without the glass, and made himself watch while what he'd foreseen became actuality. The three on the far shore were lost within the abrupt, concerted advance of the whole mass of Valde toward the shore. Those Valde nearest the river balanced for a moment on the brink. Then they leaped down into the shallows and all that could be seen anywhere near the barge were the snatching motions of pale, long arms. The bait had been taken.

Bronh saw the three packets rounding the bend downriver and was annoyed at the intrusion. She'd been sitting on a

knoll for almost two days among a throng of insingers.
Through the insingers, she'd been teaching the Valde who
they were—what they'd been, back to the beginnings, and the
terrible wrongs that had been committed against them by
their enemies who had first stolen the land from them and
then even stolen them from themselves, destroying their culture and altering their very flesh.

When the first of the packets had come into sight, Bronh
had been remembering Fathori for them and with them: the
little sanctuary, the beautiful place. In response to Bronh's
suggestions, descriptions studded with sense-images, the insingers persuaded the multitude to turn from the immediate
to the ancient, to the memory that lived in Bronh alone.
Through the Singing the lost beauty was called back from the
ashes of its incineration. Bronh took them strolling through
the luminous glades, into the drifting fragrances of strange
blossoms where the musics of air moved through the incurved
leaves of flute trees beside Isrimmon.

The packets spoiled it. Bronh opened her eyes to Morgaard
and saw the Valde stirring as awareness of the Arduners' intrusion spread among them. Bronh saw Pedross' banner.

She took the hands of the *in'marenniath* nearest her, a
young man, and said, "They are nothing to us, and less than
nothing. Deaf outlanders, invaders, no different from the first.
Only yourselves-together matter. There'll be a time to notice
and silence them. Not yet. Not now. There is no place for
them in Fathori."

Gradually the ripple of disturbance faded, and the Valde
were called back into the recreation of Fathori, the Dream-
wood, cherishing its daysinging, forgetful of all else.

Then the shared imagining was shattered again, and with
finality. From the reappearance of individual motions, visible
realizations of discomfort, Bronh knew that their endurance
had failed and the Singing had been broken. It would be
hours before she could call them all again into the tale of the
years, the whole becoming of the Valde.

With a cold and thorough indignation Bronh arose stiffly to
see what had been responsible for ruining Fathori. All she
could discern was some sort of disturbance down at the shore
nearest the rock where the packets had moored.

"What is it?" she asked the insingers rising around her, blocking her view.

"Food. Bread," replied one, vaguely. "The *sa'marenniathe* have brought, are throwing us, are baiting us. . . . There is no one intent, but many. There is bread for us. . . ."

"Take it, then," said Bronh. "Take it all. There is nothing anywhere that is not under your hand. There is food aboard the packets, too. Take it."

The insingers moved away from her, and Bronh saw hands reaching for weapons. She was satisfied. The interruption would be removed, the interlopers silenced, and the Valde better able to maintain the Singing with the nagging distraction of hunger at least muted. There was still a long way to go from Fathori to the full turning-together, the total repudiation of all strangers, which would culminate in her own death. Bronh bent to feed the coals in her firepot.

As always when the Singing ended, Poli went through a sequence of exhausted depression, loneliness, and hunger, in successive layers. It seemed to her, during those first moments of disorientation, that she'd awakened from a wonderful dream of a childhood forest—trees large and marvelous beyond imagining, unending benevolence, beauty, and protection—into an adult awareness that somebody had killed: a large kill, enough for everybody. Then the sense of the vast mass of people around her, in touching distance or within sight, made her know that was impossible: no kill could be so large as to satisfy them all.

People were moving toward the river. Early in the pauses, it was safe to do that, to drink and fill what containers there were. Everybody had learned the rhythms of the Singing now, and the Singing itself had become increasingly purposeful, less random, as people learned to find their balance and the flow of the harmony within it. After all, they themselves *were* the Singing.

There was a drift of wood smoke, and then a startling, totally foreign sound: the repeated shrieks of steam whistles rolling and re-echoing from the facing heights. Poli became more alert then and reached out through the relative unanimity of Valde to the chaotic angers and fears of *sa'marenniathe*. It seemed there were a lot of them, partly because there was no pattern to their self-singings, each deaf to the others, the whole utterly inharmonious. But in this cacophony, Poli heard people that she knew—Pedross' cool, abrupt cadences, one of the bakers, whose shop was across the street from their household, Marlena Singer having hysterics, and Sua stubbornly concentrating on standing her ground and on forcing the surrounding Valde to take notice of her, pay attention.

The immediate fight was over bread. The fundamental antagonism was over difference. Poli was aware of Pedross bringing his archers out onto the packets' decks, then she could see the marines themselves and the arrows striking the Valde who'd crossed to the long granite slab. Pedross was surprised: he hadn't thought they would chance the water.

Poli thought, with leaden certainty, *It's begun.*

And the whole mounting volume of anger, hurt, and fear that intensified steadily in spite of the ambient exhaustion, the whole keening tension of battle joined, Sua was trying to stand against by her own sole self, without even the inspeaking to focus her attitudes into speech. Refusing to be either enraged or frightened, trying to control companions who were both, she was demanding to be noticed, taken account of, recognized. When people pushed past her, she became a little angrier. When her deaf companions distracted her, she became a little less sure. When passing Valde struck out at her or at those frantic companions, she became a little more hurt, a little more frightened. Her balance was tipping, and the fall inevitable.

Poli summoned enough energy to call out in the inspeaking, *She's mine. Let her be!* and her will and desire made those nearest Sua turn a little wider as they passed. Poli called, *Who knows me? Who knows the half-blooded children of Ardun? Who has known kindness and liking beyond the Thornwall? Who would not see a child killed for the sake of some bread?*

And her calling roused a response. Those who were so inclined made a separate motion within the downward momentum, gathering and holding around the three near the shore. It wasn't the Singing but only battle, and each Valde took whatever action seemed best according to individual needs and natures.

230

Around Sua formed a widening circle of Valde too tired to be roused to fight, or concerned for any of those at risk, or reluctant to face the flight of arrows, or familiar enough with the noisy confusion of outlanders to find it insufficient cause for reactive rages when a less troubled course drew them. For almost as many reasons as there were people, they stopped and were unmoved by the tumult around them. Arriving among them, Poli made her way through to the open space under a tree where Sua was, and Nora Baker—late of the Choral Hating Society—and a wounded authoritative frightened man, an Arduner too, whom Poli didn't recognize.

Poli said, "Sua," and Sua turned and knew her, with welcome and relief and entire acceptance.

"I *knew* it!" Sua declared, grabbing and weeping on her shoulder. "I *knew* it! Where's Da?"

Poli got a knife from someone and cut through the shoulder seam of Sua's shirt, using the sleeve to bandage a cut on the outside of Sua's upper arm. Everybody was meanwhile moving gradually farther along the bank, away from the fighting, and Sua and Poli in the midst of them. The Baker woman and the man made haste to stay within the protecting circle. Poli glanced at them coldly, annoyed by their fear and their incomprehension. But she didn't care enough what became of them to prevent them from following.

"Where's Da?" Sua asked again, while Poli knelt at the edge of the shore to drink.

Poli felt the circle of attending silence that still surrounded Bronh, the other *sa'farioh* up on the knoll. She also felt the numb silence that was within herself, where the continual shifting of moods and attitudes, Jannus' selfsinging, should have been. She remained unpartnered, alone. But she said only, "I don't know, Sua."

"He should *do* something about this," commented Sua, with a general wave and a judgmental scowl. "I tried to make them see it was only us, but they wouldn't."

" 'Only us,' " replied Poli dryly, "depends on who you are. If you've been opening the door to whoever says 'It's only me,' I'd advise you to stop. . . ." Looking to the two terrified Arduners with diminishing dislike, Poli collected the remaining strips of cloth, climbed back up the bank, and saw to the bandaging of the man's cut hand. Poli felt a vague wry

231

amusement at the fact that the Baker woman hadn't recognized her yet as the "arbiter's fetch" she'd spent whole nights trying to hate into disappearance.

But they'd come, and they'd tried, and risked themselves to try to deliver their gift of bread and Poli found she bore them no malice.

She told them, "Nobody will hurt you if you stay close. It was just a bad time to come visiting."

The man nodded, clasping his injured hand in the other, saying, "We are beholden to you, Mistress Poli."

The Baker woman went white and fainted dead away.

Three farspeakers had been trapped with their backs broken beside an inferno that dropped gobbets of molten rock upon their flesh: these were the untiring, wracking shrieks of the steam whistles' panting, inescapable agonies, an affront to the very bones.

And there was a pack of weasels which trees had betrayed with snares, or the ground with staked pits, or clear pools with poison. They jerked out their separate uncomprehending rages, sometimes with wit and shrewdness, sometimes in frenzied impaled thrashings, each deaf to the others and thirsting for escape or revenge on the betrayer, or rank, foul with the terror of impending death. These were the *sa'marenniathe*, the Unhearing.

Poli had never suffered nor even imagined such an assault on the ears of the body and the hearing of the heart together. There was injury merely to be near it. She, the Valde around her, Sua, and the two Arduners moved upriver, interposing other lives, the shielding indifference of trees and other vegetation, between themselves and the unendurable cacophony howling from the rock.

Like almost everyone else, Poli had been learning how to block out and ignore horrors in the past weeks. Distance helped, and weariness, and rapport with nearer companions. These presently made of the fighting, to her and her companions, a force not unlike a particularly violent and concussive storm they endured under a roof with all doors shut.

But the intangible walls had windows; and across an incurving of the river, Poli saw forming a concerted attack on the three packets.

Insingers had no walls and no protection from the wounding chaos of the storm. No lightning struck that did not strike them, in full, searing intensity. So they became lightning, and struck back.

They were not troopmaids, who'd known discipline and deliberation in violence. And they'd fled inward, away from the worst of what was happening behind them in Entellith and the southern margins of Valde. Hardly any of them had ever known disharmony greater than the ripple of a few *sa'marenniathe* passing in calm toward the Summerfair, a seasonal disruption easily sorted and reconciled within the vastness of the whole daysinging. *This* could not be reconciled, however, or by any means brought to harmony any more than could the throatless yelling of the insensate steam whistles. In a reaction as reflexive as a hand slapping down on a spark that landed on one's arm, the insingers struck out as a group to silence the intolerable, destroy it in outrage and the shock of their wounding.

With weapons or with none, they launched themselves from the shore and, in two swarms, curved toward the packets. If they'd concentrated their fury on a chosen one, they could not have been withstood and would have gone from water deck, to cabin, to stair, irresistible as wind. With the Singing to support and direct them, they would have had the judiciousness to have waited for enough archers to move down to the shore to supply covering fire while they were at their most vulnerable, in the water. But they didn't, and marine archers on the upper decks skewered them like fish in a tub. Those that got an elbow or a knee latched over the water deck of whatever packet happened to be nearest were never enough in any one place to overwhelm the numbers of the defenders. The insingers were thrown back, killed, wounded, scattered; and on the all-but-untouched center packet Pedross stood in the wheelhouse and controlled the defenses with signal flags and periodic blasts on the whistle.

Swimmers turned and dove, or were carried, drifting, with the current, away from the packets. In their hundreds they staggered and aided each other to climb the deeply undercut bank and began their retreat. What they had failed to silence, they fled.

And with the withdrawal of the insingers' scalded sensibilities, the daysinging altered to a cooler, more settled anger. There were more Valde than Poli who knew how to mount a proper attack, how to organize and arm and wait for advantage, and strike with measured force when that advantage came. The anger arose, less through the insingers, than because of them. Insingers were *always* protected, cherished: it wasn't uncommon for a whole region to go into mourning at the loss of one of their *in'marenniathe*, who had lighted and colored everything with individual and irreplaceable perceptions, so that even the shadows were changed at the absence. And now, not one *in'marenniath* had been lost but a score, and countless wounded to the death, either through the injuries themselves or through the slower wasting of the turning-away. The Haffa, the stolid ones, freemaids and deserters together, partnered themselves to the Awiro and to whoever wished, and entered the fight none of them could see the end of.

The empty barge at the shore was tipped up on its side to become a barricade against arrows descending from the packets. Burning twigs were passed hand to hand from Bronh's knoll and fires kindled. Strips of cloth were torn to be tied around a growing collection of arrow shafts. Those who could attend steadily and with comprehension to the whole shape of the fighting without being distracted by a particular death, who were best able to tolerate the ambient hurt, rage, and fear, won deference from the rest. The whole daysinging was changed—less frantic, more settled, violence acquiring pauses and rhythms that could become accustomed things, tolerable, almost ordinary. A new balance was shaping: almost imperceptibly, battle was becoming war.

Poli, seeing so plainly how events were moving into the predicted grooves, cried out against it; but she was no farspeaker and could not affect this new partnership among folk agreeing to become both attackers and attacked. She turned away from the shore.

The hooting of the whistles rose, thin and faint, to the ridge that was the south rim of Morgaard Vale. Jannus looked down through thin clouds, past the spiny tops of evergreens furring the lower ridges, and still down to the broad meadow that flanked the river, where the packets were.

Jannus looked down from his height; and the Shai, aloft, to whom the valley and the pass it was part of were no broader than a crack in a lumpy platter, looked through his eyes and told him what they saw.

It would be settled, the Shai evaluated, by sundown at the latest. As soon as the light failed enough so that the shipboard archers could no longer find targets, there'd be Valde swarming over the lower decks by the hundreds, and the fighting would be hand to hand, while it lasted. Pedross, not being a total fool, wouldn't allow it to come to that: before sunset he'd cut cables and begin the retreat that could not thereafter be stopped short of the coast. The object lesson would have been achieved, the predictions validated. The Shai was not displeased at the prospect.

To Jannus both the motions and the Shai's interpretations remained remote things, distant as seasons seen passing in meaningless sequence. The Shai's view encompassed it all. Jannus had no part in it save as an available and conveniently placed set of eyes uncolored by the distortions of individual perspective. Without any sense that matters could or should be otherwise, Jannus nevertheless experienced a growing diffuse restlessness and began casting about for alternatives.

The Shai complied with five or six other lines of action, but they all ended up with somebody dead: mostly, a considerable number of somebodies. —Everything ends up with somebody dead, contended the Shai, with his persuasive dogmatism. —It's always that way, eventually, within mortal matters. That's the way things are. It's just a matter of where the least hurt lies.

—The lesser of the two evils, Jannus finished, without much interest, for they'd had this conversation before.

—What's the alternative: not choosing at all? Or hoping it would all go away? It's the way things are: entropy. The Shai appended a full contextual definition including half-lives of elements, solar output and decay rate, receding planetary systems, and erosion. —There's entropy, declared the Shai— and there's the Rule of One in the time between, until everybody ends up dead: myself included. That's all there is, the only alternatives.

One thing, at least, was certain: that was what the Shai

235

saw, and all he was prepared to see. But Jannus began wondering whether he himself might be able to see something else, something that didn't end up with slightly fewer people dead than alive. But for that, he'd have to get closer.

With no clearer sense of purpose than that, Jannus began finding his way down the crooked descending folds.

Eventually he began to pass among the outermost clusters of Valde encamped, fireless and shelterless, in broad clearings Jannus was accustomed to seeing filled with colorful pavilions. Some of the Valde noticed him: eyes lifting, gaunt faces turning. One said to him, "You are like the other," sounding puzzled.

Jannus supposed the man meant Bronh. "Yes," he said, and waited. But when the people only continued to look at him, he turned and went on. No one else spoke to him, nor did anyone attempt to hinder his passing.

It was so unlike the reaction he'd expected, so unlike Entellith, that it made him think he might be going the right way, doing the right thing.

The Shai considered that altogether absurd, to guess at one's purpose from one moment to the next by a species of divination and expect anything of value to come of it.

—You go on juggling the Rule of One, Jannus responded—and I'll juggle whatever I can find that makes sense to me.

The Shai communicated a burst of information on cointossing, auguries by means of entrails and bird-flight, astrology, scrying, and a host of other foolish methods of consulting the physical world about situations and choices.

Jannus didn't argue, having no arguments of his own to offer against that absolute certainty. He just kept moving, imagining the waves of perplexity and attention moving outward from the line of his passing.

When Jannus reached the valley's broad green floor, about five hours remained of the Shai's estimate. He surveyed the fighting for a while, finding that arrows were passing back and forth between ships and shore with regularity, like a trade, as possible targets offered themselves incautiously on either side. The packets and the shore seemed two opposing citadels, neither side willing to desert its secure fortress to risk a decisive encounter—not while the light lasted. The packets' hooting now seemed to him more of a deliberate annoyance than a signal of alarm. But fire arrows were beginning to arch over the rock toward the packets.

Jannus circled the fighting and went down toward the river's edge. He dipped his water bag full first, from habit, then drank from his own cupped hands. This near its source, the Morimmon was clear and good and always tasted of snow even into midsummer. He'd remembered that, but not the taste itself. He scooped another few handfuls until he was no longer thirsty, capped the water bag, and then just watched the wavering surface of the water, thinking of scrying and all the other curious ways people had ever used to find out what needed doing, and what would come of it.

When another reflection appeared on the river behind his own, he asked without looking around, "What does Pedross think he's about at the moment?"

"You shouldn't be here," Poli replied, in the cold voice she reserved for mobiles and suchlike *sa'farioh* creatures that had no business *being* at all: things that could pass unscathed only because most Valde had forgotten whatever they'd known about such creatures as Teks and mobiles, and the rest were in awe of mere novelty.

It was about what he'd thought she'd say.

It didn't hurt, this expected unwelcome. He couldn't be hurt that way; and that, alone, marked the enormity of the change.

Nevertheless, his sense of what he was doing evaporated altogether. He was left among a collection of isolated, unrelated facts, and processes grinding toward their predictable ends—all of it quite clear to him, none of it making any sense.

He wasn't where he should be. Otherwise, he'd be able to see how it all should be fitting together. Frowning, he stirred at the river with two fingers, asking, "Do you know where I should be, then?"

But when he looked around, he found she'd retreated beyond breathtalk distance. So he guessed she was operating by elimination too, the way he was. She only knew who and what he wasn't, that he should have been; she knew *not here*, but not *where*.

237

Jannus asked the Shai how long it would be before it hit him, this meeting. It didn't hurt; but it was going to.

—Perhaps never, depending what it's worth to you to avoid it, replied the Shai. —You can turn Tek altogether. There's a Simon body left over: you could take that next. Is that what you want?

All Jannus wanted was to discern what it was that he was supposed to be doing. —In the ordinary way of things, he persisted—how long before the feeling comes back?

—It should have begun already, replied the Shai. —But you've never conformed to any "ordinary way of things" as long as I've known you. Individuals can't be predicted with any accuracy. If they could, I'd not be in need of a mobile.

A child, touching Jannus' arm and then darting away, roused Jannus from absent attempts to make a mark on the water. The child had just wanted to find out if he was real, this strange *sa'farioh* thing that *was* there, but *wasn't*.

Jannus didn't mind. It made sense.

The child, now clinging to an adult's leg, had begun crying. Wondering if his moving had frightened her, Jannus went back up the bank and asked the father what was wrong. The man's ivory-tipped weaponry identified him as being of the local Morgaard kindred: most such had acquired the breath-talk. Nevertheless Jannus couldn't seem to make himself understood. Even more than he'd realized, Valde depended on the *farioh*'s counterpoint to comprehend anything said aloud.

Behind Jannus, Poli's voice commented, "She's hungry, that's all. Everybody is."

Jannus touched the child's head tentatively and she didn't duck or flinch away. He wouldn't have wished to frighten her.

Poli found herself forced into pendulum swings of approach and retreat. Near him, she saw the changes—the features remolded ten years too young, mocking her with memory: *not* the face she knew with her own immediate knowing but an untimely Newstock specter that didn't belong to her and never had, all the shared changes destroyed by a single blankly abstracted look. It wasn't only the *sa'farioh* emptiness but the visible change of manner. It wasn't only that she couldn't hear him; it was that, in some fundamental sense, he wasn't there, not even for himself. She saw no reflection of herself, no consciousness of relationship in his still, dark eyes.

And as soon as she was away, she saw the likeness, and was hotly envious of Sua's freedom to grab his arm and drag him off to talk to the two stranded Arduners. Poli knew exactly how that arm would feel under her fingers, knew his walk, knew the very back of his head and the motion of his breathing with an immediacy that drove her back again within hearing of his voice, which she found herself holding her breath to hear, unwilling to miss a single word because it was so much better than the nothing she'd had.

The Arduners, who scarcely knew him, put the external changes down to the absence of the accustomed beard, deciding with only faint perplexity that he must always have been *much* younger than they'd supposed. The nearby Valde considered him to be merely a species of walking omen, like Bronh, of which nothing but presence and influence was to be expected. And Sua, after the first moment's check at hearing his voice and after being told he wasn't just the newest item in the Garin-Simon sequence, took him so for granted she scarcely saw the outward changes at all. Any reaction, short of outright attack or persistent rejection, she was prepared to interpret as his usual diffident interest. Only Poli felt the full extent of what he'd lost, and become.

And whether she regarded him from nearby or across a distance, she felt a shivering expectancy which went on and on, so that it became a kind of tension, a kind of desperation, a kind of hunger, and she frequently forgot about the battle for several minutes at a time, just watching him.

The attraction drew her, and the angry hurt and frustration drove her away again. But, either way, there was only the one measure of distance, the one direction.

When he wandered off downstream, she followed because she couldn't have remained behind. He settled on a stump about thirty paces beyond the grove, apparently to have a better view of the rock and the packets, his head turning to follow the course of a fire arrow. Poli reached out and touched him, and the shoulder was solid and warmly familiar to her hand. But the turning face was a stranger's, without either startlement or curiosity.

He said, "It should rain soon. The Shai says it's—"

But she was already saying, "All those years I couldn't hear you, and it was still all right. . . ."

"It's different now," he replied, after a moment. "What you hear is what there is. I didn't expect I'd be a nuisance to you. Don't take any notice, past what you can help. . . ."

The voice was so exactly his own. Poli circled the stump, settled on her heels before him, and began to touch him with a frowning deliberation—his face first: the roughness at the hinges of the unshaven jaw, the nose that had known no injury, the indentations at the temples, the sober line of dark brows. Then her blind hand found the shape of the collarbone, the upper ribs, and the angular resistance of an elbow, as though expecting to find some tangible injury; but the pressure, the contact, was its own reason. And the body under her hands knew very well what she was about, and began its own responses. Presently he stirred, but only to capture her hands within his and hold them against his knee, remarking quietly, "And what would that prove: that it's not Tek meat?"

"It'd prove. . . . I've been alone, and I'm *still* alone, right now, and it's *too hard*—" Her voice failed her; she bent her head onto the bundle of hands, breathing unevenly.

"I didn't expect it would bother you so," he said finally. "Don't hurt yourself, reaching for what's not there. If the meat were enough, any meat would do. This is the Summer-fair, still, after all. There'll be somebody to suit you better— water into water, the way it ought to have been for you. Look, Poli: look what I can do now."

As she raised her head he slowly lifted both hands from hers and held them wide for a moment, then rose and walked on into a farther grove without looking back.

Now it was fire arrows.

Through the long-glass, Pedross saw a steady circular motion as Valde from the nearer heights drifted down to drink and then retreated, making way for others. Within sight of *White Gull*'s wheelhouse, children were chasing each other among the trees and a few adults were placidly fishing. Others, incredibly, had gone to sleep. Being hated was bad enough; being ignored was worse.

That was one of the major strangenesses of this battle, from Pedross' point of view: the apparent ability of those not directly involved to act as if nothing unusual were happening. The illusion persisted that if only he jumped into a rowboat and sculled out of the direct line of fire, he could settle down with a flashing line, or paddle in the shallows, until he was ready to come back and be shot at some more. He satisfied himself with pulling the whistle cord every few minutes and sending echoes rebounding from the surrounding heights.

Devorn Ault, Pedross' commander of marines, watching signals being waved from *Kam's Luck*. He reported, "Their boiler pressure is rising. A jammed valve, at first guess."

Leaning on the curve of window overlooking *White Gull's* bow, Pedross directed, "Have it shut down, then, and fixed— if it's fixable by sundown."

Devorn acknowledged the order and went to the door to speak to the signaler, who began waving his flags squeezed into the angle the wheelhouse protected from diagonal fire from the shore.

Though sunset was the absolute limit, there was a use, in Pedross' view, in delaying the retreat as long as possible. He'd come to demoralize the Valde and show strength, to impress them with the difficulty of fighting an entrenched and fore-warned enemy. The failed boarding attempt, the fact that the packets were still moored there and hooting at them in spite of several hours' attempts to dislodge them, might at least buy some of the time to prepare Ardun he'd come to win. Certainly it was providing a wonderful object lesson on "the gentle Valde" for the Loyalists aboard. That might help, when the time came to evacuate Ardun. . . .

Devorn called Pedross' attention to smoke darker than the smoke from the stacks, rising from the middle foredeck of the *Lady Marya*. Marines were crawling out, flat, with buckets hoisted on lines from the stern. Some pushed tables or benches before them to protect them from the archers on shore. All the firefighters were marines because all the Loyalists and the majority of the ships' own crews had been stowed safely away, under guard, in the messrooms to avoid distractions and abortive mutinies. Pedross always preferred to fight in one direction at a time if simple forethought allowed.

If any of the packets caught fire in earnest, the sunset limit became academic. The ships were moored too closely to escape a general fire aboard any one of them. They'd have to cast off immediately, transferring the complement of the burning packet as quickly as possible. Any who failed of the transfer would have to enact Pedross' fantasy of striking out for the shore and receiving whatever welcome they'd find awaited them there.

Neither Sua nor the two surviving Arduners, whom he could spot from time to time with the long-glass, seemed to be suffering any ill treatment; Sua's luck appeared to be still functioning to that extent, at least, though it did *him* no good. . . .

Pedross demanded a report on the boiler repair on *Kam's Luck*. The packet couldn't be sitting disabled if the fire aboard the *Lady Marya* proved impossible to control. *Kam's Luck* had been wreathed in hissing expelled steam for quite a while; between the smoke and the steam, Pedross was lucky to have a clear view of the shore for several minutes together. The message came back that the stopped valve had been located and was being removed. The estimate was an hour more before the chief engineer could start getting steam up again. Pedross got the hailing horn and shouted to the firefighters, who increased in numbers and energy. Pedross couldn't help thinking about the inexorable progress of the Aihall fire, scarcely a tenday ago.

Arrows were rattling down on the upper decks of the *Lady Marya*, arching high over the fume to fall straight and skewer somebody to the deck. But none of them that Pedross could see sported a clout of flaming fabric. Lowering the glass, he watched hard for a few minutes as a freshening breeze pushed the smoke clear of the wheelhouse. None of the arrows rising toward *White Gull* seemed to be smoking either. Only *Kam's Luck* was still receiving fire arrows.

Through the glass Pedross scanned what he could see of the shore down there and quickly located the smoke of the fire at which the Valde were kindling their shafts. And while he watched, there was a rising puff of steam in that place and then no more smoke. And between two trees he saw a dark man turning, carrying something, moving along behind the barricade.

Pedross grabbed the hailing horn again and tilted the window just enough to get the horn's larger end outside. But before he could call, a shaft ricocheted through the gap under the windowframe and buried its head in his reinforced leather cuirass. Pedross checked the angle, to make sure that deft archer had no chance to hit his face or anything vital unless an arrow came right down the horn, and he'd risk that. He shouted, "Quiet, below decks!" He had to repeat it three or four times before he got anything like obedience. Then, except for assorted engine noises and bumps and voices carrying across from *Kam's Luck,* the weird silence of the whole valley again reached him, unchanged since mid-morning.

"Jannus! That you? Hey, Jannus!" Pedross left the horn wedged into the window and, moving safely aside, put the glass to his eye and found the man again—he'd stopped and was facing the rock. It wasn't very like, but it was surely a Bremneri, and who else could it be? Pedross yelled through the horn, "Can you swim out? I'll send a boat for you."

Jannus shook his head and turned away, and Pedross dragged the horn back in and slammed the window just as another shaft struck it and bounced off. Pedross reached up, grabbed the whistle cord, and blew a whole series of demanding hoots. But the Bremneri kept moving away.

It could be a mobile. Either way, whether or not, the man would be in contact with the Shai and might be able to supply a means of breaking this downhill standoff more decisive than by dousing fires. With one Tek heat weapon, with one gigantic flash like that which had blinded the squad waiting to ambush Bronh, Pedross could inflict some real damage. With *Sunfire,* he'd have power and leverage instead of arrows and faulty valves and a defense base about as secure as a flagpole.

But Pedross' reach wouldn't extend that far; and if the Shai wasn't willing to bring *Sunfire*'s resources to the packets' aid, it surely wasn't for the lack of a polite request. Pedross had made this foray against every opposition Simon's advice could interpose and now had to conclude that he was entirely on his own—for the first time in his life, he realized, save for the few months' interval between Secolo and Simon.

He wished he could find some way to get Jannus aboard, if only for the sake of comprehending company. And of course there might be pressures that could be brought to bear. . . .

243

But, no. He was far better, he decided, without anyone brought unwilling aboard his flagship who'd possess such a unique, searing, and explosive method of saying *No*.

On her knoll, Bronh was increasingly displeased, and every time one of the packets emitted a teeth-gritting screech, her disfavor grew. The archers' duel had consumed half the afternoon without any positive result, and she couldn't persuade the Valde to attempt another boarding. The strategists now in control of the fighting knew they had only to wait for nightfall for the boarding to become both safer and more effective.

But after half a day's interval, the Singing might be ready to resume, even in spite of the insingers' departure; and Bronh wanted no outside distractions, as loud and jarring to the Valde as the steam whistle blasts were to her, remaining to mar the rite that would follow then.

The sacrifice was prepared: all that remained was its accomplishment.

Then word reached her that the shore fires had been put out by the other *sa'farioh*, and nobody willing to prevent him, protected with the same protections she had laid down for herself in preparation for this day.

Bronh took up the handle of her firepot and descended from her knoll, determined to break the present stalemate as soon as possible even if that meant doing it herself.

Before she'd gone halfway to the river, it had begun to rain—a thin mist carried before the advancing line of flat clouds darkening the farther reaches of the pass. There, the rain was visible, greying all the greens, moving in a steady curtain, shading brightness but absorbing shadow as well. But, thought Bronh, even wetted packets could burn, if a protected floor or wall could be well-caught. And it didn't take a large flame to set dry wadding on an arrow alight. She covered the top of the firepot with a chip of dry wood from the rough sack slung at her side.

She and Jannus knew each other at first glance because each stood out so markedly from the surrounding Valde. Bronh said to the former troopleader walking near her, "Kill that *sa'farioh*. He is nothing to you-all but an enemy."

It would have been better if the Valde could have been persuaded to attend to the removal themselves. It would have been good practice and a good precedent. But Bronh was prepared to manage it herself. Handing to a Haffa on her left the firepot and the protecting chip, Bronh took from a loop of the Haffa's troopmaid's harness one of the small missiles called dagger-darts. Holding it hidden behind her wrist, Bronh took care not to cut herself against the slender blade or its needle point coated with a thin, resinous paste that caused quick and prolonged unconsciousness.

"Have you brought your bond?" Jannus asked of her as she moved nearer.

"What bond?" she asked.

"I'm told you have a firepot. In five minutes it'll be the only thing alight. It'll do, for your part of the bond."

He seemed to regard it as some trivial lowlanders' dispute, with bond posted on both sides to buy impartial ajudication. Bronh tipped her head and surveyed him, wondering if he were really that much of a fool.

Before she had come within ten paces he started walking along ahead of her, the Valde moving away between and around them, leaving clear space.

"You can throw in some wet bowstrings, if you want," he continued, "but personally I don't think they'll be worth much, either way."

"Your recent associations have given you an inflated notion of your own importance," Bronh rejoined, following steadily, casually. "This isn't *Sunfire*—"

"No," he cut in, "it's the Summerfair and the season of Choosing."

"No more," contradicted Bronh harshly. "Never, anymore."

"I do hear you," he said, and stopped, leaving her path to the riverbank and the barricade open.

Setting fists on hips, Bronh stopped too, inquiring, "Do you set yourself up to hear this thing, and to tell everybody what's fit, and where the injury rests?"

"Oh no: not me," he disclaimed at once.

"Then who are you proposing to set up as arbiter—to sort this all out tidily—the Shai? *Pedross*?"

At each scornful proposal he shook his head, and the rain had reached them, falling in whipping sheets. "Where's your firepot, Bronh? You Haffa, who's the one . . . ?"

He began circling, his eyes shifting from Bronh in short quick side glances to scan the first few Valde ranked around them. Bronh followed, objecting, "You have no part in this, no power. *You!*"

While he was looking at her, she pointed beyond him, a commanding gesture, emphatic and unexpected: and as he looked aside, she moved.

The body of the dart was thick enough to serve as a haft, and there was no necessity that the weapon be thrown. Still misdirecting attention with her eyes and her pointing left hand, she struck him with the dart in her right, solidly, between the proper ribs on his left side, as deeply as the blade would go. He was already pulling away, freeing the dart she held tightly, but Bronh didn't strike a second time. She wasn't particularly interested in killing him unless as a demonstration, a precedent. He'd only come back, even if after a delay. Rather, she'd prefer to immobilize him, prevent his further interference.

Blinding, she thought, would do nicely. And, even rebodied once already, he was still lowlander enough to need considerable time to willingly discard a present body, however maimed, and face the imagined horror of the incendiary.

The dagger-dart would be long and sharp enough to empty an eye-socket quite nicely.

Bronh stood clear and waited for him to fall.

Sua had seen her at last, the she-troll who'd been her enemy from the beginning. She'd thought it had been Poli barring her from the troll hill, but she'd been wrong. She hadn't known then what she knew now, about trolls.

The crowd of Valde backed into her in making a clear space, but she jabbed and pushed to be able to see what would happen. And her da was talking to the she-troll in a flat sort of voice, flat even not counting the queer sound of it that was in the troll's voice too, when she answered him, only the troll was angry, and let it show. Then it started absolutely pouring, but nobody moved under the trees so Sua stayed too, making rounds of her hands to look through because it was raining so hard.

Somebody bumped her, and it was Poli, her face white as

chalk, but her mam didn't seem to have noticed her. Sua took Poli's wrist and, when that didn't work, pinched her arm.

Poli muttered, "I can't, I'm barred—" and then gave Sua a ferocious shove that knocked at least one person down and sent Sua staggering out into the circle. Sua was swinging around to find out why Poli had shoved her that way when she saw how the troll and her da were facing each other. There was something wrong about the stiff way both of them were standing. When her da started to turn aside and then fell, Sua knew what one part of the wrongness had been. And when the troll took a step, Sua was in no doubt about the other part.

The troll hadn't been looking for anybody to kick her, *hard*, in the back of the knee, and sat down suddenly. Sua knew to watch the hands, to learn what to look out for, and stamped on the wrist of the hand holding the dagger-dart. But the troll lady was *strong*, and the wrist lifted under Sua's foot and nearly tipped her over backward. Some Valde were trying either to grab or steady Sua then, but she twisted free of them and kicked the troll-lady under the chin because legs were longer and stronger than arms, provided you could keep one foot steady under you while you did it, and it was lucky she'd kept her shoes on or she'd have surely sprained a toe or even her whole foot.

Then there were people moving all over, the circle breaking, and Sua moved fast enough to keep her da from getting stepped on; the she-troll, Sua hoped they walked all over.

Sua tried to help her da up but he was too heavy and didn't move, and there was a really bad second when Sua thought he was dead. She bent down, feeling for the motion of breath, and found it. But her hand came away wet and with a smell she would never forget: it would be that room, and that awful woman, and Garin dead at the foot of the stairs, to her, forever. She turned her head away and threw up, which hurt because she'd scarcely eaten a thing since sunup, and the rain got into her nose and made her sneeze.

Something moved down by her knees, and she found her mam there, finding out the same thing Sua had.

"It was a dagger-dart," Sua offered, feeling helpless and upset. Poli had pulled the shirt back, and the blood was washing down into the grass but not washing away, though

Sua couldn't see any wound, only the blood, and the smell was beginning to make her feel dizzy. . . .

"Bite your tongue," Poli directed, and Sua did and felt much better except that then her tongue hurt. Poli was holding Jannus' shoulders up off the grass and seemed to be listening to his breathing. Abruptly, she told Sua, "Come on. We have to get him away from here, right now."

He wasn't helping, so he was hard to lift and harder to carry. But the three of them were much of a height, and Poli locked one of his arms around over her shoulders and put her free arm around behind his back, and Sua did the same, since Poli was on the side where the blood was.

After they'd gone a way with the wind slashing at their backs, Poli said suddenly, "It's no use, she'll only come after him, and nobody will stand between."

"I will," puffed Sua, wondering why Poli didn't, and Poli looked around at her measuringly.

"No," decided Poli. "Hold him steady a minute."

Sua couldn't, not by herself, so they instead laid him down on the rough grass of the bank and then Poli stepped down and they eased him carefully over the edge, in the little space before the water started.

Poli directed, "Think about something, anything other than this, as hard as you can, and don't come near here or look at the river. But don't go too far, and when I call, come running. That's good." (Sua was thinking about how wet she was and how much she wished she'd stayed home.) Poli muttered, "If they can't hear him, she can't find him—at least not right away. . . ."

"And what if the troll comes?"

"Then do whatever you can," Poli replied shortly, climbing back up the bank. She went away upstream, then waded out, heading straight for a long distance before she let the current begin carrying her in a long swing toward the packets. Sua wasn't watching, not really.

Poli had gone for a boat to get Jannus clear in, and had taken the long, roundabout swim so she'd have time to hail first before some marine decided to try shooting at her for a boarder. Sua had figured it out all by herself.

As Jannus was returning toward consciousness he was

aware that it was getting dark and that there was a wall beside him on the right and a roof above him.

—What's happened? he asked the Shai.

—How should I know? came the response, the only sharp thing in a blurred sense of drifting.

—Is this *Sunfire* again?

—It's a stationary packet moored, in all probability, to a rock in the Morimmon in Morgaard Vale.

She hadn't killed him, then: Bronh. And somebody had taken him aboard one of the packets, out of her reach. The sense of disconnectedness seemed to be intensified by putting those two thoughts together; so, as further distraction didn't seem important, Jannus asked for a conceptual description of what was wrong with him. But the Shai couldn't tell him. The implant monitored only the nervous system and, almost exclusively, the brain. The Shai knew no more about his injuries than he himself could feel, though the Shai promised him a fairly good observational analysis as soon as there was enough data.

—What do you want done in regard to replacement meat? the Shai wanted to know. —Tek, or another replica?

This body hurt. Jannus had no affection for it, no more expectations to conform to, and other expectations he didn't want to provoke and then cruelly fail of fulfilling. —The Tek meat. It can look like Simon, for all I care, or anybody. It doesn't matter.

—I don't think you're likely to require rebodying on the strength of present injuries alone, commented the Shai—but it's a thing I ought to know.

Jannus rested awhile, still no more than halfway to waking. He asked presently, —Is it still raining?

—I can't tell, through the overcast. . . . Jannus, if I were to leave, would you want to come?

Jannus tried to get his mind to handle that odd invitation.

—I could keep you in meat almost indefinitely, continued the Shai—and in a few centuries I ought to have made some kind of contact with the parent culture that the Teks sprang from to begin with: that, or another like it. In such an interval it seems quite likely they would have spread out nearer than they were when I set out, in *Sunfire, as Sunfire.* . . .

—Leave? responded Jannus finally.

—It's one possibility. Be my own mobile, in a scale broad enough for the power to be commensurate and effective, and work minimal distortion on its own effects. The tone of that remark was pensive, wistful, and immensely grim. —Poli told me once to shell myself. I can't do that. But I can take the shell with me.

—But what about the Rule of One?

—Gravity doesn't need enforcing, nor the processes of entropy. If the Rule of One is what I've always believed, it will be served and work its particular changes wherever there's life, without need of my help. And if it isn't, then what does it matter what one individual does? I only have to please myself, if only gravity, entropy, and a few other physical processes need be considered. . . . Could you stand some conceptual input about what it would be like?

—All right, agreed Jannus dubiously, and it became almost like dreaming, with strange perspectives moving around him and endless unchanging time passing. . . .

—You don't have to absorb all that, the Shai roused him at length by remarking. —You just have to decide whether, if I decide to go, you want to come.

Implicit in the offer was the wish and the hope that he would. But Jannus had come to the end of his curiosity, and beyond; and he'd been forced farther into the strangeness already than he could tolerate. He could imagine and visualize hard vacuum and how a world would look from orbit. But the spaces between the stars were farther out than he could stretch himself. It was like the Singing. It had nothing to do with him; and he had no real wish to understand it and none whatever to share it.

The Shai said to him —Before I go, *if* I go, I'll ask you again. It would be the end of the link, in practical terms, at least. . . . But you don't have to decide now, while it's so hard for you to think clearly.

But it wasn't a matter of thinking, and they both knew what Jannus' answer must eventually be.

Sitting quietly in the cabin, waiting for Jannus' dart-sleep to pass off, Poli could hear the body's silent voices of injury. It wasn't *farioh*, but it wasn't silence either. It was *part* of the selfsinging: the body's part, muttering in shocked restlessness at the absolute bottom limit of what she could, by steady attention almost to the intensity of trance, overhear and know.

Grass was louder. Nevertheless, the mutter was there.

He wasn't lar to her. The final proof of that had been her own inability to break through the unanimous will not to interfere when he'd faced Bronh. If they'd been lar, nothing could have prevented her from crossing that barrier.

She was, she supposed, free. He'd wanted that for her, even against her own will, and now even the tight tether of his demanding, anxious attachment had been cut and he could lift his two hands from hers and walk away.

It was very strange. It was like being nobody, invisible, with no reflection at all, as was said of witches in regard to running water.

She didn't know why she was here, smack in the middle of the swooping terrors of the Choral Hating Society, just a wall away, except that there was nowhere else she wanted to be, no other concern as strong.

She checked the dressing over the wound and added another pad. Used as missiles, dagger-darts seldom did more than temporary injury. But the narrow blade had been driven home to its full length and at least touched one of the major blood vessels. Jannus had coughed blood for a while, which Sua couldn't stand—she'd escaped to the Loyalists next door in the mess hall, and hot food—but that happened less often now, and the external bleeding seemed to be diminishing, as well. Poli didn't like the lack of color in his face. But she'd done all that she could while he remained unconscious and unable to swallow anything to speed the healing or help make the lost blood back.

Jannus' eyes blinked, but their gaze was unfocused and his head didn't turn toward her. The body continued its dazed monologue. Then Pedross came in—it was his cabin, after all—and Poli lost the truncated, partial *farioh* in the wash of urgency and impatience Pedross brought with him. Poli wasn't perturbed to lose the thin inner voice. She didn't have to hear it, now, to be sure it continued, independent of her knowing.

Pedross came across the cabin, laid the back of his hand quite gently against the side of Jannus' forehead, and considered the basin of discarded stiffening pads of stained fab-

251

ric. He remarked to her quietly, "I'm deciding now whether to run or to stay—and, if I stay, what there is to stay for: because none of my people—my marines," he corrected himself, with undertones of dubious connectedness to non-marines, "will swallow an order like that without an awfully good reason. They know the shape of the thing as well as I do. I've got no mobile, no Valde left in my service. What I've got is you. So what do you know that's a reason not to cut cables and run? What about the Singing?"

Poli listened and presently told him what she learned: "Everybody's exhausted. Since the last spell ended there's been one disruption after another and hardly anybody's gotten any rest at all. I don't think there are many who could even manage trance, much less support the Singing. . . . And, of course, the insingers are out of range of all but the far-speakers now, and that—"

"Explain that."

"The insingers: those who focus the Singing most easily and hold it together. They're gone, down the pass, and the last thing they want is any more contact with you or yours, whatever's happening here. That try at boarding hurt them badly—"

"Those were the insingers?" Pedross interrupted, and Poli nodded. Pedross was furious for the opportunity missed for the lack of a Valde to tell him what he'd been facing.

"So without them," Poli continued, "I wouldn't expect the Singing to rouse again tonight."

"Then I can expect boarders in the water again within half an hour. That tears it." With a sharp gesture of termination, Pedross started back for the door.

"What have you got," inquired Jannus' drowsy voice, making Pedross swing back, "to serve as your part of the bond?"

"What?"

Jannus repeated, "Your bond. What would you put up to have this thing settled, either way?"

"If you want to play at—" Pedross began sharply.

"To get a hearing," Jannus started, shoving up on an elbow. Then he noticed Poli and fell silent: trying, she thought, to make sense of her presence. Maybe asking the Shai, she thought with a certain wryness. Then Jannus resumed, "To get a hearing, you need something of agreed and appropriate value to stake on your end of it."

"Something of—" To Poli, Pedross directed a frowning incredulity that demanded whether Jannus was wandering in his wits, or whether he himself was, to stand listening while the time was passing. "With Ardun at stake, and every breathing soul aboard these three ships, and likely everything short of deep water and the isles, and you ask if—"

"The bread won't do," remarked Jannus meditatively, and leaned back against the pillow, folding his right arm across his forehead. "You've mixed the meanings of that too much already. Nor the packets, or whatever your Loyalists could tune themselves to. Something else."

Pedross considered with his head tilted, then went toward the cot and with an effort dragged from beneath it a rectangular block the size of a footstool, red stone with sooty streaks and smudges. "There's that," he remarked, "and there's me. And that's all I have the right to put at risk."

Carefully, Jannus rolled onto his side to look at the block, then raised his face inquiringly.

"It's the Founding Stone of the Aihall," Pedross explained, nudging at it with the side of a boot. "I had it found and dug out after the fire, and fetched it to remind me why I was coming and putting up with the Loyalists. . . . Will that do, for my bond?"

Without answering, Jannus rolled flat again and shut his eyes. After a moment he said, "Poli. Can you tell some of the Morgaard folk—the neutrals—that bond's been posted on this side, and the bond required on the other is Bronh's firepot, and no other fires to be made or tended on shore till the thing's settled. . . . Is it still raining?" he asked suddenly.

"It let up a little while ago," replied Pedross absently, watching Poli. "Everything's soaked past danger of fire arrows, though, or we'd have been about twelve miles downriver by now. . . ."

Poli was sorting through the countless *fariohe*, identifying herself merely as the speaker for the *sa'farioh* and calling for any neutrals to attend and answer her concerning a proposed major judgment.

Gradually, responses gathered and found harmony and there was a firming, broadening sense of attention. She then passed on the terms of *seeking* terms, the bond posted and the bond required. She inspoke it several different ways because specifics were always variably translated from the inspeaking and Poli wanted to leave no possibility of mistake.

The neutrals then, in turn, sent the query out to discover how the larger balance rested: whether the two *sa'fariohe* should again face each other or not. Consensus swirled and formed. The Valde, the whole mass of them, were inclined to hear whatever was to be heard, for the sake of the Stone laid to found Ardun. For the *sa'fariohe* and the Stone, they'd attend.

"They accept your bond," Poli told Pedross, who grinned broadly with a sharp clap of inner exultation.

"But you have to talk to them," Jannus told him, hitching up on his elbow again to look over to Pedross.

"No, you'll manage—" Pedross began.

"No," Jannus contradicted. "It's not mine to do. I think it's yours. Isn't it?"

"I don't know. . . . Maybe. . . . Yes," decided Pedross, abruptly sober and uneasy, with the sense of taking firm hold of something that had teeth. "It's mine. Where?"

"The mooring rock would do," commented Jannus, and added, "Stone laid on stone. That makes the right sort of sense."

That was what had made Lifganin and the Fallows wilderness: the Valde prohibition against stone being laid on stone within their boundaries.

"Yes," Pedross mused, "I'll speak for Ardun, for all us damned invaders, everything since the Laying of the Stone."

He went out to call some men to help move the Stone out on deck and, from the passageway, his voice went on about a loading boom because he didn't trust the gangway to support that much weight and it would be a pure pity to lose the block now.

Poli lifted the new pad and found it not yet badly stained. "What's to be done?" she asked quietly.

"They may need the cargo boom for me too," Jannus remarked, using his left arm to try to push himself upright. Poli helped him, and he got his feet on the floor but didn't try, yet, to stand. Presently he said, "You don't have to—"

"I'm a Haffa of the troops, a freemaid and First Dancer,

254

and a Valde of Ardun. Where else should I be?" she responded calmly.

"That's for you to say," he conceded, after a moment.

"Yes," she said. "It is."

Just because Bronh had claimed the right of the eldest to
speak first, Pedross didn't consider that the Tek would be
thereby entitled to the undivided attention of the Valde—not
if he were willing and able to divide it.

You didn't have to learn the whole of the inspeaking, he
judged, to be able to project some simple message instead of
the random noise so disliked by the departed insingers. Therefore, some of the time before moonrise, he spent in the mess
hall with the Arduners, all of them learning how to make the
proper sequence of imagined feelings which would communicate what Pedross said. They used drum-taps to keep
more or less together, at least beginning and ending each sequence of image/attitudes in unison.

The Loyalists didn't want to take instruction from Poli.
Pedross himself would have agreed to some less emotional arrangement: with Poli next door, say, and Sua running back
and forth to report the results of their efforts. But Poli
wouldn't have it. It had to be face to face or nothing. And, as
she was the only Valde available, Pedross supported her, as
did Territ and Sua. So Poli sat before them like an implacable choir director while, singly or in groups, they tried to
make their message coherent. Poli pointed at people, saying
tersely, *yes* or *no*, while Jannus wandered idly around the gal-
ley end of the mess hall with what Pedross considered an an-
noyingly saturnine expression, nursing his side and being no
help whatever.

But the inspeaking was apparently a personal thing. Each
sense/image was different with each speaker and could be
drawn only out of one's own attitudes and experience, in-
tensely subjective. It couldn't be taught: only felt, only
learned. The images Jannus used—*had* used, at least—
wouldn't work for anybody else. There was no way for Jannus *to* help. Nevertheless, Pedross resented Jannus' detached
observation and disliked having only Poli's word for what he
was communicating. For all he knew, he was broadcasting
some mortal insult or an ingenuous announcement that he

255

was a little yellow flower or a sample of excrement. But somehow Pedross didn't dare demand further validation, from Sua, of what Poli asserted; and anyway, who could then verify that Sua wasn't lying?

Better to trust, hope for the best, and try to make the images speak.

We're here now (sense of rightful belonging, home, stable footing, the presence-pressure of folk going in one direction): *you've been changed, but so have we* (motion of wind, motion of wave, the lift of a keel rising to the wave it cut) *and we didn't ask for it either* (the perplexities of growing, the advent of desire, the mystifying distances that separated himself from all others); *we must take each other for what we've made of each other, or one of us will surely die. . . .*

That was Pedross' own version of what he wanted to say, hoped he was saying: shaping the message from personal things to the rhythm of a drum.

Turning aside finally, he demanded of Jannus, "And what does Grandda Troll make of our odds?"

Jannus quit sipping soup and offered a distant expression. "Let him worry about that."

When Pedross persisted, Jannus mentioned that he wasn't a speaking-tube, to carry somebody else's chat. "You're not," Pedross agreed. "You're a firebomb and as helpful as toothache," and slammed off to block out what he meant to say in words he himself could at least hear.

At moonrise Bronh was sitting on the rock, surrounded by a *hafkenna*. One of the smaller girls, a farspeaker, was to act as Fair Witness and translate what Bronh said into faithful and accurate inspeaking for the Valde on both sides of the river. A throng of insingers would have been better, but the multiple bonding that linked members of the *hafkenna* would do almost as well. The *hafra* who had ceded Bronh the company of his pack was on shore, directly opposite the stone: the young *in'farioh* would be telling him what Bronh said. In so doing, the farspeaker would be telling everyone else, as well.

Bronh could have requested an older farspeaker, one with a more sophisticated acquaintance with the nuances of breathtalk: in Bronh's terms, one more contaminated by alien influences. Bronh preferred the child, with her bony scraped knees and gnawed fingernails. One didn't expect children to interpret complexity or attend to the boring intricacies of rational sequence. The child would keep Bronh mindful of her audience.

Bronh's firepot sat in the center of the island, guarded by a pair of the neutrals: Morgaard-dwellers, by their style of dress and carved ivory weaponry. From time to time they fed the coals in Bronh's firepot with dry chips furnished by Pedross, as he'd furnished the rowboats which had brought Bronh and the Valde dry-footed from the shore. If he thought to impress Valde with his scrupulousness, Bronh thought, he was a fool: Valde would know the intention behind the gesture and despise him the more.

He was positioned on the far side of the neutrals, sitting on the Founding Stone of Ardun.

Farther along, below the crown of the rock, were Poli and Jannus, whom Bronh unreservedly hated for persuading the assembly to this shared hearing. That he was *sa'farioh* prevented him from opposing a farspeaker's coercive influences against those Bronh would bring to bear, but it had given him the status to force this confrontation on equal terms which he in no wise merited. His arrogance entitled him to share her immolation, Bronh had decided. She was willing to grant him at least that much of what was due a Tek. . . .

The one crucial blunder had already been made. She'd been given, without even argument, the right to speak first; and afterward, Bronh thought, there would be no speaking at all.

There was no need of lanterns or torches. Pedross' bright hair, Bronh observed idly, would make him a splendid target when the killing resumed. The moonlight shimmered on the water and the young farspeaker told Bronh that there was a readiness for her to begin.

"Do you-all remember Fathori?" she asked the child, not attempting to make her voice heard beyond the water.

"We remember," replied the girl after a moment.

"Fathori was made to pay a blood-debt," said Bronh. "The debt had been owed since the time of Gaherin, a Tek. Do you remember the Teks now?"

"Some of us remember," said the girl, "what you told us."

That was their curse: to shrug off the pain of the past. Bronh had to teach them otherwise, so that they would be fitted to their revenge. Patiently, she explained, "A Tek: one of the invaders who made pets of you in the great silence of the High Plain where nothing grows of itself, and the day-singing and the nightsinging alike are the sounds of wind on dry stone. Do you remember the Teks?"

"We remember."

"This Tek warped you-all, as trees are warped by wind, and set you so near the timberline that most died and those that lived were changed. Boy-children became fewer and fewer, and you-all were dying. That is a great blood-price, a great wrong committed against you-all by that Tek, and by all Teks who neither knew nor cared what was done or what would come of it. And the proof of it was Fathori, built out of afterguilt, a bribe later Teks paid themselves to forget what they had done to you. And some of them were satisfied with the price, and forgot, and went into Fathori and were lost there. And from them sprang the Fishers and the An-drans, the Sea-people who care nothing for Valde, forgetting the crime and the blood-price and believing they owe nothing to you-all. But all they have was yours, stolen so shamelessly that their children's children claim it as though it had been theirs from the beginning. But it was yours, and you must not forget it: for the blood-price has never been paid. To this very night, the debt you are owed has waited like a spring under rock that breaks the stone at last and bursts forth."

On the packets behind her, a drum was tapping. Bronh waited a few measures for what she'd said to circulate and reach everyone, so that they could feel the heat of the brand before the brand itself that would mark them beyond any careless, expedient forgetting. Facing the vague blur of faces that was all her inadequate senses could know of her beloved Valde, Bronh continued, "There was another Tek who did *not* forget. And that Tek went among Valde wherever they were, in the days after the Rebellion's end, and tricked them. That Tek said, 'See the Bremneri that were lar to the Valde scattered from Fathori after its burning? See how the Truthtell has divided them, the men from the women? Valde must go among them and be as a wall between them; and the Haffa shall go, and the Hafera shall not. And whatever Haffa

258

will not go in her growthyear and for ten summers thereafter shall be Awiro and unpartnered all of her life.' The Tek told them this so that most of the Haffa, who were born without brothers, should die and the Hafera, who had brothers and bore more sons, should live. But Tek didn't tell the true reasons; and because the Tek was *sa'farioh*, the Tek spoke only words to them and they knew nothing of the lie and so believed. For they themselves knew of the strife among the Bremneri, which is, in fact, among all the Unhearing, Truthtell or no, so that they are a continual misery to each other and the *in'marenniathe* cannot abide them. So the troopservice began, and the Summerfair, and the Lore of the Change.

"And the Haffa went, and sometimes a hand of tens returned and sometimes less. Most died, either through heartsickness at being trapped among the *sa'marenniathe*, or by the quarrels of Bremneri with each other: for the Bremneri cared nothing for their troopmaids. The men hated them, and the she-Traders, the Truthtellers of the riverstocks, merely used the troopmaids as bricks to wall in and protect their power, caring nothing for the bricks themselves. And none of the troopmaids knew that she had been sent so that she *would* die, and have no Haffa children. She believed the lie that the price, the fault, was with Valde and not with the *sa'marenniathe* who had stolen her away from her very nature, her very form. For she, and you-all, had let yourselves forget that the blood-price *still* had not been paid. It grew heavier with each generation of Haffa troopmaids gone ignorant to the ground, or returned too dark-hearted for briding. But gradually the Haffa became fewer, and the Troopcallings came to last the whole of the Summerfair before enough were gathered to fill the numbers needed for the troops, and outlanders began to bend the Summerfair to their own purposes and intrude, yet again, on what was rightly a matter of yourselves-together. . . .

"What is the Lore of the Change?" Bronh demanded suddenly. "When will it come?"

Across the water and from all sides, Bronh was answered: "It will come when it comes, in its proper season, on the wind."

"And who will say it, and confirm it?"

"The wind's voice will say it."

"And what will be the marks of the season of the Change, that you may know it by?"

"The *in'marenniathe* will begin the Singing, and all who hear will answer it, and we will all be changed."

"And what will be the price of it?"

"Taking the fire into our own hands," answered the multitude and the farspeaker beside her on the rock.

"Do it, then," said Bronh. "For I am Windvoice, and I tell you that the fire is the will to remember and be revenged. The fire is *farioh*, the lives of yourselves-together that you must take into your own hands however it may burn you. I am Windvoice, and I confirm you in the beginnings of the Change. But you must take the fire into your own hands. For I am also the last of the Teks. I am the one who lied to the first of the free Valde in their bewilderment after the Rebellion. No Haffa has gone to the ground in Bremner, or Awiro been unpartnered, except by my sole will. The blood-price will be paid. Now. By all of us who are not Valde. Take what you are owed!"

The drum tapped its slow rhythm and all the girls of the *hafkenna* turned their faces toward Bronh in unison. She knew then that the brand had been hot enough and had seared its mark. She'd roused the full Singing without need of the insingers. All Valde were one in hatred of her.

Feeling a kind of ecstasy of completion, Bronh rose to her feet waiting for the first arrow, the first upward dagger-strike. She called into the moonlight, "Cast out whatever is strange among you, all stranger-enemies with their own purposes that are not yours. Take what you are owed. The blood-price must be paid!"

And yet no arrow had whizzed down nor hand been lifted against her. They needed present provocation to force response in kind—still restrained, perhaps, by the irrational awe of a *sa'farioh*. She had to make the enormity of her betrayal of them for the sake of their survival clear in some way that could not but reach them. She found one of the leaf-bladed daggers by its pale white shining and used it to cut the cord that had fastened it to a child's motionless wrist. With the knife's point she pricked the child on the hollow within the fold of the elbow, behind the ear, at the side of the nose: to make them know how little the injury of one meant compared to the health of the whole, and make them know they must never trust or be in such awe of anyone hereafter.

But the girl's staring grey eyes looked blankly past Bronh and the child made no attempt to defend herself or strike back.

Bronh cut one child in the hollow of the shoulder and another in the neck. And still she continued unpunished and alive, with not only the blood-guilt to bear but actual blood wet on her fingers so that she had to hold the knife haft tightly. In her rage of frustration and torn by the bond of mutual hurt, Bronh underwent a change beyond her controlling but not against her will. All restraints were broken and her deepest feelings flamed forth into the night, a silent blaze of inward agony and desire which only the *marenniath* could know. She ceased to be *sa'farioh* and became, as had all Teks before her, a Screamer.

Reaction was immediate. The *hafkenna* recoiled, wrapping their bony arms around their heads, rocking and crying out wordlessly. And Bronh moved among them, stabbing at the children randomly until her hand and arm were caught and held. Bronh let the knife fall, awaiting the return blow.

But a man's uninflected voice told her quietly, "You have to stop now, Bronh: you're hurting them."

In the full strength of her fury, Bronh broke the hold. She seized Jannus around the throat and pulled him into a toppling, bruising fall onto the rounded edge of the rock. They rolled into the cool black water. Bronh dragged him down.

It was hard to move amid the Singing. Poli felt heavy, as if there were an immense weight of inert will to be shifted in just getting a foot under her and pushing herself erect. With dreamlike slowness she walked along the ridges of the rock to where the two *saffariohe* had hit the water. The surface of the river was dark with the moon behind her. There was nothing to be seen.

Without the insingers, the Singing was a balance rather than a flow. And the force of individual desire could affect that balance, shift the still point of convergence. Still with that awful, encumbered slowness, Poli pulled the Singing into an attention, focusing the almost infinite rapport on a thing she alone knew: the truncated *farioh*, the body's voice of hurt. The Loyalists' litany was a distraction: the Singing shut it out. Trees, fish, waterfowl were likewise banished, and the small life among the grasses, then the grasses themselves, all dismissed, ignored. Without the all-accepting openness of the insingers at the center, the Singing became a purposeful trance of listening.

And, in the silence, she heard that thin and partial voice of the body's dread and struggle for breath. But there was another voice, as well: or, rather, another part of the same voice. Almost beyond the range of the *marenniath* and perhaps only to be heard at all in moments of great stress, it was the strange immanence Poli had sensed once before. Unaware of itself, as outward-looking as the body's voice was self-regarding, the strange voice was pure sorrow and bereavement.

Jannus, grieving for Bronh.

When she'd heard that alien voice before, Poli hadn't liked it. It had made her uneasy, to feel there was anything in Jannus beyond her reach, isolated and unknowable. Now she heard it with a kind of wonder: for that day in the Aihall Square had been the other side of the gap. A death had come between.

The last of Poli's reservations melted. Nevertheless she was not bound. No imprinted intimacy coerced her. No Valde could be lar to a *sa'farioh*. She knew him now; but merely knowing required of her no response and contained no necessary relatedness.

He'd gotten free of Bronh somehow, Poli judged: no such grief could arise without certainty of loss. And the bodily turbulence was calming. The river was quiet, and the near shore, at least, no great distance. He should be able to manage to get that far, on his own. . . .

The water was far more dangerous to her than to him, impeded as she was by the inertia of being tied to so many others, each individual motion an effort. If she could only *hear* him, fully, to know how he was faring. . . .

But she knew anyhow. He had no care for himself, the high voice said. He didn't care enough to fight the water and the pull of the current and the pervasive conviction or loss, abandonment. And two deaths would be one too many. It was nothing from the two ragged extremes of *farioh* that told Poli that: it was simply the knowing of insight, of imagination. Twice would be too much, and the only way afterward, Bronh's way—the love that recognized itself only as control, that courted, finally, only its own ending at the hands of its victims. People could become Teks, and Teks, Screamers, one death at a time.

Poli hit the water in a long shallow dive and presently found the surface again. But it was too hard to separate herself—her balance and her own motions—from the vast interrelatedness of the Singing. Coughing, she walked water and opposed her will, her desire to be separate, free of the Singing: and the brittle, exhausted rapport collapsed. But the fall back into isolation was almost a greater burden, filling her with lethargy and the wish to be still and just drift.

Sculling with one arm, she turned in a circle. Without the strength of the immense focused trance behind her search, she could hear only absence, silence, now from Jannus: she didn't like that. Back on the rock, Pedross was beginning his lecture on the interrelationship of peoples and how much he missed his signalers. His clear, carrying voice was backed by the variable inspoken harmonies of the Loyalists offering a renewal of their wistful, ignorant idolatries. The shore had begun to seem very far away, and the water, almost warm.

She called out, "Jannus, make a noise, *do* something, or you'll drown us both! *Do* something!"

She kept moving her heavy arms in the heavier water. Then somewhere off to her right, toward the northward bank, there was a splash—the sort of sound a leaping fish might have made. Poli leveled herself in the water and partly swam, partly floated toward the sound but could see nothing against the dark of the old landings.

"You ought," she began, and then had to cough, "you ought to be able to see *me*, at least. Make a noise!"

Her foot swung into a submerged stone and she twisted, tucking the foot behind her other knee. Weeds swirled and intertwined around the motions her arms made.

"Back this way," came his quiet, emotionless voice. Poli saw him then. He was settling part-way up a slant of hewn blocks slimed with water mosses. He stretched down an arm, but Poli was content not to attempt the climb. She groped and found an underwater part of the slant where she could rest without needing to swim, only her head above water.

"They're gone," Jannus reported, after a moment, with what Poli might have taken for indifference had she known him less well. "Bronh and the Shai both. He asked me if I wanted to go, just a little while ago, asked me. . . . And Bronh. She could have helped all sorts of ways, about the Singing, and the troopservice, and how it's all to be sorted out. But she wouldn't. She—"

"She was too busy trying to drown you."

"That's nothing. I was just in the way. . . . She couldn't swim a stroke, Bronh," he mentioned, with the same desolate offhandedness. "Just sank, and hung on. I couldn't make her see, reach her. . . . I don't know what else I could have done. She was the last. It's such a waste."

"The Shai's gone? Why? How?"

"He made a bet with himself, over this. If it had gone anything like his predictions, he'd have stayed. But there were too many individual variables, and the predictions just frayed away to nothing. So he's leaving. Going away. . . . With the moon so bright, I can't even see which star it is that's moving, that would be *Sunfire*. . . ."

That would mean the link broken, and no bodies beyond the one he inhabited. Poli savored and sorted the ramifications that touched her. Jannus might grieve for Bronh all he pleased and regard the Shai's departure as a desertion, but he was free of them and eventually he'd know it. Poli herself was jubilant.

She reached up and touched the back of one of his hands. It was cold, and he was shivering.

"Come on back in the water: after the first, it gets to feel almost warm. . . . Or we could walk ourselves warm," she proposed, when he didn't respond.

"You go on."

She twisted fully around to see him. He was looking at the sky, his face lifted to the bright moonlight. She said, "What are you going to do, then—sit on the landing stones all night and wait for sunup?"

"When you've gone wherever you're going," he replied, looking down with shadows for eyes, "I'll try to think what I'm going to do."

"What makes you so sure I'm going somewhere?"

"Poli, you've always been going somewhere," he pointed

out with tired simplicity. "Here. Among Valde. To the Summerfair. I took up arbitrage to begin with so we'd have a reason to come every year, together. . . . But that's done. You're not lar to anybody, yet not apt to die of it any time soon: forty years or so, with luck. . . . And it's still the Summerfair. You—"

"I heard you, in the water," Poli interrupted, "your *farioh*."

"You did?" He sounded thoroughly startled.

"The high part and the low part. Just the middle missing."

"The middle: out of ten, everything from two to nine, right?" he demanded, with the abrupt derisiveness of relief. "But you could *hear* it . . ." he added, again troubled. "It must be starting, then. It doesn't feel any different. But I'd better—"

He broke off and began searching out footholds on the slippery blocks, moving toward shore. Taking the easier way, Poli merely pushed away from her resting place and swam until she could wade. Reaching the shore ahead of him, she leaned on the bank's upper rim. Losing the water's support, her body felt slow as stiff mud in the cool air.

"What must be starting?" she asked him.

"The *farioh*, the feeling. The Shai said it would revive, eventually. . . ." Jannus stumbled, caught himself, and stepped backward down into the mounded rosettes of fat, cabbagey weeds. He started walking downstream, both hands poked into his pockets, his left arm tight against his ribs: the dagger wound still hurt.

But before anything else began to hurt, before he lost his detachment and his inner silence together, he meant to have gone as far as possible from the observation of any Valde and herself in particular. That was plain enough. Poli sighed and pushed herself to follow.

It took him perhaps forty stiff paces to realize that he had no supplies, no shelter, no path to follow; that he probably couldn't walk a whole hour without falling down, what with the after-effects of the dart salve and the wound; and that there were a few thousand hypersensitive insingers ahead of him, farther down the pass.

Poli had known it would come to him without need of any arguments from her.

He wheeled, looking toward the lighted windows of the moored packets, but there was no escape that way either. The swim, across the whole width of the river, was more than he could have managed alone. And he looked up toward the heights, along the pass toward the High Plain, where nothing, now, remained alive. Then his eyes lifted toward the sky.

He turned aside, and Poli didn't know *what* he was thinking of now. He seemed to be searching for open ground, away from people and overhanging trees. And she realized that one drastic escape from exposure and hurt together still remained to him.

She never moved faster in her life.

She grabbed him around the shoulders from behind. "Don't even think it. No."

"It doesn't matter," he replied, trying to shrug out of her grasp.

"It does, because I say it does. No. Twice would be too much. Don't even think of it."

"It's none of your business," he retorted tightly.

"It's my business if I say it is. Or else why am I soaking wet, tell me?"

He turned between her hands to face her, demanding, "What do you *want*?"

"That," declared Poli, "is the right question. First, I want you to swear to me to put this notion clear away from you."

"It would be worse than Bronh—a farspeaker, besides. It would be Entellith and the blood-price, together. I won't—"

"Who are you afraid will get hurt, even if that happens: you, me, or them?"

"Things are just starting to settle," he said, not answering her question, "and it's *got* to settle. I got him this hearing—"

"Oh, it's for the sake of Pedross' signalers?" she rejoined, with ironic skepticism. As long as she kept him talking, as long as she insisted on being there, he wouldn't do it. And certainly not for the sake of Pedross' signalers. "That much, that's settled already. Look: they're starting to scatter."

She turned him to see the hillsides in soundless motion. On nearer ridges small moving groups were briefly silhouetted against the sky, among the trees. Closer at hand, there were the swish of people brushing through vegetation, silencing a

266

succession of scraping insects, and the occasional sleepy wail of a child.

"Leaving," he commented; and the single curt word told her he hadn't understood.

"They're going home. They can stand the Singing now, live and move within it, and even put it aside if there's no in-singer near. And that's what they came to learn. So they're going home."

"And what about Bronh's blood-price?"

"That's not now. That's gone. And there's a lot of us so *sick* of being pushed into things by the 'emotional sur-round'. . . . first the Singing, then Bronh——. She was trying to do it again, take all the choices away, and at the *Summer-fair*! We make our *own* choices, and abide with the results, and *nobody*——" Controlling her vehemence, Poli added, "There'll be trouble yet over Lifganin and the Fallows. But not war: only trouble. Something for arbiters' sessions. We've won," she added simply. "Now, will you swear?"

What he said sounded like, "Oh damn——." He slowly sat down on a patch of soggy ground, folded his arms across his knees, and bent his forehead onto a wet sleeve.

Kneeling beside him, Poli remarked, "That wasn't exactly the swearing I had in mind."

"All right, I won't. I swear it. He's almost out of range anyway. Everybody's going. . . ."

"Not everybody. There are still the Morgaard folk and the people of Entellith, the ones most concerned with Ardun and with the Summerfair. And the young Haffa in growthyear, and the Awiro, and those returned from the troops, and the *hafrae* whose girls are grown and gone. . . . It's going to be a memorable season for marriages. . . . It's *still* the Summer-fair, and the season of Choosing. Now, the second thing I want is for you to listen to me. Why is it you always have to be driven into a corner before you'll just listen?"

"I'm listening. You're not saying anything."

Poli smiled a little and leaned against his bent knees. "All right, I'll say something. I'm a freemaid. Not lar to anybody, and yet not like to die. I have my choice of anyone here that suits me, and that I suit, and you have no say at all about it, as though we were fresh-come from Newstock and me with

Ansen Dibell

my bridestone and the last ten, eleven years never happened. That's so."

"That's so," he acknowledged without inflection.

"And me raveled back out of our children's flesh, the loving all undone again."

"You're still not saying anything."

Poli shifted and laced the fingers of a hand through his. "That's the third thing," she said. "I want you. And I want to go home."

"That's two things," he remarked, but encircled her with an arm and gathered her closer to his sore side with a careful pressure. After a slow moment he said, "Nothing makes sense otherwise. . . . I guess you're used to me."

They'd worn each other to fitting, she thought, but that wasn't why. The thought of Bronh came to her, and of what that profound relatedness had become, at the last. And she began to think of the worn paths of difference and accustomed responses still channeling her own approaches to Jannus, and his to her. And the end of that path was Entellith.

They'd each passed through their separate fires; now, on the far side, it was time to walk new ways, by choice and not by habit, and to leave the scarred paths to the seasons' healing.

It would have to be words, to reach him and make him know. Therefore she said quietly, "You are dearer to me than any other thing alive. If you were *sa'farioh* forever I'd still choose you and call until you could answer me. I've broken the Singing to come to you now, without your ever calling. No lesser thing will ever prevent me. We are not lar. We are something else. We'll have to find out what it is that we are and will be. You won't have to hang on anymore—at least, not alone, by yourself. I'm not going anywhere, except where we go."

He bent his head against hers, and Poli heard it then: no more than a faint humming scarcely distinguishable from the renewed scrape and buzz of surrounding insects. It was the beginnings of the middle, the silent part: everything from two to nine. Any distance away, she wouldn't have been able to hear it at all. But she wasn't any distance away.

She leaned closer, altogether at ease. After a while she remarked, "I've had enough of Valde to last me the whole rest

268

of my life. I like words, and silence between. I'd like," she reflected slowly, "to learn how to read. And I'd like to see what
kind of shoving would be needed to move the Summerfair to
Ardun. There's space enough, on the flood plain west of the
city, and it's too wet to be built on anyhow. . . . It *should* be
on the border, not two weeks' hiking away. After all, it's ours
too. And there's still the need for a meeting place, and the arbiters' sessions, and Fair Witnesses. . . ."

After she'd wandered a while among the possibilities she
felt ahead, Jannus broke in quietly, "How would you like to
be governor of Ardun? I can see a way that could happen."

Poli thought about it, trying to imagine why Pedross would
ever consider such an appointment. "I know he'll have to
have somebody, but that's a lot of bribe to throw away for
nothing. What have I got that he'd pay that kind of price
for?"

"Direct contact with Valde, for one thing. A reliable
bridge. And the things you want, for another. . . . And he
could trust you not to raise an army behind his back, which
is rare enough, just by itself. And of course, there's value for
value: he owes us."

"For the hearing?"

"That too. . . ." said Jannus uncomfortably, and stopped.

So he'd done something else. "All right—what?"

"Well, the fact is, I made it rain," he admitted. "I saw how
things were shaping and had the Shai seed the clouds and wet
everything down a bit. It was only rain, after all. And I
ended up having to put out the fires by hand anyhow, when it
took so long in coming. . . ."

The fact of even so unnoticeable an intervention troubled
him. But Poli pressed the heel of her free hand into the soggy
turf, marveling. She had as a backrest a man who'd commanded weather. "*Only* rain?" she teased.

"Better that than a wind of poison or fire," he replied
flatly.

"That's so," Poli admitted, and then began to think. Without the rain, the packets' cables would have been cut in
midafternoon, beginning the retreat and the end of Ardun.
The insingers would have returned, and Bronh would have
had the unopposed, undivided attention of the Valde for her

incantations of love, betrayal, and vengeance, with the stranger-scarred insingers weaving the flow of the Singing.

Value for value, she thought. That one rainstorm should be well worth the Stone of Ardun.

"I'd like that," she agreed presently, and then they turned their talk to other things, sharing the warmth of their nearness.

When nobody was paying any attention, Sua slid out of the mess hall and wandered the length of the water deck, feeling wistful and lonesome. She groped in a pocket for a piece of bread, then changed her mind. She was becoming more discriminating, and there were times, like now, when she wasn't even actively hungry. She'd begun to wonder whether the body had at last become satisfied with its burst of stretching and would just stay the same and not make a nuisance of itself so she could learn it, and herself.

She sat on a big coil of rope, glad of the quiet. Whenever the breeze backed, she caught phrases of whatever Pedross was calling through the hailing-horn, but mostly it was quiet. Then she heard a muted wooden *thump,* and a rope flipped around the bottom of the deck-rail post not five paces from her. Instead of hollering and running away, she went to the rail to look over.

A man in dripping clothes, standing spread-legged in one of the channel marking boats, was casting brisk half-hitches in the mooring rope he'd put around the post. Alerted, he looked up, and it was absolutely Garin. A grin lifted his wonderfully rough features into a quizzical greeting that was a question as the boat swung slowly around to the end of its tether.

"Saves me peeking in windows," he remarked, just loud enough for her to hear; and the combination of deepwater lilt and troll flatness made Sua shiver all over with recognition and sheer gladness. "You ready?" he asked, gesturing openhanded at his stolen boat.

Her own unsurprise told her she'd always expected it, against all sense—as soon as she'd begun to know that trolls could and generally did come back. *Not,* this time, as a haunted old man who liked to keep people terrified of him but what, in spite of himself, had looked sometimes out of Simon's eyes to meet hers. Now she knew what it was, that she'd been waiting for.

She slid between the rails and held on, balanced on her toes on the very rim of the deck. When his hand supported her, she found the seat-board in the stern and sat down, all in the one quick motion, because one person standing up in a boat was already one too many. The half-hitches were pulled free almost as swiftly as they'd been cast. The rail, and the packet's side, and the squares of lit windows all in line, began to drift away, smaller against the dark hillside that seemed to grow and stretch like a cloud.

Pedross was going to be just furious when he found out. Sua thumped at the stern seat for sheer delight, and grinned. But they kept their escape quiet: not until they were past the rubble of the old landings did Garin begin dipping the oars as though they were light as skimming-spoons: after all, he wasn't an old he-witch anymore but a young waterman with an easy hand for ropes and oars and boats, just as he should be.

Curling her ankles together under the seat among the wet bundles she could feel piled there, Sua picked out the knot in the cord that she'd made from the blue bandana. She held the crooked, grimy string a moment so he could see it, then rubbed it into a wad and bounced it away into the river. The oars paused, dripping, clear of the water, and Garin cast a look up at the sky, remarking suddenly, "It's so quiet," as if he'd just noticed it. And when he resumed his stroke and regarded her again, there was a soberness about his eyes that hadn't been there before. Sua began softly humming: a Smith tune, for all that it was about boats and rowing. The name of it was "The Water Is Wide." And so it was, and the banks far away and still, and the high hills beyond for walls.

"What would you like to know?" he offered presently. "Why Grandda Troll decided he owed me a life? What took me so long, coming down from the High Plains? Whether it'll rain on us tomorrow? How I propose to keep you from starving?"

Sua shook her head, still humming: none of those things was she the least bit concerned about.

"Then what can I make you? A compass? A small electrical fire? A lie? A small fortune? But you've got ten thousand

271

marks in your own right," he reminded himself, "though it might prove a bit hard to get at." He meant, because of Pedross. Sua didn't care: she'd never wanted the money anyhow, or to be collected. They'd all been collectors of one sort or another, all the Masters of Ardun, back to the Laying of the Stone: everybody knew that. But Garin was going on, "So it'll have to be some other toy. I'm all out of lightnings. You name something."

Again, Sua shook her head, smiling to herself. She wanted no toys, not even lightnings to spin off her fingertips.

"Then what use do you have for a second-hand reconstituted copy of a troll, Mistress Sualiche?"

He knew perfectly well, or he wouldn't have come back for her. He was just being shy and tiresome. Trolls weren't that much different from anybody else, Sua thought: they just wanted to be sure they were welcomed and loved.

She leaned to catch hold of the oar shafts. Against no resistance, she shipped the blades on either side of her seat, and the boat coasted quietly on the patient midstream current.

His clothes were still soaking wet from his swimming out to steal the boat, but that problem was easily solved, and the slotted floor panels weren't especially splintery though Sua wouldn't have cared much if they had been. She was too busy teaching and learning the magics of contact and of touch which bodies offered in partial amends for the tiresomeness they were generally inflicting. It was enough.